The TOWER

JEAN JOHNSON

BERKLEY SENSATION, NEW YORK

THE BERKLEY PUBLISHING GROUP
Published by the Penguin Group
Penguin Group (USA) Inc.
375 Hudson Street, New York, New York 10014, USA

USA I Canada I UK I Ireland I Australia I New Zealand I India I South Africa I China

Penguin Books Ltd., Registered Offices: 80 Strand, London WC2R 0RL, England
For more information about the Penguin Group, visit penguin.com.

THE TOWER

This book is an original publication of The Berkley Publishing Group.

Berkley Sensation Books are published by The Berkley Publishing Group.
BERKLEY SENSATION® is a registered trademark of Penguin Group (USA) Inc.
The "B" design is a trademark of Penguin Group (USA) Inc.

Berkley Sensation trade paperback edition ISBN: 978-0-425-26222-1

An application to register this book for cataloging has been submitted to the Library of Congress.

PUBLISHING HISTORY
Berkley Sensation trade paperback edition / May 2013

PRINTED IN THE UNITED STATES OF AMERICA

10 9 8 7 6 5 4 3 2 1

Cover art by Don Sipley.
Cover design by George Long.

ACKNOWLEDGMENTS

This book is dedicated to the men and women who graciously allowed me to torment them with a tabletop gaming version of the Tower's traps and tricks a few years ago, in preparation for writing this book. To Peter "Why yes, I am a rocket scientist," who inspired me to include actual science puzzles among the traps; also, thank you for teaching your love of science and critical thinking to your students. To Steve "Let's put another tombstone tattoo on my character's arm" for his great sense of humor even in the face of so many deadly monsters and lethal traps, both in mine and others' games.

To Rachael for coming up with the gloriously perfect motto for the Healer's Union (local 442): "We Don't Heal Stupid." To her mother, Chris, for nearly killing me with laughter over the crystal ball incident, among many, many other moments of hilarity over the years. To Chris' late husband, Glen; may he enjoy many a fine game with Gygax and Arneson in Heaven, and finally get to "destroy Dresdin's hat." And of course, to every other person I've had the pleasure of gaming with, either as a fellow player or as their games master.

I particularly want to thank my cousins Kat, Karl, and Kevin, who introduced the rest of our generation, over thirty-two years ago, to a game where imagination, the luck of a die roll, and cooperative storytelling opened all of our minds up to never-ending worlds of wonder, challenge, and creativity. Tabletop RPGs have allowed me to test out ideas, practical and absurd, in a safe environment long before I'd ever need to face similar troubles in real life, or have a chance to write about them. They have helped me to learn the value of common sense and caution, and the joy of having good friends at my side, watching my back as I watched theirs. I definitely would not be as good at storytelling today if I hadn't played. (I also wouldn't know how to survive the zombie apocalypse, otherwise.)

My thanks, as ever, go to my beta ladies, Stormi, Alexandra, Alienor, and NotSoSaintly, who put up with all the behind-the-scenes stuff with grace and understanding. And lastly, my thanks to you, the reader, for being willing to pick up and read such an unusual twist on the typical romance novel.

I hope you enjoy this unique start to my new series, the Guardians of Destiny.

Jean

PROLOGUE

NIGHTFALL CASTLE, EMPIRE OF NIGHTFALL

Eyeing the prophecy scroll in her hands, Hope shook her head and rolled it back up. Some of the old doggerel which her personal goddess, Nauvea, had expressed through her was quite cheesy, compared to real poetry. She also had no idea what a Vortex was—well, she knew what a *vortex* was, a swirling funnel of something, like water going down a drain, but she didn't know what that particular prophecy meant by using that particular word. She certainly couldn't remember when her scribe had written it down.

Two centuries from this world's perspective was a long time for a prophecy to be forgotten. Even just five years from her own perspective was enough to have forgotten most of these old messages,

particularly after having to deal with the cultural and techno-
logical complexities of an entirely different universe. But she was
back home now, in a safe and sane world of perfectly normal magical logic, rather than a crazy world that was almost entirely tech-
nologic.

The latest heat wave had passed three days ago with the start
of the Convocation of the Gods, but the attics of the old palace
were still quite warm. Wiping a bit of sweat from her forehead
with the back of one hand, she reached for another scroll with the
other. Hope—formerly Duchess Haupanea—wasn't actually *looking* for prophecies. Instead, she was trying to find the last piece of
legal business she had signed before her involuntary exile to
another world.

Her secretary, Giolana, had put one copy in the office of the
Desalination plant and one in her private quarters, in a cupboard
that held her important documents. The contents of that cupboard and a couple of others had long since been rummaged
through, moved around, traded, swapped, and finally exiled to
the myriad attic spaces of the sprawling wings of the palace. She
needed the original, not a mere copy.

"Hope?" a welcome, male voice called, words echoing between
the stone struts and wooden beams dividing the bays of the attic
space in the western wings. "Are you in here? Helloooo?"

"I'm in here, Morg!" she called back, unwrapping another
scroll. Scrubbing at her face again, she unrolled the parchment
and squinted at the words. She had brought a lightglobe into the
attic to provide a decent amount of soft white light, but the writing on this scroll had started to fade.

Oh! I remember this one, she realized. *This is one of the ones where
that batch of ink was mixed wrong . . .* She started reading it, wondering if she should take the time to copy it with better ink so it
would last longer, or if she should just try to see if anyone knew if

it had come true in the intervening centuries. It wasn't a bad piece
of doggerel prophecy, at least.

> *"City's Delight, Island of Sins,*
> *Choose the path that balance wins,*
> *Hostess fades and soon retires;*
> *Select the Host whose help requires*
> *Virtue's—"*

"There you are!" Dropping into a crouch next to her, Morganen leaned forward, scooped her dark curls back from the side
of her face, and pressed a kiss to her tanned cheek. Then frowned
at her sweat-dotted face. She had donned shorts and a sleeveless
top—fashions from the other world well-suited to a warm
climate—but he didn't object to her bared limbs, just the signs of
her discomfort. "Why are you so determined to sweat up here
while reading these things, when you could've just brought them
down into a spell-cooled room downstairs?"

She rolled her eyes. "Because I wasn't thinking? Besides, I
thought it'd be a quick trip. Most of my contract scrolls should have
been in the same cupboard, and not jumbled up with all my old
prophecies. The Katani Council needs to be smacked with the
indemnity clause from the delay in the old Portals being shut
down—which the Empire will have to pay for, since it was that idiot
mage's fault they took so long to shut the Portals down—but I'm not
sure they'll accept anything *but* the original, which I think was the
one Giolana sent to my quarters. Or the one I gave them was the
original. I remember the one in the Desalination office is a copy.

"Help me find it, will you?" she asked him. "Two will make
the work go faster. I want to give it to Priestess Saleria, the representative from Katan, so she can ask Kata and Jinga to authenti-
cate it as the original before the Convocation ends."

"Ahh, how very smart of you," Morganen praised, grinning. "If the Gods of the Empire approve it as a true contract, and They verify that the delay that caused the destruction of the Desalinator was the Empire's fault, the Council won't have any means of protesting your indemnity claim. So, it's among the scrolls in *this* cupboard, right?"

"This cupboard, that one, and I think that chest over there," Hope told him, pointing at the other two pieces of furniture. She wiped again at her forehead and cheeks. "I don't know if they got mixed up in any others, but I recognize these bits of furniture as having come from my chambers, back when they were still mine."

"First, I think I should give us both a cooling charm." Flicking his fingers, Morganen murmured under his breath. Cool air rustled through the furniture-crowded space, rippling old cobwebs and swirling a bit of dust out the way. He wrinkled his nose and muttered another spell, this one stripping all the dirt from their surroundings. Compacting it into a thick ball, he dropped the floating orb to one side with a solid thunk, then opened the chest she'd indicated.

"Oh, bless you," Hope sighed as the wind gusts cooled her down. "That's faster than an air-conditioning unit . . . Speaking of which, we need to get Koranen to make some air-cooling sigils before he takes off for Menomon, something we can activate at a touch."

"If he doesn't have the time before he leaves with Danau, I'll chat with Trevan and we'll work something up," Morg promised her. Flicking his long, ash-blond braid over his shoulder, he picked up one of the scrolls from the chest, speaking as he untied it. "I think I remember Wolfer tossing these in here, back when we cleared out the dome chamber for Kelly's use . . . Nope, not a contract."

He started to scroll it up again, then paused. Frowning, he read the lines of verse quietly to himself.

Hope glanced at him when he muttered, and smirked a little. "Addictive, aren't they? Little tantalizing puzzles waiting for time and circumstances to unveil their meanings, warnings, and clues."

"*This* one could almost apply to recent events," Morg told her, unrolling it further so he could tilt the parchment her way. It wasn't particularly long, but it was eight verses. "The pattern of five lines per verse is very much like Seer Draganna's verse of the Curse of Eight, the ones we just suffered through. The first line of each verse ties them all together, with the remaining four lines speaking of a specific event."

"That's not uncommon when an over-arching prophecy is about seemingly unrelated events that actually are intertwined," Hope said, checking the next scroll in her hands. "Doesn't necessarily mean it's about us, though."

"It mentions Painted Lords, which we've just dealt with . . . and a Painted Lady," he allowed. "Plus a Darkhanan Witch, a Voice—which might or might not refer to Evanor's song-based magics—plus an island city and royalty . . . though I sincerely hope this bit about a '*Groom's mistake and bride's setback*' doesn't refer to *us*. Especially as I still haven't wed you, yet. Though it could've referred to Dom and Serina's troubles right after they married . . . except he's the third brother, not the eighth."

"Ah, but the precursor line speaks of Guardians having a goal. You're not a Guardian, nor are the majority of your brothers, so it couldn't possibly be about you and me," Hope pointed out, tapping the first line of the final verse. "Besides, we have all the Gods and Goddesses on hand to bless our union . . . and my heart-sister Kelly to make sure They toe the line when it comes to those blessings."

Morg chuckled. "Better her than me. I think they respect our new queen all the more for *not* having magic, yet still being fearless as she faces Them. Okay, so it's not in this scroll." He rolled it up and retied the ribbon, then looked at the other scrolls stacked around her crossed legs. "Does it go in a special pile?"

"This one here, since it has several verses referencing different known locations," Hope directed him, patting a small stack of scrolls. She wiped one last time at the sweat on her forehead, since the air was now comfortably cool around both of them. "The Dragon verse probably means the Draconan Empire . . . and the Harper, I think I overheard one of the priests or priestesses mentioning that as their title. I'm hoping to ask a lot of our Convocation visitors about these prophecies, to see if any have been fulfilled already, or if they know of any budding circumstances that might match. We only have a limited amount of time to question people about these things before the Convocation ends."

"A Seer's work is never done," Morg teased. He set the scroll in his hands on the pile indicated, then reached for a fresh one. "Now that your Goddess is back, we'll have to get you a new scribe to follow you around. Or maybe some sort of Artifact that can record your words, like Evanor's brass music tokens, so your new prophecies won't be lost."

"Just keep looking for the indemnity contract," Hope ordered lightly. "We'll have plenty of time to record new prophecies when they come along, but with all the Gods and Goddesses here, with Their attention focused on the petitions being laid before Them, it's highly unlikely They'll speak through any Seer for the duration of the Convocation. And even if They do, these are old prophecies. Either they've come true already, or they have not. I can only make enquiries to see if they have. The Council, on the other hand, is a pain I can *do* something about. Something I can help you with."

Nodding, Morganen leaned over and kissed her, then shifted back to select and unwrap the next scroll. "And that help is deeply appreciated, my love. If and when these prophecies do come true, we'll probably only know it after the fact."

ONE

When serpent crept into their hall:
Danger waits for all who board,
Trying to steal that hidden tone.
Painted Lady saves the lord;
Tower's master's not alone.

VALLEY OF THE TOWER, EASTERN AIAR
SIX OR SO MONTHS EARLIER

One of the mirrors arrayed on Jessina's desk shifted, revealing the image of a blond man in his late forties. "Topside Control, this is Base Maintenance."

"Go ahead, Base Maintenance," Jessina stated, her voice smooth and calm. It was in her job description to always be calm while on the job. So was Brennan's.

"We're having some problems with the main power fluctuating. Are you doing anything special up there?" Brennan asked.

She carefully looked over the array of enchanted Artifacts and gizmos framing each mirror along her broad, curved desk, then at the other stations around the control room. Shaking her head, she said, "No, everything's the same as it was. Status normal."

"Well, we're losing power to the nonessentials," Brennan told her. "I'm getting reports from repair teams that the rooms and corridors not currently in use have been shutting down in Standby mode. It's starting to make getting from point to point difficult behind the scenes. We've had three teams temporarily stranded so far, though we did get them out again with a local override."

"That's . . . not good. I'll try to see if I can track the reason from up here. You look for a reason down there," she directed, and turned in her chair so that she faced a different mirror. Sliding her fingers down the edge of that mirror and the one next to it, she activated both. "Middle Maintenance, Top Maintenance, this is Topside Control. Base Maintenance is registering a slowdown in responsiveness from the unused sectors. Double-check and report. What's your status?"

Middle Maintenance was overseen by Heral. The man was as dark-skinned as Jessina, and could have passed for a cousin in a pinch, though they each originally came from two separate kingdoms along the southern coast of Aiar. He grinned at her, his teeth flashing white. "Eh, it's probably just repairer's syndrome; with the Master away, the Tower will play, and all that."

The woman on the screen to his left scowled. "I heard that, Heral. Don't even joke about it! If the Tower is actually acting up, and the Guardian's not here to handle it quickly, we could *all* be in serious trouble. Jessina, should we send for him?"

Jessina wrinkled her nose. "He gets out so infrequently, and he was so happy to have the chance to go shopping in a big city. He was going to meet with his printers, too. I'd really hate to cut his trip short if it's just a false alarm—if anything sudden happens, yes, absolutely, I will contact him, Wenda," she promised the leader of Top Maintenance. "But let's see first if this is more than just a bobble on the charts."

"It could be something one of the player teams has done," Brennan offered from the still-open mirror to her left. "Like that explosion last year that broke through three levels and damaged the water and sewer lines? That locked more than a few rooms in place for a bit, and not all of them logically connected to each other."

"I don't have any such explosions registering on my Artifacts," Wenda said, "but then it could be a non-blatant piece of wild magic. I'm going to order my teams to double-check they have their emergency packs with them, just in case they get locked up, until we can get the Master back."

"They should anyway; it's standard operating procedure," Jessina stated. "I will *not* have a preventable accident on the day when I've been left in charge. The Tower will play *nice* while the Master's away, or it'll learn not to mess with me a second time!"

Brennan chuckled at that absurd statement. Heral laughed outright. Even Wenda smiled a little; Jessina was a good mage, a strong mage, but she was not the Mistress of the Tower. She wasn't the Guardian of the magical source powering all the many rooms, corridors, halls, traps, tricks, and the very important safety features that made the Tower so compelling to watch even while it was so dangerous to play.

For all that the locals took pride in the Tower, mages from halfway around the world paid dearly to see adventurous and hardy souls brave its many dangers . . . the pay-per-show scrycasts of those adventures were not the purpose of the Tower's existence. The Tower's traps were meant to be very lethal. They could be modified so they weren't quite so deadly, but only by the Guardian, the Master himself.

Their employer had done so, making a few adjustments so

that the Tower would run smoothly in his absence. Only then had he stepped through a mirror-Gate to the nearest main city for a day of shopping and negotiating for his latest book on the nature and ways of certain aspects of Gating-based magic. Even when he was here, the Tower was usually quite stable under normal operating conditions. There shouldn't be any reason for some of its sectors to have problems. At least, not serious ones.

Still, it was Jessina's job to make sure those problems were found, identified, and handled, one way or another. Disturbing though the implications were, she went about the task of contacting various subdepartments, asking for signs of any anomalies, slowdowns, changes, and so forth. She did so calmly, though she did hurry. If there was a problem, she wanted to know exactly what it was before contacting the Master on his one day away from the Tower in nearly a full year.

Kerric Vo Mos stood with his feet braced, his shoulders squared, his hands on his hips, and just breathed. Inhaling lungful after lungful, he dragged in the wonderful scents of the farmer's market here in Sendale. The stalls were teeming with piles of ripe vegetables, pungent herbs, brightly colored berries, butchered meats, mounds of fruit, and fresh-caught fish . . . He could have gotten similar fare in the town located a short distance from the base of the Tower—and had, in the past—but there, he was treated with deference. There, he never had to pay for a thing.

Sometimes a man just wanted to pay for a damn apple, and take pride in being able to do so, and *not* have his perfectly good coin refused.

Here . . . well, here, almost nobody knew who the short, curly-haired man in the plain brown tunic and dark brown trews was. He wasn't Kerric Vo Mos, Guardian of the Tower, Master Mage

and Author of Dozens of Tomes. He had been that august per-
sonage earlier this morning, but that was when he had been handling his publishing affairs. Right now, he was just plain—

"Outta the way, youngling!" an elderly woman snapped,
whacking him on the boot with her cane hard enough to make
him hop a little. It stung, since the wood had connected with the
anklebone under the leather, but he didn't scowl or curse. Instead,
he grinned and gave her an exaggerated bow as he stepped aside.

"Of course, Mistress! My apologies for delaying your day's
tasks," he offered as suavely as he could.

She eyed him, snorted, and hobbled on, cane thumping the
cobblestones lining the market square.

The day was a beautiful one, warm but not overly hot, with
puffy white clouds drifting by in a beautiful blue sky. The edges
of that sky were crowded by timber-and-plaster buildings with
tiled roofs, but no matter which way he turned, he could not see
the mottled, cream-and-white walls of the Tower looming over
his head.

Grinning, he turned in a circle, enjoying the view yet again,
then wondered what sort of delights he should look for first in the
farmer's market. Fattened liver mousse, or beautifully marbled
cheeses; perhaps there was even a fruit-ice vendor somewhere
nearby. Such things were usually sold by some enterprising, low-
powered mage who could freeze and shave water with a simple
pair of spells for vast profits in the summer.

Such as today, a glorious, warm, early summer day. A fruit-ice
was definitely not out of the question. Rubbing his hands together,
Kerric eyed the stalls and booths and tents and wagons, trying to
spot what he wanted. Something out of place caught his eye: a
man walking with two books in his hand, gesturing at them as he
talked to the lady at his side. The tomes looked a little old and
worn. Curious, Kerric moved closer.

". . . I think I should've bought the Elgin Ves Troth edition, too, but it was in such terrible shape," the dark-haired man was saying.

Kerric perked up at that, and stepped into their path. "Excuse me, milord, milady," he apologized by way of introduction, "but by any chance are you talking about a bookseller?"

"Why, yes," the middle-aged man stated. He nodded back the way they had come. "Go that way about eight or nine farmers, to the first big left-turning, and cut over to the next aisle in the market and head right, further down the way. You can't miss it."

"Many thanks!" Lifting his hand in farewell, Kerric hurried that way.

He was shorter than the average man in Sendale, and barely as tall as the average woman, which made it hard for him see where to go through the crowds attending the market. Still, the square set of his broad shoulders, his confident, erect posture, and the deft way he dodged between passersby allowed him to double back and take the left-turning when he passed it, then allowed a dash to the right to get ahead of a mother and her gaggle of four or five children.

Their shrill whining for treats as the woman and her herd passed a pastry stall made him wince. He didn't dislike children; they were important to the world, and could be pleasant if their parents taught them the hows and whys of good manners. Some were even quick-witted and charming. But they were not allowed in the Tower for very, very good reason. The end result of that sensible prohibition meant Kerric wasn't used to dealing with them.

Ah, they stopped at a fruit stall, something about cherries. Gods bless you, woman; you have the patience I lack. Hurrying onward, Kerric spotted the bookseller. The old man had a large cart of them, most in bad condition, but Kerric didn't care. He didn't have a lot of free time for reading, between his duties as Master of the Tower and his interest in experimenting with magic and writing down his observations in tomes meant to help others . . . but he did love to read.

There was indeed an Elgin Ves Troth in among the baskets of books, and it was in deplorable condition. The pages were wrinkled and the ink smeared from having been soaked; hints of mildew bloom stained the cover, which was falling apart; and three of the quires would have to be re-stitched together to hold all the pages in place . . . but much of it was still readable, if one went slowly and carefully. However, what might make it worthwhile was that it was a treatise on the Gods he hadn't read before, always a plus.

Kerric fancied himself a modern-day Ves Troth in his own field of expertise, since the man had wielded his pen with a deft touch of humor as well as a liberal splashing of truth. The book was in bad shape, yes, but he did have the tools to repair it. The trick was finding the spare time to tend to the tome, if he bought it.

". . . Master Kerric? Master Kerric!"

Kerric turned. He couldn't see who had shouted, but the voice was familiar. At the third calling of his name, the owner of the voice dodged a set of market visitors and came into view. The sight of the beanpole-tall, beanpole-skinny, dark-haired Seanus made Kerric wince. The pendant straining in the young man's fist made him curse. And the frantic look on the apprentice mage's teenaged face made him want to hit his forehead with the tome still in his hand.

"Master Kerric! Thank the Gods I've found you!" Seanus gasped out, stumbling to a halt. He braced his palms on his knees, careful not to drop the locator-pendant, which swung toward Kerric in defiance of gravity, as it was enspelled to do. "Trouble at the Tower . . . !"

"I *know* that, Seanus," Kerric muttered, regretfully setting the book back in one of the baskets. "Fire, flood, rioting, or did something collapse?"

Oddly, Seanus glanced around the mostly mindless crowd. His brown eyes were so wide, the older man could see the whites surrounding the youth's irises. Seanus held his breath for a moment, then leaned down and in, close enough that his breath hit Kerric's ear in an anxious gust of warmth.

"Someone'sstealingtheFountain'spowers!"

The jumble of consonants and syllables didn't make sense for a long moment. When it did, the oath that burst from Kerric's lips silenced most everyone within a good fifty feet. It was loud, it was vehement, and it accompanied a dark scowl of anger. On his one day off of the year—!

The mother back by the fruit seller quickly clapped her hands over the nearest boy's ears, her expression even more affronted than most of the other adults', while her other little ones stared, bewildered by the fuss. An elderly couple blinked in shock, the old man pressing his hand to his chest. Assorted middle-aged and younger adults gave him wary, offended looks. Kerric ignored them all, mind racing. There was too much between him and the local Mage Guild. Too many bodies, too many buildings, too many streets . . .

"*Tessoloc!*" Snapping his hand down, Kerric cast a flight spell on himself. One moment he was on the ground next to Seanus, who was still trying to recover his breath. The next, he jerked up into the air and soared toward the east, heading for the green-tiled roofs of the Guild. From there, he could catch a mirror-Gate into the Tower itself. Hopefully. If things had gotten to the critical stage . . .

If the situation *had* deteriorated that far, he would have to pick a mirror in the village, one of the ones at the Adventurer's Hall, or maybe the mayor's office.

Landing in the small courtyard, Kerric hurried inside without bothering to close the front door. Most of the Guild's business was conducted upstairs, but the main floor was devoted to the most profitable of the services provided by the local Mage Guild: the ability to open Gates between distant locations via large mirrors.

The receptionist, an apprentice mage with pale blond hair cropped so short, he almost looked bald, gave him a startled look. "Master Kerric? I heard that someone came tearing through here earlier, but—"

"I need a mirror, right now," he ordered, digging into his pouch. Tossing a handful of gold crownai on the younger man's desk, he didn't bother to count them. "Which one's free?"

"They're, uh, they're all busy. It's summer, the traveling season. I *can* schedule you in half an hour, I think," the apprentice said, looking down at his appointments ledger.

"Your schedule can hang itself. I'm taking the very next mirror—and if the Guildmaster has a problem with it, tell him he won't get any scrying feed from the Tower for a week!" Kerric stated bluntly, already striding toward the Departures corridor.

The rooms on the far side of the reception hall had mirrors reserved for Arrivals, to make sure those traveling from mirror-Gates in neighboring regions to the mirrors of Sendale's Guildhall would not be trying to cross into a mirror opened into a third location. Picking the first room for departing travelers, Kerric stepped inside just as a quintet of well-dressed bodies started carefully hopping over the cheval-style frame of the open mirror. Father, mother, and three roughly teenaged children passed through.

The mage in charge of opening that room's mirror frowned at Kerric. His lack of recognition told Kerric that he wasn't one of the mages here at the Guildhouse who watched the scryings from the Tower. "Excuse me, but you don't look like a clutch of nuns from the Starranos Temple, and they're next on the list. Not *you*."

"That's because I'm not. I need to get back to the Tower immediately, and I'm commandeering your mirror for it." The pot of powder he wanted was on the table next to the frame of the large cheval-style mirror. Grabbing a handful, Kerric cast it at the permeable surface, chanting the Gating syllables in a strong voice that echoed off the walls of the modest room. The words shifted the focus of the mirror from whatever Guildhall the previous group had paid for as their destination to a mirror in the castlelike command structure at the top of the Tower—

The mirror shattered in a flare of greenish-gold light. Both men flinched, personal shields snapping up instantly, Kerric's in transparent gold, the other mage's in green. Thankfully, they weren't needed; the cheval stand had subtle warding runes carved into its wooden frame. Fragments of silvered glass hit an elongated, egglike shield and bounced back, falling and sliding down the curved, blue-glowing surface into a pile an inch from the floor.

"Bastard!" the other mage cursed. "You cast the spell wrong! What sort of incompetent—"

"*Silence.*" Kerric glared the taller man into obedience. He wasn't tall, but his will was strong, his sense of command imposing. "That was *not* a mis-cast mirror-Gate."

"I don't care who you think you are—" the mage began again with disparaging heat in his tone, only to be cut off again.

"You *should* care. I am Master Kerric Vo Mos, *foremost* living authority on mirror magics, and Guardian of the Tower," he stated slowly, crisply. The other man lost some of his belligerence, choosing to gape at Kerric instead. Most people didn't expect the Master of the Tower to be . . . well, short. Kerric was used to it by now. He pointed at the shield-wrapped stand. "*That* mirror was destroyed by the Tower's defenses. I can tell because of the greenish cast to the explosion's energies.

"Someone is attacking the Tower, and with myself *here*," he added, jabbing his finger at the ground, then at the mirrorless frame, "instead of *there*, I am now unable to stop it from killing anyone who tries to Gate in . . . *or* out. There were eight teams of adventurers crawling through the Tower when I came here this morning, and over two hundred personnel who are now trapped inside. Lives always take precedence over objects, because objects can be rebuilt or replaced.

"I'll send payment for the mirror when I can, or send a better replacement, but I'll have to commandeer another mirror immediately to deal with this," he finished grimly. The other mage opened his mouth to protest. Kerric cut him off, lifting a hand in dismissal as he turned back toward the corridor. "To the *village*. I'm not an idiot."

"Are you sure?" the mage called out as he left. "Because it sounds like your village is *short* one!"

Ten or so years ago, Kerric might have taken that as a personal insult on his height as well as his intellect. Fifteen years ago, he would have been insulted outright. But over ten years ago, he had traveled to the Tower to study its translocational arrangements, the ways the myriad passages, corridors, chambers, halls, caverns, stairwells, and rooms not just connected to each other, but interconnected. The life he had been given, the opportunities, made such things unimportant by comparison.

The next room had a merchant with five porters bearing huge bundles strapped to their backs. Upon seeing Kerric enter, the female mage in charge stopped herself from casting the Gating powder, choosing to frown at the new arrival instead. "Can I help you . . . wait, Master Kerric? Is that you?"

"Yes. Penambrion Village, to any of its mirrors. It's an emergency," Kerric stated brusquely.

"City Hall, then; I have the mirror for the burgher's office already connected to this one," the woman stated after only a hesitation, and cast the powders. The merchant and his stevedores flinched from the harsh shout of her spellwords. She sounded like an upset raven instead of a roll of thunder or a battle cry, but the spell worked. The image shifted to a familiar view.

"Now see here!" the merchant spluttered while his hirelings frowned and Kerric strode forward. "I paid good money to be mirror-Gated today!"

"I'll open the Gate to your destination in a moment, milord," the lady mage soothed.

Hopping through, Kerric ignored the icy, prickling sensation of transversing hundreds of miles. Some days it burned, some days it felt like swimming through mud, and most people unaccustomed to the inner-ear lurching felt at least a touch of nausea. Kerric was immune to that latter effect, thankfully. Behind him, sounds from the mirror cut off. In front of him—off to the side, actually— a frantic-looking bureaucrat quickly set down her mug on her desk and hurriedly stood so she could move to meet him, her blonde braid frazzled, her tunic freshly damp from where she had spilled a drink on it.

Like his, it was cut in the local style, fastening down the front in a row of decorative knots, with high-cut slits on the sides to help vent the summer heat. The matching trousers were short enough to bare half her calves, much like his, but where he wore plain browns, she wore brocaded shades of blue. "Master Kerric! Oh, thank the Gods," she breathed, touching his arm and tugging him away from the arrivals mirror. "I don't care which ones—I have Jessina on my mirror right now, and things are *really* bad in the Tower."

"So I surmised," he muttered, gratefully taking Sylva's seat at her gesture. The burgher gestured toward a pot of tea sitting on an enchanted brazier stand off to one side, but Kerric waved her off. He wanted answers from the Tower, not tea from the mayor's office.

The dark-skinned manager of Topside Control spotted his face in the connected surfaces and sighed in relief. She didn't look quite as flustered as the blonde, but she did look worried. That was not a good sign.

"Praise Amaz, you're back," Jessina muttered, before launching into her report. "Five hours ago, we started having difficulties with power fluctuations. It took us almost two hours to confirm the problem lay at the power source itself, not from anything external or internal. Apprentice Fisly was still inside on watch, but by that point, the warding shields had snapped up around the middle sector."

"Fisly's not strong enough to fix whatever's been happening," Kerric stated. "And if she's trapped in there, she'll have no food or water until we arrive."

Jessina shook her head. "She managed to get herself out when we realized no one else could get in to her. She's holed up in a refreshing room a few chambers away." Biting her lip, the normally unflappable woman hesitated, then added, "I cut the audio spells to all outgoing scryings, and broadcast a warning to everyone to get to a refreshing room. There's fresh water, food dispensers, and furniture in the outer lounging rooms. I figured that would be the safest place for everyone not Topside.

"Shortly after I did *that*, all the rooms started to realign, and the lesser traps started turning deadly again. Just a few here and there, but . . . I'm sorry, Master Kerric, but over fifty percent of the Tower is now live. Probably closer to seventy by now. It started from both the heart and the base. We noticed it in the base sector first, but Fisly was able to report her observations on the source of the problem once she reached safety," Jessina added. "She says it looked like the tampering was coming from one of the other Fountain communication lines. It sounds from her description like an external takeover through those channels."

"Which one?" Kerric asked, narrowing his eyes.

"Menomon." Jessina gave him a sober look. "From the echoes she heard, she said the voice tones were right, but it didn't *sound* like Guardian Sheren . . . and that it sounded like one of the Fountains farther down the line was having difficulties of its own."

"Fisly has a good ear for both tone and nuance," Kerric murmured, half to himself. "I'd be inclined to trust her observations. So, either Menomon or one of the ones farther down the line was being taken over, and *our* Fountain got caught in the backlash."

"I'm not so sure, Kerric," Jessina countered slowly. "It's not just the shields on the Fountain Hall locking things out. Corridors and rooms have been realigning. Specifically, in the patterns *you* left on my desk in the 'just in case' folder. *I* think it may not have been Guardian Sheren at all, but rather someone pretending to . . ."

Her image turned fuzzy and her words garbled for a moment.

". . . attacking *our* Fountain as well, like a spider at the heart of a web," she finished . . . then frowned. "Did your end just turn fuzzy?"

"Yes. I think you're right," Kerric said quickly. "That means the Tower is going to block all communications in a moment. Broadcast a reminder to stay in the refreshing rooms wherever possible, and have everyone just sit tight. I know what to do on my end, but it's going to take many hours, if not days outright. I . . ."

The mirror fuzzed, streaked, and wobbled several times . . . and resolved into a reflection of his own face. His fist thumped on the desk surface, then stroked the frame for a moment. He smacked the desktop again when the mirror remained a mere reflection.

"Dammit," he muttered, dropping his head into his other palm. "My *one* day off in a year, and *this* has to happen."

"What do we do now?" Sylva asked him, brow furrowed in worry. "If someone is trying to invade the Tower remotely, how can we stop that if there's no one left in the Fountain Hall?"

Straightening up, Kerric shook his head. "*We* don't. The Tower just did it for us. Its defenses are designed to cut off all communications from magical sources if it's ever put under a Guardianship attack, in order to force a ground-based assault. That way our patrons cannot try to wrest away our control of the flow of the scrycastings in any way. You have to be at the Tower itself, physically there, to get into the chamber to take it over and form a new Guardianship bond.

"But *don't* tell anyone that," he ordered, rising from her desk. "We have far too many mages among the various adventurers who throng the Tower day after day, year after year. *Your* job is to get the village organized to contain and quell any panic. You can start by helping the Adventuring Hall contact everyone who has a scrying contract with us."

Sylva blinked, and quickly sat down at her desk. "Oh, you're right! They're going to be *furious* at the loss of the adventuring shows—oh Gods, how do I contact Senod-Gra?" she asked him, blinking up at the half-disposed Guardian. "They're literally on the far side of the world from us, and they're our biggest subscriber! Three whole Fountainways dedicated just to bringing them round-the-clock images . . . and with the Fountainways now cut off—!"

Kerric clasped her shoulder. "Contact who you can, *burgher* Sylva," he directed her, reminding her of her position as second in command to the village mayor. The mayor himself was currently off visiting relatives somewhere, taking advantage of the fine summer weather to travel, leaving Sylva in charge. She was competent, but she did have a little crush on Kerric. "Senod-Gra and other points out of mirror-range will just have to suffer until I can regain control of everything. Oh—order a replacement full-length mirror for the Mage Guild in Sendale. The Tower defenses broke the one I tried to connect to Topside Control."

She nodded, calming down a little, then shot him a worried look. "Right, I'll do that. But, *can* you get in there? You took over the Tower at Guardian Felesten's express invitation. You were *let* into the innermost chamber. You may have been the Master of the Tower for the last decade, but . . . forgive me, Kerric, you're no adventurer."

"No, I am not," he agreed, squeezing her shoulder before letting go, "but I *am* still a powerful mage, and I have ten years' worth of experience in watching and managing the Tower. *Your* job is to reassure everyone that everything is under control, and that our scrycasts will resume schedule 'soon' . . . but be vague on exactly when that 'soon' will be."

She nibbled her lower lip, wincing a little. "I think I'd be more convincing if I had an actual cover story, milord. They'll want to know *what* we have 'under control,' and some of the Tower's clients will be very persistent about it."

Mind blank, Kerric tried to think of something. All he could think of was the need to remember the progression of traps and tricks pre-aligned into the Tower's defenses. Most of them he could navigate more or less on his own, save for one repeating trap. It would render any mage unconscious within just a few seconds, which meant he would need to take one non-mage along with him, to literally drag him free of the trouble-spot.

No, he realized, wincing, *that should be "save for two traps" . . . I forgot about the other one. Which means I'll need a female to come along. One who doesn't find me repulsive.*

Under any other circumstance, most adventuring teams consisted of three to seven people, depending upon factors such as difficulty of the adventuring route, lethality of the traps, objective of the adventure segment . . . but this was a trek meant to penetrate the very heart of the Tower. Anyone who came with him would see the actual tricks needed to get inside, and that meant the more who saw it, the more chances there were for word to get out of how to navigate those tricks. That could lure unscrupulous mages into attempting to get into the innermost sanctum, and not just from among those who came here to make a name for themselves as adventurers.

Such a slip would waste too much of his time in trying to thwart and keep them out. Right now, he had plenty of time to conduct research in his favorite areas of interest, interspersed among the day-to-day needs of managing the Tower. He would either have to close the Tower to all adventurers—a very difficult prospect, considering the prosperity of the whole region depended upon the Tower's scrying clients, including all the people who helped maintain the place and staffed the Adventuring Hall—or give up his writing time and probably his writing career, with the attendant risk of innocent staff members getting caught in all the cross fire.

No, the smaller the party, the safer they'd all be in the long-term.

"I have it! Two rumors," Sylva stated, startling him with her exclamation. "The first one is the official reason, that there is an emergency maintenance issue cutting a whole swath of rooms off from the rest of the Tower, not just one or two. So you're going in personally as Master of the Tower to perform maintenance yourself. The *second* rumor is that you've been privately bet by an unnamed, wealthy outsider to run the Tower yourself . . . but as the Master, either you're running it without scrying because you don't want anyone to see you fail, or because the bet requires total anonymity, at the request of your sponsor. A private scrying, as it were."

"Not bad," Kerric praised. "But both are a lie. What if someone demands a truth-scrying?"

She gave him a smug look, and pulled open one of the drawers of her desk. Fishing out a white disc from the interior, she held it up in her right hand, and extended the left to him. "*I* will bet you—very, very privately—that you cannot make it all the way to a very specific, very private goal, without any outsiders scrying on you."

He stared at her for a moment, then chuckled. Patting her shoulder, Kerric clasped her hand. "I'll take that bet, O Wealthy Anonymous Patron." Shaking her hand, he gave her a mock bow. "Be prepared to lose, for I intend to get into the heart of the Tower . . . and with it on lockdown, no one can scry anything inside its walls."

"Oh, I'd *better* lose. Because if I win, it'll mean you're probably dead," she shot back tartly, "and I don't want that."

"So what will the wager be?" he asked her as she returned the Truth Stone to the drawer.

Sylva blushed and smiled shyly, fussing a little with the papers on her desk. Finally, she offered diffidently, ". . . A dinner date?"

"If I lose, which includes not making it to the heart because I die, I cannot go on a date with you," he quickly pointed out. She'd tried asking him out before, but Kerric knew Sylva wanted not just a prospective husband, but children somewhere down the line. He did not. Still, she tried now and then.

"I know. Which is why I'm counting on you not to lose." She snuck a shy look at him up through her lashes.

She was pretty, smart, competent, neither too young nor too old, and quite good at managing the needs of the little town of

Penambrion, which everyone else called the Tower Village. But he just wasn't attracted to her. He wasn't going to tell her that, though. A simple date was a small price to pay for quelling rampant rumor and speculation.

". . . Right. Good luck with the clients," Kerric muttered, heading for the door.

"Good luck with the Tower, Kerric," she called out after him.

TWO

꘠

Lifting a hand in farewell, he headed out of the building. It was a modest-sized structure, built of solidly mortared stone and pretty red roof tiles. It was also dwarfed by the Adventuring Hall next door, an imposing structure crafted out of patterned colors of granite and white-glazed roof tiles, a structure easily six or seven times the size of City Hall. Administering the needs of the village was a simple task, compared to organizing the constant flux of would-be adventurers, men and women who wanted to try their luck against the traps, tricks, and puzzles of the outer layers of the Tower.

He didn't go into the Adventuring Hall just yet, however. Instead, he detoured to the nearby fountain for a drink and a rest. For a think, as well. Planning, as his tutors and teachers had always instructed him, was the most important first step in any task. Planning involved gathering information, assembling supplies and assistance, and organizing each stage of a task.

Kerric knew every trick and trap in the tower, and remembered the pattern which would lead to the innermost heart, but he would need help. Preferably a woman as skilled and knowledgeable in combat and trap-navigating as he could get ahold of, and hopefully one who was also trustworthy. And one who was not a mage, of course.

Thankfully, there were a large number of women willing to dare the dangers of the Tower time and again. The staff would have made notes on each adventurer's conduct—mostly to try to determine who would make a good candidate for recruiting into the Tower staff once they were ready to retire, or into the Adventuring Hall staff. Kerric could use those notes to winnow the lot down to a trustworthy list of females to approach. Thankfully, copies were kept in both the Tower and the Hall, since the staff in both locations needed ready access to the information.

These adventuring parties were merely a profitable side effect of the Tower's existence. At some point in the distant past, a Fountain singularity, a spark-sized hole between Life and the Dark, the place where souls passed through on their way to judgment and the Afterlife, had been released into the world. And somehow, it had wound up high in the sky over the broad valley and the village of Penambrion a couple hundred miles from the eastern coast of the Aian continent.

Fountains literally poured magical energies into the world like a fountain poured and splashed water. All living animals cast off magical energies into the aether; normally, they soaked into the plants that fed the animals, including his fellow humans. This was the circle and the cycle of magic, just as the circle and cycle of the weather included evaporation, clouds, and rainfall. But sometimes a bit of that magic got dragged into the Dark when a soul was released from its body, and that energy in the Dark had to go somewhere. Such things could be vented by tears in the

Veil, the barrier between life and death and even other planes of existence, or could be pinpricks.

Such things could be caged in special crystals, but they had to be constantly moved or they would eventually slow, stop, and anchor themselves permanently in place. Which was why it was so puzzling to have one stuck high up in the sky. Not a few feet, not a dozen yards, but hundreds and hundreds of feet straight up. Normally, the extremely strong mages who mastered their energies moved them into caves, or castles, or other defensive structures that already existed. In this case, the Tower had been built *after* the singularity had come to rest so puzzlingly high, spilling its excess of magical energy all over the broad local valley.

The Tower had been erected fairly quickly, too, to contain and control those energies so they wouldn't warp the people living down below; magic in excess could be crudely shaped by a non-mage's will, but those wills were usually untrained, and so the end results often ended up mangled, making everything worse. Fountains had to be controlled by a Guardian for the safety and benefit of all.

True, the land had grown lush and ripe with overgrown, magic-fed plants, and the vegetables and fruits of the local gardens had become legendary for a while for their size, but the animals had started to mutate. The energies needed to be controlled. And because no one had been able to hide the Fountain's existence, the Tower had been filled with numerous defensive and offensive layers of protection to ensure it would be too difficult to capture by outsiders. That, however, had been a good seven hundred years ago.

At some point in time roughly four hundred years ago, the Guardian of the day had been putting up with would-be Guardians constantly trying to surmount the difficulties . . . and had started broadcasting scryings of their unsuccessful attempts to his fellow mages. The popularity of the scrying broadcasts had grown rather quickly, and the Guardian had seen the potential for profit. Rather than trying to discourage such attempts, he had turned it into a formal business, enlarging the Tower and stocking certain rooms with valuable things, such as coins, weapons, armor, and enchanted objects, paid for by the mages and their non-mage patrons, who wanted steady access to such entertaining scrycastings.

Those risks and rewards were confined to the lower levels with easier, less lethal traps at first, but as the lure of that wealth brought in more and more outsiders, more and more of them grew rather skilled, penetrating farther into the mazelike structure, particularly as the original patterns became known. So some predecessor of Kerric's had come up with the idea of sectioning off all the rooms and corridors at their doorways with special doorway-Gates which could be swapped up on a whim by the Guardian. The Fountain, of course, powered both the scrycastings and the enchanted doorways. It left the land less fertile than before as more and more magic was diverted, but the income from the scryings more than made up for it.

The flexibility of the arrangement allowed the subsequent Guardians to actually plan various routes. Different levels of difficulty could be assigned to those routes, and different styles of games could be devised. Some were along the lines of "get in, grab a certain item, and get out again" while others were a case of "rescue the victim"—who was usually a Tower employee—or "see how many traps you can disarm in X number of hours."

After four hundred years, and with paths which could be realigned nearly at will, there were a *lot* of different games and configurations people could run. Adventuring in the Tower was the single most popular activity for a good thousand miles around, even beyond the extent of most scrycastings. There were even scrycast relays, mirrors hooked up in tandem to extend the range, and the images could be sent along the Fountainways.

Adventurers could sign up as a group, or as individuals who would be put into a pool and selected by lottery based on their skill sets, levels of expertise, and the types of adventures they had signed up for, or any number of variations. But they all had to check in here, at the Adventuring Hall. Anyone caught trying to sneak into the Tower unauthorized was presumed to be a thief of some sort, with the nearest traps rearranged by the various Maintenance departments to be turned lethal.

It was inevitable that they had clients who would pay for scryings of such things, but Kerric and his predecessors had made sure such clients paid dearly. And every single would-be adventurer had to sign legal contracts to hold the Tower, the Adventurer's Guild, and their various employees free of responsibility for any damages they suffered or incurred while adventuring in the Tower. No one was forced to go inside, and no one could be forced to go inside, so whatever happened to them was of their own free will.

Which means I'll not only need to find a female adventurer who isn't a mage, one who is capable of keeping her mouth shut, but also one who is highly skilled at navigating the tricks of the Tower, and willing to go in on a two-person team. Three-person teams are usually hard enough as it is, but with only two, everything grows extra hard. Plus she'll have to be physically strong, to drag my frame through that one particular trap . . . and single, for the other trap. Interested in men, for that matter.

The thought of *that* trap made him blush. As Master of the Tower, he normally just rerouted any doorway he opened or passed through with a pulse of his power, unless the configuration had to remain consistent for some reason. Such areas were usually the living quarters up at the very top, or if someone was using a particular passage or room during a game. Normally, he could override such things at great need . . . but not this time.

There were nine concrete, physical paths leading upward from the base of the Tower all the way to the very top. The trick lay in choosing the right entrances among the thirty or so doorways that could be accessed from the ground floor. Two of those were maintenance stairwells, connected to various rooms and chambers on different floors via carefully concealed secret doors. Those paths did not necessarily connect to the heart of the Tower, however.

Two more simply led from the base to the top, and the last five led toward the heart. Only a few of them crossed each other's path at certain points. Of the five that led to the heart, they joined together at different points until only one final stretch led through a set of very deadly traps to the Fountain Hall, the hidden heart of the Tower.

As Guardian, he knew which of those five paths was the easiest. Technically, the two maintenance stairwells were the easiest, but by now they were sealed off by the Tower defenses. Short of blasting giant holes in the Tower itself—which would cause an entirely new host of defensive measures to activate—there would be no way for an outsider to get into them. Whatever path was chosen, he and his companion would still have to face the formidable defenses lurking inside.

Beyond the white-tiled roof of the Adventuring Hall rose the mottled-cream bulk of the Tower. He could see the balconies and windows from here. They looked like enticing shortcuts, but he knew they weren't; their doorway-Gates were designed to loop back in on themselves in self-defense.

No, the real paths to the heart of the Tower—not the top, which he could reach by simply levitating all the way up—started at the bottom. And the best path to finding the right woman for his adventuring companion lay in the personnel files of the Adventuring Hall. Cupping his hands for one more drink at the fountain, Kerric wiped his mouth on his forearm and headed for the steps up into the Hall.

At least I can pick locks, so she won't need that in her skill set. I'll need to pick up a couple sets of tools from the supply master, though. I should probably pick up some knives or daggers, just in case. The physical fighting, that'll mostly be her job, whichever woman I pick. She'll need to be an outstanding warrior, too, since I'm not the best combatant in the world. Damn, I can't remember who was scheduled to go into the Tower this morning. I don't think any of them were the top fighters. I know I'd have remembered if a big-name adventurer-lady like Shalia or Myal or Terrend went in, so hopefully one of them is free. I do know Nafiel is taking the day off for certain, though he's a fellow male and both of us are straight, as far as I know . . .

"Master Kerric! What is going wrong within the Tower?" someone called out from the reception hall the moment he entered. "What's happening?"

Heads turned his way, not just from the staff managing the front chamber, but from the men and women lounging on the benches and chairs, many of them in armor with packs of traveling gear and supplies at their feet. Kerric quickly went into Master mode, shoulders square, chin confidently up, his strides solid and purposeful. Raising his hands, he quelled their concerns before the others could add their own queries.

"Rest easy, everyone. The Tower is just undergoing a bit of emergency maintenance. It will take a little bit of time to settle out," he admitted, "but I know exactly what to do and how to do it, so it will get done. In the meantime, consider this a little rest-break from the normal hustle and bustle of things. Relax, have some fun, and I'll see about requisitioning a nice meal for everyone on the Tower's bill if this stretches into tomorrow, to apologize for the inconvenience."

"Uh, Master Kerric?" one of the women lounging in the front hall asked, her tone hesitant but her hazel eyes earnest, almost pleading. She rose to her feet, taller than him by a handspan, clad in fighting leathers, her ash-brown hair pulled back from her face by a leather band across her brow. "You're the one in charge, right? I . . . I have a friend in the Tower right now. I was a little late getting here, so she went on ahead without me, and . . ."

Kerric dipped his head, acknowledging her fears. "All adventurers inside the Tower were instructed to move to a refreshing room shelter area. I'm sure your friend did exactly that. Once inside a refreshing room, she'll be perfectly fine while she waits for the necessary repairs to be made. She might get a little bored of dried meats and crackers from the food vending cabinets, but she'll be alright.

"If she wasn't smart enough to find one immediately . . . Well, everyone who enters the Tower accepts the inherent risks. And yes, that includes Tower personnel, from the lowliest cleaner all the way up through even me," he added deprecatingly, touching his chest.

"Master Kerric, I have a question!" a man called out.

Giving him and the others a slight bow, Kerric continued toward the back halls, where the copies of the files on every currently active adventurer were kept. "I'm afraid there's quite a lot for me to do in order to get the Tower back up and running properly. We'll do our best to get everyone out again, but things do break down from time to time, and so maintenance must happen. Try to enjoy the day off, everyone!"

Flicking his hand in a friendly wave over his shoulder, he disappeared through a door marked with a brass plaque that read

Authorized Personnel Only. It meant escaping to safety, but only relative safety. He wouldn't be queried by adventurers, but the men and women on the other side of that stout panel would also have awkward questions for him to deflect.

The head of the Adventuring Hall would need to know what had gone wrong. Sylva, of course, already knew. And those with whom Jessina had spoken would already know. The rest would only get the two scenarios proposed by burgher Sylva. It was the only way to quell the wrong sorts of rumors.

Rumors were rampant in the Honey Spear. No sooner had Narahan Myal pushed open the door and stepped into the tavern than she heard at least five different reasons why the Tower was locked down. She had to duck a little to get through the doorway without feeling like she was going to smack her head on the lintel, but she was used to doing that. She couldn't duck the noise of all that speculation, though.

A huge chunk of rooms had swapped entrances and frozen up, with no access in or out. A special team of adventurers was making a run for some sort of fantastic treasure. A small army of would-be thieves had managed to infiltrate the structure to steal the various treasures meant for honest, hard-working adventurers. An extremely wealthy patron wanted a private adventuring run. An extremely wealthy and perverted patron wanted an erotic adventuring run with scantily clad males and females competing for . . . things that made her ears burn.

Thankfully, the men and women joking about that one carried it clearly to the point of absurdity, and the game broke up in ribald laughter and deep sighs of denial. Myal *had* heard of certain rooms in the Tower of a very adult nature, and that such things were traps, but those rooms were almost never run. When they *were* included, it was announced to all, and any adventurer who chose that particular scenario had to sign additional waivers. Not to mention they had to prove they were at least twenty years in age, and wear contraceptive amulets. The local age of consent was sixteen, but the rules of the Tower decreed an adventurer had to have a bit of experience in such matters to be able to handle them maturely. Or at least had enough time to give the consequences some decent thought.

A variation on the "erotic adventuring" rumor made its way around again shortly after Myal had snagged one of the servers and requested whatever was hot and ready for her supper. She'd heard the one about someone betting the Master of the Tower to run the tricks and traps himself on her walk from her three-room tenement to this place, but this version had the Master of the Tower running the gauntlets stark naked.

She blushed just thinking about that. She, like many other adventuring favorites, had dealt directly with the Master of the Tower from time to time. Most of those "meetings" had been mirror-based. The administrators in the Adventuring Hall would call for specific players during special events requested by patrons when they wanted to see their favorites perform, or had a particular form of gauntlet in mind, but sometimes the Master would make those requests or outline those runs himself.

He was rather handsome, with his exotic curly brown hair, lightly suntanned skin, and those nice gray eyes . . . but it wasn't right to think of the man naked. He worked very hard to make the Tower entertaining, exciting, and even fun, despite its many dangers. Myal didn't think it was respectful to . . . to think of him as a sex object instead of a man. Everything she had learned since coming here had only increased her admiration of the hardworking Guardian and his equally hardworking staff.

Five years ago, she had arrived on the eastern shore of Aiar as part of a Mendhite merchant ship's crew. As they had made their way up the coast, offering Mendhite spices and seeking out exotic local versions to take back, word of the Tower and its adventurers had reached her ears. Being who and what she was, Myal had felt an itch of curiosity about the place. Wanting to test herself, she had parted from the crew at the nearest port, found work as a caravan guard headed west, and wound up here in Penambrion, the Tower Village.

She wasn't the only Painted Warrior at the Tower, but at the moment there were only three, herself and two men, and she was the best of them. There were always more male adventurers than females, particularly among the non-Mendhites; if one wasn't a mage, capable of shielding and augmenting one's abilities, then an adventurer had to rely on strength and stamina as well as skill. In just about every land she had visited by sea, women were expected to be more interested in more peaceful pursuits, such as raising children, administering a government, or making a house into a home. Such things didn't leave much time for adventuring and life-risking, after all.

Myal wasn't tied to a job, a hearth, or a cradle. She wasn't interested in amassing vast amounts of prestige or money, either, though she had purchased expensive enchantments for her boiled leather armor and her weapons. She had also bought a few comforts for her tenement, like the custom-sized bed to fit her Mendhite-sized body, and she made a habit of eating someone else's cooking on a regular basis. Little things, though, nothing big.

No, she was here for the challenge and the fun. She could afford to spend her excess money on finding and buying copies of various Aian books to be shipped all the way back to the Great Library. She could also donate to various local charities, such as the disaster fund for the local farmers of the broad Penambrion valley-basin, whose crops were occasionally ruined and homes flooded by heavy rainfall. It had been a very wet spring, and the communities for miles around had been deeply grateful for the support from the adventurers who chose to live here permanently.

"Ah! Myal the Mendhite!" The hearty baritone voice was more than familiar; it belonged to Nafiel, self-styled Aian barbarian, and the single most popular adventurer, period, of the entire Tower. He raised his mug of ale to her. "So what do *you* think is the real reason for the Tower being locked down?"

They weren't being remotely scryed. That was the deal with the villagers, to protect the privacy of their daily lives; no scrying was allowed anywhere but within certain chambers in the Adventuring Hall, and of course in the Tower itself. That rule also protected everyone's privacy in their off-hours, including hers. Nafiel wasn't being hearty for the mirrors and their patrons; he was simply that way all the time, public or private. She knew he came from a land to the west called Pasha, where the people had chosen a God and Goddess who represented passion in its many forms.

Accepting the plate of sliced beef, mashed roots, and steaming buttered vegetables and the mug of chilled Aian tea brought by the server, Myal considered his question. Nafiel, having adventured with her multiple times, hushed a few of the more impatient patrons of the Honey Spear, and waited for her to speak. He may have been boisterous by nature, but he was also polite.

"I think . . . given the age of the Tower," she allowed, "that it is quite possible several of the rooms have 'locked up' like joints seized with inflammation. Some of the rumors from those watching the current adventure groups did say that the rooms and corridors have realigned themselves unexpectedly. And it has been said that the Master appeared in the Adventuring Hall personally, so the situation must be quite grave to involve him on the outside."

"Nah, s'not the real reason," another man dismissed, sipping from a glass of wine. He had dyed his shaggy hair in stripes of white and black, and had dyed and stitched his leathers to match, making him look like a *zevra* from back home. He wasn't Mendhite, but he had heard about that land's wild horses from one of the others within the first few days of his arrival, and had decided to create an outlandish outfit to catch the eyes of the scrycast viewers, and the name to go with it.

"It makes the most sense," Myal stated. "The Tower is old. Even with the Fountain powering it, spells do eventually wear out. Or so I understand; I'm no mage."

"No, but you're the next best thing to it," Nafiel chuckled, lifting his mug in salute before drinking. Like Zevra, he was in his working clothes, which were nothing more than furred boots, a furred loincloth, and a plethora of enchanted armbands, necklaces, rings, and even earrings to make up for all the lack of armor. His gimmick was leaving his rather large and very well-muscled chest, arms, and legs as bare as possible; the Tower had a *lot* of lady mages paying right and left to watch him as he worked his way through each gauntlet. Rumor also had it he paid mages to remove his chest and armpit hairs by spell, so that no female patron would have her view distracted from all those flexing muscles.

"Nah, nah, meant th' Master bein' on the outside," Zevra corrected, waggling his spread hand as if to erase the misunderstanding. He sipped his wine, then grimaced. "Nah, *I* heard he'd gone off to th' city on a trip. Things went rump-up while he was gone, an' he got locked out."

His suggestion was met with far more catcalls and derisive noises than mutterings of agreement. It wasn't just loyalty on the part of the locals and the regulars. Every once in a while—about two, three times a year—some idiot-mage came by, demanding to have an Arcane Duel with the Guardian of the Tower. Master

Kerric allowed it only after the would-be challenger paid a hefty fee . . . and then usually drove the challenger to his or her knees within minutes. Sometimes one-handed. Those, too, were broadcast for a fee.

Zevra quickly held off the worst of the grumblings. "Just sayin', must be pretty bad f' the Master t' get locked out, s'all. Or just bad luck 'n bad timing crawlin' into bed together."

And just that easily, they were back to the sexual speculations and accompanying innuendos. Myal rolled her eyes and focused on her meal. Not that she had anything against sex; it could be enjoyable enough with a good partner. But it wasn't her favorite leisure-time activity. For her, that was writing up text versions of the various adventures she had in the Tower, trying to find just the right phrase to describe what she had done in a way that conveyed what had really happened.

It wasn't easy, and she couldn't claim to be the best at it, but she enjoyed it all the same. Most Mendhites wrote, but then their religion centered around She Who Records, the Goddess Menda, Scribe of Heaven and Creator of the Written Word. Every land Myal had ever visited knew that writing had begun in Mendhi, and most knew of the Great Library in Mendham.

With translation spells and pendants and even certain expensive potions available, reading was an activity that could be enjoyed by a traveler wherever she might go, and writing was a good way to share that traveler's observations on other lands and cultures. And with Painted Warriors, well, those who didn't stay in Mendhi often took up a life of wandering and non-Tower adventuring, and many of them sent back written tales of what they had seen and done in their travels. It was as much Myal's religious and civic duty to write down her Tower-based adventures as it was her pleasure.

She wasn't Master Kerric, whose skill with the language was a pleasure to read, but she wasn't bad. Her short stories, hand-bound and copied by a local mage, were enjoyable enough that her fellow adventurers and some of the villagers always asked when the next one was due to be distributed. *I should get back to writing about rescuing Prince Samel from the Demon-Summoners,* she decided. *I have notes for three more beyond that; I've been falling behind on my writing. If the Tower is really as locked-up as everyone thinks it is, I could easily have two, three days for writing that are free and clear of any patron requests for my presence on the next few runs.*

Mind made up, she ordered a pocket-pie to take with her for her dessert, adding a couple extra coins as a tip. The fruit-filled pastry the server brought was hot enough that it stung her fingers. Shifting her right hand in a scooping, swirling motion, Myal focused on the tattoo inked around her littlest finger, activating it. Immediately, the heat from the pie ceased bothering her. It was still very hot, fresh from the oven, but the writhing, flamelike lines of the tattoo protected her from being burned.

Having them inked into her skin had burned, too, if in a different way. The hands, feet, and face were the most sensitive parts of the body for tattooing. There were spells to dull the pain and make the process of being inked bearable, but Painted Warriors did not, and could not, take the easy way. The pain was part of the process, part of bonding the spell-tattoos to body and will.

Her littlest right finger controlled variations in heat when she activated it. Her littlest left controlled and grounded shocks. The subtle pale brown tattoo around her left eye, which blended into her deeply tanned skin, permitted her to see through the simpler sorts of illusions, and the one that stretched from her throat to her right ear and her right eye in pale blue gave her the ability to understand languages both written and spoken.

The bottom of her left foot had a sigil that would allow her to walk on a delicate surface, such as thin ice, dried leaves, or even water, without breaking through, provided she concentrated. The right one had a marking that would allow her to walk on and cling to any surface, whether or not it was horizontal, though the rest of her body was still subject to the effects of gravity. Her spine had a twining vinelike design that would heal most injuries in minutes—though it took its toll on her in other ways—and her biceps were circled with bands that gave her extra strength and extra speed. And those were just a handful among the dozens pricked into her skin.

Unfortunately, there wasn't a tattoo inked anywhere in the world which would make her stories write themselves. Or make her tell them better, or get her noticed by a printer, or . . . or allow her to write them while soaking in a nice cool bath. She didn't know of any tattoos that would allow her to dictate to a quill and page located a safe, dry distance away.

Nor did she have any tattoos that would get her home any faster, though the heat of the day looked like it was finally beginning to cool down. Five years of a wandering seafarer's life followed by five years in this temperate climate had robbed her of the ability to tolerate extremes of humidity and heat; Mendhi was much closer to the Sun's Belt than the valley around the Tower. Not that today had been especially warm or muggy, but a cool bath did sound good.

She wasn't the only one seeking her tenement. A man in a brown outfit stood at the door to Shalia's quarters, knocking on the stout wooden panel. Made of red brick and pink mortar, the building had a row of doors on the ground floor, and a set of stairs leading up to a balcony with more doors, and a third one above that as well. Her place was on the second floor, a bit warm in the summer, but quite comfortable in the winter, what with the fireplaces from the other residents' rooms lending their heat to the building as a whole.

Shalia finally answered the knocking just as Myal came within a few lengths of the curly-haired visitor. Opening the door, the muscular blonde leaned her head out, her body clearly wrapped in a sheet for clothing. Myal blushed. Shalia did not.

". . . Yes?" she drawled.

Before the man in brown could say anything, a taller man, bare-chested and bare-legged, appeared behind the blonde. He kissed her shoulder and wrapped an arm around her waist, making the adventurer giggle. Myal knew his face, but couldn't for the life of her place a name to it. Not with such a big, leering, smirking grin in the way.

"Uhh . . . never mind," the shorter man, the visitor, stated. Belatedly, Myal recognized *him* by his voice and his brown curls, though she hadn't seen his face yet. Master Kerric Vo Mos cleared his throat, cheeks slightly pink, and dipped his head. "I see you're busy, so I'll not bother you. Have a good night—both of you."

Turning, he started to stride away, and almost smacked into Myal. Shalia looked like she wanted to linger and listen; like Myal, she had dealt with the Master of the Tower before. The man in her quarters had other ideas. Still kissing her shoulder, he tugged her backward and firmly shut the door. That left Myal face to . . . well, breast to face with the Guardian. She had met him far more often by mirror than in person, and each time in person it was a bit of a shock to realize how short he was, even for an Aian. Handsome, confident, with a mind both fair and strong, but shorter than any Mendhite man.

"Master Kerric," she murmured politely.

He looked up, blinked, and gave her a bright smile. "Mistress Myal! Just the woman I wanted to see. At least, you were next on my list, since Shalia is obviously occupied," he added, gesturing vaguely over his shoulder. "Could we perhaps have a little discussion in your quarters?"

"Of course," she agreed quickly, gesturing at the stairs. "It's the second floor, middle tenement."

"I know," he agreed, nipping up the stairs with the quick tread of someone used to going up and down all over the many, many levels of the Tower. "I made sure to check the address at the Adventuring Hall."

"Is this about the Tower, then?" she asked, following him up the steps. He didn't answer her. At his silence, it occurred to her that if the Master was *here*, looking up the residences of adventurers but not wanting to talk openly about it, then there was something going on which he didn't want anyone else to know. Quickly changing the subject, she asked, "So how was your trip to, uh, Seldane?"

"Sendale," he corrected lightly. "And aside from being cut short just as I hit the marketplace, not bad. The worst was finding a first edition Elgin Ves Troth just as I was called to come back. I didn't have a chance to buy it."

"Elgin Ves Troth?" she asked, moving ahead of him so she could fetch out her key from the pouch on her belt and unlock her tenement door. "Who is he?"

"A pre-Shattering authority on the Old Gods of Aiar," Kerric stated. She gestured him to enter first; he bowed politely, and preceded her into her sitting hall. "Not all of the regional Gods and Goddesses are the same ones that were worshipped prior to the Shattering of the last Convocation of Gods and Man, you know. It's fascinating to read about the old ones, and compare and contrast that with the new beliefs that have sprung up—most of the Gods and Goddesses around the fringes of the Empire have remained the same, and in a few scattered spots through the interior, but a good half of them are completely new."

Nodding, she closed the door and twisted the upper knob, locking out any would-be spies. The locking mechanism had been etched with various runes by the landowner, giving each resident privacy as well as security. "There. We're shielded from scryers and eavesdroppers. Please, sit. Can I get you anything to drink? Water? Tea? I don't keep anything fermented on hand."

THREE

"Water will suffice, thank you," Kerric replied, glad the tall foreigner was willing to be discreet. He watched her set the pastry in her other hand on the low table in the room as she crossed to the far door, and followed the sway of her hips, subtle but graceful, as she left to find him his drink. Shalia was a lovely enough woman, but blondes were fairly common around the Tower, particularly the farther north one went. He'd seen scores pass through the Adventuring Hall over the last decade.

Myal the Mendhite was not a blonde, and not common. He admired her tall, strong figure as he always had, covertly from under his lashes, and hoped his proposal wouldn't offend her. He'd take any woman along who agreed to his codicils, but it definitely wouldn't hurt to take one of the few he was actively attracted to, and not just found attractive. He could make love to the latter, but if luck was on his side, he could make love *with* the former. If she didn't find him repugnant.

Once she was out of sight, he looked around the front room, taking in the different things she had used to decorate it. Mostly the wooden-paneled walls were hung with scrolls painted with Mendhite characters and ink-washed images in subtle shades of pastels and grays, but there were a few trinkets from her adventurings. Having drunk a very expensive translation potion early on in his apprenticeship to the previous Guardian, Kerric felt his eyes twitching as they tried to adapt to the foreign runes at a single glance. Phrases about honor, vigilance, respect . . . insights into the values his hostess found important.

Dragging his gaze away, he looked at the other decorations. He recognized a bright gold and scarlet shield from among a shipment purchased three years ago for gauntlet prizes, and a feathered mask that had been worn by a fellow adventurer during a contest that had pitted group against group. The winners had each "counted coup" by claiming one item from the losers in that gauntlet game, so that must have been her claim.

The rest of the color in the room came from a worn Sundaran carpet on the floor, a plethora of bright cushions on the low divan, and the warm glow of the setting sun through the glazed windows behind the divan. Maneuvering around the low table in front of it, he shifted a few cushions and settled himself on the padded platform while she disappeared through one of the other doors.

He had a glimpse of a room with a writing desk and a stack of booklets before she came back with a pitcher and two mugs. Setting them on the low table, she poured water into both, then gestured for him to take his choice while she sat down next to him. Selecting one, Kerric sipped from it, enjoying the cool liquid. It was refreshing after a warm, hectic afternoon. It also reminded him that he had eaten recently, but he didn't know about her.

"Have you had supper yet, Mistress Myal?" he asked politely.

"Yes, I just came back from the Honey Spear. I usually eat there," she confessed. Then gave him a sidelong look and added, "There were a *lot* of wild rumors going around the tavern tonight. About the Tower being locked down."

Kerric grimaced, cradling the mug in both hands. "I was hoping to quell those."

"I presume you're here because you wish to discuss my, er, participation in the . . . maintenance issue?" she asked delicately.

He blushed. She blinked at him. Clearing his throat, Kerric dug into his own pouch, fishing out a bracelet. He lifted it between them. "This is a mild geas Artifact. It will compel you to keep from repeating in the presence of anyone else whatever is discussed for the duration that you wear it. Would you be willing to put it on for a little bit? And hold a Truth Stone?"

Myal eyed the curved, rune-chased scrap of silver, unsure of his intent. "I suppose so." Holding out her hand, she accepted the bracelet and fitted it onto her left wrist. It was a bit tight, but not uncomfortably so. "Where's the Truth Stone?"

He pulled that out as well, clutching and testing the white marble disc first. "I am covered in blue fur." Uncurling his fingers, he revealed black marks on the palm-sized bit of stone wherever his skin had touched it. Clutching it again as the marks faded, he stated, "I am Kerric Vo Mos."

The Stone was unblemished, pure white. Catching her hand, he turned it palm-up and placed the Truth Stone in her palm. "Ready?"

Myal clutched it and nodded.

"Topside Control believes someone in the distant city of Menomon broke into Guardian Sheren's Fountain Hall and tried to use it to take over the Tower Fountain," he stated bluntly. He gave her a moment to recover as her eyes widened, then continued. "The Tower is designed to lock down *all* forms of access and communication in the event of any change of Guardianship. This prevents it from being subverted remotely, because once that lockdown occurs, the only way to regain control is to either be on hand in the heart of the Tower, or to run the gauntlets in person, from the ground floor all the way to the heart of the Tower. When I took over, the lockdown took only a few minutes of time, because I was there in the Fountain Hall with my predecessor. This time, however, because *I* was in Sendale on the one day away I've had in a year, I couldn't stop it from happening at the heart of the matter.

"If I am to regain control of the Tower and its now *very* lethal traps . . . I need to run those gauntlets myself," Kerric confessed grimly. "And I need to do it before any other high-powered mage wakes up to the fact that the Tower *is* vulnerable to a change in Guardianship. I don't know how you feel about the way I've run things," he added in an aside, "but I do know most of the locals say I'm doing a good job, so I'm not inclined to just hand it over to whoever gets there ahead of me. Which means I need to get in there first."

"Oh, no," Myal quickly agreed, clutching the Stone. "You're doing a great job! All the adventurers believe so, too. Tonight, when someone dared to suggest you weren't on top of things at the Honey Spear, he was shouted down by three-quarters of the inn, and even *he* agreed it was unlikely. You're well-loved by almost everyone here in Penambrion."

He blushed again, and the corner of his mouth curved up on one side. It revealed a dimple in his cheek, a sight she found fascinating.

"Well, thank you." He then made a show of craning his neck to look at the Stone in her hands, and she uncurled her fingers, showing the lack of even a trace of gray on the unblemished Stone. That earned her a chuckle. "Thank you, *indeed*. But there's still a chance someone with too much ambition and not enough understanding of the way things work could get his or her hands on the Fountain . . . so I've come to you . . . after trying a few others . . . to see if you'd be willing to help."

Myal considered his words, frowning softly. She gave him a wary look. "What's the catch? If I'm not the first adventurer you've approached, and the others have turned you down . . . what's the catch?"

He blushed again. Rubbing at the back of his neck, Kerric cleared his throat, sipped at his water, and didn't quite meet her gaze. "There is more than one path . . . at least initially . . . to get to the Fountain Hall. The path I'd *prefer* to take, the one with the least lethal hazards . . . has a particular hazard that . . . ah . . . Well, it is a bit . . ."

She waited patiently while he fumbled to a stop, frowned a bit, then sighed heavily and muttered something under his breath. He sipped again. Myal wanted to be patient, but her curiosity was also rising. Master Kerric had never struck her as a man prone to blushing, yet here he had done it four or more times in nearly as many minutes. "Go ahead and say it. Whatever the hazard is, just speaking of it will not give offense."

Nodding, he dragged in a deep breath, faced her, and asked bluntly, "Would you be willing to make love with me?"

Her jaw dropped. Blinking at him, Myal wondered if she had heard him right, but no, his face had turned pink again under its light tan, yet he was also gazing at her steadily, soberly with those fascinating gray eyes of his. To cover up her confusion and shock, she sipped at her own mug. When she felt she could speak again, she asked, "Uhh . . . what circumstances will prompt such a need? Since we, ah, have only worked together infrequently, and never, um . . ."

Rubbing at the back of his neck again, he gestured with the

mug. "The other paths require three or more people to success-fully navigate. The easiest one to take would only require two adventurers, myself and a highly skilled non-mage such as your-self . . . but it requires undertaking through part of the Seraglio gauntlet. That's the, ah, erotic section. Pheromone filled gas-traps, desire-based geases . . . and a particularly nasty psycho-logical trap that requires a person to already have a, er, dedicated partner in order to successfully resist the spell's efforts to ensnare the adventurers and hold them in place, and . . . well . . ."

Blushing, he shrugged again. Myal nodded, not quite under-standing, but then some traps just had to be experienced to see how they worked. Kerric cleared his throat, continuing.

"Well. Time, as I said, is an important factor, since once we're inside, we'll have no idea if anyone else will be trying to sneak in as well," he reminded her.

That made sense . . . and confused her at the same time. Myal frowned at him. "Then why did you try asking the others, but with the implication that you were turned down?"

"Because I'm not looking for a wife, and most of the women I asked assumed this meant I was automatically going to propose to them afterward." He had the grace to blush a little harder this time at such blunt words, blush and apologize. "I'm sorry if that implies I wouldn't value any moments of intimacy we might share, but I am the Guardian of the Tower. I do not have the time for all the trappings of marriage . . . and the Tower is no place to raise a child. That's why I've refused to date adventurers; the few times I tried, they assumed that I'd want to settle down, raise a family, and be someone, well, other than *me*."

"That . . . wouldn't be a concern with me," Myal murmured, thinking of the tattoo encircling her navel, the one empowering all the rest. *Impossible, even.* Out loud, she said, "I can understand why you'd not want to be entangled in that way. As the Master of the Tower, your job is to keep adventurers *out* of the heart. It'd be a conflict of interest."

"Mostly only if that adventurer were a fellow mage," he amended, checking the Truth Stone more discreetly this time for darkness. Nothing stained the pristine marble. "A non-mage would not be much of a threat to the Tower's control, and a dedicated, professional adventurer such as you even less so. I sorted out a list of women who have been here for at least a full year, and have shown every sign of wanting to stay here near-permanently—the kind of women whom the Adventuring Hall staff have already recommended as making potential future employees, when they're ready to cease risking their lives in the gauntlets and settle down to help manage and maintain the Tower's games."

"Oh. I hadn't considered joining the staff," Myal admitted, thinking about it, "but I suppose I very well could. I certainly know more traps and tricks than anyone outside of Nafiel and maybe a dozen of the others. I've also offered suggestions on ways to improve or alter some of the gauntlets I've run . . . unless that's . . . what's the Aian word . . . hubris?"

"You see, *that* is something I could use," Kerric told her, shifting to face her a little more. Their knees almost touched as he gestured. "Someone whose mind is on the *Tower's* needs, and not on their own personal . . ." He stopped, abruptly realizing just how unflattering that sounded. Wincing, Kerric gave her a rueful smile. "I apologize, Mistress Myal," he said. "I did not mean to trivialize anything we would share if you went with me into the Tower. I may not want to turn my life upside-down for a relationship . . . but I would cherish any time spent with you, and I would not take any lovemaking we did for granted.

"In fact, it would have to be *above* a trivial, grab-whoever-and-go-at-it liaison in order to break through the geas involved with the least chance of failure. Which brings me to my next

Truth Stone question. Do *you*, ah, find me attractive enough for lovemaking?" he asked. Again, his lighter skin turned pink along his brow and cheeks.

It was her turn to blush. Her skin wasn't as dark as that of those who lived along the southern coast of Aiar, so she knew he could see it. Gripping the Stone, she spoke bluntly, braving the truth as she braved far more deadly hazards in the Tower. "I do find you attractive, and I do hold you in high esteem. And if *you* find *me* equally attractive, I would not be . . . adverse to sharing lovemaking with you."

Uncurling her fingers, she showed him the all-white disc. He nodded slowly. Biting her lip, Myal shrugged mentally and added more to her statement, once more holding the Stone.

"I'm not looking for anything permanent, either. I . . . like my life as it is." That was safe enough to say truthfully, and a brief flick of her fingers showed it was indeed the truth. Honesty prompted her to add, "I've never really thought about working for the Tower or the Adventuring Hall, but I am flattered to be considered. As dangerous as it is, this is a . . . a fascinating thing you have here. The Tower is truly unique in the world. I am glad to be a part of it. If I can help you regain command of it, I'd be happy to help."

Again, he checked the Truth Stone. Again, it was blemish-free. Kerric felt relieved. Myal the Mendhite was imposingly tall, exotically beautiful, and very competent. She had been fourth on his list of top five choices of women to approach, and fourth only because of the path he'd had to walk to get to each woman's residence. Myal was one of his top ten favorite adventurers, for those times when he had a chance to sit down and watch the various gauntlets and games on his own private mirrors. Graceful, competent, gorgeous, courageous . . . Kerric hoped she was the right woman for his needs.

"Good . . . good." Taking the Stone from her hand, he clasped it in his fingers. "For the record, I find you admirable, lovely, and intelligent. In no particular order. And your help will be deeply appreciated." Revealing it for a moment, he showed her the all-white sides, then pressed it back into her hand. "Now, answer me this very important question. If I take you with me on a run for the Fountain Hall at the Tower's heart, will you do everything in your power to ensure we arrive there safely, and that I regain control of the Fountain as its proper Guardian?"

"I promise," she agreed, clutching the Stone. Opening her hand, she showed him it was still white, then gripped it one last time. "*I* am covered in blue fur." Fingers shifting, she showed the black marks on the surface, proving the Truth Stone was still working correctly.

The smile he gave her was warm, relieved, and rather handsome. "Good. Good! How soon can you be ready?"

Myal quirked one eyebrow. "How soon? Do we not get a good night's sleep, first?"

Kerric shook his head quickly, his shoulder-length curls bouncing with the movement. "The sooner we get going, the sooner we can get there. If we need rest, I can set a spell that will speed-trance us, but I'd like to get started right away. The longer we take, the more risk there is that someone or a group of some-ones will dare the Tower anyway, despite the lockdown status. There are plenty of adventurers who have made a point of study-ing the stories and the scryings of past attempts, and in those records are at least partial details of the successful routes one could take to the Fountain Hall. I want to be several jumps ahead of anyone else on this. As it is, I've already spent a couple hours looking up and sorting through a list of possible partners."

"I suppose that makes sense. You're lucky I've already eaten, or we'd be delayed that much longer," she said. "Do we need to pack food supplies? How long is the route?"

He grimaced. "We'll need a few rations, for safety's sake. I cannot guarantee more than three refreshing rooms along the route, so don't count on vendor cabinets—not to mention those refreshing rooms might already be occupied by refugees. There *is* one spot for a solid meal, but just the one. And it all depends on how quickly we get through each of the traps, and how wounded we are, and how long we may have to rest. But I can guarantee the absolute shortest anyone could ever run a five-man team through this route will be a full eight hours, if not longer.

"With just the two of us, it could be anywhere from twelve hours to two days or more. It depends on just how far into emergency mode the Tower defenses have been pushed," he finished.

"Then I'll get my armor, and make up a multiday pack. Ah— do *you* have any armor?" she asked, eyeing his brown linen tunic and trews.

Kerric winced again. "No. I'm not a fighter, and even if I were, it would have been stored with the rest of my things in my quarters deep inside the Tower. I'll have to go dig through the odds and ends from the armory at the Adventuring Hall. Meet me there," he directed her, rising to his feet. "I'll leave word at the front desk they're to pass you into the employees' section, and they'll let you pack up whatever supplies you think the two of us will need. We'll also be approaching the base of the Tower through the maintenance tunnels, which link from the Hall. I don't want anyone to know I'm going in until it's too late for some ambitious mage to speculate, grab a pack, and try to follow us— oh, you can take off the bracelet, now."

Nodding, she removed the geased piece of jewelry from her wrist and offered it to him. He accepted it back and offered his hand in return.

"From this point onward, you can talk about the fact that the two of us are going into the Tower to repair it," he told her, giving her a point o

spell otherwise co

in that I don't want

Myal nodded. Acc

feet. Escorting the Ma

unlocked it and let him ou

against it for a long mome

moil of emotions his words a

then gathered her energy, p

started running through a men

need based on her five years of ex

At least Kerric had the fore

his head like a second ski

all along the edges

his head like the edges

His breastplate

had brace

She hadn't run the Seraglio g   but she had
heard rumors. And from the sound o   master of the Tower
knew every inch of what they had to face. As for the rest of it, she
was fairly confident she knew most of what awaited the two of
them, or at least could handle any surprises. She just didn't know
how well a non-fighter could handle the dangers of the Tower,
even if her partner was the Master of the place.

Kerric was her greatest concern for their safety, now. Traps,
she knew. The enigmatic, handsome Guardian, she didn't.

The Guardian looked a little . . . odd, the next time she saw
him. Actually, he looked a bit silly.

Eyeing the Master of the Tower in his selected pieces of
armor, Myal quickly stuffed her tongue between her molar teeth
and bit down. The pain kept her from so much as twitching her
lips, never mind outright laughing. She didn't know what the others in the Adventuring Hall thought of his outfit, because she had
been taken down a long set of stairs and nudged through a door
into a subterranean hall lit by suncrystals embedded in the ceiling. She only knew what *she* thought of the matter.

...ght to get a helmet, but it fitted
...l, and left his brown curls poking out
...ke a demented, curly-haired bit of fur trim.
...looked a little bit large and a little bit long, and he
...rs laced on his wrists, with the opening gaping just a
...e too much and the knots placed a pair of holes short, proving
the wax-stiffened leather had been crafted for someone with
thinner forearms than his.

The brass-and-leather strips skirting his thighs from waist to
knees, however, *that* made him look absurd by local standards.
While Mendhite war-kilts were not too dissimilar, here at the
Tower, leather strip skirts were usually reserved for female adventurers running the lighter, less deadly gauntlets. Those were the
ones where the audience cared more about the agility and grace of
the adventurers, and the flash of nubile bare legs, rather than the
complexity and dangerousness of the traps involved. Myal wore a
variation on the same mostly because they were similar to the
war-kilts she had been trained to wear, but she wasn't used to seeing them on a non-Mendhite male.

At least he kept his trousers and tunic on, she acknowledged. *I
hope he remembered groin protection too. Particularly if we're running
the Seraglio, as he claims. He'll want those bits to arrive intact.*

Her own armor actually bared more skin than his, but in her
case it had to, as some of her tattoos worked best when not muf-
fled by excessive layers. She had a close-fitted helm, breast and
back plates, shoulder and elbow guards, bracers, and a strip skirt
of her own, but underneath the skirt lay thigh, knee, and shin
guards. The segments of hardened leather weren't overly large,
but they covered enough of her body to cut down on major inju-
ries. None of it had brass plating, unlike his, but all of her armor
was rune-carved with spells to help guard against major injuries

above mere scratches, bruises, and strains. The rest, her spine tattoo should be able to heal.

That did bring up a question about his own capabilities. "Master Kerric?"

"Just Kerric," he directed her, lifting and shrugging into the backpack provided by the Adventuring Hall workers. "You adventurers don't waste your energies on such formalities when you're running a gauntlet, so why should either of us when it's just you and me?"

"Then you may call me Myal," she acknowledged. "Kerric . . . what sort of healing knowledge do you have?"

"Enough that I could've made a living as a semi-competent village healer," he admitted, adjusting the lay of one of the buckles on his breastplate so that it didn't pinch under his backpack strap. "Not so much the herb-lore to augment my abilities, but enough to set bones, seal wounds, and banish infections. I can even reattach a severed limb, if it's done swiftly enough. Plus I have a good knowledge of the various poisonous traps of the Tower and their antidotes." Poking a thumb over his shoulder, he indicated his pack. "I have a spell-cushioned pouch of vials with all the antidotes and antivenoms we'll most likely need. Hopefully we won't actually have to use them."

That relieved her. Not just that he had the pouch, but that he'd *thought* of needing it. She nodded. "Good. I have tattoos that can cleanse poisons, but if you have specific antidotes, those always work faster and are less exhausting. I also have almost a hundred feet of silken rope, bandaging, a trio of sticks for splints, and some painkiller possets. Do you have gloves?"

He nodded, patting the pouch at his waist, the belt for which he had slung over the front of his strip skirt. "Waxed to prevent poison contamination. I don't have any fancy tattoos."

"What about a map?" she asked next.

Kerric shook his head, then tapped his temple. "It's all up here. *Nobody* gets a full map of the interior, not even the maintenance crews. Partial maps on crystal tablets, yes, but not full ones. For one, it wouldn't work under normal conditions. For another, it's a security hazard. The Tower is broken up into three major zones with a handful of people in charge of each, but nobody gets to know the whole thing except the Guardian. The maintenance crews are issued tablets that rely upon passive scrying spells built into the Tower stones, with a set radius of so many yards and so many floors, but that's it. They have no way of discerning a path all the way to the heart of this place."

"Then I'm glad you picked up that helmet," Myal told him. "Your head is our most important asset, because you're the one who knows where we're going and what we'll have to face—you *will* tell me in advance, I hope? I work better when I know what to expect."

"I'll do my best," he promised. "Ready?"

"As much as ever," she murmured, and followed the short man as he strode down the stone-lined passage. The Tower Village had been built no closer than a quarter-mile from the base of the Tower, and the Adventuring Hall on the side of town closest to the structure, so the walk wasn't technically all that long. It just seemed that way in such a long, straight, dimly lit tunnel.

Kerric Vo Mos might not have been an adventurer, and was nearly a full foot shorter than she was, but he set out at a brisk pace that caught her by surprise. One swift enough that it forced her to trot a little to catch up. After their paces fell into a two-steps-for-her and three-for-him rhythm, she eyed the swift-moving mage.

"Shouldn't we pace ourselves, rather than race on ahead?" she asked. "Starting early and quickly is fine, but if we're climbing the height of the Tower, and you said you could only guarantee three resting areas, we don't want to exhaust ourselves. This is not to doubt your confidence in knowing the route, but I've run weeklong gauntlets and you have not."

He craned his neck to look up at her, then shook his head, shrugging a little. "Actually, this is the pace I normally walk. Is it too fast for you? I can slow down if you like."

Unable to think of a good reply to that, Myal shook her head. She hadn't actually ever seen him walk anywhere for any real distance before now. Just a short walk up to her tenement, and short movements within the Adventuring Hall the few times they had been together in person before. Giving it a bit of thought, she realized she had just assumed that a short man, with short legs, would have a short and thus slow stride. But he looked to be in his mid- to late thirties, which meant he had been walking this way for a long time.

As it was, he was probably used to walking fast to keep up with anyone who had longer legs than him. She certainly didn't have any trouble. In fact, it was a bit of a relief not to have to slow down for once. And a relief not to have to walk over the cobblestone road that led to the flagstone-paved foundation ringing the base of the Tower. The road was getting a bit old and weatherworn, with the cobbles rounded and rutted from generations of use and centuries of weather; at night, the walk was a bit hazardous in certain spots, even under torchlight. By comparison, this dry, clean corridor was flat and level. With the suncrystals veining the rock of the ceiling, shedding a somewhat dim but serviceable light, they reached the far set of stairs fairly quickly.

Those stairs spiraled up to a short hall with a set of doors; Kerric picked the one that was obviously locked on the inside. Letting them through to the quiet, cool night air, Kerric carefully shut the door again, making sure it latched. When it did, it blended almost perfectly into the stonework of the tower. Accustomed to searching for secret doors, Myal marked its location in her mind.

She didn't know if she would ever need such knowledge again, but one never knew. Some of the games she had run had been won with her fellow adventurers and her "cheating" by using the hidden maintenance corridors and stairs. Namely the ones where the exact gauntlet rules in use did not specifically exclude such things. This run . . . somehow she doubted they would be able to cheat via the maintenance tunnels.

The door he led her to was typical of most of the base entrances of the Tower. It had a broad curve of shallow steps leading up to a sort of porch or dais, a recessed, stout door with a pointed top, and enough room for two average people to pass through the door without touching each other. It was also tall enough that she didn't feel like she had to duck to go through. Only a few of the passages and chambers in the Tower were shorter than average; most of those were strictly trap-related.

Myal glanced around, hoping no one had seen them. It was past sunset by not quite an hour, and most everyone was back at the village. But not everyone. She could see a few others as shadowy figures on the creamy granite paving stones, thanks to the pale white light of Brother and Sister Moon creeping their way across the starlit sky.

A couple groups had gathered near some of the other doors spread out along the broad base of the tower. Some were adventurers, their dark forms moving in ways that told her they were drinking and speculating about what had gone wrong. Others were pacing, arms folded, heads tilted up to look at the imposing edifice; those would be either fellow employees or loved ones of the personnel trapped inside. They were here because they were worried, not just curious as to what was going on.

She returned her attention to Kerric when he mounted the steps. To her surprise, he didn't do what most employees did when they started a gauntlet by opening up a door to an adventuring party; he did not place his hand on the bronze plate above the lever for the latch. Instead, he fished out a set of metal tools and prodded at the opening of the lock below the latch.

For a moment, she wondered if he even knew what he was doing. Most mages did not learn mundane, non-magical ways to open locks. But with a faint, audible click, he shifted one hand to the lever and pushed down, swinging the door open, then extracted his tools with the other. To her surprise, he was as fast as any lock-picking adventurer she'd been teamed with over the years. *Well, so the Master of the Tower has more than magical tricks up his badly bracer'd sleeves . . . Good.*

"In you go, milady," he murmured politely, holding the door open just wide enough for her to slip past. "There won't be any traps for the first twenty feet. After that, we're on our own—and this is your last chance to change your mind. Once this door shuts, the only way out is by completing our task . . . or by waiting for someone to carry our bodies out."

"And miss out on a chance to run the Tower *with* its Master?" she muttered back, smiling. "If you hadn't noticed, I am already crazy enough to adventure repeatedly." Taking him at his word about the immediate lack of traps, she stepped into the Tower, letting him follow at his own pace. A few seconds later, the door clanked shut behind them, the locking mechanism reactivating with several *clacks*.

Like many other such entrances, the first room wasn't large, just an area big enough to have served as a tenement sitting room, save that it had no furniture. At the far end of the empty chamber, a stairwell led up. Like the service corridor, it was dimly lit, though brighter than the darkness outside. The whole Tower was riddled with suncrystal veins, which drew in daylight from the Tower's surface, storing excess sunlight for illumination throughout the night.

In corridors, stairwells, and halls, it was almost never truly bright, and not always in each chamber, but it was rare for a room in the vast structure to be completely dark. When it was . . . there was always something dangerous lurking in the depths, usually some sort of monster, sometimes some sort of trap. Most were very complex illusions, but rumor had it some of the beasts and guardians were real creatures. Mortal or magical, it did not actually matter; they were just yet another obstacle which adventurers had to navigate.

She had two small lightglobes in her pack, strung in fine mesh nets so they could be carried by hand, or by tying them to a shoulder guard or something. They weren't the standard, head-sized spheres, which when struck illuminated at a level of brightness comparable to the firmness of the tap. These simply turned on or off, requiring a hard, swift double-rap to start or stop. That way they could be hung from bits of armor to free up both hands, without worry that the slightest jostling would reduce their illumination. Expensive, but necessary.

Other tools of the adventurer's trade had been stuffed into her backpack as well. It wasn't as if Myal lacked the room for it; she didn't need more than a single change of clothes, and she didn't need a bedroll. Unless a chamber or a trap was specifically designed to be overly hot or overly cold, the whole of the Tower stayed at a steady, reasonable temperature all year round. Curling up in a corner might be a little on the cool side, but it would still be comfortable enough to allow sleep.

Provided they could find a safe corner. If the Tower had realigned itself to protect the Fountain that powered it, yet provide a direct path to it, then that path was going to be perilous indeed. Myal had entered herself in only a few of the extremely lethal gauntlets.

She had done so strictly for the challenge and the thrill once her skills had improved to the point where she felt the risks were manageable, and only with fellow adventurers she believed she could trust to do their parts. But not in the last year or so . . . and not with a mage who admitted he was no warrior, and hadn't made a daily, weekly, or even monthly habit of running the Tower, as far as she knew. Staring at the line of steps ahead of them, she wondered how bad this trip would be.

Kerric knew how bad it would get. Memorizing all the direct paths to the Fountain was something he did once every turn of the seasons, at solstices and equinoxes. All previous Guardians of the Tower had done so, for just such an emergency. This wasn't the first time someone had attempted to take over the Fountain energies from outside, after all, and not the first time someone had tried to control it via the Fountain ways connecting the various singularity-points.

"Right," Kerric half-muttered to himself. With only a handful of weeks between himself and his last memorization, and almost two score of such sessions under his belt, it didn't take long to organize his thoughts. "The first five traps and tricks are . . . a common gas trap on the stairs, designed to make us sleep. That's the first one, forty-two and forty-three steps up. It's a straight flight, and the gas acts quickly."

"I see," Myal murmured, considering the implications. "So if we trigger it, and we succumb, we fall down not just to the steps, but quite possibly tumble all the way down, and run the risk of breaking bones, or even our necks."

"Exactly. The second trap is the Danger Sign. It's a bronze plaque, similar to all the rest that mark various riddles and warnings," he told her. "*Don't* read it. The runes are enchanted to explode the moment your mind makes sense of what they say."

Myal nodded. It was common for all of these traps to be given a code name. No one knew if the adventurers had come up with them first, or if the Guardians had, back when the Tower was turned into the adventuring show it was today, but everyone used them. They made good mnemonics for remembering and differentiating each peril. "The third?"

"The Hourglass Pit," he told her.

"I know that one," she said. "In fact, I ran into it five games ago. Unless there's anything different I should know about this version?"

Kerric grinned. "Nope. I remember watching that one with you in it, and it's the one with the sand, not the one with the oil. You're welcome to sift through the sand in your shoes for diamonds and other gemstones once we get free if you like—actually, any treasure that isn't an illusion, you can keep, though I cannot guarantee you'll have access to any refreshing room with a bank depository, and *no* guarantees it'll be transferred from the Tower to the Adventuring Hall's depositories. At least, not while the Tower's locked down."

"Fair enough," she agreed. "The fourth trap?"

"Wasp Hitting the Mage Shield." At her puzzled look, Kerric explained. "There's a pit with spikes on the bottom, and it's just narrow enough you can jump over it if you take a running leap . . . but there's an invisible shield-wall hanging down to the level of the pit opening at about the halfway point. So you splat against it like a bug on a mage's shielding and drop onto the spikes."

"Ah—we call that one the Pit Stop," Myal told him. "I've encountered it many times."

"It's a common one. Not every pit will have them, but it's a popular way to stop someone from crossing with careless arrogance," he agreed. "The last one in the first set is The Door That Wasn't." Again, his label earned him an odd look from her. "It's not a door. It's a shield. We'll need to fight something on the other side. On the bright side, once it's down, it's down and won't reset for at least an hour, so I'll have a break to list the next chain of hazards. So. Ready?"

She checked the fit of her weapons in their sheaths, a sword at her hip which she'd had enchanted to cut through all but the toughest of armors, plus several daggers tucked into belt and boots. Giving her backpack a careful shrug-and-jiggle to make sure it was well-balanced, she nodded. "Ready. Steps forty-two and forty-three, you said? Are the walls trapped as well as the steps?"

"Only for about a foot or so along the bottom," Kerric admitted.

"Then I'm ready. You first, or me?" she asked.

He grimaced at the question. "I know all the traps, and I've even *repaired* a number of these traps, but I don't run them like you do. So you first, if you don't mind?"

FOUR

Nodding, Myal crossed to the steps and started up them, counting quietly with little flexings of her fingers. Closing the fingers of her right hand, she counted to five, then opened them up again to ten, and closed her left thumb. A second time curled her left index finger at twenty, and the middle at thirty. At her ring finger, she stopped. "Step forty. Can you fly?"

"As well as you can wall-walk," he told her. "I'd be doing it the whole length of the stairs, but this is just the start of a very long trip, and I don't have access to the singularity anymore to bolster my own reserves."

Myal nodded, looking back at him. Amusingly, she realized that with him placed just a few steps behind her, his head was at the level of her rump. He seemed to be fascinated by it, and blinked when she spoke. "A lot of inexperienced adventurer-mages don't realize they have to conserve their energy on long gauntlet runs. It's good you know what's needed."

One step, she could skip easily. Two steps would be a stretch, even for her long legs. She *could* do it, but that ran the risk of accidentally triggering the trap. Bending her right knee, she balanced that leg lightly on her toes, then twirled her leather-clad ankle and foot, activating the dark purple spider-tattoo inked into the sole. The movements didn't have to be blatant; she could activate a pattern's effects within a split second if needed. But they were imperfectly powered if she didn't take a bit of time, and usually of shorter duration that way.

Feeling a touch of warmth and a faint tingling in her soles and palms, she turned to the right-hand wall and put her right foot on the surface. It clung firmly through the leather of her boot, though she knew she could lift it away again at will. Stretching out her left hand, she braced it on the far wall, then pushed and lifted her left foot to join the first.

The staircase was narrow enough that she had to hunch in with bent limbs as she pressed in both directions to hold up her weight, but at least she wasn't trying to hold herself horizontal by just her own muscles. Ignoring the sideways tug of her braided hair, backpack and armor, she shuffled her way by hands and feet up the slope for a good ten steps, then carefully lowered one foot at a time, righting herself once she was safely past the trapped stretch.

Turning to check on Kerric's progress, she found the short, brown-armored mage floating just behind her with all the effort of a dandelion puff on a warm day. He gave her a brief smile and settled himself on step forty-eight, gesturing at the rest of the steps. "Danger Sign, and Hourglass Pit."

Myal nodded and turned to climb the rest of the stairs the normal way, relaxing her painted powers with another flex of the sole of her foot. It wasn't magic like a real mage had, just a facsimile, but it was as effective in its own way, and just as exhausting, since she couldn't tap into any other energy source than her own life, her own fertility.

Which meant conserving her own energy was just as important as Kerric conserving his. The top was a good forty more steps up; many of the ground-level entrances had access rooms at or near the ground floor of the Tower, but even with just thirty visible doorways piercing an area the size of a walled town, some had to go up so that they didn't open into the same rooms.

A few also went down, since the Tower foundation stretched deep into the valley floor. Probably all the way down to the local bedrock, just to be able to support the sheer weight of the place. Or rather, it may have been grown from the bedrock on up, given the smooth, seamless stretches of granite and basalt she had seen here and there. If she'd been a mage of great power—with access to that Fountain hovering up in the sky—that was how Myal would have built the Tower. Solid rock for the foundation and framework, and everything else added in afterward.

Reaching the top step, she saw a pool of light just up ahead. The suncrystals enmeshed throughout the Tower, no doubt grown when it had been built, formed a thicker spot than the narrow ribbons of before. The result was a brighter patch of corridor. The light from that thicker vein gleamed off the reddish-beige metal of one of the ubiquitous Tower plaques.

Mindful of Kerric's warning, she resolutely stared straight ahead, her attention fixed firmly on the next task, and *not* on trying to read the raised letters cast into the bronze surface.

"Good girl," she heard the Master of the Tower breathe.

Twisting to glance back over her shoulder, she retorted, "This isn't my first time in the Tower. And I'm not a girl."

He quickly held up his hands. "I'm sorry; it was honest praise, and not meant to sound condescending. I've known maintenance mages, experienced ones, who haven't been able to resist looking, even knowing they were going to have to pass things like this. That, and 'good woman' doesn't roll off the tongue so well in Aian." He grinned mischievously, showing what he must have looked like as a teenager. "Feel free to call me 'good boy' if you like."

She thought about that as they approached the next obstacle, a door with a lever-style handle and a lock placed above it.

"Fair enough, though I'd say you were a man, not a boy," Myal finally allowed, stopping in front of the door. "Even Nafiel has fallen for a simple trap or two in the last year."

"And we received great feedback from the betting houses in Senod-Gra over those mistakes, too," Kerric told her. "Fortunes are made and lost as to whether or not our top stars will fumble along the way—and yes, that does include you. The Guardian of the City of Delights enjoys discussing the . . . effects these games have on her people's livelihoods."

The end of his statement fell a bit flat, tone-wise. Myal gave him a curious look. "You don't sound happy about that."

"Oh, I normally am, but . . ." Kerric grimaced. "Every hour we don't have the ability to send scrycastings is an hour we're not entertaining our patrons. The biggest of which is Senod-Gra. There's a maintenance clause built into each contract, but it's only for a limited duration. Once we exceed the full-day mark, we start losing income."

"So why not take in a full crew? Three people at the very least?" Myal asked him. "Or rather, four, if the Seraglio gauntlet requires couples to get through it?"

"Because *this* is the easy path, and the easy path means having to go through Cabbage, Goat, Wolf," he stated flatly.

"Ah." He didn't have to explain any further. She'd been caught in that one a few times before, as the Wolf, and as the Cabbage. She hated being the Cabbage, and didn't like what she had tried to do to her adventuring partners as the Wolf. She couldn't imagine what it would feel like to be the Goat, the one stuck in the middle. Thankfully, taking only two people on this trip negated that particular nasty trap because it required a minimum of three people to activate the spell. "If Cabbage, Goat, Wolf is the easy path . . . just how nasty are the others?"

"Twice to five times as nasty—but that's not to say this one is a garden stroll," he warned her. "One of my predecessors realized it would be best if a Guardian who found him- or herself locked out had an easier path to get back to the heart, but *easier* isn't *easy*. Oh, and past this door?" Kerric added, holding up a hand in caution. "There will be multiple-choice paths to take, once we get through the Hourglass Pit. We have to make sure we take the *right* path."

"Understood." Myal eyed the door, then him. "Can you tell if it's locked or trapped? And if it's trapped, can you disarm it? I can do a bit of pickwork, but not the really complex stuff."

He nodded quickly, his curls trying to bounce below the hardened leather cap squashing his hair flat. They could only jiggle a little, a sight she found strangely amusing. Composing herself, Myal listened politely to his reply.

"I know every single one which can be disarmed magically, plus how to pick all the locks manually. And I know which ones will explode if you do them the wrong way. It takes a while to memorize everything, but I've been at it for nearly ten years," he told her. Placing his hand over the lock plate, Kerric murmured under his breath. A modest but audible *chachunk* proved his words. Free hand going to the handle, he pushed down on the lever. "For example, the door to get into the Tower must be opened non-magically on this route, or it changes all the settings by routing us through a doorway-Gate set just inside the outermost doorframe, sending us to an entirely different track.

"This lock, however, leads directly to the Hourglass Pit, and it can be opened either way." Pushing the door, open, he showed her the modest room inside. Round and smooth with the crazed lines of suncrystals piercing the upper curves, it was shaped something like a bell jar, save that the peak of the tall ceiling had a funnel-shaped hole about a foot in diameter. Gesturing for her to enter first, Kerric followed Myal inside, and carefully closed the door.

Immediately, the door vanished. Without hesitation, he strode across to the far side, hands digging out the tools from his pouch. The moment he crossed the center of the room, a hissing sound rushed down from that hole. Within seconds, it turned into a broad spill of sand. The mage ignored the cascading granules, focusing instead on a small hole placed just above a fist-sized iron ring.

Myal felt the air in the bell-shaped room swirl up around her, racing toward the ceiling as the falling mass of sand displaced it. Fine strands of black not caught up in her braid wafted up against her cheeks, tickling her skin. Tightening her left ring finger, the one with the green and brown turtle inked on it, she moved toward the sand-fall. Already it had formed a mound bigger than a footstool, but she stuck her right hand under the falling spray.

With the tattoo hardening her skin, the abrasion of all that sand didn't harm her. The larger chunks of stone did sting, though. Managing to snag two of them between her slightly spread fingers, she shuffled away from the growing pile, now the size of a cushioned chair, and joined Kerric. He grunted and grabbed the ring, pulling it up on its hinge and giving it a twist. The smooth rock cracked and swung open, allowing them to escape into the dimly lit corridor beyond. Closing the door on the hissing trap, Kerric grinned at her. "Did you get anything good?"

Myal shrugged, dusting off the stones. The lighting was a bit too low to tell exactly what color they were, either blue or purple, so she simply tucked them into her pouch. "I'll find out later. Let me get the sand out of my boots."

She started to stoop to unbuckle her shin guards, but Kerric touched her arm. "Please, allow me. Mage, remember? *Silicamundic!*" he commanded, one hand stretched toward her feet, the other toward his own. Sand whipped out of her clothes, bundled up into a sphere at the height of her knees, then floated off to the side and settled on the ground at a gesture from his hand. It promptly collapsed into a little pile. A tiny, similar ball of grit removed itself from his boots as well, joining the first. "There. That wasn't too harsh on your skin, was it?"

Belatedly, she realized her skin was still toughened. Flexing her ring finger again, she shook her head. "No, I had it guarded against the sand."

"Good. Next up is . . . ?" Kerric let his tone turn it into a probing question for her. As much as he knew she had to harbor doubts about his abilities to run this particular gauntlet, and needed reassurances he wasn't going to get both of them killed, *he* needed to know she was paying attention. Not paying attention would also get them killed.

"The Pit Stop." She smiled shyly when he blinked at her teasing. "Try to leap across the pit, and it stops you."

"Wasp Hitting the Mage Shield," Kerric retorted lightly. "It's like a wasp zooming in on a mage, only to splat against their shield-spell."

Myal gave it some thought as he started to lead the way. "I think Pit Stop is more accurate."

"Well, it is shorter, I'll grant you that," he allowed. The corridor was short, making a left turn. Located just a few lengths past the corner, the pit in question was now visible. About as long as Kerric was tall and stretching from wall to wall, it looked to be about twice as deep as it was long. A forest of spears filled the bottom half.

This time, he didn't use his floating spell. Moving up to the edge of the pit, Kerric extended his hand, murmuring. A pool of mist formed just above the spear-heads. It thickened, rising up in slow, eddying waves. After a few lapping movements, the waves solidified into smoke-translucent steps, one set at each end of the pit. The air, however, felt uncomfortably dry; the mist was a solidified mass of all the humidity in reach.

"There. No need to walk the wall on this one. I'll go first." The steps were narrow. Descending sideways, he stretched out his hand, felt for the unseen barrier and its bottom edge, then carefully ducked under it, straightening on the far side so he could climb out again.

Myal followed as soon as he was clear. Following his lead, she reached out her hand, bracing her descent on the invisible wall, then ducked under it. Kerric offered her his hand as she navigated the narrow steps on the far side. Accepting it, she nodded at the wooden panel blocking the far side of the corridor, roughly three lengths away. "Right. Fifth is The Door That Wasn't, you said?"

"It's big, it's ugly, and it varies from day to day as to *what*, exactly, is on the other side of that 'door,'" Kerric warned her. "And that 'door' is warded against magic. But only the shield, so I cannot strike whatever's holding it from in front. That means the opening moves are all yours, Painted Warrior."

"Then I'll knock on it with my sword hilt, slip through the moment it opens, and turn whoever's holding it so you can take them down, Mage," Myal returned briskly. Grasping her sword hilt and her scabbard, she unsheathed the broad, slightly curved blade. Its width was somewhere between a saber and a scimitar for weight behind each blow, yet the tip came to a point fine enough for stabbing. Looking at the door with her left eye, she wasn't sure but she thought the shield-door was glowing faintly. "Illusion, right?"

"Oh, definitely an illusion," Kerric reassured her, flipping his hand to disperse the mist in the pit. Moist air wafted their way, allowing him to breathe deeply without his sinuses feeling like they were going to crack. "A very solid, very mean, very cranky illusion. You don't have to feel guilty about killing it, but *don't* underestimate it. You'll only have to worry about living people if we cross a still-adventuring team along the way, or maintenance personnel, or if we had a third person for Cabbage, Goat, Wolf, or . . ."

She looked back at him over her shoulder, wrinkling her nose. "You are *so* very cheerful, Master Kerric."

"Just Kerric," he reminded her, and nodded at the door. "Go on, give it a good knock, and let the what's-it-today know we're here."

Flexing her right knee, with its gray-and-black bull tattoo, she sized up the door, backed up, skipped into a swift charge, and whirled at the last moment, thrusting her leg hard behind her so that her heel slammed into the stoutly built panel with all the power of an actual bison. The *bang* forced the panel back with an audible grunt from its wielder. Twisting, she darted forward, ducking low as the owner of the door that wasn't a door growled and straightened.

The room beyond was fairly large, about the size of the Honey Spear. The thing which she had just kicked back was a caricature of a man melded with a mountain, with craggy sandstone skin, mossy dark green hair, gray scale armor like cracked and crazed shale, and a shield taller than Myal. Which was only fair; she only came up to the middle of his thigh at best, and that while he was crouched. Like the two of them, the ogre-man was clad in a strip-skirt, breastplate, and guards for his arms, shoulders, and legs.

Unlike them, he had no shoes covering his feet, though they were so callused and the nails of his toes so clawlike, there was no need for further protection.

Leaning to one side as she entered, the ogre grabbed the trunklike haft of a giant mace, its head a squared-off knob of spiked steel, and swung it at her. Faster than she was expecting.

Her right bicep flexed instinctively, activating the green, red, and black braid of ink encircling her arm muscles. Everything blurred for a split second, then slowed down from her perspective, giving her time to haul herself out of the way. Spine arching, she leaned back from that swift, swiping blow. The mace-head whooshed just over her breastplate. Spinning, Myal whirled out of the way and slashed at the back of the ogre's nearest knee, above the straps holding his shin guards in place.

At this speed, strength didn't matter, just the angle of her blade versus his unguarded flesh. The modest curve of its edge sliced deep into his tendons, setting off a gravelly roar of pain with a hint of a rocky avalanche rushing down a mountainside. With more of that same speed, the ogre whirled to follow her as she continued her traveling spin, slashing again with his mace, though he limped as he did so. This time, she dove and tumbled along the floor, feeling a bit of a wind from his missed attack. Using her momentum to tumble up to her feet in a low crouch, she prepared to duck, dodge, or leap his next attack.

"*Spetulignessum!*" Kerric thrust out his hand as if he was throwing something, and his hard cry jolted through the ogre. Or rather, the glowing spear of energy he had just hurled through the giant's ribs. The barbed head protruded from the front of his chest.

He coughed, and blood bubbled up from his punctured lung. Staggering, the ogre tried to swipe at Myal again, his club traveling in a low, scooping arc. This time, she flexed her left bicep and leaped upward, high and hard with great strength. Boots landing with a thump, she watched the mountain giant stagger a second time, cough and wince, then collapse with a *thud* that she could feel through the floor. Myal approached the ogre warily. When the monster didn't move, she wiped her sword on the mossy green hair, sheathed it, and flexed her muscles again, relaxing her abilities and the drain they made on her life force.

"My compliments to your illusionists," she murmured, heart still racing a bit. Then wrinkled her nose, catching a whiff of the dead ogre's rank sweat and blood, and the relaxing of his bowels. "Sincerely, my compliments. My left eye tattoo normally lets me discern illusions in the gauntlet games, gauging how solid or ephemeral they are, their weaknesses . . . but this one looks very solid and real."

"It's as real as magic can make it, now that the Tower is in full defense mode. It is otherwise a great pity that all means of scrying on this trip have been blocked out, because this run would have made for high interest among our watchers," Kerric murmured, skirting the fallen body. "What *we're* facing is the Tower at its best. Or worst, depending on your viewpoint. And these are some of the easiest dangers we'll face."

"Right. So what are the next few traps?" Myal asked him. The door on the far side of this room wasn't a door, so much as it was just an opening. The frame for it was made of the same stone as the rest of the corridors, discernible only by the crack edging the doorway. According to her guide, the Gate built into that doorway wasn't going to be active, so she peered into the broad corridor beyond without crossing it. "I see . . . a large bronze plaque on the wall, a lever a little bit past it, a long pit filled with some sort of liquid, and an iron grate in the middle of the pit, blocking us from getting across."

"That's the Rowboat and Brick," Kerric told her. "After that is

Herding Cats, a set of stairs beyond it will be trapped with the Snowball Effect . . . with three separate trigger points to be circumnavigated . . . then we have to cross the room with All That Glitters Is Bone, and one of our many infamous Junk Room Riddles. Number Four, to be precise. You can safely cross the threshold. There are no traps between us and the Rowboat and Brick."

"I feel sorry for all those brute-strength adventurers who come here thinking they only have to swing hard and fast to make it through alive," Myal murmured, stepping cautiously into the long, broad corridor. "They'd get through this one, but I've seen the looks of confusion on some of their faces when they've met up with your Junk Room Riddles. Your predecessors were downright devious, insisting anyone wanting to breach the Tower had to be able to think as well as fight."

"Those 'dumb brute' scrycastings are actually quite popular," Kerric admitted, following her. "Particularly the comedic ones— and the ones who are smart enough to play it up for the watchers are assured a steady job as adventurers. Mainly because we tone down the danger levels for those."

"I'm . . . too shy, I guess," Myal stated, trying to pick out the right word for it in Aian. "Retiring? Not . . . ah, flamboyant. That's the word. I am not flamboyant enough. One of the Hall employees asked me if I could play up the humor and such, but . . . it's not me. I *have* a sense of humor," she added, slowing her steps so that he caught up with her, "but I came here to test my skills, not to entertain. I take it too seriously."

"Well, some people like a good comedy, and others enjoy a good drama," Kerric allowed. "The Hall staff are very good at figuring out within just a few runs which adventurers are suited for what kind of a run. Some can do more than one kind, but they don't all have to do it that way."

They stopped next to the plaque. The lever was located out of their reach, halfway between the edge of the pit and that iron grate. The long pit was actually quite shallow, only about a finger-length in depth, but it was filled to the brim with a clear liquid. The smell in the air told Myal what that liquid was.

"An oil pit? Let me guess: if we get the riddle wrong, a torch drops into the pit, and this whole corridor roasts us alive?" she asked.

Kerric nodded. "In the 'safe' version, the torch is an illusion, and lowers slowly on a chain from a hole behind that grate. We get the real torch version, which will be dropped swiftly if we're wrong." He lifted his chin at the plaque. "Don't touch the lever just yet. I'll give you a chance to guess the riddle, since you are a smart adventurer."

"What will I get if I guess it right?" Myal asked him, curious.

Kerric opened his mouth, closed it in thought, then finally shrugged. "Well, I *was* going to offer the usual, a bag of coins or whatever after we get out. But since we're going to be facing the Seraglio gauntlet at some point . . . how about a kiss?"

If he hadn't offered it so matter-of-factly, Myal would have wondered at his real motives for bringing her along. As it was, however, she felt a little bit insulted that he'd treat kissing her so casually. Hands shifting to her hips, she stared down at him. "How do I know your kiss is *worth* a correct answer?"

Kerric lifted his brows, not expecting that particular challenge to his offer. He could have boasted, he could have argued, but the truth was . . . Shrugging, he admitted freely, "I don't know if it is or not. Some women have quite enjoyed my kisses, and wanted more. Others were only mildly pleased by them. I suppose you could have a free one right now, if you like. But just the one."

The absurdity of the bargain made her chuckle. Hands slipping off her hips, she shook her head at him. "This is ridiculous. A kiss isn't worth a bag of coins."

"Nor are you a whore, to trade for one," he agreed quickly, wanting to make that point clear. "But we do need to build up some, ah, physical trust between us." He reached up to tuck the edge of his finger under her chin, caressing it a little. She permitted the touch, looking down at him. Kerric realized at that moment just *how* tall she was, and an unhappy thought crossed his mind. Lowering his hand, he asked, "Or is it because I'm too short?"

Myal stared down at him. "Kerric, *every* man in this land is 'too short' by my people's standards, if you gauge it by that. Even most of the adventurers; Nafiel himself is among the tallest of those, and I am a thumb-width taller than *him*. But I am *not* interested in him, I am not interested in my two fellow Mendhites—who are taller than me—and I have occasionally enjoyed a moment of . . . of intimacy with some of my fellow, *shorter* adventurers. I have learned that height is no guarantee of pleasure in such matters.

"It is the truth to say that it is a man's *skill* that makes him good or bad at being a lover." A pause, and she added lightly, "I will take that free sample, and see if a kiss per riddle is worth it."

It was his turn to chuckle. Not for long, though; Kerric lifted his head as she stooped. Cupping her cheek, he guided their lips together. She didn't make it a quick kiss, either, though it stayed soft and tenuous at first. Moving his lips against hers, he nibbled slowly on her bottom lip, then gently traced the upper one with the tip of his tongue.

A soft sigh escaped her. He did have some skill, Myal decided. Grateful this wasn't going to be too awkward, she nibbled back, sliding her own hand under his chin. Their height difference was a little distracting, but not insurmountable, and his taste was sweet and slightly minty. She wondered if he could taste the spiced fruit from her dessert, though it had been eaten over half an hour ago. She prolonged the kiss, encouraged when he met her lips with just as much interest . . . until a stray thought crossed her mind.

Breaking it off, she straightened, shaking her head a little to clear it.

Not knowing why she ended the kiss, Kerric lifted a brow. "Come now, my kisses cannot be all *that* bad?"

"No. It was very nice." She gave him an awkward smile. "No, it just occurred to me I was kissing the Master of the Tower. And it felt . . . unreal."

"I am *also* a man," he reminded her, his own hands going to his leather-stripped hips. "I deserve as much pleasure as any other man should hope for in the presence of a beautiful and willing woman."

She ducked her head shyly at the compliment. "A rather big and unpleasant-looking woman."

"A beautiful woman," he corrected. "With the exotic appeal of a far-distant foreigner, exciting and lovely. Plus you are talented, competent, and intelligent."

"I meant my tattoos," she told him. "They're not exactly lovely."

"They are. They make you a beautiful, *colorful* woman," Kerric clarified.

Myal realized that he didn't get it. He didn't understand that a non-mage Painted Warrior was . . . less than appealing, back home. On the one hand, that was a very flattering compliment, that he didn't care she was infertile. On the other hand, he probably didn't know her tattoos made her infertile, and that might cause a problem down the road.

"Kerric . . . the tattoo that empowers everything," she said, gesturing at the one surrounding her navel, "that one is responsible for making me infertile. It makes me . . . less than a woman, back home."

He frowned at her words. "That's a pile of turds. Why should that make you less than a woman? You're still an adult female, and I find you attractive. As for what other people might say, they do not speak for *me*. I can do that myself."

His assertions warmed her, soothing part of the old ache inside. Except this is supposed to be a one-time liaison, and he did say he wasn't looking for long-term attachments, she reminded herself. *So I shouldn't worry about the needs of any long-term interest . . . and not plan for any long-term interest in me.*

Something in her didn't like that idea, having to acknowledge this was all ephemeral and temporary, but that was alright. It wasn't the first time she'd known that reality and wishes wouldn't coincide. She had chosen to become a Painted Warrior with a full understanding of just what she would be giving up in recompense.

Turning to the plaque, she examined it, grateful that this one at least wasn't going to explode in her face when she did so. The message cast in raised letters on its surface was fairly simple, and didn't even rhyme, unlike many of the riddles found on similar plaques elsewhere.

A man in a rowboat rows to the center of a small lake. In his rowboat is a large, heavy brick. He tosses the brick overboard. Does the level of the water in the lake go up, or down?

A glance at the iron lever showed it sticking out perpendicular to the wall, parallel to the floor, in a neutral position. The socket in which it was set was a longish, curved slit, giving plenty of room to push it up or pull it down. The trick was, she had to be either standing in the shallow, long pool of oil to move it, or clinging to the wall next to it.

Kerric waited while she read the plaque, then looked at the lever. Finally, he asked, "Well? Do you know which it is?"

"I am no mage, to be taught the ways and the workings of the world," she confessed. "But I *am* a former sailor. And I have loaded many a longboat, and occasionally tossed something heavy overboard. I say the water level goes down overall . . . because if you toss something heavy overboard, the boat goes *up*, and is no longer displacing a large amount of water. Something heavy enough to sink, like a brick, displaces a *lot* of water in a rowboat, but only a little bit when it goes over the side."

He grinned at her, and crooked his finger. Relieved she had figured it out right, Myal bent over to accept her prize. This time, the kiss wasn't tenuous. This time, he cupped both of her cheeks, and engaged her lips thoroughly, sharing his pleasure in her wits. She felt a little dizzy when it finally ended and her face felt warm with a blush, when he finally allowed her to straighten. Gathering her wits, she focused on the task at hand.

"Should I . . . ?" Myal offered, gesturing at the lever. Oil in her boots would be better than sand, unless they encountered a fire-based trap.

"I'll get it. Stay here," Kerric told her. A gesture and a snap froze the surface of the oil in a variation of a popular liquid-hardening spell known as the glasswater spell. A narrow strip of the oil solidified, allowing him to walk along the edge of the wall. "If we'd been wrong and chosen *up*, the gate would have risen, but only after the torch dropped, igniting the oil.

"As it is, since that *is* the right answer . . ." Grasping the lever, he flexed his muscles, hauling down on it with a hard *clunk*. The gate did not move, but a section of wall next to the plaque did, swinging open to reveal a set of stairs. "There's a lever upstairs that opens the gate without the torch, and a bit of treasure. You can have whatever you like of the treasure, but be mindful of how much you can carry."

Myal nodded. Rejoining her, Kerric gestured for her to go up the steps first. She did so, he noted, with a touch of caution, eyes wide, head cocked slightly to listen, feet testing each step for a brief moment before committing her weight. He knew this particular stairwell wasn't trapped, but she had several good habits. One of them, the mark of a seasoned adventurer, was being wary and watchful in new territory. Not every trap was used in a gauntlet, nor every puzzle or riddle, particularly if it was part of a physical path to the Fountain Hall.

Unlike the last one, this stairwell was short. It doubled back up over itself, emerging in a room of only about ten feet square. Until now, the lighting had been low and gentle; this room had larger veins of suncrystal. They illuminated a longish, footstool-sized chest on a pedestal in the center of the room, and a small lever off to one side. Kerric crossed to the lever, but did not yet pull it.

Myal eyed the chest warily. Such boxes were normally locked, trapped, and tricked. She couldn't see any sign of a lock, or even a latch, though. Drawing her sword, she prodded the gap between lid and base with the sharp edge of the weapon, and eased the top up. Nothing happened, no poison needles or gaseous hissing. Just a glint of light reflecting off gems and metals, and the rich gleam of velvet lining the case.

"A dagger? Is it enchanted?" she asked her companion.

Kerric shrugged. "I haven't the faintest. I'm not in charge of restocking these things anymore, and this particular trap-and-treasure hasn't been used since I don't know when. But I do know the chest isn't trapped. This is one of the rare honest reward-rooms, with contents that are not an illusion."

"I'll trust you on that," Myal murmured, eyeing the dagger. "But is the *knife* a trap? Is it cursed, will it cut my hand, or does it require magic to unlock its potential?"

Kerric shrugged. "I honestly have no clue. I could try probing it with my magic, if you like. Or you could pick it up and just hang on to it until we're done, then check it against the Topside inventory list."

She thought about it for a moment, frowning, then shook her head and flipped the lid shut again. "I think I'll pass. I have good daggers on me already, and one of them is enspelled to return to my hand on command. I don't need another." Resheathing her sword, she looked at him. "I'm ready to move on."

FIVE

ꞑodding, he pulled on the smaller lever. They both heard a
chunk and several seconds of rattling echoing up the stairs,
the sign that the gate was being raised. This time, Kerric led the
way. "Step lively; the gate has been enchanted to reset after a
minute or so. Stick to the left-hand wall, too; that's where my
altered glasswater spell has hardened the surface."

"Thank you," Myal told him. He glanced back up at her, so
she explained. "For easing the way for both of us."

"Don't worry, you'll be pulling your own weight soon enough,"
he dared to tease. Then sobered a little, muttering under his
breath, "And *my* weight, too." Clearing his throat, he reminded
her of the next trap. "Get ready to herd cats, milady."

This door had two locks. The first one, he unlocked with his
tools; the second, with a spell. Once both were undone, the panel
swung open of its own accord. Inside was a well-lit chamber,

about twice as big as the treasure room had been . . . and teeming with cats. Twelve of them, to be precise.

Twelve sleek, fluffy, large, small, dark, light, spotted, patchwork, or mottled cats . . . but otherwise quite common house cats.

Myal paused on the corridor side of the threshold, blinking at the felines. "You weren't jesting, were you?" she finally asked. "We actually have to *herd* cats?"

Kerric, already inside, gestured her impatiently to enter. "Come on inside; this is one of those tricks where you cannot begin to solve it until all the doors are closed."

Stepping over the threshold, she moved aside so he could shut the door. Immediately it latched. Not with two locks, but with twelve that *snick*ed and *ka-chunk*ed into place, turning from vertical to horizontal. Off to the right was an identical door, also teeming with twelve locks. Or rather, with the knobs that normally were used on the inside of a room by its occupants to lock out the rest of the world. There were no keyholes, and no bronze plaques on any of the room's four walls indicating what they were supposed to do in here.

As she looked around, one of the cats came up to the two of them and sniffed at their boots. The moment the tabby finished stepping all the way onto the patch of carpet under their feet with all four of its paws . . . one of the locks behind her *snick*ed again. Myal spun around, eyeing the twelve knobs. Eleven of them were parallel to the floor. The fifth one up from the bottom was now perpendicular, angled up and down unlike its brethren. After sniffing for a few seconds, the tabby purr-rubbed against Kerric's boot, then wandered off the carpet again. The lock on the door clicked, returning to the horizontal position.

The weaving wasn't much bigger than a single person's bed. Nor was it the only rug on the floor. There was another one arranged in front of the other door. Two cats sat on it, one of them grooming its shoulder, the other hunkered down with its paws tucked under the chest, making it look like a cat-shaped loaf of bread, though the nearly-white calico's tail-tip kept twitching while it watched the other felines.

All of the cats glowed faintly to her left eye. Myal quickly looked up at the row of locks. Two were vertical; ten were horizontal for the far door.

"I see," she murmured. "We have to get all twelve cats onto that other carpet all at the same time, don't we?"

Kerric sighed and spread his hands. "That's why it's called Herding Cats."

"Did you at least bring some cat-mint to lure them?" she asked wryly.

"Better. A stasis-sealed packet of fish." Unslinging his pack—three of the cats came over to sniff at it, and two triggered the locks on the first door—he dug around until he pulled out a parchment-wrapped bundle covered in runes.

Myal was familiar with those runes; stasis spells had been one of the earlier inventions of the mages of ancient Mendhi. She couldn't craft any herself, but she had used such papers, and rune-carved boxes and cabinets, multiple times herself. Watching him break the wax seal holding the packet shut, she noticed the cats reacting to it within moments. The nearest ones looked up at the crack and rustle, then strained their muzzles upward, nostrils sniffing and whiskers trembling, ears aimed forward.

"Here, you take half," Kerric offered, holding out the unwrapped paper.

"Let me hold it while you get your pack back on," Myal countered as more and more of the cats noticed the fishy scent. Lifting the paper, she cradled it in her hands while he quickly slung the heavy pack back over his shoulders.

Kerric reached into the parchment and pulled out a hunk of

pink-broiled fish, then stooped and started walking around the room, luring the cats. Myal stooped as well, crinkling the paper slightly to ensure she had the attention of roughly half the cats. She reached the carpet first, felines rearing up on their hind legs, meowing and trying to paw at the paper, noses still sniffing away.

When he came back to her, all but one of the cats had been lured by the smell. Myal finally put the paper on the ground, letting him dump his half of the tender, flaky fish on it. Quicker than expected, Kerric dashed off the carpet, scooped up the last, napping kitty, and carried it over to the rug. It woke up and *rowrr*ed in protest, but he had it set on the carpet before the mottled orange and black cat could actually do more than hiss unhappily.

The moment it touched down and the last lock *snick*ed itself into the open position, Myal quickly hauled the door open. The cats were forced to scatter as the panel swung inward, but that was alright; the locks clicked when they scampered out of the way, but the dead bolts couldn't seal the exit now that the panel was free of its frame. Kerric toed the paper out of the way, then followed her into the short hall beyond. Once the door was shut, the same dim level of lighting from before prevailed.

Myal looked at the closed door behind them. "Those cats were just illusions, right?"

"Yes—don't worry about the fish being left to rot," Kerric added, guessing what her concern was. "The spells are complex enough that the bits they 'eat' get shuffled off to the Tower's sewer system. They'll continue to eat it, too, until it's all gone," he said. "When this is all over, I'll also leave a note for the Bottom maintenance teams to check it and the other rooms for cleanup."

"Right. Where are the three trigger points on these stairs?" Myal asked, lifting her chin at the next obstacle.

"Seventeen, nineteen, and thirty-three, out of fifty-two steps," he recited, eyes lifted to the ceiling while he reviewed what he had memorized.

Repeating the numbers to herself with little curls of her fingers, Myal started climbing. When she reached step sixteen, she skipped the next—easy enough with her long legs—then the one after that, and kept going. Behind her, Kerric hopped over the intervening trigger points. As soon as they skipped thirty-three, he spoke up again.

"You do realize that Junk Room Four has a riddle, right?" he asked, watching her strip-skirt armor sway as she climbed the remaining steps.

"You did mention that, yes," Myal replied politely.

Rolling his eyes, Kerric joined her at the top of the stairs. A short hall and a door awaited them. "I meant, if you get the riddle right, would you like another kiss?"

She blushed and smiled, ducking her head. "Yes, please. Is the door locked or trapped?"

A lift and swirl of his hand sparkled energy over the latch. The door swung open. Beyond lay another well-lit room, though it had no cats and no carpets. Piled in the center of the room was a mound of gold coins, jewelry, trinkets, goblets and plates and more. Ropes of precious pearls, colorful, faceted gems, unsheathed blades of highly polished crafting, even what looked like the edge of a cape trimmed in luxuriously thick white fur, all lay mounded in the center of the room.

This wasn't the Junk Room; this was the trap named All That Glitters Is Bone. The wealth glittered under the glow of the sun-crystals streaking the ceiling. Both of them ignored the pile, skirting the edge of the room carefully. "All That Glitters Is Bone" was easy enough to decipher; if either of them touched so much as a single coin of it, the entire treasure would transform and rise up as an army of skeleton warriors. Only those adventurers without any common sense or self-control would fall for such an easily avoided hazard.

The door beyond the pile unlocked with a bit of magic as well. It led straight into the next room. This one wasn't quite as bright, though not as dimly lit as the corridors had been. It was a very strange room, rectangular and somewhat narrow, and the most normal thing about it was the stone pedestal in the center, with a bronze plaque topping the surface. The least normal thing about the room was the walls. Hundreds of knobs and levers poked out of the walls, each one tipped with an object that had been glued or nailed or screwed or welded in place.

Myal eyed the objects. She counted a rope sandal, a baby's leather teething ring, an empty wine bottle, a book, a pair of scissors, a stuffed rabbit's foot, a little hand mirror, and more, and those were just the nearest objects sticking out from the wall to her right. Joining Kerric by the pedestal, she bent her attention to the riddle, and read it aloud.

"Ones and twos, we fall from above, dropping into the past. Plus our world is oft' overturned, allowing us more time to last."

"Well?" Kerric asked her.

She shook her head. "Far too easy, given that first room. We need to look for an hourglass. Do you know where it is, or should I take the right-hand wall while you take the left?"

"It's not a timed trap, so I didn't have to memorize the location, just the answer," he admitted. "So, first your kiss, then we'll the search for the hourglass."

Myal started to lean down for the kiss, but Kerric had other ideas. Catching her hand, he lifted it to his lips. Nibbling lightly as he worked his way toward her arm, he paused every once in a while to lick a bit of her fingers, the yoke between them, the lines of her palm. The play of his tongue against the tender skin of her inner wrist made her squirm and flinch.

Looking up, he raised a brow. "Something wrong?"

She blushed. "It's . . . ticklish. It tickles. I thought you were going to kiss me on the lips?"

"I thought you might enjoy this more," he countered lightly. "But if you like, I can work my way up there. Eventually." Dipping his head, he nibbled her thumb into his mouth, and sucked.

Her blush deepened. Myal wasn't accustomed to . . . this. Whatever this was. He kept his eyes locked with hers as he slowly suckled again, and again, a pulse of unexpected pleasure washed through her. Clearing her throat, she sought for something to say. "Ahhh . . . what comes after this, when we find the . . . the hourglass?"

Pulling his mouth from her thumb, Kerric licked his lips. As fun as it was to seduce her—particularly with the way her tanned cheeks blushed so charmingly—they did have a task to perform. "Oh, after this is the Cookie Trap, then the—"

"—The *Cookie* Trap?" Myal asked, chuckling. "*That* old thing? You weren't kidding when you said this was the *easy* route," she scoffed. She started to tug her hand free, but he tightened his grip slightly.

"A tonne of fresh-baked cookies can still hurt if you're caught under them when they fall," Kerric reminded her. "But beyond it is the Towel Trap, which lasts for four more rooms, not including the plain traps, and some of those are quite deadly."

Sobering, she dipped her head, acknowledging the moment was serious. "Alright. Cookie Trap, Towel Room . . . and then what?"

"One Foot, Two Foot, Red Foot, Blue Foot, which are a pair of pit traps of different depths, plus a spike trap and an ice trap," he recited, releasing her hand so he could recall the exact order without distractions. "Then the Seven Jewels Trap, which is the first room of the four required by the Towel Room Trap, with the Rushlight Trap for the second room. Rushlight is followed by the chasm trap of Rope, Bridge or Swing, followed by the third room for the Petrification Chamber. The one after that is a trap we have to trigger instead of avoid, because it lands us on the Scales of Justice for the fourth room in the series."

Myal blanched. Eyes widened, she stared at him. The Scales of Justice was one trap which no adventuring party cared to encounter, particularly one with members who were either substantially different in size such as herself and Kerric, or an odd number of participants.

"Yes," Kerric confirmed, catching her unsettled gaze. "The Scales of Justice is one of the rooms. And after *that* one, we have to face Greed Hurts, so either we kill all the gargoyles on the platform and recover our wounds before we move on from the Scales, or we have to risk getting poison into our wounds. Thankfully, by that point, we'll be free to discard our towels."

She frowned. "Discard our towels?"

"They're enchanted toweling cloths," he explained, gesturing. "You have to keep them with you for at least the next four rooms—slung around your neck, tucked into your belt, whatever and wherever so long as it's on you and visible, but not hidden in a bag—or you get sent back to the starting point. If you get sent back, you have to grab a fresh towel and run the gauntlet all over again from One Foot, Two Foot all the way through to Greed Hurts. Without our towels on hand at each step of the way, we're stuck in an infinite loop—and if I keep my towel but you lose yours, I get to move on, but *you* have to repeat all the tricks and traps. Or I'll have to repeat everything on my own, if *I'm* the one who loses his cloth."

Myal shook her head slowly. "I have never heard of that particular trap. Why a towel?"

Shrugging, he spread his hands. "It's on the list of infrequently used tricks, so I'm not surprised you haven't heard of it. As for why a towel, I have no idea. It was created long before my time."

She considered that. Her hand still tingled a little from the effects of his nibbling. Folding her arms, Myal thought it through. "At what point do we get sent back? The moment we drop the cloth, or . . . ?"

"The moment we try to go through the next doorway," Kerric told her.

"Then we just check before we open each door to make sure we have both towels on hand," she told him. "Does it still work if we drop the towel then pick it up? Or do we get sent back?"

"I'm . . . not sure," Kerric was forced to admit, thinking about it. "I've never actually run the room myself, remember?"

"Fair enough," she agreed. "If one of us drops a towel, then both of us drop it, and we restart everything together. But better to knot it around our belts if we can."

"Agreed." He started to turn away, then looked back at her and crooked a finger, beckoning her head down to his level. When she bent over, Kerric kissed her on her cheek. He smiled when she pulled back, a surprised look on her face. "That's for being smart. You'll get more kisses as we go on, I'm sure."

Chuckling, Myal unfolded her arms and turned to start looking for an hourglass on a handle or lever. "You make me wonder what I should look for in your own actions, to reward *you* with a kiss."

"Oh, surviving a trap with pure physical skill, probably. Or being undeniably handsome, though you'd have to stop kissing me at some point over that one, or we'd never get anywhere," he quipped, searching the right-hand wall. He was rewarded by another chuckle, and grinned over his shoulder at her. "You should laugh more often. You have a beautiful voice when you're happy."

She ducked her head, keeping her attention on her task. "You flatter me."

"No, it's true. I even brought a Truth Stone with me, if you'd like to see it for yourself," he offered, peering at handles with various things attached to their ends. Rag doll, magnifying lens, grease pencil, wooden button, coil of linen thread. "Your voice is soft, like velvet. And you don't waste it when you speak. When you have something to say, you say it. Nothing superfluous."

Myal was glad they were working with their backs to each other. "I'm . . . shy. I guess. I'm better at writing what I want to say. I can take my time, that way."

"Oh, that's right; you've written those little pamphlets on the gauntlets," Kerric recalled, stooping to peer at some of the levers down low. "I'm afraid I haven't had a chance to read any, though I have heard good things from those who have. I've been caught up in my research—I don't know about you, but the trouble with being a writer is that all your leisure time seems to get eaten up by research. Or at least mine does—hey, here we go! I think I've found it."

Marking her place mentally, Myal turned and crossed to his side of the narrow room. Stooping, she eyed the handle he pointed to, but carefully did not touch. The bow-tie shaped glass was no bigger than her thumb, but the bottom of the two bell-shaped lobes did hold a fine white grit. "It's not very big, but it *is* an hourglass."

"Ready?" he asked her.

Myal drew in a deep breath and recited the next chain of steps. "Cookie Trap, Towel Room, One Foot, Jewel Trap, Rushlight, Rope choice, Petrification, the trap to the Scales of Justice, and Greed Hurts . . . right?" When he nodded, she did as well. "Then I'm ready."

Grasping the knob with the hourglass affixed to its tip, Kerric twisted it. With a click, the door hidden behind all those rods swung outward, a line of the levers tilting inward among their brethren in order to clear the opening. Another dimly lit corridor lay beyond. This one, however, had half a dozen doors within the first sixty feet, two side-corridors, and a stairwell leading up at the far end.

Myal eased into the corridor, eyes scanning everywhere for any sign of a trigger for the promised trap, down along the flagstones paving the floor, the blocks of stone that made up the walls, even the ceiling. Kerric carefully closed the door behind them, then strode forward. And stopped, hearing something behind them. Returning to the panel, he pressed his ear to its surface.

". . . Did you hear something?" she finally asked in a whisper, not willing to move until he identified where the trap was located.

He nodded, a frown pinching his brow, and spoke in a whisper as well. "I heard voices—at least three. Sounds like they're working on solving the trap."

"I was afraid someone might have followed us," Myal whispered back. "Looks like someone did. Let's go."

A swipe of his hand and a murmur of a spell flung a glowing green web onto a patch of stone no different than any other in their path, save that it was past the second door and the first turning to the left. Once they had hopped over the blocked trigger point, he dissolved the barrier with a snap of his fingers. "So much for the infamous Cookie Trap."

"They're fresh-baked, but a tonne is still a tonne," she agreed.

Picking the third door, just before the right-hand turning, he pulled out his lock picks and went to work. As soon as the latch clicked, he pushed the door open and moved inside, giving her room to enter. Swinging the panel shut, he caught it at the last moment and closed the door gently, quietly, then twisted the knob above the latch to re-lock it.

Myal, looking around the room, took in the layers of fresh and faded linens hanging from the hooks on the bench-lined racks down the middle of the room. Narrow, painted metal cupboards with yet more hooks lined the walls, and a door with a glazed window in the upper half stood at the far end. If the cupboards had been made from wood instead of glazed metal, and the linens made from plain bleached muslin instead of the various hues and patterns she saw, it would have looked like one of the changing rooms for the practice salles of the Adventuring Hall.

That, and the other main difference was one of the Tower's ubiquitous bronze plaques hung next to the far door. There was almost always a bronze plaque in this place.

"Pick a towel, tie it on, and let's go," Kerric whispered, one hand touching her elbow, the other her hip as he edged past her. Or rather, her buttock. He blushed a little when he realized where his hand had brushed. "Pardon me."

"You like my rump, don't you?" Myal asked as casually as she could. She reached for a faded blue cloth patterned in bleached-out flower designs. "You keep staring at it."

Face warm, Kerric cleared his throat. "Well, it's a magnificent rump, firm yet rounded, and you move it very gracefully. A man would have to be blind or dead not to notice it."

He plucked a yellow and green cloth off one of the hooks. Working it under the strap of leather holding his pouch over his armor, he carefully knotted it in place. A glance at her showed she was doing the same. Grabbing three more towels, he carried them to the far entrance, where he carefully draped them over a hook next to the door in such a way that they obscured the plaque as much as possible.

"There . . . now if they follow us in here, they might not see that, and get stuck in a repeating loop. Ready?" he asked.

She nodded, so he flipped the knob keeping the second door

locked. While he did so, she shifted the towels just enough to read the plaque, something about counting fingers and "*. . . what gets wetter and wetter, the more that it dries,*" an obvious reference to toweling cloths. Gently readjusting the fabric, she re-concealed the plaque and followed him into the corridor beyond the door. Which was only glazed with frosted glass from the perspective of the inside of the changing room, and was nothing more than a solid wooden panel on the other side.

Once they were through, Kerric closed the door quietly, and relocked it with his tools. "Right. Best way to get across this hall is via the ceiling. Got your sticky-feet ready?"

Myal nodded—and found herself inverted with a swirl of his hand, her body lifted feet-first to the ceiling. Flexing her ankle, she touched the stones, felt the soles of her boots grab hold, and started carefully walking.

"Watch your hair!" Kerric hissed at her as her braid started to dangle and sway free. "Crouch a bit, if you can. The four traps can be triggered at just above knee-high on you, thigh-high on me."

Grunting, she scrunched her legs and stomach muscles until she could touch her hands to the ceiling as well. Crawling in an awkward, dangling way, she headed down the hallway. "How far do we go?"

"Around the corner to the stairs," Kerric murmured. He floated right past her as he did so. The cheating, magically empowered . . . cheater floated right past her, blithely ignored each of the two doors on either side, and took the first left.

Shuffling upside-down after him, Myal turned the corner and pulled her feet free so that she dangled toward the steps where Kerric now stood, then flexed her foot again while concentrating to cancel the effects of her violet spider tattoo. That let her hands drop as well when the faint tingling sensation ended. Landing lightly, she balanced on the steps and lifted her chin. "Next?"

"Lady-adventurers first," he offered, gesturing her up the stairs.

Myal smirked. "*You* just want to stare at my rump."

"Guilty as charged. The Jewel Trap is a riddle trap," Kerric warned her, following her up the steps. "Don't touch any of the pedestals until we've picked the right one. We want the left-hand fourth landing. So . . . tell me about the childhood of Narahan Myal. Any parents or siblings back in Mendhi? What did your family do for a living?"

"Four brothers, three sisters. I was third-from-youngest. We farmed. Mother and Father raised ducks and chickens, grew quinoa and gourds, and harvested nuts in the fall, and twice a month Mother would take us down to the beaches to dig on the neap tides for clams and hunt for crabs," Myal said. She moved steadily, not swiftly, pacing herself so that she could speak freely without feeling winded. "Great-Uncle Narahan Jomen was a Painted Warrior. He had been a quinoa farmer like Grandfather, but then became a sailor. He was the one who introduced Mother to Father. She had lived in a fishing village where his ship stopped on its trading route along the coast."

"I've seen maps of the Mendhite coastline. I can't imagine anyone *not* becoming familiar with the sea, in your home country," Kerric quipped. "It's all inlets and coves, little islands and peninsulas, and lakes all over the place, if the map I saw was in any way accurate."

"Lakes, hills, mountains, inlets," she agreed. "Legend says our Goddess created so many lakes and ponds and puddles and lagoons so that She would always have a place to dip the Brush of Creation." Curling down her ring finger as she reached the next landing, she nodded at the door on the left. "This should be the Jewel Trap."

Kerric pressed his hand to the latch plate, focusing his magic.

The door clicked and swung open. "So what is this *kinwa* stuff? I've had a lot of things imported to the Tower over the years, but I don't think I've heard of that one.

"Quinoa is a common grain. It's not a grass grain like wheat or oats or rice, but we grow it, harvest it, thresh it and winnow it, and wash the grains and dry them quickly—you have to wash them because under the hull, they're coated in something like soap, and can cause stomach-cramps," she added, following him into the next chamber. Like some of the others, it was brightly lit, making her squint and shade her eyes protectively. "But once washed and dried, you can cook them like your oats for porridge, or grind them into flour. It's very tasty."

"I'll take your word for it," Kerric murmured, shielding his own eyes. Walls, ceiling, and floor had all been painted a bright shade of white. Even the pedestals, six of them arranged in a circle around a seventh in the center, had been coated. "I see the maintenance crews recently whitewashed this room—how did you learn the Aian tongue?"

Myal raised her brows at the out-of-the-Tower question. She tapped the tattoo stretching from her eye to her ear to her collarbone, all on the right side of her body. "Translation tattoo. Some Painted Warriors apply a tattoo for one or two foreign languages on their bodies. Some even have five or six inked. I braved the pain of a face-tattooing to ensure I would understand *all* languages I encountered, as thoroughly as if I were a native."

Kerric frowned at that, but more in a thoughtful way than anything. He tapped his lips with a finger, then pointed at the plaque on the central pillar. The outer six each bore a huge, gleaming gemstone fixed to the tops of the slender columns, but the central one was a riddle-plaque cast in bronze. Each jewel was as big as two fists pressed together: a clear diamond, a golden topaz the color of pale honey, a scarlet ruby, a grassy emerald, a sapphire the color of the evening sky just after the sun has set, and a glossy, iridescent pearl. The plaque, of course, was plain bronze, with the letters polished from years of dusting and cleaning.

"This one sometimes trips up non-native speakers. I can admire anyone who learns a language the hard way, word by word, but their vocabulary doesn't always cover enough to solve this riddle. On the other hand, some translation spells don't translate the writing quite in the way it was intended, which can also cause problems."

"How so?" Myal asked. She glanced at him as she paced around the outside of the pillars, careful not to touch any. There was enough room to slip between them to read the central post and its sign, but she remained outside, mindful of the potential for traps.

"Well, if your language is like that of Senod-Gra, it's ideographic; symbols represent whole ideas. If it's more like Aian, it's phonic, where symbols represent sound-fragments," Kerric said. "As he went about conquering and unifying the many disparate lands and peoples and languages of Aiar, the first emperor of the ancient Empire, Ai-kan Fen Jul, realized that using symbols for whole words might allow the people of one area to communicate with the people of another area through writing, but it would only be used by those who knew how to read and write.

"A written, symbol-based language would never unify the spoken versions, and without that unity of speech, the *people* would never unify," he continued, warming to the subject. The Tower was no Great Library of Mendham, but it did have a substantial number of pre-Shattering textbooks on various subjects. This was one of Kerric's favorites, the ancient days of the First Emperor. "So, Ai-kan decreed that words should be broken down into their individual sounds, and created a cross-continental version of common words found in most of the various languages. That became the language for both government and trade, which eventually became the main tongue. These days, it's a very rare corner of the continent that speaks anything else besides Aian in everyday life."

Myal nodded, seeing where the Master of the Tower was going with this. "I see. If your method of translation warps whatever you see into a version of your native tongue, you might miss the original writer's intentions. Mendhite was originally all about the symbols, not the sounds, but over time, we came to realize it was smarter to use the sounds as we encountered new peoples, new lands, and new ideas, all of which required new words.

"Memorizing thousands of word-symbols is tedious enough, but memorizing hundreds of thousands would be near-impossible for everyone. Thankfully, my tattoo translates a written language as if I were the native speaker of that language. It has even allowed me to appreciate written puns, and cultural jokes," she added, mouth curving in another of her shy smiles. "The pain of being inked has been more than worth it, over the years."

"Yes, I would imagine being tattooed onto your very eyelid would be quite painful," he agreed, grimacing at the thought. "I heard in passing from another Painted Warrior a few years back that the bigger the tattoo, the more powerful the magic imbued into it. Does that count as well when it's the pain endured in the inking process?"

She nodded. "Hands, face, feet, inner elbows, backs of the knees, wrists, ears, throat, navel, spine . . . These are all places of great power. Pulse points and joints, major muscle groups . . . and the *chakrasa*, the focus points along the torso where certain magics are most powerful. The primary one is the navel, which gives magical abilities to those who have none. There are even some who have shaved their heads and inked their scalps, only to let their hair regrow so that they can hide extra powers. Others keep their heads shaved, baring their marks proudly."

Kerric eyed the tall warrior with her long black braid. He shook his head after a moment. "I'm sorry, but I simply cannot imagine you bald. Not since you were a newborn baby, and probably not even then."

She ducked her head, smiling. "I don't know if I had hair on my head or not when I was born. I never thought to ask my mother that. I don't remember my younger brother and sister's heads, either; I was too young myself to pay attention when they were born."

"Well, as fun as it is to learn more about you—and I do hope to continue learning," Kerric added, "—but we should check the riddle. Don't touch the outer columns," he reminded her, watching her slip between them. "What does it say?"

Myal read the plaque silently to herself, then recited it out loud. *"If you cut off my head, I may shake your hand one day. If you cut off my tail, I may hide in a tree. If you cut off both my head and my tail, you'll probably be stuck with two of me. I am the only safe thing in this room."*

"Well?" Kerric asked as she stayed silent after her recitation. "Do you know what the answer is?"

Frowning softly, she turned to eye each of the gemstones. "You spoke of the Aian language being phonic, bits of word-sounds. Since this isn't a normal gauntlet, but rather one you have ensured will be traversed swiftly and easily, your comments have something to do with—ahah! *Pearl*." She stated it with confidence, turning to point at that pedestal. "The first one, I didn't get, but the last two, if you take away the L, you get PEAR, which is a fruit that grows in a tree. And if you take away the P and the L, you get EAR, which come in pairs."

"The first one, take away the P and you get EARL, which is a type of nobleman," Kerric told her. "Hence being able to 'shake your hand' even with his 'head' missing."

"Clever," Myal praised. Moving around the bronze pillar, she approached the pearl one. "I just touch it?"

"A compartment will open below the pearl; you may take whatever lies within. Just don't forget to find and press the lever inside," he told her. "Unless you want me to do the honors?"

She smiled with a touch of pride this time, lifting her chin. "My riddle, my task. And I'll have my kiss out of you, now."

"Oh, well, if you *insist*," Kerric joked, heaving a mock-sigh and rolling his eyes, though he did grin at her. He waited for her to clear the ring of pedestals, then lifted up on his toes and met her descending lips.

SIX

This time, the kiss was a relatively brief one. Myal pulled back with a small frown and a worried look in her eyes. It was prompted by the differences in their heights, and the memory of one particular man about three years back, a fellow adventurer whom she'd tried kissing before. He, too, had been shorter than her. "You don't mind that I'm so tall, do you?"

Kerric arched a brow at her. "Milady, I have *always* been short. I was short as a boy, I am short as a man, and when I came here from two kingdoms over, half the native-born women in this valley were and still are taller than me. Most adventurer-women are taller, period."

"That doesn't bother you?" Myal asked, thinking of the previous fellow she had kissed, a man with the pale skin and light blond hair of a far northerner. He had been exotically handsome in her eyes, but standing a palm-width shorter than her, he had been uncomfortable having to kiss *up* when kissing her.

"Oh, it used to. I even thought about using magic to lengthen my body," Kerric admitted, rubbing the back of his neck. His helm got in the way, so he pulled it off, fluffing out his curls for a moment with a tousle of his hand. "I went to a Healer-mage to see what could be done about it. He told me it *could* be done, but that it would be like stretching anything else out of its proper shape. My bones would always ache, my joints would twinge, and that was just if I lengthened my legs and my arms.

"My feet would have problems, too, since they'd have to grow to keep my balance, and there are dozens of little bones in them, all of which would hurt with every weather change. And if I messed with the size of my torso, I'd have digestive problems and worse." He shook his head, frowning into the distance off to her right. "It wouldn't be worth the constant problems that would plague the rest of my life. He *did* show me a few easy levitation charms—I've never needed a stepladder since—but since I can't go around floating for the rest of my life, it was just easier to accept that I am who and what I am.

"Like you," he added, flicking a hand at her armored body. "Yes, magic could make you permanently shorter, or you could figure out a tattoo to do it temporarily, but there would always be attendant problems in the long-term, and it wouldn't be *you*. I don't know about you—and I hope you feel this way about yourself, too—but I *like* who I am. Yes, I had to work harder because people often overlook or dismiss shorter people, but it seems to me that the too-tall have their fair share of stares and unrealistic expectations. So I'm not going to be bothered by it.

"Um . . . unless it's a literal pain in the neck for you," he finished, eyeing her uncertainly. "If it is, I can start floating. I'm just trying to conserve energy."

"Or I can take a knee, on every other kiss?" Myal offered, dropping to the right one so that she had to look up at him instead of down. That made him chuckle, which made her grin. This time when they kissed, her neck and back didn't feel the strain so much, though there was enough difference in their heights that she knew he was probably feeling some of it.

This time, without his hair being confined by that silly but necessary cap, she could feel the curling ends brush against her skin. It was a sensual, subtle caress, particularly when he tipped his head just a little bit more, deepening their kiss. Sighing softly, she wrapped her arms around his waist when he looped his around her shoulders, ignoring the stiffness of their various bits of armor in favor of enjoying the closeness of his embrace.

She knew these intimacies were a deliberate choice, that they were necessary to get through a complicated-sounding trap. Foreign or familiar, Myal also knew enough about men to know when one was lying to her, and the Master of the Tower was being as honest as he could, given the secrets she knew he had to hold back. At the end of their kiss, he pressed his lips to her forehead and murmured something. She looked up at him in silent inquiry, and he smiled with one corner of his mouth.

"Oh, I just said *Enshil-ka*. It's a word one of my fellow Guardians taught me. It literally means 'your wave has rolled me,' but in the Menomonite culture, it means 'your beauty rocks me.'" He ducked his head a little, but didn't stop looking at her from under his lashes.

Honesty prompted her to speak. "I'm actually not all that pretty. Not ugly, just average for a Mendhite woman."

"And I'm short, but you still think I'm handsome," he retorted.

"What makes you think I think you're handsome?" Myal asked, smiling to show she was teasing.

"Because *you* have been checking out *my* backside," he reminded her.

She smiled and shook her head, looking up at him. "Not your

rump. Your *legs*. That strip-skirt armor you wear isn't much different from a proper Mendhite kilt. You have very nice calves."

"What, you don't think I look silly in it?" Kerric asked, twisting a little so he could peer down at himself.

She bit her lip, but couldn't quite muffle her chuckle. "I didn't say *that* . . ." At his mock-affronted look, she pointed at the curve of boiled leather in his hand. "It's the helmet. It squashes your hair into an odd fringe, and flattens out all those handsome curls."

"Well, I need it, even if it makes me look silly." Scrubbing his fingers through his locks, fluffing up some of the natural wave, he added, "That, and it makes my scalp itch."

"But it's needed," she agreed, watching him scrape his hair back and squish the brown curls under the boiled leather cap. "The next one is the Rushlight Trap, yes? Another riddle trap? Another chance for a kiss?"

"Yes and no. It's a timed trap. We have exactly sixty seconds to decide on a solution, thirty seconds to carry it out, and sixty more to get out of the room, so I'll handle the riddle, since I already know the solution," he warned her. Kerric offered her his hand. She accepted it, letting his stout but strong body help haul her to her feet. "Beyond it is Rope, Bridge, or Swing. That one, you can take a stab at. We'll have the time for it."

"I think I know that one," Myal murmured, dusting off her knee armor. Crossing to the pedestal with the giant pearl, she touched the creamy orb. A crack appeared in the pedestal just below the top. It eased out like a tilting drawer, one filled with yet more orbs; these were the size of beans and peas, and some of them were strung together on silken cords.

They felt cool and smooth against her fingertips as she wiggled her digits into the mass, trying to find the lever. Brushing up against something lumpy, cold, and decidedly not a pearl, she pulled it out, revealing a necklace that should have belonged in the diamond pedestal, since most of the gems strung in white gold were clear-faceted jewels that sparkled in the light of the suncrystals streaking the ceiling. Three thumbnail-sized pearls had been set between the bejeweled links, though.

Kerric recognized it. His brows lifted. "Congratulations. Those three are rainbow pearls—you can't tell because there isn't any direct sunlight or moonlight to make them glow with rainbow tones, but I remember approving that necklace as a Tower treasure. Each pearl is worth the cost of a large castle, and the diamonds could fully staff it for four, maybe five years per segment. You could retire in quite a bit of comfort off of that one piece of treasure alone."

She frowned at the necklace with a thoughtful expression. Kerric held himself still, wondering what she was thinking. He hoped she would stay with him all the way through, and wasn't thinking of just taking the necklace and turning back. She could change her mind at any point up until the trap for the Scales of Justice; once they triggered the chute for that, there was no easy way back.

Sighing, Myal shook her head. "I don't have a use for a castle. I could afford to go home with this and buy a very nice home, but there is nothing back in Mendhi that draws me there. I have friends and I have fame here. I have a *life* here, not there."

Dangling it over the opening, she dropped it back into the bin, then dug in again. A click opened a door off to the left. Stirring up the bin, which went down as deep as her forearm was long, she buried the necklace.

"Careful," Kerric warned her, half teasing, half serious. "An attitude like that just might get you formally employed, here. And you *are* free to take the necklace. It would look lovely on you."

She shook her head. "I don't have anything pretty to wear it with."

"Well, I'd offer to take you shopping myself, but going *shopping* is what got me into this gauntlet," he quipped wryly. "Although I could have some high-quality tailors bring their wares here to Penambrion for you, as a thank-you for helping me."

Myal hesitated, then dug into the bin. Once again, her fingers found the diamond-strung necklace. "I'll take it, for now. But I'll keep it *only* if you find me something pretty to wear, and only if it really is pretty on me."

He grinned and bowed. "Fair enough, fair lady."

"I thought fair ladies meant blonde ladies in Aian culture?" Myal asked, tucking the necklace into her pouch.

"It was a play on words. And you're not the darkest-skinned adventurer lady in the valley," he pointed out. "There are at least two from the southern coast kingdoms, and a good dozen on the staff, if not more. Ready for the Rushlight Trap?"

"Ready."

Opening the door, Kerric ushered her into the dark, dank chamber that formed the next room. It was stone-lined, not plastered and whitewashed, and there was a nasty metallic taint to the air that spoke of blood spilled, the kind that had never been completely cleaned. The source of the smell was apparent; there were three doors out of this place, including the one they had just entered. In front of each was a stained patch of floor, the cracks between each block dark with dried blood. Some of the blocks had small, deep holes, also crusted with unpleasantness.

Overhead, Myal spotted matching holes, and a broad crack that suggested that huge blocks slammed down, possibly with spikes descending as well, or maybe jutting up from below. The lighting level in the chamber wasn't very good, so it was hard to tell. Even as she peered around the gloom-filled room, Kerric strode straight to the pedestal in the middle of the rounded chamber. Snapping both fingers, he simultaneously lit both ends of a lumpy, oil-soaked reed sitting on a longish metal dish.

Joining him, she read the plaque below the dish, polished raised letters gleaming faintly in the dim lighting.

I burn out in exactly sixty seconds. If you wish to proceed safely and stay alive, burn me in exactly thirty. But hurry if you do, for in sixty more, I will come back and kill you.

The rushlight, she realized, was indeed burning that fast. It was too lumpy to have been split evenly lengthwise down the middle, and gauging where to cut it in half crosswise would have been a hard task to judge. By igniting it at both ends, he guaranteed it would burn out in the required amount of time.

While she read the riddle, Kerric dug out his lock-picking tools, heading toward the door on the right. He glanced over his shoulder, counting down silently in his head. The moment the two reddish-yellow flames met and winked out, sending up a puff of oily-dark smoke, he slipped the tools inside and started counting under his breath. One to prod and twist, one to press and hold. Again a gentle prodding, and a slide of the other one to hold that bit down as well. Attempting to unfasten this lock by magic would cause the very deadly traps overhead to go off.

At twenty-one, Myal had joined him, though she carefully stayed out of range of the stained patch of floor. At twenty-seven, the last bit of the mechanism had been eased through. Twisting the knob, Kerric pushed the door open and stepped smartly through, turning to let Myal out as well. "Out" was the right word for it. Though the rocky promontory they emerged onto was located inside a rough-hewn chasm deep within the Tower, the sound of the door shutting didn't even echo.

This wasn't the only rift in the thick, tall block of chamber-riddled stone, but it was the most impressive one. It stretched far out to either side, giving the impression it existed somewhere other than the Tower itself. In fact, it gave the illusion that they could *see* Penambrion off in the dark somewhere, as if there were a big chunk of Tower wall missing, though it actually wasn't. Anyone attempting to leave the Tower by going in that direction would find themselves dead rather quickly under the lethal conditions of the Tower on lockdown.

Luckily, Kerric and his partner weren't going to leave. The rocky peak onto which they had emerged rose a good eighty feet from the cavernous, rubble-strewn bottom, with the ceiling at least another fifty or sixty more above them. Lit by a patchwork of jagged streaks of suncrystals growing out of the spires and peaks around them, the chasm showed bridges, balconies, chains, and more. Suncrystals crossed the chasm like beams of fattened lightning; others gleamed like shards of light embedded in the stones. Despite their presence, the place wasn't even half-lit over most of its expanse, leaving the landscape grimly dotted by patches of light.

He knew the vast chasm was at least part illusion; it was in reality several much smaller chasms connected to each other via elaborately built Gate-frames. Under normal circumstances, they could have taken a shortcut by literally flying or climbing up to a higher spire, cutting off some of this tedious traveling, fighting, and puzzle-working. Unfortunately, what they currently saw were projections that did not actually, physically connect. Not safely, not directly. Not without a Master of the Tower back in control.

That meant they had to take the long way through . . . and like any good adventurer, Myal had already climbed the rugged path to the platform at the top of the peak. Catching up to her, Kerric found her reading the plaque at the edge of the balcony.

There were actually three ways to get across, here. The first, a trio of long ropes off to the left, which had been between this balcony's edge and a peak a fair distance away; the thickest of the three ropes had been fastened at floor height, while the other two flanked it at waist height. They were tied to rough stone posts on either end in an inverted triangle position, forming a very unsteady means of crossing the rift. There was the bridge itself, of course, narrow but sturdy-looking despite its rough-hewn appearance and lack of railings. It stood open and inviting. And there was a single rope, hanging from a suncrystal shaft that crossed the gaping chasm. It lay draped over the near-side railing to the right of the bridge. Between the bridge and the rope meant for swinging across the rift sat the plaque, fastened to the railing.

"*In the change of a song, the traveler is dry, the duck is wet, and the fault is crossed. Worlds can be straddled, ends always met, yet when it is washed, the journey is lost*," Myal recited. It didn't take her more than a moment to point at the bridge. "Clever riddle. If I didn't know anything about composing music, I'd be lost, too. But the middle of a song is called a 'bridge.' I learned that when my ship stopped for trade and provisions in the coastal kingdom of Garama, where music is as worshipped as writing is back home," she murmured. Glancing over at Kerric, she asked, "What happens if we used the ropes instead of the bridge, either to balance and walk, or to swing our way across?"

"Lightning trap," Kerric said. "It doesn't fire until you leave the balcony by a body-length, but once it ignites, it doesn't stop scorching you until you let go of the ropes and fall out of range. It doesn't stop even if you regain the balcony; it just keeps firing until you're dead or beyond its grasp."

"Charming," Myal muttered, eyeing the air around the bridge. Maybe it would come from the suncrystal shaft, or maybe from the air itself. Or there could have been enspelled chains intended for conduits hidden in the mottled patches of light and shadow; it was hard to tell. She dropped her fingers to the towel still knotted around her belt, and glanced at Kerric, checking for his. Both were still firmly in place. "What do I need to know about the Petrification Chamber?"

"One of us will be turned to stone," he told her, as casually as he would have said, *One of us will wear a red tunic.*

She gave him an alarmed look. "Turned to *stone*?"

"Oh, it's quite simple. The other person, the one not petrified, just keeps going. Don't look back, just get through the next door . . . which may be locked," Kerric admitted. "I didn't memorize anything specific for getting through it, like using just magic or using tools, or just breaking down the door to get through, so you should be able to get through it in whatever way you can manage without problems. You'll have a good fifteen feet on the other side of the door before you'd trigger the Scales of Justice, so just go right on through the door, then shut it and wait."

"I'm not leaving you as a . . . a stone statue in one of these rooms," Myal argued, slashing her hand between them. "That would be wrong, and dangerous, and you're the *only* person who knows which path to take!"

Her voice echoed off the chasm walls. Kerric caught her hand between his, hushing her. "Shhh. It's alright. As soon as all the companions of the victim have passed through to the next room or corridor or whatever, the petrified person comes back to life and is free to leave the room and join them."

". . . *Hello?*" The voice startled both of them, echoing up through the chasm. The reflections of it off all the hard surfaces made the gender indeterminate, either a tenor man or an alto woman. "*Is someone out there?*"

Rolling his eyes, Kerric drew in a deep breath and hollered back, speaking slowly and as clearly as possible to ensure his words would be understood despite the way they bounced off the peaks and ravines. He wasn't sure, but it sounded like they were somewhere near the rift in the outer wall, which meant they were very close to dying if they went the wrong way. *"Yes! This is Tower Maintenance. Please remain in a safe location. The traps are particularly deadly in this sector! Do not try to climb outside! Remain calm. We should have the Tower fixed within a day or so. Please remain in a safe location!"*

His bellow echoed off the irregular stretches of rock and smooth-hewn stone, reflecting from balconies and projections alike. It took a few moments, but he got a reply.

". . . Okay! We'll stay right here!"

Dropping his voice to a much quieter level, Kerric lifted her fingers to his lips. "At least most adventurers are sensible about maintenance problems." He kissed the back of her hand, then turned it over and kissed the palm. "There. Your kiss for getting the riddle right."

Disappointment made her mouth turn down at the corners. "That's not much of a kiss."

Amused, he smiled at her. "Are you pouting? Is the great Myal the Mendhite, Myal the Magnificent, veteran of a hundred and more gauntlet runs, actually *pouting*?"

Flustered, she started to deny the very thought, then blushed and tugged at her hand, still caught in his grasp. He didn't let go. She sulked a little more, and finally admitted it. "Yes. I am."

Grinning, Kerric kissed his way up her inner wrist, covering her skin from bracer to inner elbow. He lingered at that last spot, teasing her flesh with the tip of his tongue. As he thought she might, she squirmed at the ticklish touch, grinning. "There you go," he murmured, releasing her. It was the other arm from the last one. "Count that as a bookmark. I'll get to reading the rest of your body soon enough. And don't worry about the next room. It's nothing more than an elaborate stasis charm."

"Kerric?" Myal asked quietly as he started across the bridge, keeping her voice low enough that it wouldn't echo or travel far. He glanced back at her, but didn't stop; her tone hadn't implied the need for that. "What do you mean, reading the rest of my body? Yes, I'm covered in tattoos, but you couldn't read them like a fellow Painted Warrior could."

"Ah, but there *is* a way to read that involves touch. It's what the blind do, or did, before the Empire collapsed," he told her, leading the way across the chasm. "Not every kingdom retains the old ways, but the Tower has a massive library, Topside, and they had ways back then of imprinting heavy paper with a special kind of raised-letter writing."

Myal thought of the cast bronze lettering on the plaques, the way they stood out, literally, from the surface. "Yes, but I don't have letters cast into my skin."

"True, but you do have goose-bumps," he said. "Especially when I tickle you."

The absurdity of that, coupled with his comment about raised-letter writing, made her smile. Kerric Vo Mos, just plain Kerric, was turning out to be far more amusing than she'd thought. Until now, Myal had only ever dealt with Master Kerric, the Guardian of the Tower. This, however, was a glimpse into the man behind the job.

Reaching the far balcony, he went straight to the door and tried the knob. It opened easily. Holding it for her, he entered behind Myal, stealing a quick peek at her armor-skirted rump. And bumped into it as she stopped moving not more than a body-length into the plain, small, stone-walled room. Mid-stride, too, with her hair and skirt frozen while swaying. Her lungs didn't move, her eyes didn't blink. She was as frozen as a perfectly preserved, skillfully painted statue, save that a real statue would have toppled over mid-stride, or needed some sort of subtle extra means for support in that particular position.

Well, better her than him. *He* knew the trap was temporary. Giving her upper back a gentle pat—to have patted her rump without her knowledge would have been wrong—Kerric moved around her and tried the far door. It was unlocked, thankfully. Opening it, he stepped through and shut the door behind him.

Kerric took the moment of privacy to scratch an indelicate itch under his leather and brass armor, then leaned against the wall. Waiting for the trap to reset, he unlocked the door from his side without opening it, then reviewed the next few steps after Greed Hurts. Before he'd thought through more than twelve rooms ahead, the door opened and Myal poked her head through.

"Ah. It was me that was petrified, wasn't it?" she asked. He nodded, and she shrugged philosophically. "A relatively harmless trap, compared to the Rushlight one. Still have your towel?"

"Yes, as do you. And they can't all be deadly," Kerric offered lightly. "That one is designed to delay a group, because if you come in with someone you cannot leave behind—say, someone skilled at healing, or picking locks, or whatever—then you're going to waste time trying to unfreeze them before you realize you're being forced to abandon them. And by that point, the Guardian has had ample time to marshal more forces into place, in a real invasion."

Thinking about that, Myal offered another solution. "Or the Guardian could use it to figure out if the frozen person is the most important member of the group by how the others act, and then they can work to neutralize that person. If not, they can neutralize one of the others and see how they react to that."

He grinned at her. "Well done! I could definitely use someone as smart as you on the inside. Let me know when you're ready to retire from the adventuring side of things."

Pleased by the praise, she shrugged. "I'm not *quite* ready to retire, but I'll think about it. Now . . . the Scales."

"Yes, the Scales. And we're obviously not the same weight," Kerric pointed out. "I may be stout for my height, but you're both tall and strong. Your side will dip down fast, while mine will rise. I don't dare levitate until you're off of yours, either, or you won't be able to make the leap to the platform. Which, of course, will have gargoyles on it. Statues that will animate and attempt to attack us, flinging us off to the floor far below."

She nodded. "With the poles greased, and without other teammates to try to even out the load . . . Well, I'll try to come out of the chute in a controlled tumble, and see if I can aim for the platform. Unless you think we should climb down the chute? Maybe use a rope if there's a place to tie it? Or have you levitate us both?"

Kerric shook his head. "If the Tower weren't in shutdown mode, maybe that would work. But it is, so these chutes will be spell-greased, and the trapdoors at the bottom won't open unless we hit them at the right speed. The one thing in our favor is that both platforms will have a great deal of mass to them, in the expectation of three or more adventurers coming along. They should move a little more slowly than we've seen in past gauntlet scryings, even if we are two different weights."

"They should, but I will not count on that," Myal cautioned him. "Neither should you."

"True. Well. We'll both see how good our reflexes are, won't we?" he asked rhetorically. "Ready for the drop?"

"No, but that won't stop me," Myal retorted. "I hate falling. I hate it more, knowing I cannot stop it from happening. Let's go."

"Right, then. Here goes. Stay close. The weight of at least two people will trigger the floor trap," Kerric stated. "After that, we know what to do."

Gesturing her to join him, he headed up the corridor. They passed two doors, it turned left, they passed a third—and the entire floor dropped out from under them. Both yelped, even though they each knew it was coming. Kerric reflexively levitated within a body-length, then forced himself to cancel the spell, sliding and tumbling after Myal. Armor and backpacks scraping, they twisted and slid, until a loud *snap* made her dart off to the left and him to the right as a leverlike section flipped over the moment she skidded past.

If he hadn't been aware of the very lethal trap awaiting them, Kerric might have enjoyed this chute. As it was, the moment he dropped a second time, he tensed, hit the metal grate with a loud grunt, and twisted to get himself upright and oriented even as the platform started to rise under him. Just as he did so, he watched Myal uncurl from her own tumbled landing, and launch herself like a cat springing for a bookshelf. For a moment, his side of the Scales jolted upward from the force of her leap, then the grate reversed course, sliding quickly downward.

Overhead was a mess of spikes, designed to slot into the holes in the grate supporting him. Down below lay the same, yet more spikes designed to impale the unwary. Fingers snapping, Kerric floated up off the sinking platform. At the same moment, Myal hit the edge of the platform at waist height. One of her hands hooked around the talonlike paw of one of the half-dozen winged beasts perched there. Just as it looked like she was going to haul on it to pull herself up, it shifted, shook off her fingers, and made her slip.

Breath catching, Kerric willed his body to soar in her direction, using his mind to push the energies holding him aloft. The platform in question was a good twelve feet or more from the Scales and the vertical, cagelike bars the Scales used as guides as they slid up and down. It was also at least fifty feet above the spike-covered floor. Somehow, Myal managed to bunch up her legs and touch her toes to the platform—and let go with her hand just as the gargoyle stretched its wings, twisted, and snapped downward, no doubt intending to bite open her skull. Its granite beak *clacked* shut on empty air.

Myal swung free, saved by the feet now clinging to the underside of the solid stone shelf. Braid dangling over her head, she drew her sword and braced herself. The gargoyle curled over the edge and slashed with a talon. Dodging, she grabbed the hilt in both hands and jabbed downward—upward in relation to gravity.

Blade-tip stabbing under one of its feet, between it and the platform, she wrenched and heaved. Caught off-balance, the gargoyle tipped over, knocked into the second statue—which woke it up—and twisted, trying to get free. So did Myal, twisting the steel blade like a broad prybar so that it tipped the gargoyle forward, off the platform. It snapped its wings open, no doubt intending to fly, perhaps even come around to snap at her again, though she quickly relaxed, dangling upside-down out of its way.

Instead, Kerric got in its way. Not physically; he was no fighter, and had backed off from the platform the moment he knew she was anchored to its underside. Instead, he shouted a word. The stone beast rehardened mid-glide, and *clanged* into the bars, before dropping straight to the ground four or so floors below. It shattered with a loud, echoing *crunch*. He snapped his attention to the second gargoyle, which was nudging its fellows awake with thunking slaps of its hand. They weren't overly large, about the size of a child of four or five, but between their tough hides and their sharp beaks and claws, the six-limbed monsters were dangerous.

Panting, blood rushing to her head, Myal considered their options. "Can you freeze the rest?"

"Only for a few seconds," Kerric said. He dodged as the second launched itself, and snapped the same word. "*Dolomus!*"

Wings caught in an upbeat, it dropped more or less like the rock it was, and smashed on the spikes at the bottom of the bar-lined cage where his platform slid.

"They have the power of the Fountain to break through any compulsion, and I—*dolomus!*" he snapped as a third launched itself at him, croaking like stone grinding on stone. It fell, but not completely. "Dammit!" he swore as the beast recovered mere feet from the spikes and the rubble of its companion. "They're getting faster on blocking it. I'll have to think of another spell."

"Think faster! Dodge that one, and try to distract the others while you're doing it," she ordered, sheathing her blade. She curled her body so that her hands brushed the wall behind the platform. Another twist brought her dropping down—and now *she* was a target for the one laboriously flapping its way higher, sort of hovering its way up with gray stone wingstrokes.

The thing about these massively complex illusions, a lesson which experienced adventurers learned, was that they were all based on simple rules. Many rules, but rules all the same. Without magic, stone the size of these gargoyles was far too heavy to fly. With magic, it could have simply levitated and just hurtled straight at them, smashing them against the walls . . . but while the Tower's Guardians wanted to *guard* the singularity empowering the place, they had to give people a chance to get into the heart of the Tower.

More than that, simple blocks that flung themselves in straight lines were boring. They were not entertaining. So, these gargoyle statues had wings and claws and beaks. They might have arms as well as legs, but they were enchanted to "fly" to get where they wanted to go, and they were enchanted to have "reflexes" so they could dodge adventurers. But those reflexes would only be so fast.

Tensing certain tattoos, Myal scrambled up the wall on sticky hands and boot-covered feet, shuffled over, and bull-kicked the nearest gargoyle just as it turned to attack her, using both of her feet. She almost clipped one of the others, but that wasn't her intent. With that strong a double-kick, the stone monster flung across the way and smashed into the far wall, wings and one limb breaking. Landing with her feet on the top of the platform, she released her hands, spun, and ducked under the slashing claws of the next stone beast, the fifth one.

Arm hooking around one of its legs, she flexed her left bicep, activating great strength all across her body. It had a second in which to squawk as she whipped it off its feet, continuing her spin, and then she flung it like a disc in a tossing game from back home at the third one, which had recovered from Kerric's spell. They cracked into each other, literally chipping off chunks from the thinner parts, talons, wings, a wrist, but they didn't fall; her aim had been slightly off.

Still, they did lose altitude, and that gave the two adventurers a break. Kicking sideways to shove the sixth and final gargoyle off the platform, she shouted, "Kerric! To me!"

He responded as fast as any of her previous adventuring team-mates, zooming in straight for the door, tools in hand. Taking up position at his back to guard him while he worked, Myal pulled a trio of chain-connected sticks from the holder on her pack. The flail-like weapon came not from Mendhi, but from a kingdom that bordered her homeland. She had learned to use the farm-implement version for threshing grain, and had learned to use the weapon version on board one of the first ships she had worked.

The gargoyles learned quickly that a section of ironwood staff, swung with great force and speed, could indeed chip off more chunks of stone as she bashed them back from the pair, keeping them from landing any blows.

"Done!" Kerric gasped, pushing open the door and darting through. She smacked another of the trio and backed up—just as three more gargoyles materialized on the platform, and the sounds of approaching, yelling voices warned her that someone else had sprung the Scales of Justice trap.

SEVEN

As soon as he slammed the door shut, she looked at him. "Did you hear that? Did you hear them coming?"

Kerric nodded, grimacing. "Dammit—I don't know if they're just opportunists, or if they're deliberately following us. I suspect deliberately. There have been too many alternate choices they could have made. As much as I *don't* wish anybody who enters the Tower permanent harm, I'm very glad the Scales are so deadly and time-consuming to defeat."

"They're tracking us somehow," Myal pointed out. She turned to face the rest of the room, mind racing. The room was filled with coffer chests, the kind built to hold money. She had no desire to open any of them, given the name for this room, Greed Hurts. All she wanted was to get through alive, to help out Kerric, who was quickly advancing from the category of work acquaintance to friend. "I have a tattoo that makes me impossible to track, either by physical or magical means, but it only works for me and anything I carry. Do you know any spells that do the same?"

Kerric shook his head. "I've never had a reason to learn. There's this stretch, and a stretch coming up with *lots* of side paths—you can carry me on that—but it's not for another seven, eight rooms. Speaking of which, we have to find the Oh My Gods The Fireball Trap, and then—"

Recalling a round of tale-telling from some point in the last winter at one of the taverns, Myal interrupted him. "Isn't that the one that Rick the Archer likes?"

Snickering, Kerric nodded, making the ends of his curls bounce under his cap. "Yes, *that* trap."

"Wait—don't talk," she ordered him, holding up her hand.

The doors in the Tower were so thick sometimes, an adventurer couldn't hear anything short of an epic battle in the next room over, but there *were* other magical ways of eavesdropping, from enhancing one's hearing to dredging up echoes out of the immediate or near past. That meant anything they said could be overheard by a competent mage.

There was one solid way to stop it from happening. Stooping, she flexed her left bicep and scooped him up like a very overgrown child. Startled, he clutched at her shoulders. A good thing, too, since that let her free one hand from his waist. Lifting her hand to the back of her head, she felt up under her hairline at the back of her skull, and pressed.

Sparks tingled over her vision. Satisfied, she returned her hand to his back, the other under his buttocks, carrying him on her hip like a basket in the marketplace. "*Now* we can talk and not be overheard, either by spell-sensitive ears, or by someone scrying the immediate past," she stated, wending her way carefully through the chests sitting on the floor, on pedestals, and on shelves at the edges of the room. "What comes after Rick's Favorite Fireball Trap?"

Kerric caught immediately what she meant. Arms around her shoulders, legs around her hips, he considered the ramifications. He hadn't been carried like this since he was a child, and he was now a full-grown man. Adding packs and various bits of armor didn't help, but he understood what she was trying to do. "That is a damned powerful spell, milady, if it can seal off conversations from time itself."

"It's not a spell. It's a tattoo, and it simply focuses my life-energy to perform a task. Which means I can only do this for a short period of time before I get a massive headache." Angling her body by the door, she waited to see if he would pull out the tools he had tucked away. Kerric just waved his hand over the doorplate, murmured something, and the door unlocked and unlatched itself. Even while touching him, she couldn't sense his magic in use, not unless it affected her directly. She just wasn't a mage.

"Right, then. After . . . ah, Rick's Favorite Fireball Trap," he allowed, chuckling at the new name for it, "we'll pass through Ring, Mirror, Comb, which isn't a trap but rather a set of tools we can pick up and use."

"Like the towels?" Myal asked, meaning the cloths still knotted to their belts. The corridor beyond the room had a good five or six doors in view.

"Yes, except that if we lose one, we don't get sent back, we just get into a lot of trouble. We want the fourth door on the right. It's trapped but I can disable it with a spell. After Ring, Mirror, Comb is the one trap that makes this approach impossible for a mage to attempt on their own," he told her, gray eyes meeting her brown ones with a serious look that bordered on somber. "It's possible for a single person to get through the Seraglio, if the love of their life is waiting for them outside the Tower, but this one corridor—or rather, the three versions of it we'll have to cross at different points in the gauntlet—makes this 'easiest' path impossible for me to cross on my own.

"Beyond that is a flight of stairs with a ramp trap—you know the kind, the stair treads tip down and it forms a magically greased ramp. We'll have to float up that one, because it has too many trigger points," he warned her. "It's another spot designed to slow down adventurers, should they try to disarm each trigger instead of fly."

Passing the third door, Myal stopped in front of the fourth on the right. She waited until he opened it, then stepped inside. The bedchamber-sized room was plain and square, with nothing inside it, not even another door. Not that this meant anything. Most doors in the Tower were hidden magically until the correct answer to a riddle had been applied. Remembering what the archer had said, she carried Kerric straight into the middle of the smallish room.

Fire exploded around them. She winced a little reflexively, but breathed slowly and steadily as the flames billowed and roared, washing over them like elemental demons. Finally, the "attack" died down, leaving both of them unharmed. If either of them had screamed and panicked, *then* the flames would have had real heat to them. Kerric, she was pleased to note, did not panic. *Of course,* she thought, *he knows exactly what to expect, but still . . .*

It deserved a reward. Leaning over, she kissed his cheek. At his surprised look, she smiled. "That's for not fussing about me picking you up." Another kiss, this time on his lips, and she pulled back. "And *that's* for not panicking."

"Hey, I'll have you know that the first rule of the Tower Maintenance Staff Handbook is '*When something goes wrong, don't*

panic!'" he quipped. And kissed her back. "That's for *you* not panicking. Now, the step after the Fireball, Mirror, Corridor, and
Ramp traps is yet another Junk Room, Number One Hundred
Seventeen, and beyond that is the lift room with Cabbage, Goat,
Wolf. And after *that* is our first refreshing room break. Now,
head back out into the corridor, turn left, go two rooms on the
right—the middle room on the left as we came this way—and
we'll pick up the items we need."

Myal frowned at him. There were now two doors out of this
room, she noted. "Back out the way we came? But if that other
group is there . . ."

He nodded, understanding her confusion. "We had to trigger
this trap to disarm a very *real* trap many rooms ahead. If they're
out there, I can cast an invisibility illusion on us."

"But that could be tracked by magic," she countered. "I can
make us invisible for a short period of time in a way that cannot
be tracked. But only a short while. Where do we go after picking
up the mirror, ring, and comb?"

"Back up the corridor in this direction, take the first left, the
first right, and a door at the base of a set of stairs. That's the trap
that I cannot cross," he warned her. "You'll have to stop carrying
me at that point, because the moment I enter that room, I'll drop
unconscious. *Any* mage will succumb, and the stronger they are
as a mage, the faster they will fall. The corridor is a hundred feet
long, and closed by doors at either end.

"Get me into the next hall, and I will recover within minutes,
but I will be useless to you . . . and *you* had better not use any of
your tattoos while you're in there," Kerric said, giving her an earnest look. "I don't know if you using them will count as magic or
not. If it does, you will fall unconscious the same as me, and
nobody will find us until the Tower has a new Guardian and
Maintenance can once again scry and roam safely."

Sober, Myal nodded. "Then I'll just carry you as far as the door at the bottom of the steps, but we will have to be quick, since this trick comes at a price for me. Hold on to me for a moment."

Kerric tightened his grip. She freed both hands for a moment, touching the back of her head. A faint grayish light rippled over both of them like a cascade of water, turning the appearance of their limbs as clear as glass.

"Try not to make any sounds," she whispered, quickly returning her hands to his body, supporting his weight. "You'll have to unlock the doors."

"They're not locked," he whispered back, freeing one hand from the glasslike woman holding him. Opening the door to the fireball illusion room, he carefully closed it behind them, aided by the way she pivoted when she stepped through. The hallway was empty for the moment. Backtracking, they reached the second door, which was indeed unlocked.

The reason was simple. Any experienced adventurer would be very wary of anything that seemed easy or risk-free. A large number of these rooms were locked, even trapped, but not every door. And some of the unlocked, non-trapped doors hid far worse dangers than the Rushlight Trap and the Scales of Justice.

This room, however, hid nothing more than a large closet-sized room lined with shelves, with about thirty or so items arranged carefully on the shelves. It took him only a few moments to locate the wooden comb, the braided gold ring, and the little silver hand mirror. Myal watched him pick them up and stash them in his pouch—requiring a bit of awkward balancing on her part while he moved—then headed for the hall again. Both froze at the sound of one of the doors opening.

Myal took a risk and stepped into the corridor itself, turning as she did so. Unfortunately, caught off guard, Kerric didn't quite catch the door lever in time. Forced to leave it open, they found themselves staring at a quintet of slightly bloodied, bruised, grim-looking adventurers. One of them was a man in a black robelike tunic similar to the one Kerric had worn earlier, though its knotwork buttons reached all the way past his knees, and not just to mid-thigh. He was frowning in concentration, holding a glowing, triangular-shaped crystal in front of him. After only two steps, it winked out.

"Damn," the man muttered to his companions. "I've lost the trail."

Myal took advantage of his speech to back up a few steps. She froze when he stopped speaking. One of the other two men spoke, giving her a chance to move again, backing up toward the side-corridor which Kerric wanted them to take.

"He must be using some sort of magic to meddle with our tracking," the tall, muscular, armored adventurer stated. None of them were overly famous, but Myal remembered him. Barric, that was his name. A good fighter type, fairly intelligent, but he played a little rough on the practice field for her taste. One of the two women looked familiar, but she couldn't place the curly-haired blonde.

"That door is open," the blonde woman pointed out tartly. Clad in shades of green and beige leathers, with a strung bow slung over one shoulder, she would have looked more at home in a forest than in the granite halls of the Tower.

"Could be a trap," Barric murmured.

The other woman was short and clad in mottled dark grays that would make her blend into almost any patch of shadow, including a scrap of cloth wound around both her hair and her face, leaving only a strip of golden skin visible. She ghosted toward it. Myal backed up a few more steps, glad she was now fully out of reach. Crouching, the woman examined the entrance to the shelf-lined room without touching anything, then peered at the modestly lit contents of the shelves.

"Dey took a few tings," she stated, speaking with a non-Aian accent. "Or maybe it's vun of dose traps vere you are supposed to put something dere. I dunno."

The man in the robe pulled out another crystal, this time a clear rectangle roughly the size of his face. "Well, we'll just have to solve this particular puzzle with a little help from this Maintenance pad."

At the sight of the crystal tablet in his hands, Kerric tensed and bit back a curse. He let Myal carry him all the way to the foot of the stairs, then released her and dropped to his feet, body returning to full visibility. He clenched his hands to contain his rage, while she pressed the back of her head with both hands and panted with relief. She looked at him and frowned.

"What's wrong?" she breathed as quietly as she could. Her head had started to throb, prelude to the headache that always accompanied the full invisibility of that particular tattoo, but she was concerned about the fury hardening his normally friendly features.

"That bastard of a rat's son was hired three months ago as a Maintenance mage," Kerric hissed. "Said his name was Torven. The others are probably taking advantage of the lack of scrying to loot the Tower, but from what *he* said, he probably wants to follow us all the way t—!"

Quickly pressing her finger to his lips, Myal lifted her head at the door behind him. It had a bronze plaque next to it with the simple, ominous warning, *Magic cannot help you, here.* "Hush," she breathed. "Let's get through this next trap and find a safe place where you can rant."

Nodding, he grimaced, turned to the door, then looked back at her. "Remember, no tattoos."

She nodded and relaxed all her muscles, shaking them out slightly. Nodding in approval, Kerric opened the door, took three steps inside—and dropped with a sigh. Myal checked herself even as she tensed her muscles to leap after and rescue him. The *whumpf* he made didn't quite echo down the hall, but it did make her nervous, thinking that it might have been overheard. Relaxing herself again, she made sure all her tattoos were quiescent, then moved inside, quietly shut the door, and stepped over his body.

Turning around, she crouched, checking him for damage in the dim light of the corridor. *Nothing worse than a bruise on his chin*, Myal decided. She turned him over onto his pack-clad back, hooked her fingers under his armpits, and started dragging him down the hall.

He wasn't kidding about the length of the thing; halfway along, she had to pause to wipe sweat from her brow. Three-quarters of the way, she had to reflexively check herself to keep from using her tattoos; the one time she started to use the left tattoo band for extra strength, she started feeling woozy. Fortunately, the moment she released the use of it with a thought and an arm-twitch, the dizziness faded.

The far door, as promised, was unlocked. Beyond lay another stretch of corridor, this time perpendicular to the hall that had knocked out Kerric. Pulling him into the new passageway, Myal quickly shut the door, then crouched over him again. Hand patting his face, she tried to rouse him gently. It took longer than she liked, minutes instead of seconds, but he finally roused with a deep breath. Eyes snapping open, he gazed up at her for one brief, wary moment . . . then slumped in relief.

"Thank the Gods," Kerric muttered. "Thank you so *very* much for hauling me. I *hate* that trap . . . It's like falling down a never-ending well of darkness, and it *drains* a mage, even if we aren't using any active spells."

"Any *active* spells?" Myal asked, her mind catching on that word. She helped him to sit up, and pulled her waterskin free so he could have a drink. So both of them could, which she did after he took a good swallow, taking it back.

Kerric nodded as she drank. "Mages—trained mages—always have passive spells on themselves. Mostly shields, and a way to ground excess energy into the earth in case something happens that causes their power to surge, or in the advent of an attack. I did my best to remove most of them, but some of them are so deeply ingrained, so instinctive, it's near impossible to undo them and stop using them.

"*This* is why I've been conservative in using magic," he confessed. "I could fly both of us through these corridors and traps, shield both of us, and be unaffected by the majority of them . . . but having to cross three of *those* halls from a Netherhell?" Kerric took back the waterskin for another drink. Swallowing, he shook his head. "No . . . I'd be utterly unable to face the final challenge at the end, drained too much to survive. But there's no choice. There are three of these on our path, which means I desperately need your help to survive this trap." He paused, then lifted his brows. "Mind you, I'm happy for your company either way."

"As much as I am beginning to like you very much, the more time I spend in your company," Myal told him, taking back the skin so she could help him to his feet, "I'd rather you *did* survive."

"I already knew I wanted you to survive," Kerric told her, releasing her hand somewhat reluctantly once he was upright. He liked the way she felt to his inner senses, calm and steady with none of that inner buzzing most mages had.

"You're not a professional adventurer," Myal murmured, eyeing him. "But you *are* proving to be a good partner."

"I'll take that as a high compliment from a professional. Give me another moment to regather my energies," he told her. "Then we'll fly up the stairs to the next stop, which is Junk Room One Hundred Seventeen—it'll be *my* turn to carry *you* up those steps."

She snorted a little in mirth at that idea. Kerric lifted a brow at her, both of his hands going to his hips.

"You don't think I can do it?" he challenged, giving her a wary look.

"No, no, I am certain you can," she quickly reassured him. "I was laughing at how much my limbs would stick out on either side while you did so. Like trying to carry a really long pole sideways through a doorway."

Grinning ruefully at the amusing thought, Kerric shook his head. "I'll try not to whack your head or your feet on anything. Besides, I was going to have you hop on like a backpack. Here, let me put mine in front."

Suiting actions to words, he shrugged out of the pack, hooked his arms through the other way so that it rested against his chest, then turned and bent over a little, fingers fluttering near her hips.

"Hop on," he ordered. "I'm stronger than I look. My stamina's only good for a magical marathon, not for a footrace, but then it's my magic that'll be carrying both of us, not my feet."

Taking him at his word, Myal climbed onto his back, letting his hands hook under her knees for additional support while she looped her arms around his shoulders and grabbed the straps of his pack for support, rather than throttle his neck. To his credit, he didn't grunt when she climbed on, though she did hear his breathing deepen a bit, and he did stagger two steps while he was adjusting their balance.

"*Zamatu*," he ordered, coaxing his powers into an egglike envelope. To lift himself required but a thought and a flexing of his will. To lift someone else as well required more effort to form the magic into doing what he wanted from it. "*Tessoloc!*"

They lifted off the floor, floated for a second, then raced up the winding steps. Which, sensitive as they were, still *clunked* and flattened into a long, slippery ramp even though neither of them had touched a thing. Landing a few feet beyond the top, Kerric cancelled the spell and let Myal climb back down. Magic couldn't solve everything in the Tower, but the two of them had just climbed eight or more levels in less than one minute.

Of course, they had fallen down the chute at least five levels to the Scales, and would climb and fall several times more as they progressed. There was no path straight up to the Fountain Hall at the heart of the Tower; indeed, they were about to rise again once past the next room, and would lose more levels somewhere after that. Returning his pack to his back, Kerric strode for the first door on the right. A bit of magic unlocked it, permitting him to escort her into a chamber lined with portraits, and a single pedestal in the center of the long, rectangular space.

Myal went straight to it, quickly reading the lines.

I can be long, or I can be short, I can be grown and I can be bought. I can be painted, or I am left bare. I can be round, pointed, and square.

Mindful of the men and women potentially still following them, Kerric ignored the pedestal with its riddle about fingernails, and went straight to the painting in question, a lovely, pale blonde lady in blue velvet and brocaded silk in the layered-robes style of the far-off Draconan Empire. Her hands were crossed in front of her in such a way that they displayed her—

"Fingernails," Myal stated, satisfaction in her voice. Each nail on the upper hand had been painted in a different style of cut or color. Kerric turned to look at her. She had a pleasant alto voice, not high but not too low, and more used to speaking softly than bellowing commands, though the Mendhite had proven she could give orders quite well when needed.

"Well done," Kerric praised. He tipped his head at the portrait next to him. She nodded, so he touched the lady's fingernails. The frame clicked and swung open, and the two stepped through into a foyer. There was no other word for it.

Tiled marble squares had been laid in the floor, shading from light in the middle where the plaque-topped pedestal sat, to dark at the edges in a faint checkerboard pattern, and dark polished granite around the edges. Potted plants sat under pools of suncrystal-focused light—real ones, since there was no hint of a faint glow to them. Three sets of double-panel style doors awaited the two adventurers, and a small bronze plaque had been hung next to each set of doors with two buttons set in it, one with an embossed arrow pointing up, one with an arrow pointing down. A larger, fourth plaque had been set between the middle and left lift doors.

"If they follow us," Kerric murmured, mindful that the mage in the group behind them was no doubt still trying to track their path, "then they get what they deserve. Topside Control told *everyone* to stay put, even the Maintenance crews."

Myal nodded. While he pressed the middle of the up buttons, she read the plaque. In three neatly cast lines it said:

I will eat you! Eat or be eaten? I am eaten.

The last time she had stepped into the lift-box, she had nearly killed one of her traveling companions. The rage of the Wolf had swept through her, making her draw her sword against her target, the one overcome by the conflicting desires of the Goat, who wanted to destroy the Cabbage, but was terrified of the Wolf. The Cabbage had crammed himself into a corner and cried, cowering in fear from the Goat even as she, the Wolf, had backed the other woman into a different corner.

Only the last-moment grappling of one of the other two in their five-man party had turned the blade in her hand so that the flat struck the woman's head, not the edge. The moment they had wrested it out of her control, the Goat had gone for the Cabbage with fists swinging, and since it took both of the non-affected members to hold Myal down, the man who was the Cabbage had been badly beaten before the doors finally opened and they were able to toss Myal through and go after the girl afflicted by the Goat part of the spell. The male adventurer who had been the Cabbage had needed several healing spells, and had ended up refusing to go on any more runs. Even Myal had hesitated after that one.

This would be a nasty trap for just three adventurers, who had no one sane on hand to try to separate the rest, and even nastier for six, since that meant two sets would be affected. Both Goats would go after both Cabbages, not just one of them, and so on. The one time she had seen the attack be a non-lethal one, viewed on a scrying mirror in the Adventuring Hall that was replaying great moments recorded in the Tower's history, still stood out in her mind.

The intent of the spell was to make either the Wolf or the Goat want to "devour" the Goat or the Cabbage respectively, and the adventurers playing the Goat and the Cabbage had been lovers, so the Goat had frantically kissed the crying, cowering Cabbage instead of attacking her while the others in their party had restrained the Wolf. But that was a rare instance. Normally the Wolf had to be forcibly restrained from killing the Goat, and the Goat kept away from the Cabbage, with no such bond of love between the pair to morph the "devour" imperative from killing to kissing.

The lift dinged, the far right frame lighting up in a pale green. The green, she knew, meant up. Pale pink meant down. The box-like little room inside, which slid up and down a long shaft in the Tower, was now here.

Following Kerric inside, she felt her shoulders tense in antici-pation, and had to remind herself there were only two of them. Thinking about that time when Goat and Cabbage had kissed made her think about the kiss she was owed. She waited until he selected the right button from all the dozens displayed on the panel, though, letting the doors shut and the box of a room sway as they headed up.

"So. Is this where I get my kiss?" At his inquiring look, she reminded him, "I did solve the riddle before you touched the painting."

To her surprise, he winced, blushing, and covered his face with his palm. "Tinnea and Jathris . . . oh, Gods . . . Two workers from Middle Maintenance."

"What?" Myal asked him, confused.

Kerric wrinkled his nose ruefully. "They shut down the lift doors under the pretense of 'maintenance needs' and rode it up and down several times while making love. I had to fire them, because this thing was supposed to be in use for an adventuring group. That was back in my first year of managing this place."

She could imagine why such a thing would bother him. Kerric was a conscientious Master. Taking his wrist, she gently pulled his palm down from his face. "That was then. This is now," she stated, leaning down for a kiss. "That's one from me. You still owe me one from you."

Chuckling wryly, he hooked his free hand around the back of her neck, tugging her back down for another kiss. He didn't release her until the lift bell dinged again. When he did, he mur-mured, "Block the doorway, will you?"

She stepped into the foyer—nearly identical to the one down below, save that it had three plain doors, not one, and just one lift, not three—and stretched her arm over the opening. The lifts had two sets of doors, an inner set that traveled with the box and an outer set that kept the shaft from being accessed. There was some sort of magic in the tiny gap between that not only raised and lowered the boxy room, but kept the doors from closing and crushing her arm. While she waited, Kerric patiently pressed every single button, starting with the floors higher than this one, and then hitting the button this floor again . . . and all the ones leading back down to the bottom-most floor. Myal smirked, realizing why. His words confirmed it.

Satisfied, Kerric shooed her into the foyer, allowing the lift doors to close. "If nothing else, that will delay them a good ten minutes waiting for that thing to get back. The Maintenance crews call that a *shavott*-delay. I'm not sure what language *shavott* comes from, but it means making the lifts stop on every single floor. Torven, the traitor, will want to push the up button if he and his crew are following us. The doors will open, but if they don't realize it's going down, that's an extra-long stretch of time where they'll have to ride it all the way down and back if they get in."

"Yes and no," Myal pointed out. "With every button pressed, all the other two have to do is shove the three affected ones out the nearest door—the Cabbage, if no one else, since they'd just cower in a corner. Push out the Cabbage, and the Goat will follow."

"And the Wolf will follow the Goat . . . and the spell controlling their emotions will be broken," Kerric agreed. He picked up her hand and kissed it, then twined his fingers with hers. "You, milady, are quite smart. Now, let's hit the refreshing room while we can, and while we have a little bit of a delay."

Which of the three led to a refreshing room was obvious. All refreshing rooms had a large, friendly, masklike face carved and painted onto their doors. Their layouts varied a bit, but there were always at least three rooms: the lounge, where there were long couches, stasis-preserved food in vending cabinets, and sometimes banking depository boxes to alleviate adventurers of loot-based burdens on long gauntlet runs; the ladies' refreshing room; and the gentlemen's refreshing room.

Those latter two rooms had little stalls with water-flushed privies, counters and sinks with toweling cloths and soap, and at least one stall in a corner with a clever showering pipe in the exotic Natallian style, a horizontal pipe pierced with holes that would rain water down on an adventurer who needed to get cleaned up for some reason. Similar stalls were available in the changing rooms of the Adventuring Hall for post-practice cleanups.

There was no bank depository box in this particular refreshing room, but there were four people in the lounge, two men and two women. They were seated around the low table in front of one of the couches, playing a card game. Three had the dark skin and dark hair of the southern coastline, where civilized kingdoms thrived in spite of the collapse of the old Empire, and one had the reddish hair and freckles of someone from the far northwestern coast, or perhaps from overseas to the east.

Her companions merely had to look up, but with her back to the lounge door, the redheaded woman had to twist around from her seat on a cushion laid on the floor, just to see who had entered. Once she did so, her hazel eyes widened in recognition. "Master Kerric!"

She wasn't the only one to scramble to her feet at that. The others widened their eyes and swiftly stood, too. Hiding the urge to grimace, Kerric turned it into a wry smile instead.

"Please, sit down. Relax," he told them, gesturing for them to return to their card game. Their faces were familiar, but he couldn't remember their names off the top of his head. "If you hadn't noticed my armor, well, I'm afraid I have some bad news and some good news. The bad news is, what's wrong with the Tower is bad enough, I have to go in personally to fix it. The *good* news is, at least this way you know it'll get fixed right the first time, eh?"

One of the two men chuckled, his teeth gleaming white against his brown lips. "Aye, I remember the infamous Refreshing Room Break from three years ago—two teams got into a heated free-for-all, and all the water mains broke, sewer as well as freshwater, on the, what, sixty-seventh floor?"

"Ninety-seventh . . . and the ninety-sixth, and the ninety-eighth, and a couple of rooms got flooded on the ninety-fifth floor, too," Kerric half-joked.

"What sort of problem is it, Master Kerric?" the other woman asked. "Is there anything we can do to help?"

Kerric only knew this quartet somewhat. They were steady adventurers, but not flashy, attention-catching ones. Out of the corner of his eye, he saw Myal gesturing at the ladies' half and nodded slightly, letting her know he had seen her intention. Most of his mind was on the redheaded woman's question. Quelling panic on the outside of the Tower was one thing, where there were far too many civilians, opportunists, and more. These men and women were *in* the Tower, at a particularly dangerous time.

So he gave them a half-truth. "Well, I'm not going to go into details of how or why, but the Tower thinks it's under attack, which means it's removed a very large number of the safety features that are normally put in place to prevent unnecessary and excessive risks to life and limb. This is why even the normal Maintenance crews have been asked to find a safe place and stay put."

The redhead gave him a bemused look. "But—begging pardon—you're not an adventurer, milord." She peered at the door to the ladies' half, then at the entry door behind him. "And you're here with only *one* other person? Or are the rest waiting outside?"

He spread his hands, shrugging blithely. "Well, I am the Master of the Tower. That counts for a lot more than you'd think. And you saw who I came in with. The two of us make an effective team."

The man on the couch, the one who had chuckled, grinned outright. "Myal the Mendhite? Prettiest beanstalk in the valley? How much of her presence is because you want to climb the Tower, and how much because you want to cli—"

Two sets of cushions whacked him from either side, both from the other two south-coasters. Kerric chuckled, not too offended. "Well, she is lovely, but it's her adventuring talents and her quick wits that please me—you know, there *is* something the four of you could do. There's a certain group of adventurers that have been trying to kite in on our heels, take advantage of the Tower's prizes while the system's broken. If they get up here, can you delay them?"

"Delay them? How?" the redhead asked. Like the others— like most of the adventurers who came to the Tower—she was clad in leather armor. Partially clad, since most of it was stacked at the end of the couch with her partners' gear. She glanced at it, then at Kerric. "As in fight them?"

"Preferably not," Kerric stated flatly, holding up his hand. "I'll deal with them once I've fixed the problem with the Tower. There's no need for anything other than a Tower trap to deliver an admonishment until then. Just . . . talk with them, delay them politely, ask them questions, that sort of thing. Even a few minutes' delay will help. There's no need to confront them aggressively, and that's only *if* they make it this far. Above all, *don't* risk any of these traps yourself.

"As I said, the Tower thinks it's under attack, which means a previously mild jolt from a lightning spell will now stop your heart. *Your* first priority is to secure your safety," he reminded them. "These idiots are thinking only of getting riches; they aren't thinking of keeping themselves alive long enough to enjoy them . . . and if they keep following the Mendhite and me, the odds are, they won't survive."

"Do we get paid for this?" the second man, the one who hadn't spoken yet, asked Kerric with a touch of dry humor to leaven the request.

Kerric shrugged. "I'd pay you a gold each per minute you delayed them, but I'd have no idea how well or how long you'd delay them. Even the scrying mirrors have been cut off by now."

"Only a gold a minute?" the first man asked, giving Kerric a dubious look.

"Well, I'm not asking you to *fight* them, just talk with them to delay them. Anyway, it's up to you, but just keep in mind how dangerous it is now, out there," he warned the adventurers, tipping his head at the outer door. Not the one behind him, but the one ahead, the other door out of the lounge at the far end of the room. "Don't stray too far from this refreshing room. You're in the safest spot in the Tower right now, and that's the most important thing. Now if you'll excuse me, it's been a long climb, and it's only going to get longer if I don't . . . *you* know."

With a polite nod, he headed for the gentlemen's half of the actual refreshing rooms. Thankfully, no one was in there at the moment. It gave him a few minutes of privacy to slump his shoulders, scrub his face, and regather his wits after he attended to his body's needs.

Facing himself in the scrying-warded mirror over one of the

sinks, Kerric stared into his gray eyes, bracing himself for the next stage of their climb. The riddles would still be a mix of easy and hard, but the closer they got to the heart of the Tower, the traps would grow closer together. Some would be overt, some would be insidious, and too many of them would be lethal to the unwary and unprepared.

But at least I have Myal with me. I'll need to step up the romance— no hardship there, he thought, a smile breaking through the gloom of having to fight his way back into his own stronghold. *She's bright, quick, tall-dark-and-lovely, and doesn't seem to mind me flirting with her. Always a bonus.* Frowning in the next moment, Kerric eyed his face, wondering if he should shave away the hint of stubble dusting his jaw.

A rub of his hand convinced him it was getting a bit raspy, this late at night. While he didn't mind wearing a beard in the winter, this was summer, making even the thought of one too hot and itchy. It also wouldn't do to abrade a woman's skin with excessive beard-burn. The spell was nothing more than a cantrip, so familiar and so easy, it just took a moment of thought and a snap of his fingers. Jawline now stripped smooth with nothing more than a brief, stinging tingle, he focused on reviewing the next set of steps in his head while he washed his hands.

We'll have to fight our way through the Flying Flaming Poodles Of Doom, then disable the Party Parter trap, followed by the Garden Of Misfortune—I must remember to pass Myal an apple from my pack, he reminded himself, *and eat one as well, myself, so we aren't tempted to pluck and eat any of the fruits in that one.*

So many traps ahead of them, and so little time, with that damned Maintenance mage on their trail. Kerric had only given him a cursory interview, leaving the testing of Torven's magical abilities to others in the Maintenance staff. He wouldn't have thought the man strong enough to endure the surging powers of a Fountain, but then he wouldn't have thought the man ambitious enough to enter the Tower when it was forbidden, either.

If they were here for the wealth hidden away in the Tower's many rooms and chamber, well, he didn't give a damn about the money, or the jewels, or whatever they might run across. Such things could be easily replaced once the Tower was scrycasting again. He'd have to arrange for some sort of special gauntlet run, a scrycast for free to make it up to all their patrons for the lost viewing time, but they would be back to business as usual soon enough.

If, however, that group of five adventurers was in the Tower to get Torven all the way to the Fountain Hall, to attune *Torven* to the energies of the singularity, that was a danger Kerric could not allow. It was possible the other mage had hidden how strong he was from his testers, appearing to be weaker than he really was. If that was so, Kerric had to get to the Fountain first, to attune himself and command its energies once more.

The Tower was big business, too big to be managed by an ambitious upstart who had only been working here for a few months. Kerric had originally come here seeking to learn about the way adventurers were transported seamlessly from one room to the next, one corridor to the next. It was a small-scale version of the great Portals everyone had lost with the Shattering of Aiar, and the resulting damage to the world's aether. They were permanent, unlike mirror-Gates, but they could be rearranged at will by the Master of the Tower like a mirror-Gate. Fascinating magic, really . . . but then he had been tapped to apprentice to the previous Guardian as more than just a Gating technician, and that was that.

A Master had to be compassionate toward the adventurers running the gauntlets of all those tricks and traps. He—or she, since there had been Mistresses of the Tower before, and there would be again someday—had to be able to promote new adventure scenarios, and placate sometimes touchy patrons. He had to be able to direct others in the maintenance and repair of all those tricks and traps, and be able to step in to manage their restoration himself.

Above all, however, the Guardian of the Fountain had to be a good person deep down inside, so that the vast powers spewed out of the singularity-point would not fall into the hands of someone selfish, greedy, or outright evil. All Guardians chose their successors carefully, whenever possible. Kerric hadn't even considered himself in that category, being content to trade his skills as a mage in the maintenance of the Tower in exchange for access to its vast library of magical, mechanical, and architectural knowledge.

The previous Guardian, Master Jonas, had kept an eye on the younger man, and finally coaxed him into taking on more and more responsibility, overseeing the business side of things as well as the magical side. But he hadn't told Kerric he was grooming the young mage for his own position until Jonas had been certain that Kerric truly cared for the people of Penambrion and the outlying farms of the valley, as well as for the adventurers and workers in the Tower. Its magics influenced everyone within a hundred miles, after all, not just those who ran or maintained the gauntlets and scrycasts . . . which meant its magics could be used *against* them by an unscrupulous mage.

No, he decided, wiping his hands on a soft towel. *This Torven's arrogance has lost him any chance that I'd consider him for an apprenticeship. As my old Academy teachers used to say, a mage must think things through not once, not twice, but thrice to consider all the implications of a particular action . . . particularly when our actions can change the face of the world beyond all recognition. We have a duty to wield our power carefully.*

Liars and cheaters don't understand that some shortcuts are just

*wrong, particularly when applied for all the wrong reasons. Whatever
this man thinks he can get out of the Tower besides a few trinkets, I will
stop it.*

Emerging from the gentlemen's room, he found Myal waiting
for him, her face freshly scrubbed, her hair re-braided, and a tiny
packet of smoke-dried fish in her fingers, purchased for a few
silver scepterai from the vending cabinet. She was chatting with
the others, and doing more listening than actual speaking, asking
questions that led the four men and women to eagerly relate the
adventures they'd had so far in the Tower.

Displaying a level of tact Kerric could appreciate, Myal noted
his arrival, asked only two more questions, and brought the rem-
iniscing to a gentle end, adding, ". . . but I'd love to hear more
from you once we're all safely back in the village. I'm not quite as
fancy a writer as the Master, but I do have those little booklets of
gauntlet-stories. You might have seen them in the merchant stall
in the Adventuring Hall, the *Tales of the Tower* booklets."

"*You* wrote those?" the dark-skinned woman asked. "Oh, I
love those! It was the story of *Fael's Party and the Waterfall in the
Tower* that helped me and my group survive the Sucker Punch
trap! Hey—if you think I have stories worth putting into print,
I'd be happy to tell you everything I know."

Myal blushed and smiled, quickly cutting her off before she
could gush further. "I'd be happy to write them down when we all
have the time. For now, as the Master said, keep yourselves as safe
as possible. We'll do our best to put the Tower back to what it
should be as soon as we can."

One of the two men shook his head. "I don't know how much
just the two of you can do, if the Tower's gone too protectively
mad and dangerous for a group of four to be in it, but I know you,
Myal; you're one of the best. And with the Master, well . . . *I'd* pay
to watch him run a gauntlet, and I'm an adventurer, not a patron."

Chuckling, Kerric touched Myal's elbow, guiding her toward the second of the two doors leading out of the lounge, opposite the one they had entered. "I'll keep that in mind, if I ever need to run a special viewing for our clients. Be safe, milords, miladies. This way, Myal."

Murmuring a few farewells of her own, his partner followed him back into the perils of the Tower. A blessing, all things considered, that the Mendhite was still willing to endure the rest of this trip with him. A blessing she was a good companion, too.

EIGHT

ours later, Kerric was laughing so hard, he kept having to wipe tears from his eyes in between casting bolts of pure force at the animated skeletons attempting to attack them. A couple got past him, jumping on Myal's back, but she merely grabbed each in turn, hurtling them against a wall so that the bones shattered, dissolving into piles of dust and shards.

"Oh Gods!" he gasped, trying to catch his breath. "Wh-what did you say to *that?*"

Myal grunted, flinging another skeleton off her back. The enchanted rack of bones jerked on her pack and scratched her arm in an attempt to cling, but at least half of him went flying across the room, and when that half broke, the rest of him crumbled into rubble. "*I said . . . that if he wanted me to be . . . his brood-mare, he wasn't good enough stock—ha!*" she yelled, whipping her sword around so that the flat smashed through another skeleton's skull, "*—to breed with me! Then I said—incoming!*"

Warned in time, Kerric thumped the air, smashing a bolt of power onto the overgrown, ogre-sized bone monster bearing down on them. It staggered wobbled, and collapsed. He prompted her when she kept smacking their attackers. "Then you said . . . ?"

"That if he was just looking—*ungh*—for a whore, he couldn't *afford* me!" She grunted with the effort of slicing through another skeleton's lower leg bones with her steel blade. Never having been a Healer, she didn't know what to call them, but there were two per shin, and they cracked like dry tree branches under her blows. A backhand smashed the skull, collapsing the skeleton. Only a few were left. "I then said if all he wanted was a cook or a pot-washer, he couldn't afford to *hire* me, because I certainly wasn't going to be his *slave*! *Hai!*"

One of the last two skeletons had grabbed her braid mid-spin. Gritting her teeth, she whipped her blade through the ribs and spine of the other one, then whirled tattoo-fast with a flex of the colorful band around her right bicep, flinging the skeleton off by sheer speed. It barely missed Kerric, smashing into the wall next to him.

"*Hey!*" he protested. "I'm *agreeing* with you, here!"

"Sorry. I can't control when they let go," Myal apologized, straightening up from her spin. Breathing hard, she looked around the chamber. Bone shards lay all over the floor, in some places ankle- and even knee-deep. "Is that the last of them, for this one?"

"Uhhh . . ." Kerric glanced over at the golden numbers hovering near his right shoulder. "Ninety-nine. We have one more to go. Probably another big one. And that was the single *lousiest* proposal I have ever heard in my entire life. '*You* will do me the honor of becoming my wife.' What an *ass*! Someone should've checked his brains to see if a mage secretly swapped them with a donkey's," he scorned. "I'm surprised you didn't break him like one of these skellies. Did he not *once* think of you as a fellow human being?"

Myal shook her head. She blotted at something trickling down her brow, and blinked, discovering it was blood. Her head didn't hurt much beyond a bit of a stinging throbbing sensation, and she knew even a tiny scratch on the scalp tended to bleed profusely, so she didn't worry too much. The concerned look Kerric gave her and the soft exclamation was a balm, though; she held still while he hurried over, hands lifting with a faint glow of greenish energies as he touched each wound. She could have healed them easily with her spine tattoo, but his concern pleased her. It did not, however, distract her.

"*Coagidermic*," he muttered, gently brushing his fingertips over the scratches just above her hairline. "There. You'll need a wash, but you won't bleed anymore."

"Good. Duck," Myal ordered. He stared at her for one brief, blank moment, then dropped into a deep squat. She slashed through the air over his absent head, cracking her blade into the horselike jaws of whatever-the-skeletal-thing-was. It had wings and talon-tipped legs in front, the head and hindquarters of a horse, and a tail like a snake's, ending in a barb-tipped bone at the back. Her blow cracked the head right off its spine, forcing the rest of the body to collapse. "*That* would be the full One Hundred Bones."

"Well done," Kerric praised her, glancing over his shoulder as he recovered from his crouch. He dusted himself off, then muttered over a few of his own scratches. "Thankfully, the next two rooms are *much* easier to endure. Well, relatively. We'll have to be very careful to help each other with the next one, but the one after that is a piece of cake. Or pie, or pudding, or ice cream, your choice."

Myal mouthed his words, repeating them to herself. Her brow cleared. "Oh no . . . not the Banqueting Hall?"

Her tone was far more humorous than dolorous. Kerric

chuckled and kissed her chin, the nearest bit of her face in reach, since she had solved his own little riddle. "Oh *yes*, the Banqueting Hall. I'll presume you saw the replays we occasionally show of 'Team Rogue' clearing the riddle in two seconds flat?"

"I thought it was one second, myself," she quipped, smothering a yawn behind the back of one hand. Mindful of the sword in her other hand, she returned it to its sheath. "So, what lies between us and the Banqueting Hall? Mind you, just the thought of that place is driving me mad with hunger. It's been a while since I had that smoked salmon jerky, and that apple you gave me. I could use some food to wake me up. Not too much, though, or I'll go to sleep." Catching herself starting to babble, Myal shortened what she had been about to say to a simple question. "How many hours have we been at this?"

Kerric sighed. Removing his cap, he let it drop to the floor so he could ruffle his fingers through his curls, scratching vigorously. As soon as he felt relief from the itching, he spoke. "Probably about five or so, by now. Doing this at the end of a long day was *not* my idea, I assure you. I do have a spell I can use on both of us to speed-sleep us, giving us the equivalent of five hours sleep in fifteen minutes, but it's best to do that after we've eaten."

"So let's move on to the next trap," she told him. "You keep changing the subject, rather than say what it is."

That made him grimace. "It's a bad one. On the plus side, we *can* get through it safely, if we work together."

"Kerric," Myal stated flatly, giving him a hard look. "The *trap*?"

"The Canal Trap." He winced, waiting for her reaction.

She stared at him, then turned, walked over to a stretch of wall with the least amount of bone-rubble at its base, and thumped her head against the polished granite stones. "Goddess . . . Goddess . . . Goddess . . . I *hate* that trap! Those three stupid songs get *stuck in my head for days!*"

Kerric quickly moved to join her, hand going to her shoulder. "Myal, it's okay. We just have to stick our fingers in each other's ears and distract ourselves."

"That doesn't work! I've *tried* sticking my fingers in my ears!" she argued, turning back to glare down at him. "I can still hear the tunes when I do that, and if I can hear them, I am going to climb out of the boat and attack those stupid wooden golems, and they'll kill us both, because you're not strong enough to keep me in the boat!"

Catching her hands, he lifted them to the sides of his head, where he pressed her fingertips against his flesh in emphasis as he spoke. "Not in our *own* ears. In each *other's* ears." Uncurling a finger on each hand, he tucked them into his ear canals just firmly enough to cut off part of his ability to hear. "If we do *this* to each other, we will not be able to hear the music—it's a hidden cheat worked into the song-magic. Plug your own ears, you can still hear and be affected. Help your companions by plugging *their* ears, and each of you, so plugged, won't hear a single note of any of the tunes, though you'll still be able to hear each other speak. It's yet another reason why I couldn't take this trip alone."

He pulled her fingers free and kissed her knuckles in apology for manhandling her. Myal studied him warily, not sure for a moment she could believe the solution was just that simple. It had to be, though; Kerric had proven himself right at every step along the way.

It *couldn't* be that easy, though. She didn't trust easy solutions, and for a very pragmatic, physical reason. "Won't that be awkward, though? Leaning over against each other, arms all tangled up, trying to get our fingers in each other's ears?"

"It's a case of two birds smacked with one spell," he countered. "I figured if I could sit on your lap, we'd more or less face each other, fingers in the other's ears . . . and then just spend our time kissing. That way we wouldn't even have to *see* the golems, since even their gyrations can be considered hypnotically aggravating. Particularly when they do the hand-signs for that one song, the one about the bunny?"

He shuddered. So did she. "*Ugh.* Do *not* remind me. But why should you sit in my lap? Women sit in the laps of men."

"Torso length." At her bemused look, he explained. "Men usually have longer torsos than women, but if you and I were the same height, mine would be a hand-span longer. You're a full foot taller. It makes more sense for me to sit on your lap."

She sighed and shook her head ruefully. "I never knew that courting a shorter man could be so riddled with all the things you have to consider . . ."

He winced a little at her word-choice, but didn't correct her. "Well, there are some perks."

"Oh?" Myal asked.

Stepping right up to her, Kerric looked down by a few inches at most. "You do realize I'm the perfect height to nibble on *those* while making love, yes?"

She glanced down as well, and burst into laughter at the obvious innuendo. Her breasts were indeed just about mouth level on the man. "Yes, but only when standing upright."

"Oh, no, they'll be at the right height for when we're horizontal, too, I promise you," he told her.

That made her lift one brow. "You've made love to a tall woman before?"

"No, but I did get run over by a Mendhite adventuress several years back, when she was running through the village. It was when I was still a lower-ranked peon. By some twist of humor, we spun around as we fell, and I landed on top of her. She was about your height," Kerric added, waggling one hand. "Give or take a thumb-length, I think. Smaller breasts, bigger hips, and no face tattoos. A lot of your folk have come to the Tower over the years. Some for a few years, some only for a few runs or a few months before they move on again, like that one."

"That's all that happened? You tripped and landed on top of her?" Myal asked, curious. "You didn't try to court her?"

He shook his head. "She had a husband. He helped sort us out and stand us up. *He* had tattoos all over the place. And a thankfully forgiving nature, since I'd smacked face-first into his wife's cleavage. It made for a good laugh, but that was all."

She chuckled softly at that. "*Much* better than a proposal from an arrogant Netherhell . . . which reminds me, you were going to tell me about your worst proposal."

"I thought I did, a good five or six of them," Kerric pointed out. "You want more?"

"Not from other women to you. I meant the other way around. Haven't *you* ever proposed to anyone?" Myal asked him. She hoped her question came across casually enough, though her interest in the answer was acute. "I haven't . . . but have you?"

To her relief, he shook his head. "No. I'll admit I've been rather picky. Women like to throw themselves at me because I'm the Master of the Tower. And some men, too," he added, to be fair. "But at the end of the day, I am *me*. Kerric Vo Mos, not Master Kerric. I'd like to find a woman who can understand and appreciate that."

"You should have her run a gauntlet with you," Myal said. She blushed in the next moment, realizing what that revealed, but she didn't take it back. "You have a great sense of humor. We women like that in our men."

He nodded. "So you do. Of course, I have one more requirement in a potential wife that most women would refuse to comply with . . . so that's made it doubly difficult to find someone with whom I *could* spend the rest of my life."

"Oh?" she asked, unable to help herself. "What requirement is that?"

Sighing, he picked up his helmet from the floor and moved toward the far door, revealed now that they had slain the full force of this room's illusionary foes. "Most women want children. And as much as I want a woman to love me just for myself . . . I *am* the Master of the Tower," he reminded her, speaking over his shoulder. "This is *no* place to raise a child. No matter how many nurses or nannies or watchers you set, a child *will* go wandering off at some point, maybe even sneak off deliberately out of mischief, and get killed. For that reason, I will *never* allow a child into the Tower, brought or conceived.

"Unfortunately a lot of women just don't understand that, so every time a woman looks at me with stars in her eyes, all I can think is, *She's going to get a child killed.* And the corollary to that gloomy statement? I love my job more than I have *ever* loved the idea of having kids. Nor will I ever lie about it, since that would rob a woman of the right to find someone she *could* have children with." Spreading his hands, he shrugged. "So what woman would have me for more than a brief liaison, knowing all of that?"

I would, Myal thought, but the words didn't escape her. At least, not with actual sound behind the movement of her lips. Nor was he facing the right way to read them, since he had turned to the door and was now working his familiar little metal tools in the opening of the lock. Her quietness . . . her *shyness* . . . had robbed her of a good opportunity to talk about it. But in the quiet following his rhetorical query, she could at least *think* about it.

Kerric pulled the close-fitted, oil-hardened, steel-lined cap back over his hair. It bore a couple scratches from close calls in this and previous rooms, as did the rest of his armor. The same as hers bore. No, he wasn't a professional adventurer like her, and she had seen several who were better, but he was competent. She had been paired with far worse partners than him in her years here. Kerric did hang back from most of the physical fighting, but he did fight. And he made spellcasting look easy.

He could be diplomatic and tactful, polite and discreet. But he also had a wicked sense of humor, wasn't afraid to openly scorn the wrongful and the absurd, and was equally unafraid to show his admiration and respect. Part of Myal wished this gauntlet wouldn't end. Not for the danger—never for the danger—but because the more they talked, the more she realized this was the unvarnished Kerric. The man behind the scrying mirror's gloss. A man she wanted to know a lot better.

Opening the next door, Kerric led the way. The chamber beyond the defeated shards of skeletons smelled damp, echoed every sound, and reflected the beams of the suncrystal shafts in strange, veinlike patterns of their own. Just beyond a short hall, no more than a body-length, the passage met a broader one set at a right angle, one filled deep enough with water that the bottom could not be seen. Stairs led down to a small dock on the left, where a Mendhite-style gondola awaited them, each end swept up into fancifully carved beast heads from the mythology of Myal's childhood.

Kerric gestured for her to board first, but Myal hesitated, remembering her mother's lectures. Making up her mind, she greeted the ironwork at the prow with a bow. *"Ava, Aichano Ferra."* Turning, she addressed the empty oarlock at the rear, bowing to it as well. *"Ava, Aichano Forco."*

Only then did she feel right about stepping on board. Choosing the middle of the three bench seats, she looked up at Kerric, still standing in the dock. He had a puzzled look quirking his brows.

"What was that about?" he asked her.

Myal pointed. "Aichano Ferra is She Who Guards, a sort of

minor demi-deity. Not a true Goddess, but a folk hero. That's why all Mendhite *gondolae* have metalwork at the prow, to prevent damage from collisions. And Aichano Forco, her brother, is He Who Navigates. It is his strong arm and keen memory which propel the gondola through the water swiftly from place to place without error. My mother always said the prow must be sturdy and the oarlock must be strong, for the danger of either breaking would mean all the luck and the safety would drain out of the boat. So a good Mendhite greets both when she boards, and bids them farewell when she leaves."

"Ah. Well . . . *ava* to both of you," Kerric allowed, giving a short bow to the prow and the stern. "If you are ready, I will board."

Myal held up her hand. He accepted it for balance, carefully stepping into the boat. Under normal conditions, the boat wouldn't capsize at the start or the end, but these conditions weren't normal. Moving slowly, he adjusted himself so that he could turn and settle onto her thighs. The moment he did so, the gondola started moving forward. Quickly, he slid his hands to her ears, and gently but firmly tucked his fingertips into each one. She did the same, cutting off all the higher-end noises, but adding the faint thrum of the blood rushing just beneath her skin.

"Good g . . . good woman," he corrected himself, hearing his voice oddly this way. She smiled and chuckled, and the sight was so charming, he couldn't resist. Moving carefully so that he wouldn't dislodge her fingers from a sudden shift, he brought his head close to hers, and brushed their lips together. He did it twice more, then pulled back just enough to study her tattoos and the deep brown eyes they framed. He couldn't shift his hands far, but he could caress her cheek with his thumb. "Beautiful."

Blushing, Myal tried to duck her head. He wouldn't let her, choosing instead to bestow another kiss. That one led to another, and a fourth, a fifth . . . At some point, the dim ambient lighting became brighter. Movement flickered and gyrated at the edges of their vision, but all Kerric could hear was the increased beating of his heart, the rush of his breath, the soft sounds she made as their mouths met, parted, and met again.

He almost shifted his hands away from her ears, but the moment one finger started to come free, she shook her head, frowning as she pulled back. Quickly stuffing it back into place, he kissed her in apology, dusting her cheeks, nose, and brow with his lips. She bit his bottom lip in punishment. Not hard, just enough to sting, and she did suck on it to soothe the nip.

It wasn't easy, holding each other's heads, plugging each other's ears while their kisses grew more heated, more impassioned. Kerric managed to sneak peeks at their progress. One island-dotted, golem-filled cavern slid past, lushly festooned with jungle growth and dotted with richly perfumed flowers. The next one morphed into a cavern filled with a dark green forest, more temperate northern than tropical southern. He quickly averted his gaze from the gesturing constructs, and kissed Myal thoroughly.

Somewhere in there, they transited to the third cavern, the gondola swept forward by its spell, weaving this way and that to hopefully give the music-based enragement spells enough time to work their will on its passengers. Myal, however, was very good at keeping his hearing stoppered, and aside from that one slip, Kerric stayed equally careful. The third cavern was bright and cheerful, filled with colorful butterflies that fluttered, trying to catch their eyes. Aside from one brief glance, he kept his closed. She didn't open hers.

In the fourth chamber, all three songs were combined into one glorious piece of ultimate aural annoyance. Matching it visually, the golems danced in great, tiered ranks of choreography lining either side of the now narrow but still curving canal. The spell didn't translate through scrying mirrors—otherwise this trap would have been too dangerous to scrycast—but even so, the songs and the dancing and the gestures about the bunny had been known to annoy and irritate viewers anyway.

Neither of them noticed.

In fact, Kerric didn't even realize they had come to a stop in a dark and quiet place for several long minutes. Kissing—just kissing, without the ability to caress—was both frustrating and exciting. He learned he could have kissed her all day, and would have kissed her all day, except it was getting hard to breathe. And hard to just sit, literally as well as figuratively. Pulling back, he focused on his breathing for a moment, then dared to glance around.

Plain granite stones, dim lighting, no dancing or singing. Sighing in relief, he looked at Myal. She gingerly pulled one finger free, removing it from his right ear. Hearing nothing, he nodded and removed his own fingers. She sighed, too, removing her hands completely. Then grabbed him by the shoulders and pulled him close for a heated kiss, before clutching at his back. He returned it for a few moments, then reluctantly pulled away.

"We . . . we have to get out. Or it might reset. I think," he added under his breath. "I know the boat resets; I don't know if it does so only when we get out, or if it's on a timer."

Resting her forehead against his, Myal laughed softly. "So the great Guardian doesn't know for sure?"

"I have thousands of rooms, tricks, and traps to keep track of," he reminded her dryly. Rising, he climbed carefully onto the dock, then held out his hand to assist her out of the boat.

As soon as she reached solid stone, Myal turned and bowed to the stern and bow. "*Vala, Aichano Forco; Vala, Aichano Ferra.* Thank you for bringing us safely to our destination."

Kerric nodded as well. He felt a little silly, but he nodded at the boat. Mounting the steps—identical in every way to the ones they had descended—he used his lock-picking tools on the door in the alcove-sized hall. Dimness gave way to bright light, making both of them blink and wince from the difference. The scent of damp, murky water gave way in turn to a hundred different smells, each one mouthwatering. This chamber was long and somewhat narrow, a good sixty feet long, and filled with a very long, very heavily laden dining table.

Chairs lined the table, and place settings with plates, bowls, glasses, and various eating implements from the delicate forks of Fortuna in the far east to the chopsticks of Mendhi in the far west. Behind the chairs to her left sat four doors down one long side, and a single door at each end. Across from the wall with the doors was a long wall filled with glazed windows. If she pressed herself to the glass, shading it from the suncrystal lights, she knew the view would show the starlit sky outside and perhaps a glimpse of lights from the village of Penambrion. But the real view lay down the middle of the table, save for a single stand in the very center with one of the ubiquitous bronze plaques: the table was burdened with dish after dish after dish of food.

At the near end sat all the things that needed to be kept hot; platters of roasted meats, tureens of soup, Natallian *pasta* dishes and casseroles, and hot beverages; in the middle were salads of greens, mounds of breads, trays of cheeses and fruit, pitchers of drinks, and at the far end, fifty feet away, everything that had to be kept cold. Flavored ices and iced creams, aspics, chilled meats, parfaits, puddings, sorbets, and even a bucket with chilled sparkling wine awaited consumption.

Myal had seen this place and knew what to do, but she wasn't going to take any chances. Before she touched a single morsel, she moved down the side of the table until she could read the plaque and be absolutely sure. Some of these rooms seemed to be duplicates of each other, but there were subtle variations to each, some dangerously different.

"*Uninvited guests will be poisoned*," she read aloud, and looked at the Master of the Tower. It was the same room she knew about, but she couldn't help commenting on it. "Cheerful thought."

"Myal, I cordially invite you as my guest to sit and eat this fine feast," Kerric stated, giving her a courtly bow. He raised his brows at her, waiting.

"Kerric, I invite *you* as my guest to sit and eat this fine feast," she returned, equally politely. Both pulled out chairs at the same time, sat, and reached for whatever was closest of their favorites. For Myal, it was a pair of grapes, which she popped into her mouth and chewed. For Kerric, it was something slathered in melted cheese and what looked like little crumbled bits of bacon.

Chewing and swallowing, he nodded. "Okay, we should be fine to get up and move, now. The thing is," he added in an aside, "this food is *never* poisoned during the normal runs. That's because everyone who enters the Tower on a normal gauntlet has been invited to do so. But since the Tower's in lockdown mode, like the gondola, I don't know for sure if it was or wasn't altered. But I *do* know all of this food is completely safe for us to eat *now*."

"How so?" Myal asked, shedding her backpack. She picked up the nearest plate and rose with it in hand, intending to hunt for her favorites in this rather bountiful feast. Movement out of the corner of her eye proved to be him pointing at one of the casserole dishes.

"The *paprik* vanished from that one. I have a mild allergy to it," he confessed. "Not enough to kill me, so it's technically not a full-on poison, but it is enough to make my eyes water, my nose run, and my mouth burn a little too much."

"Pity," Myal murmured. "I like *paprik*. Makes my mouth feel alive."

"What, and my kisses don't?" Kerric quipped right back. "Because if they do, I'd happily substitute them for you, day or night."

The absurdity of that, and the suave charm inherent in his offer, made her tip her head back with a laugh. The soft chuckle echoed off the windowpanes, which showed a shadowy version of herself moving down the length of the table in one direction, and an equally shadowy version of Kerric moving the other way. She glanced over her shoulder at him. "Careful. I might eat *you* for dessert."

That earned her a grin. Plucking a few slices of roast beef onto his own plate, Kerric focused on serving himself a hearty meal. "Make sure you eat well. I'll be sleep-spelling us as soon as we're done—oh, I should secure the doors to this place so we'll be safe for the fifteen or so minutes we'll be locked in the spell."

"How rested will we be, compared to a full night's sleep in our own bed?" Myal asked. Then blushed, realizing she hadn't made that a plural *beds*. He didn't seem to catch it; instead, Kerric had set down his plate and dug into the backpack resting on one of the chairs.

Fishing out a piece of chalk, the Master of the Tower went from door to door, marking a trio of runes on each panel with just a few practiced slashes and squiggles. The door at the far end, opposite the one they had used, bore the smiling mask of a refreshing room door, but he marked it as well. Only when he was done concentrating on focusing his power into the chalked symbols did he answer her question.

"If you normally sleep eight full hours, it'll feel like a little over six. If you sleep six, it'll feel like five, or thereabouts. But it'll be solid-seeming sleep, even if you don't normally sleep well," he said, replacing the chalk in his pack. Dusting off his hands, he returned to piling food on his plate. "We'll need the food, too, since the spell speeds the body's healing abilities along with everything else. Once we wake up, a trip to the refreshing room, another round of food, and we'll be able to keep going for another twelve to eighteen hours.

"The only thing this spell doesn't do," he stated, spooning something made with vegetables in a lemon butter-scented sauce onto his plate, "is restore my magical reserves in a comparable amount. It'll be more like I slept for only three hours out of six, or four out of eight. But that's more energy restored than I currently hold, so it's worthwhile."

Myal finished serving herself little egg-pancake rolls stuffed with chilled fruit, and headed for the hot end of the table. A glance from Kerric ended with his brows rising. She defended her choice. "I like to start with something sweet, and end with something salty."

To her surprise, he flashed her a grin. "I think I can provide that."

She stared at him blankly for several seconds as she came near him. Then the innuendo hit her. Blushing, she shook her head, stopping next to Kerric. "*You* are naughty-minded."

"Ah, but *I* like to end with something sweet, and I think *you* can provide that, yes?" Kerric asked. He mock-snatched at her fruit pancakes.

She smacked the back of his fingers lightly, and found him hooking his arm around her waist instead. Quickly holding her plate out of the way so it wouldn't spill, she realized she had left herself open to a kiss. Myal didn't resist, though; when he rose on his toes, chin lifted, she dipped her head and met his lips with her own.

They didn't have to keep their fingers in each other's ears, but they did have to balance their plates. Neither could fully concentrate on the passion rising between them. Reluctantly, she broke away, and reluctantly he let her go, fingers sliding along her waist in a caress that would have been more effective if she hadn't been wearing her armor.

"Right. Food first," he sighed. Looking up at her, Kerric smiled slowly. "And then, dessert."

He licked his lips, dropping his gaze first to her cleavage, then lower. Blushing, Myal couldn't help the chuckle that rose up in her at his audaciousness. True, that was partially why she was here, to make love with him so they could safely get through the Seraglio section of this long gauntlet. But while she found him physically attractive, it was his personality that was beginning to charm her.

Including his sense of humor.

NINE

Searching for a way to tease him back, she spotted a small sausage speared on a toothpick in some sort of spicy brown sauce. Plucking it from the tray, Myal brought it to her lips. She sucked gently on the tip, tongue swirling out to catch the sauce as it threatened to drip from the tiny bit of spicy meat. All the while holding his gaze.

Kerric started to laugh. Shaking his head, he pointed at her. Or rather, at the little finger-sized sausage she was nibbling on so lasciviously. "Nice try, milady, but I am *much* bigger than that."

With only a brief search to find what he wanted, he plucked a thick, long, slightly curved pickle from one of the other platters and saluted her with it, grinning. She couldn't help laughing again. Turning back to the matter of food, she focused on stuffing herself fully. Not that it was a hardship; she had used her spine tattoo to heal herself several times so far, but that always came at a price. New tissue to repair or replace the old had to come from somewhere after all, and that somewhere always left her hungry.

There was more than enough to choose from, to sate that hunger. Meat that came from four-legged creatures such as lamb and beef, and winged ones such as duck and quail. Fish from freshwater as well as the sea. Eggs cooked in a variety of ways, cheeses of a hundred different kinds. Vegetables familiar and strange, cooked and raw, heated and pickled and chilled. Scores of types of bread, made from grains and seeds like wheat and rice, barley and even quinoa. Sweets that were made from ice and cream, sweets that were hot and sticky. Foods meant to be eaten with a finger, others meant to be eaten with a variety of utensils, from chopsticks and forks to little hammers and prongs for digging out the meat of crustaceans from their shell-covered hides.

Neither of them took more than a spoonful or a nibble from any one dish; that wasn't the purpose of a banquet like this. Thankfully, it was all spell-sealed to remain both fresh and at the right serving temperature for whatever it was. Indeed, each time Kerric scooped a bit of tender, flaky salmon onto his plate or plucked a radish carved to look like the unfurling petals of a flower, he could feel the faint tingle of his fingers breaching the stasis spells preserving each item.

The trick was to keep the food on or in the serving platters, bowls, tureens, and baskets. Once it was transferred to a plate, the spell ended, which meant the plates had to be checked and cleaned by Maintenance on a regular basis. If the food hadn't been spell-preserved, it would have formed a tremendous waste as dishes were forced to be rotated in and out every few hours lest they spoil and cause stomach problems, or worse. A constant feast such as this would never have been possible without the sheer amount of magic harnessed from the singularity at the heart of the Tower.

Some of these foods were imported via the Fountainways. Special purchasing agents picked by Kerric's fellow Guardians around the world looked for local delicacies and bought them for the Tower's adventures. For a fee, of course. His own agents shipped local delicacies elsewhere, including crates of fine Aian tea. But thinking along those lines made him think of the Tower's budget, which in turn made him think about how every minute they weren't scrycasting was hundreds of gold they weren't receiving from all their patrons.

We're making good time, he reminded himself, glancing at Myal. She stood down by the chilled end of the table, poking a gelatin dessert with a clean spoon just to watch it jiggle, a silly grin on her face. *She is magnificent as a partner. She's saved my hide directly a good three, four times, and indirectly many more.*

She's brilliant, swift, kind, smart, strong, funny . . . sexy as anything, Kerric acknowledged, smiling at her. A moment later, he had to smother another yawn. Even though she was half the table away, she yawned, too, in unconscious sympathy and equal exhaustion. *Damn. As soon as we're done eating, we'll be too sleepy to do anything right away . . . but I suppose there's always after we power nap and wake up again.*

That thought perked him up. As he watched, she stopped jiggling the dessert and smothered another yawn. Making his way down the table toward her, Kerric lifted his chin at the door beyond the end of the table. "Do you need the refreshing room?"

Myal thought about the question, then nodded. She set the spoon on the table, along with her used plate. "Yes, please."

Nodding, he continued past her. Wiping out the chalk marks with a brush of his forearm and a touch of his power, Kerric opened the door. A peek inside proved the lounge room was empty. Like the other refreshing room, it had three more doors, one to the rest of the Tower and one to each of the actual refreshing rooms for women and men. Murmuring a request for her to wait, Kerric checked both inner rooms. Satisfied they were empty, he returned to the lounge and warded the outer door.

"There. Now we won't be interrupted," he stated, satisfied they would be safe.

"What if someone needs the safety of a refreshing room?" Myal asked him.

He shook his head. "They should've reached one by now. If they haven't . . . well, the area right in front of a refreshing room door, and for about five feet or so in either direction, all of it is neutral territory. Nothing will attack adventurers in that zone." He pinned her with a look. "Don't tell the other adventurers that, though. It'd spoil the dangerous atmosphere we try to cultivate in here."

She smiled and shook her head. "I won't. I'll be back soon."

"Feel free to strip off your armor and relax for a bit," Kerric added, working on the buckles for his own. "The more comfortable you are physically, the more effective the sleep-spell will be."

Myal laughed at that. Backing up toward the ladies' door, she gave him a sly smile. "Is that an excuse to see me naked?"

Kerric hadn't meant it that way, but he wasn't one to refuse a good idea. Giving her a sly look of his own, he replied, "Maybe."

The door swung shut between them, cutting off most of her chuckle. He could still hear her voice behind the panel, a reminder that doors didn't guarantee privacy in the Tower, not when those doors were currently linked physically to each other. Spells could, however.

Double-checking the chalked wards on the outer door, he added an extra mark against eavesdropping, then finished removing his armor, dropping it on one of the lounge couches. Then wasted a tiny bit of magic, conjuring a hairbrush that could soothe the itch formed by the combination of the helmet flattening his locks and the sweat raised by all their exertions. Three deep scratches on the leather-wrapped, metal-lined cap had proven its worth in combat, protecting his skull from blows that had gotten through his spells.

The brush alone wasn't doing much; what Kerric needed was a bath, or at least a shower. Pulling a toiletry kit of soap and toweling cloths from his backpack, he retreated into the gentlemen's refreshing room. Adventuring was messy, sweaty, muscle-aching work. A hot scrub would feel very good. The sound of running water, thrumming faintly through the thin stone barrier separating the two refreshing rooms, let him know that he wasn't alone in that idea. On the other side of that wall, the tall, beautiful, shapely Myal was now scrubbing herself clean.

Kerric wasn't quite so tired anymore.

Turning the levers to activate both water and temperature, he imagined what that tattoo-colored body would look like with steaming water and soapsuds streaming down over her curves. That image was so distracting, he forgot to remove the cloth undershirt and shorts that had protected his skin from his armor. The feel of the damp cloth clinging to his skin made him grin and wrinkle his nose. *Fine, so the rest of me gets cleaned and dried, too . . . Maybe I should offer to clean Myal's things?*

On the other side of the wall, Myal finished scrubbing herself and her underclothes, and shut off the shower so she could wring out the garments. Activating a tattoo curling just under her sternum, one shaped like a tornado, she blew a stream of air on the garments, drying them in a rapid flutter of wind-tossed, swirling cloth. The empowered breeze fluttered the showering stall's curtain and blew away the droplets clinging to her skin.

It also tossed around her long hair, but that couldn't be helped. The sight of the dark, tangled mess in the mirror over the sink, one marked with anti-scrying runes around its frame, stirred an old memory, however. Long ago, a young Myal had watched her mother come in from the garden after a sudden wind had sprung up, and had watched her father first gently tease his wife, then offer to brush out the knots. The tenderness with which he did so, and the loving little looks her mother had given him, had left an impression on the young girl.

It was the little things that created and fostered a true sense of intimacy between two people. Her parents had done little things for each other, taken the time to both speak and listen, shared chores, given compliments . . . little things, all of which added up at the end of each day. *I think I have a comb in my bags—other than the one we picked up. I'm not sure that one's safe to use on actual hair. If surviving this gauntlet means having an attachment to each other, then we should work on forming several layers of intimacy.*

. . . I think Kerric might be the kind of man who enjoys brushing out hair, she decided, giving her naked image a critical look. The faint thrum of running water in the other refreshing room shut off, letting her know Kerric was done. Making up her mind, Myal reached for the toweling cloth still knotted around her belt. Wrapping it around herself instead, she carried her things back out to the lounge and started searching for a non-magical comb or brush in her adventuring kit.

Wrapped in his own gauntlet-borrowed towel, his own spell-cleaned garments bundled in his hands, Kerric emerged as well. He did so just in time to see Myal bending over, her long, ink-decorated legs rising all the way up the hem of her wrap, and a hint of the curves the cloth didn't quite conceal. Clothing *flump*ed to the floor, spilling out of hands no longer governed by his mind. All he could think of was touching that beautiful, tanned, tattooed skin.

Straightening quickly, Myal turned around. Catching him staring at her, she blushed and smiled. He was definitely ogling her legs now. "I thought you liked my hips more than my legs. And what about my breasts?"

"Hips, legs, breasts . . ." he murmured, flicking a hand in a gesture both dismissive and inclusive. "You're rapidly converting me to the whole package—and you're ruining my intentions, you know," Kerric added, shifting to plant his hands on his cloth-wrapped hips. "I *was* going to transfigure a separate bed for each of us, and ensure we got a good night's speed-sleep. *Chastely*, at that. But no, you just have to show up looking more delicious than all the desserts in the Banqueting Hall. If you're not careful, young lady, I'll eat you up like a midnight snack."

Myal ducked her head a little, not quite used to such compliments, but didn't hide her grin. Looking down at the brush she had found, she held it up. "I was thinking . . . if you're willing . . . you could brush my hair?"

Dragging his gaze up the length of her body, Kerric took in the tangled mass of fine black strands. If it hadn't been so windblown, it would have reached nearly to her waist. As it was, brushing it smooth would take a while . . . but it would allow him to touch her that entire time. It would give both of them a feeling of intimacy.

Kerric was no fool. Myal the Mendhite might be quiet, even shy, but she was not dumb. She would have considered that before making her offer, he was sure. Nodding, he scooped up his fallen garments and pitched them onto the cluttered end of the lounge sofa, then climbed onto the other half. Turning, he seated himself on the padded armrest, and gestured for her to take a seat on the cushion.

Brush in hand, Myal complied. "I wasn't sure if using the comb we picked up would be a good idea or not. I found a brush, though."

"It probably wouldn't do any harm," Kerric murmured, adjusting his towel so that it wasn't trapped awkwardly by the way she settled between his knees. Accepting the brush, he lifted her hair in one hand and started stroking the bristles through the very tips of her locks with the other. "But we'd have to make sure to remove all hairs from the teeth before using it, just to be sure."

"What does the comb do?" Myal asked, glad he was brushing out the tangles properly from the bottom up, rather than trying to force everything from the top down. She had learned to brush her own hair that way, too.

"It creates a barrier, one that lasts just long enough to get us through a certain room without actually fighting anything. Your hair is really soft. Is there a tattoo for that?" he teased lightly.

"Is there a spell for making yours so curly?" Myal retorted, teasing him right back.

Chuckling, he brushed more of her hair, working over a hand-length's worth with the boar-bristle brush. "Actually, there are spells for that. I don't *know* them well enough to pop one off right now, but I've seen them and others in books and scrolls." He brushed a few inches higher, then started following the brush with his free hand, petting the thick, straight locks. "Spells for hair, spells for clear skin, spells for *enhancements* . . ."

"Oh?" Myal asked. "What sort of enhancements?"

"Skin sensitivity . . . breast size . . . or lengthing the tongue. Ways to ensure two lovers are a good fit for each other, neither too large nor too small," he added in a murmur. Her hair wasn't hopelessly knotted, just a bit tangled. "Spells to make a woman extra wet, spells to make a man hard for a full hour . . ."

Myal blushed. "I, ah . . . have heard that there are certain tattoos for the same things. Even tattoos to enhance virility, fertility . . ."

"Wait, fertility?" Kerric asked, confused. "But I thought that tattoo on your belly stopped that from happening?"

Myal shook her head. "That shifts the fertility in a *non*-mage into being able to focus life-energy into magical effects. If a *mage* becomes a Painted Warrior, they can retain their fertility. The navel-tattoo is subtly different, and they can still cast spells," she explained, enjoying the soothing feel of the brush working its way through her hair, inching higher and higher as her locks untangled. "It's just very difficult to cast spells *and* use tattoo-based abilities. There are limitations to what spells can be turned into tattoos, but there are limitations on what spells can do, versus tattoos. From what I understand, a mage has to *know* a spell to be able to cast it without shaping it via sound and gesture, or augmenting it with herbs and such, yes?"

"That is correct," Kerric confirmed. His palm smoothed down her back and over her shoulders, following in the wake of each brushstroke. "Some I can cast with the ease of familiarity, others I need assistance with. And certain mages have certain affinities. Some cast easier by shaping their spells via sound or song, while others are natural alchemists, turning spells into potions and salves."

"It's similar for Painted Warriors. With a tattoo, you just flex it the right way to activate it and channel your magic, or your life-force, through the tattoo. No memorization needed," Myal told him. The brush was now at the base of her skull, her hair almost completely smoothed. She felt like purring under each stroke. Rolling her head, she encouraged him to work the brush all over her scalp. "That feels really good . . ."

Watching his hand smooth her long, black tresses in the wake of the brush, Kerric glanced over her shoulder. A silent double-take confirmed his brief impression. Her towel had loosened, giving him a lovely view of the shadowed cleft between her ink-swirled breasts. Daringly, he leaned forward, left hand stroking her hair more than the brush, now. "You know what else feels good?"

"Mm, what?" Myal hummed, enjoying the caresses.

His fingers slipped down under the worn fabric of the toweling cloth, warm and gentle. Cupping her left breast, he lifted it with the slightest squeeze, and let his thumb play over the nub at its tip. "This . . ."

She shuddered. It was a bold touch, confident. Practiced, even, for he seemed to know exactly how to gently tweak her nipple between his thumb and the edge of his forefinger, teasing her with a little sting of stimulated nerves. Breath catching, she arched her back a little, pushing her breast higher into his hand. "Ahhh . . . yes. That is good."

The movement finished loosening her towel. It slid down, sagging onto her lap. Kerric trailed the brush through her hair with his right hand, smoothing the last of the mussed strands, then ghosted it down over her curves, before very lightly brushing her right nipple with the boar-bristles. She gasped and arched her back further, pushing against his chest with her head. That forced him to tighten his abdomen against the threat of being toppled off the side of the couch.

Chuckling, Kerric brushed his knuckles over her right breast instead of the bristles. His left hand gently squeezed and kneaded. "I do believe there is another set of locks which I could brush for you, if you'd like."

The absurdity of his offer made her tip back her head with a laugh, accidentally thumping him in the chest a second time. "You—you want to brush my *nethers*?"

Overcome with giggling, she curled forward, hands covering her mouth. Rather than let himself be put off by her mirth, Kerric shrugged philosophically and abandoned the brush to the cushions. Scooping her hair to either side, he leaned forward and licked the nape of her neck, then kissed it.

"I want to get my hands on every inch of your skin, Myal," he murmured, dredging up the words he wanted to express himself with, though it wasn't easy to focus through his rising desire. "I want to stimulate every tattoo you have, and tease every ink-free patch, until you're begging me to paint you with the colors of my desire."

"You, ah, have a word with ways—I mean, a *way* with *words*," Myal corrected herself, blushing. His fingers were now brushing the sides of her ribs, tickling and teasing her skin in sensual caress. She couldn't quite dredge up a proper glare, though she did voice a complaint. "You're making my mind melt!"

"Good. All that adventuring without any lovemaking is far too unbalanced a way to live," Kerric said. Then stilled his hands, realizing he hadn't asked an important question. "Ah, that is . . . I'm not interfering with any relationship you currently have, am I?"

She tipped her head back, giving him an amused, sardonic look out of the corner of her eye. "Do you think I would have agreed if there *was* anyone right now?" Leaning back further, she relaxed against his chest and shoulder, enjoying the feelings stirred as his hands began moving again, the brush set aside. "There hasn't been anyone for months. You?"

"Almost two years, and that's counting professionals," he confessed. "Though I prefer real relationships to paid ones. It's hard to see anyone intimately when you're the one in charge of everything. There's always an inequality of power and position to worry about. Am I pressuring them inadvertently, are they simply trying to take advantage of my status and resources, will they . . ."

Myal shushed him with a finger lifted to his lips. The angle was a little awkward, but she traced her knuckle lightly over his mouth, then along his freshly shaved cheek. "I already have everything I want in my life. Except maybe getting my stories published farther away than just Penambrion."

He smiled a little at the half-tease, and kissed her knuckle.

"I'll see about arranging a chat between you and the printing house that publishes my works. No guarantees, of course, but at least you'll be able to talk. The rest is up to you and your skills as a writer. I don't write adventure stories, but I do know they are popular. Hopefully yours will be good enough for large publication."

"I hope so. It's my sacred duty to leave some sort of written mark upon the world," Myal sighed. "I know I'm supposed to worship the local God or Goddess, but Penambrion seems to lack a specific Patron Deity . . . so I worship mine as best I can."

"The Tower has a strict all-Deities-are-welcome policy," Kerric admitted, wrapping his arms around her. He turned his palms up as his forearms crossed, cupping her breasts. "We have a long-standing tradition of doing just that left over from prior to the Shattering, back when Aiar hosted the Convocation of the Gods, and too many foreign visitors still dropping by, almost two hundred years later, not to acknowledge and honor the Patrons of whoever may visit."

Enjoying the way his thumbs teased her curves and their sensitive peaks, Myal daringly asked, "Is there a Goddess of Nipples, by any chance? Since you seem to want to worship Her."

His laughter was swift and hearty, caught off guard by her teasing quip. Hugging her, Kerric released the Mendhite woman. "Up, and I'll transform this couch into something much more suitable as an altar to the God Pashon and Goddess Pashana, Patron Deities of Love and Desire. That's the closest I can think of, at any rate."

Nodding, Myal scooted off the couch, clutching at her towel. Not that she was afraid to drop it; she just didn't want to lose track of it. Finding her belt, she tied it back in place, then sneakily grabbed Kerric's and pulled it from his hips while he was clearing the belongings set on the other end of the cushioned sofa. He gave her a surprised look, then grinned, passed her his belt for the same treatment for his towel, and went to work on enchanting the sofa into a bed.

While he did so, she studied his body. He didn't bulge with muscles in the way that Nafiel did, but he was fit, a man who spent as much time moving as he did sitting. From his calves to his rump, he had plenty of muscles, thanks to the many steps and stairwells here in the Tower. The waist was trim, hips narrow compared to the breadth of his shoulders, and his back flexed nicely while he worked. There was a trio of light brown dots just below his right shoulder blade, and another small mole on his left buttock. An idle corner of her mind wondered what they would taste like under her tongue.

He flipped something her way. "Catch."

Myal caught her hairbrush, and stepped back when he gestured her to move. Within moments, the couch shifted and expanded, turning into a leather-covered, thick-padded platform, with the arms and back of a sofa still in place for its headboard. Turning, he flourished a bow in her direction, brown curls bouncing around his head and neck.

"Our bed, milady," he announced, and straightened, smirking. He knew exactly where her gaze had roamed while he worked. The Master of the Tower watched it roam now, over the curls dusting his chest, along the treasure-line that skimmed over his navel, and down to the flesh perking up in salute under such direct, warm, feminine regard. His smirk bloomed into a full grin. "See something you like?"

"Maybe," she returned with a smile of her own. Mindful of the brush in her hands, she lifted it. "Shall I use this on your hair?"

Nodding permission, Kerric padded up to her. He didn't turn around, though. Instead he slipped his hands around her hips and dipped his head just a little, kissing the upper curve of first one breast, then the other.

That was distracting. Not just for the soothing yet ticklish press of his lips, the flick of his tongue as he tasted her skin, but for the hands gently clutching and kneading her hips, and the slight brush of his manhood against her thigh. He was well-proportioned for his body, not too short, not too long, but thick enough she guessed he'd fill her nicely.

That thought made her thigh muscles clench, then part, her loins swaying toward his. Mindful of her task, she focused her attention on running the boar-bristles through his clean, spell-dried locks. It wasn't easy. By the time she had the ringletlike curls untangled and smoothed as much as they could be, her left nipple had his undivided attention. Lips and tongue alternated between suckling and swirling, nibbling and flicking.

His right arm wrapped around the small of her back, pulling them close enough that she could feel every inch of his warm body down her left side. Including the jut of his erection. His left hand distracted her in the next moment; it moved from her hip to her belly, pressing for a moment just below her navel tattoo, then shifted straight down to her mound.

Fingers sliding into her folds, he caressed her boldly, spreading the moisture that had emerged during his homage to her breast. Myal shuddered, turned on even more by his steady, smooth movements. Letting the brush drop with a clatter, she threaded her fingers through his hair, cradling the head of the man giving her all this pleasure.

Kerric Vo Mos might not have made love to anyone in a couple years, but he was by no means an amateur, or that far out of practice. Confidence, one of his first lovers had told him long ago, was a man's sexiest trait. Timing was everything, another had let him know, teaching him to move neither too fast nor too slow.

Focus, a third had lectured, was very important. If a man treated a woman like the center of his universe, focusing all his attention on the goddess in his arms . . . she'd melt just like this beautiful, tattooed Mendhite was melting.

His own mind was melting. Her skin tasted clean and sweet, with just a hint of soap. Her slick musk clung to his fingers, teasing the air in a delicate, heady perfume. Wanting to thrust against her flesh, Kerric carefully held his groin still, focusing instead on her needs, her wants. That included swapping to her other breast when she tugged on his scalp.

Leaving the left one flushed and glistening from the attentions of his mouth, he licked and nibbled his way around the right one, all while the fingers of his left hand continued their slow, steady stroking between her nether-lips. Strokes which she began to meet, flexing her hips to encourage him to move a little faster. Being a gentleman, Kerric smiled and complied.

"I take it you like that?" he murmured against her breast, swirling and lightly pinching with the fingers tucked between her folds. Not everyone was born dextrous with both hands, but he had practiced using both for many tasks from an early age. Kerric liked to think it gave him an advantage. From the dazed look in her eyes, this was yet another task he was mastering left-handed.

Myal gasped and clutched at his shoulders, one knee buckling. "*Da-zhul! Da-zhul, nafaa* . . . I mean, bed," she corrected, dredging the right Aian words out of her mind. Her translation tattoo was powerful, but it did still require concentration, and he was blowing hers away in a stiff breeze. "Need a bed right now . . . don't think you're strong enough to . . . hold me."

"Probably not," he admitted wryly. "And I do speak Mendhite; I drank Ultra Tongue years ago."

Myal blinked at him in surprise . . . then mock-clutched at her chest. Not because of his translative abilities, but because of the other thing he had said. "A man who admits to a weakness! Should I faint?"

Her teasing provoked a chuckle—and a mutter-and-snap. Scooping her off her feet, Kerric shifted her onto their makeshift bed. It was easy with her mass lightened by magic. Canceling the spell to conserve energy, he gently parted her thighs and crawled onto the bed between them, inhaling her sweet, musky scent. "Only from sheer pleasure. And it takes a far greater strength to admit a flaw than it does to boastfully cover it up, you know."

"I know," she reassured him, pushing up onto her elbows. Smiling, she shuffled a little higher on the bed, giving Kerric room to settle between her thighs. She reached for his hair, delving her fingers through the silky-soft brown ringlets. "You're one of the strongest men I've met. Strength of will and character, I mean."

Kerric grinned at her amendment and rocked back onto his knees. He lifted his arms, flexing them. "What, am I not as muscular and magnificent as Nafiel?"

That made her snort. He did have some definition to his form, but not the bulging biceps of the barbarian adventurer. "You're far superior to him. He's far too boisterous and . . . and full of himself. Nice, but full of himself. I'd rather have a man like you, who can make fun of himself, as well as be serious," Myal stated. Since he had shifted himself out of her reach, she crooked her finger. "Come here, noble writer, and dip your pen in my inkwell."

Brows lifting, Kerric asked, "Is that how they euphemize love-making in Mendhi?" At her nod, he considered the notion. "Huh . . . I like it. But I had something else in mind."

Dipping down again, he parted her thighs a little farther with his hands, and his shoulders. Breathing on her nether-curls, Kerric took the time to tease her with light little touches that traced through the dew already spread over her nethers. Just as she started to growl in frustration, he finally leaned in, closed his lips over her folds, and suckled.

Her elbows gave out. Flopping onto the leather-padded bed, thighs splaying wide, Myal moaned in pleasure. She panted, enjoying the flicking swirling of his tongue, but it wasn't enough. Tugging on his hair, she lifted his head from her loins. "Up . . . please, up . . . up here."

Kerric weighed his desire versus his lust, and matched it to her request. As much as he wanted to feel her bathing his lips in her climax, he wasn't going to deny her the chance to be filled by him. Working his way up the length of her body, he pressed damp, fragrant kisses up her colorfully inked belly, until his loins were snuggled against hers, his manhood rubbing against her slick, hot folds. As suspected, the position left him at the perfect length to place his weight on his elbows, plump a breast in each hand, and suckle each turgid nipple in turn.

Myal groaned in frustration. Bracing her heels, she lifted her hips, rubbing her folds against his shaft. "Inside me!" she ordered. "Dip me, now!"

A chuckle escaped him at the demand. Bracing his weight on one elbow, Kerric reached down between them, positioned himself at her entrance, and pushed in a little. Enough to tease. Except it wasn't just her he was teasing; the wet heat enfolding the head of his shaft made his eyes want to roll up in his head. Sucking in a sharp breath, he prodded a little deeper. Then plumped a breast and suckled hungrily on it, tugging with his lips each time he prodded with his flesh.

Delicious. That was what he felt like, thick and hard and hot, pushing his way into her sheath. A fresh moan escaped her throat; when he suckled on her areola, it connected a line of fire down through her blood to her groin, delicious fire. Delving her fingers through his hair, she encouraged him with wordless murmurs, hips lifting instinctively in rhythm.

He wasn't overly long, but his girth was more than enough to satisfy her; it put pleasurable pressure on all her nerve-endings down there, including a spot inside that made her gasp and tense. The moment she did so, Kerric grinned. As much as his body ached to pound and spill, it was those little twitches that pleased him the most. Rocking back and forth, he angled himself up into that spot, provoking a lustful moan out of the beautiful, exotic woman in his makeshift bed.

Sweat beaded on his brow, but he didn't stop teasing and tormenting her. All he did was dip his head back to her breasts and suckle, adding suction to friction. The slightest nip and scrape of his teeth finished the job. Cursing in Mendhite, she bucked under him, tugging on his curls. The sting was more pleasurable than painful. Grateful she was already experiencing her bliss, Kerric gave himself up to his.

It took a while; there were so many wonderful things about her body, the soft feel and sweet taste of her breasts, the warmth of her belly, the heat of her sheath. Feeling like he was drowning, he pounded into her as the tide rose within him. Rose, spilled, and flooded into her with a lusty groan that could have been her name. Holding himself on stiffened arms over her, he pressed his loins against hers, letting himself enjoy the way his body filled hers.

All good things had an ending. Gradually softening inside her, Kerric lowered his torso back down to hers, bracing some of his weight on his elbows even as he nuzzled her breasts. Her skin clung to his cheeks, damp with a sheen of sweat. Her fingers tangled lazily in his hair, equally damp along the scalp.

"Mmm," Myal sighed, enjoying the closeness of their aftermath. He was just the right weight on her, neither too removed nor too heavy. With her nerves still humming in delight, the silky feel of his locks was rather soothing. "I liked that," she finally said, licking her lips to moisten them. All that panting during the crux of her passion had dried them a bit. "How soon can we do it again?"

His chuckle vibrated between her breasts. Kissing one of her curves, Kerric replied, "As soon as we've speed-slept. Lie here. I'll fetch some cloths for cleaning up."

That offer made her release his hair, and untwine the legs she had unconsciously wrapped around his own. As soon as he left her, she stretched luxuriously. The cool air of the refreshing room felt nice against her overheated skin. Sprawling on the transformed couch, she relaxed into it, letting her eyelids droop.

The creak of leather and a brush of cool, wet cloth against her thighs made her slide one knee sideways, bending it to give him room to work. The intimacy made her smile and open her eyes a little. Not every man bothered with the need for after-lovemaking cleaning. Some, yes, but not all of them. She favored him with a very pleased look for his consideration.

Seeing that sexy, feline-lapping-the-cream smirk, Kerric groaned and shook a finger at her. "Don't get me started again, woman. We need our sleep, first. Both of us. You can pounce on me when we wake up. Now, go use the refreshing room if you need to," he added, lightly smacking her hip with his fingers. "You'll want to be completely relaxed and ready for sleep when the spell hits."

Grumbling a little—mock-grumbling—she rolled over, staggered to her feet, and sauntered toward the ladies' half. Her nethers felt deliciously tender, her breasts ached for more kisses, and her fingers itched to play in his hair again. For such curly hair, twining around in thumb-sized ringlets, it was remarkably soft. She wanted to touch it again.

She also wanted to sleep. Going through the motions of readying for bed—an odd thing to do, naked in one of the refreshing rooms of the Tower, of all places—Myal padded out in time to catch her lover emerging from the other half. Her lover. She smirked again, thinking about that. At a quick double take from him, his second look a chiding one, she shrugged blithely. "I'm just thinking I should have sought you out much earlier than this."

"Really?" he asked. Half of him was deeply flattered that such a sexy, exotic woman would want to make love with him again, and regretted the time lost in not doing so. Half of him was wary this was some prelude to the sort of unreasonable demands on his time that had ended many of his other attempts at relationships.

"Mmhmm," she sighed, stretching. His gaze followed the teardrop-shaped lift of her breasts, and the way they settled back down in comfortable, handful-sized curves. "You are the perfect post-gauntlet relaxation therapy. I am ready to sleep the sleep of the well-satisfied." She slanted a look at him. "You did enjoy it, too, yes?"

Her quick moment of insecurity made him smile. "Yes, I did," he said, beckoning her onto the expanded couch next to him. "Very much so. And I'd like to enjoy you again. After we've rested."

Nodding, Myal settled down at his side. Then stretched, arms over her heads, toes and legs pointed, before twisting onto her side. Her arms scooped around him, one tucking under his head, the other over his waist, cuddling him close. "I shall enjoy waking up, then. I don't normally sleep with someone, but I like touching you."

Her honesty touched him deeper than mere hands could. Looking into her eyes, mere inches from his own, Kerric cleared his throat to catch her attention, and to focus his own thoughts.

"Alright then. Pay attention, now: *Adduak. Ashtet. Belzuak.*"

Tendrils of dim golden light arced up and wove around both of them as he spoke. *"Mardenth. Comnuenth. Lanzak. Aaaaaa-dipoza,"* he finished, deliberately pronouncing the last word with a yawn.

Myal, caught off guard, yawned in response to the sound he made, as yawns tended to do. He yawned as well, his second one triggered by hers . . . and both dropped instantly into sleep, snared in his spell.

TEN

When she woke a short while later, the first thing on Myal's mind was, literally, a headache. It throbbed in that peculiar way that said she had overslept, and not the completely good, completely restful, satisfying sort of sleep. She felt rested, but not completely so. Then again, Kerric had warned her it wouldn't be quite like real sleep.

Lying there, eyes shut against the ever-present light of the suncrystals striating the lounge ceiling, she focused on her breathing and her spine tattoo. Within a half dozen deep breaths, her head felt better, allowing her to open her eyes. Nothing had changed; she still lay on her side curled up with the Master of the Tower, both of them naked, and neither having lain there long enough for the cool air to give them a chill.

Beside her, Kerric still slept, curled up on his side, cheek pillowed on her bicep, arms folded up against his chest. He didn't look like his usual self, asleep; the vibrancy of his personality had faded, leaving a solemn-looking man edging toward middle-age. Hints of stubble shadowed his jaw, and the lips that could kiss and caress her so well, that smiled so readily, were now lax.

She thought him very handsome, if exotic, with his sharp nose and pale skin. There was just one problem seeing him like this: She wanted to see him smiling in his sleep.

In one of the western lands whose coast she had visited as a sailor—Myal couldn't remember which one off the top of her head—she had heard a saying that a woman's or a man's true face appeared when they let down their guard as they slept. If that saying was true, Kerric Vo Mos looked like a man who took his responsibilities seriously, who was more concerned than he was letting on while awake, but who was not so mired in his troubles that it permanently creased his brow in a frown. Indeed, as she studied him, she found more evidence for tiny laugh-lines at the corner of his eye than she could see of scowl marks and the like.

A deep breath told her his spell was wearing off. Drawing in a second one, he opened his eyes, stared at her shoulder for a moment, then lifted his gray eyes to her face. The smile he gave her was warm, sleepy, and contented. She didn't know whether to cuddle him, kiss him, or push him onto his back and mount him. It was possible she could do all three.

Just as she drew in a breath to suggest it, his eyes snapped wide, focusing somewhere past her face. "Someone's testing my wards to the Banqueting Hall. We need to get dressed."

Myal bolted out of the bed. Spinning around to survey the scattered mess of their gear, she grabbed for her undergarments. A chuckle from her partner confused her. "—What?"

"They'll take a good twenty minutes or more to break through at the rate they're going," Kerric soothed her. Sitting up, he stretched his arms, scratched at scalp and belly, then took his time getting up, only to stretch a second time, this time up onto

his toes. "We don't have time for lovemaking, which is unfortu-
nate, but we do have time to get dressed and see who they are."

She had to trust that he knew his own spells, but Myal preferred to be cautious, and only slowed down a tiny bit. "I'd rather
hurry, just in case they turn out to be stronger than these first
few tries."

"You have a point," he conceded, and began looking for his
own things with a bit more speed.

A flick of his hand restored the couch; a trip to the refreshing
room freed them from necessary urges, and a bit of mutual help
got both of them into their armor in record time. The scent of
lovemaking still hung faintly in the air, since it had been less than
half an hour, but Kerric didn't waste magic on dispersing it; the
Tower would do that eventually with its own plethora of subtle
air-refreshing spells. Picking up his backpack, Kerric stepped
into the Banqueting Hall and hurried for the door at the far end.

Myal followed, shrugging one-shouldered into her own pack.
They arrived in time to see the chalked runes shuddering outward, jolted every few seconds with the force of whatever spells
were being applied. Oddly enough, the door itself didn't move,
just the runes. A few bits of chalk dust fell with each blow, weakening the whole—and on the fifth strike, the entire lot blasted
outward in a swirling puff of white as they watched, leaving the
solid wooden panel bare of markings.

Instinct made Myal move forward to intercept whoever might
come through the door. Kerric silently gestured her back, stepping away from the entrance as well. She opened her mouth to
whisper a protest, but he held up a finger to his lips and shook his
head. As they waited, the doorknob turned slowly. The door itself
flung open sharply a few seconds later, revealing the quintet from
below.

The clothing-swathed woman knelt to one side, knife held

ready to throw in the hand that hadn't flung open the door. The blonde archer woman stood behind her, bow strung and an arrow nocked. On the other side of the entrance the warrior Barric stood with his sword drawn and ready; the other two men lurked behind the trio, either to guard the hall or just waiting to see if they would be needed inside.

Finding Kerric and Myal waiting for them, the lead trio didn't relax. The blonde glanced at the mage who had held the maintenance tablet. "Well?"

"He's not in charge anymore. Go for it," Torven stated, shrugging dismissively.

Not good, Myal thought, tensing. She didn't strike first, though, because of two things. The first was how Kerric was standing there, relaxed and smiling. The second was, the moment the woman had permission, her fingers had relaxed their grip on her bowstring. The arrow was in flight faster than thought, faster than Myal could have moved—and just as fast, smashed itself to pieces on nothing at all.

Splintered pieces of wood puffed outward before following the dented arrowhead and tattered bits of fletching as it all fluttered to the floor. Everyone but Kerric blinked in shock. He merely widened his smile, and spoke. "By the power invested in *all* Guardians of the Tower, past and present, I hereby not only revoke your standing invitations as adventurers and maintenance personnel, I revoke your ability to *grant* invitations. This ruling applies to the quintet standing here before me, and excludes myself and Mistress Myal of Mendhi.

"Enjoy your meal." Turning, he caught Myal's hand and tugged her back down the hall by a dozen or so chairs, before turning and gesturing at the table. "Myal, I invite you to dine."

"Ah . . . I invite you to dine as well, Kerric," she quickly replied, recovering.

"*Shoot* them!" Torven ordered.

Gamely, the blonde drew and nocked another bow, while the short, kneeling woman cast her knife. The small dagger thumped into an invisible barrier a foot from her fingertips and clattered to the ground. The second arrow met the same fate as the first, reduced to a splintered wreck. Cursing under his breath, the sword-wielder sprinted into the room.

Myal tensed her muscles for speed and strength, only to find herself shoved back out of the way by one of Kerric's hands. He used the other to snatch up . . . a breadstick? It happened too quickly for her to shout: Barric came at him in an overhand swing meant to cleave open his flesh from collarbone to navel. Kerric blocked it—*blocked* it—with the skinny, finger-thick, forearm-long piece of baked goods.

The *sword* shattered. Barric wasn't the only one who gaped; Myal did, too, as well as the quartet still working their way inside. Kerric didn't hesitate. Taking advantage of the warrior's stunned pause, the Master of the Tower snatched up a larger, longer loaf and smashed it, clublike, against the bigger man's head. It thunked against the adventurer's head, and dropped him to the floor, knocked unconscious by the bready blow.

"That . . . that's *impossible*!" Torven protested.

Kerric abandoned the breadstick and snatched up a wedge of cheese. He backed up, pushing Myal back with him as he retreated. "It's a banqueting hall, Torven. The only kind of fight allowed in here is a *food* fight. Check your tablet, if you don't believe me!"

Trusting her partner's words, Myal snatched up a fistful of crackers, and began flinging them like throwing-knives with her other hand. The hard-baked squares struck the wall behind the dodging pair of women. Several bounced off, but those that struck corner-first stuck as surely as if they had been made of metal, not flour. As soon as her left hand was empty, she snatched up the next thing, a pitcher of fruit juice, and cast it off-hand at the other mage.

The container struck, but did not shatter; instead, it splashed, dousing him from face to belly in fruit juice, interrupting his spell. Her attack was more effective than she thought, though, for he started screaming and rubbing at his juice-stung eyes, coughing and spitting between howls to get the liquid out of his mouth. From the way his skin reddened and began blistering, Myal realized Kerric's command had come true: all the food in this hall was now poisonous to the quintet across from them. She snatched up a bunch of grapes and a spoonful of something gravylike, and flung the contents at the other two women, who were forced again to dodge instead of attack. The glop—spinach dip?—splattered harmlessly against the wall; the other two women weren't taking any chances that it could harm them, and had dodged.

Torven wasn't casting a spell, but instead was digging in his pack for his maintenance tablet. The moment that rectangle of crystal came into view, Kerric hissed a spellword and yanked his hand inward in a snatching movement. Caught off guard, the other mage didn't tighten his grip in time. The tablet yanked out of his fingers, flew across the room, and smacked into Kerric's grasp, leaving Torven to gape and scowl.

"What the—? If this is a food fight, that shouldn't have worked!" he protested.

"*That* was a theft, not an attack," Kerric retorted, nudging Myal back toward the refreshing room. "You might want to save your partner, there," he added, pointing at the howling third man.

Torn between attacking them and saving his helpers, Torven growled and whirled, chanting a spell to cleanse the too-acidic juice from the other man.

Myal snatched one more bit of food off the table, a slender

summer sausage, and retreated ahead of Kerric. The blonde launched a spoonful of something in their direction in return. Kerric flung up a shield spell, letting the coleslaw splatter harmlessly against the thickened curve of air. It wouldn't poison them, but there was no point in walking out drenched in sauce-covered cabbage, either.

As soon as the door slammed shut, Kerric scribbled on it in chalk, using a double set of the previous runes to lock and ward it. The chalk went back into its pouch; the bread and cheese wedge, tucked under his arm, he passed to Myal. Pulling the crystal tablet out of his belt, he eyed it, grimaced in disgust, and dropped it on the floor.

"Smash it," he ordered. Myal gave him a curious look. Kerric gestured impatiently at the tablet. "Power up that sexy leg of yours, and smash it under your heel. We don't dare take it with us, because the deeper in we go, the more the Tower will think we're cheating by using it and step up the danger levels. And we cannot leave it for those idiots to recover. *Smash* it."

Shrugging, she handed him all the bounty they had pilfered from the table, flexed the right patches of skin, and *cracked* her boot heel onto the rectangle. It shattered with a *pop* of light and a rush of heat that warmed her calf where leather boot and metal armor didn't quite cover. Thankfully, it didn't burn. Relaxing her tattoos, Myal lifted her chin at the door. "Do we lay traps for them?"

"No. It'll take them time to break through the door, time we don't want to waste. You're going to pick me up and use that anti-scrying trick of yours," Kerric told her, "then I'll tell you what our next chain of tasks will be, and we'll be on our way. We'll have to eat breakfast as we go."

"Right." Holding out her arm, Myal scooped him up onto her hip, and used her other hand to press behind her skull. She kissed him on the cheek as soon as she was done. "That's for defending us with bread."

"My pleasure. Here are the next five rooms," Kerric stated, knowing she couldn't hold him like this for long without exhausting all the energy they had just recovered with his spell. "First, we go down to the third door on the left . . ."

Myal dragged Kerric the last few inches necessary, then staggered over to the door on the hateful corridor and shut it. Bracing herself on the edge of the doorframe, she worked on recovering her energy and her breath. Her partner wasn't a large man, no, but he was solid enough that dragging his unconscious carcass yard after yard without any tattoo-based magics to help her was an exhausting task.

Partner, and lover. Between rooms filled with bits of paper that exploded on contact, statues of dragons that had to be appeased with gold, pools of flame and a snake-headed, snake-bodied woman with looks that could literally kill, they had continued to kiss and cuddle, rewarding each other for navigating traps, destroying enemies, and saving each other's skins.

It wasn't just the physical side, either. The more they talked, the more Myal really liked the Aian male sleeping on the hallway floor. The more time they spent together on this long gauntlet run, the more she wished they had time to just stop, relax, talk, and make love again. That first time had been too brief, in her opinion. Fun, enjoyable, but brief, and pretty much under his control. Watching him recover from the hall that drained magic, Myal imagined what she would do to him if she had the chance to take the lead in their next round of lovemaking.

The rapid patter of footsteps interrupted her musing. Tensing, she drew her sword, ears straining and eyes searching down each of the three corridors around them. The thumping feet grew louder, until their owner burst into view, turning a corner at a junction about thirty feet down the left-side hall. It was big, it was hairy, and it was male. Nakedly male. It—he—ran toward her, making her shift forward and brace herself between him and the still unconscious mage on the floor.

Whatever he was, he wasn't human; no human had *that* much hair sprouting all over their body, nor arms that long or shoulders that broad. The creature almost reminded her of the jungle monkeys from back home, save that it moved upright like a man, didn't have a tail, and its coarse black hair was both longer and more sparse than the fur most monkeys typically bore.

Skidding to a stop just out of slashing range, the being jogged in place, eyed her, eyed the mage on the floor, then flung up his hands and screeched at her. "AAAAAAGH!!"

Twitching at the shout, Myal screamed back, brandishing her sword over her shoulder, ready to strike and parry if it tried to attack. "AARRRGH!"

To her shock, the hairy man-thing grinned as if in approval, nodded politely at her, and slipped past while she was still gaping in surprise. He leaped over Kerric without a second look, resuming his loping run. A grunt from down by her feet returned her attention to her gauntlet partner. Rubbing at his forehead, Kerric peered up at her. "Did I miss something?"

"A giant . . . naked . . . hairy . . . thing?" she managed to offer, gesturing in the direction it had fled. "It just . . . He ran up to me, screamed at me, I screamed back, it grinned, and . . . and ran off somewhere that way!"

Kerric nodded, looking oddly satisfied. "Good." Grunting again, he pushed to his feet, dusting off his leather-skirted backside. "Good. You did exactly the right thing."

"Well, what *was* it?" Myal demanded, resheathing her sword. "And why didn't you warn me about it?"

"I didn't warn you because it's on a random patrol," he told her, removing his helmet so that he could scrub at his scalp. "I had no idea if we'd encounter it or not. As for what it is, obviously it's a Hairy Naked Thing. What else should it be?"

"You . . . This place is *insane*," Myal stated. She poked her thumb at the door they had just come through. "On the other side of that hall, we fought *hellhounds*, illusions of literally flaming, deadly dogs born and raised in a Netherhell, and on *this* side, a . . . a Hairy Naked Thing that just jogs all over and screams at people?"

Kerric grinned and spread his arms. "What can I say? I love my job. I'm almost never bored."

Caught off guard, she laughed. In fact, she laughed so hard, she sagged back against the nearby wall for support, tears leaking down her cheeks. Warm hands, callused only in the ways that said he was used to wielding a pen, not a sword, stroked the moisture from her cheeks. It was a tender touch, and as her mirth died down, it was replaced by a warmth that blushed her cheeks and curled all the way down to the bottom of her belly.

Looking into Kerric's eyes, she tried to duck her head shyly. He traced a thumb over her bottom lip, adding a sensual layer to the intimate moment. When he lifted up on his toes a little, bringing his head close to hers, she sagged lower on the wall, letting their kiss meet on more equal ground. It was soft, it was sweet, and it was over too soon. Resting his forehead against hers, he caressed her cheek again, then sighed and pulled back.

"As much as I love making you laugh and really enjoy kissing you, we still have the Gerbil Route ahead of us, followed by the Seraglio," he warned her, looking into her dark eyes. "Are you ready to continue?"

"Have you recovered from the hallway?" Myal asked him. At his nod, she agreed. "Then I am ready . . . except for one thing. What is a *gerbil*?"

"It's a small animal. Related to rats and rabbits, I think, but kept as a pet. I'm not really sure," Kerric dismissed. "The important thing is, it cuts off about seven other lethal traps from our route."

"*Other* lethal traps?" Myal clarified. "This one is deadly, too?"

"If I can't get our opponents' attention, yes," Kerric admitted. He backed up from her, turning toward the left-hand corridor. "If I can't, you'll want to toss down either the mirror, which becomes a lake, the comb, which becomes a tangled briar thicket, or the ring, which becomes a trapping spell. And toss them *behind* us, so we ourselves don't get caught. But don't use them unless we absolutely have to; I'd rather talk our way out of this next fight."

"Right. I will follow your lead," she said, pushing off the wall to follow him. "Anything I need to know?"

"We're going to land in a cage filled with sawdust. Do you have any wood allergies?" he asked, looking back at her.

"Only if it's being used to hit me. Then I'm very allergic," she quipped, making him chuckle. He opened one of the right-hand doors and gestured her to join him in a plain, empty stone chamber.

The moment the door shut, the floor gave way. It wasn't the first time. Myal crossed her ankles, locking her legs together, though she kept her joints flexible enough to bend with the curves of the chute, particularly as this one was dark and difficult to see as they descended, Kerric just ahead of her. A strange, disorienting tingle washed over her flesh at one point, leaving behind a pins-and-needles effect that slowly faded.

Their emergence in a place of bright light distracted her; a quick flex of one buttock-tattoo lightened her mass. It was needed;

she landed on Kerric, forcing an *ouf* out of him, bounced, tumbled, and skipped across a fluffy mound of sawdust curls. Hastily restoring her weight stopped her skid. Myal righted herself into a sitting position, wiped wood shavings from her face and mouth, and squinted around the chamber.

The vast, sitting-room-style chamber.

She knew it was a sitting room because there was a couch with brightly colored cushions, artwork on the walls, end tables, and a vast platform upon which their large, roomy prison cage sat. That vast platform was nothing more than a couch table, Myal realized, with the couch itself sized for someone who would have to tower a good ten or twelve floors tall in order to seat themselves comfortably upon its creamy, flower-sprigged cushions. Somewhere off in the distance, a crowd was cheering and someone was speaking, both sounding as if they were being heard from the bottom of a bucket.

Or perhaps they were trapped in one, given the scale of this place.

"Oh, no," she muttered, wincing. Pushing to her feet, Myal absently brushed off more sawdust from her limbs. "We're in the Giant's House, aren't we?"

"Yep." Cupping his hands, Kerric hauled in a deep breath and shouted. "*COOOO-EEEEE! GEORGE!!*"

"What are you *doing*?" Myal hissed. "We have to get out of this cage!"

"Exactly," Kerric agreed. He pointed at a high shelf laden with knicknacks, porcelain figures, little leaded crystalline figures, glass bells and baubles. "But as I said, we need the shortcut to the Seraglio, and that means we need to get up there. The fastest way is if they lift us up. I could fly us, but—"

"*George?*" a high, strident feminine voice called out from an open doorway off to the right. *"George! Red light, George! Go pick up whatever dropped in an' bring it t' the kitchen, there's a dearie?"*

"Bollocks t' that, Mandy; I was listenin' to the cricket match in me study!" a deeper, masculine voice called back from a hall off to the left. *"Can't th' little blighters wait a bit? Game's just gettin' good—an' why can't you get 'em yourself, woman?"*

"I've got my lil' fingers up to th' wrist in your fav'rit soda bread recipe! Cricket match'll wait; you want yer tea on time, you gotta go grab them whatsits now, an' strip' n' gut 'em fer supper!"

Myal shuddered. If this was a lethal trap, those giants actually meant it. They'd be killed and cooked in a trice. She'd heard of adventurers getting crushed, bashed, hacked in half, and even eaten alive—though she wasn't sure that last one was true; there were certain things which even the Tower wouldn't show.

". . . But they have butterfly nets for just such a chase," Kerric finished his interrupted sentence. "And the door back into our own dimension takes a bit longer to open than usual, up on that shelf. Mandy insisted on a child-proof lock on the door that leads to the Seraglio, though I don't know why, as children are never allowed to run the gauntlets anyway."

Grumblings came from the left. They preceded the appearance of a tall man—obviously, but even in proportion to the huge room he was tall—with a balding patch on his head, a bit of a comb-over, a rounded nose, and a bit of a belly on him. He strode right over to the cage the pair were in and reached for the latch to the door.

"Coo-ee! George!" Kerric shouted, waving his arms. *"George!* It's me, Master Kerric!"

Myal glanced between the two men. From the scowl on George's humongous face, he either hadn't heard, or didn't care. The barred door opened as Kerric shouted some more.

"I need you to lift us to the topmost shelf!" he called out. "Can you do that for us?"

George wasn't paying attention. Making up her mind, Myal struck swiftly. Kerric went tumbling across the sawdust-fluffed cage at her shove, and *she* got picked up first. A flex of her finger hardened her skin, toughening her body against being crushed. Hopefully. She didn't know how strong a giant of George's size and stature might be.

"Myal—*NO!* George, you put her *down* this *instant!*" Kerric screamed, righting himself in time to see the cage door being shut again. "*Myal!*"

Myal, now free of the confines of the cage, arched her back and activated the tattoos flanking her spine high on her buttocks. George turned toward the kitchen, and found himself with a rapidly expanding handful of formerly miniature human.

"*Whot th'?*" He frowned down at her.

Myal poured more of her concentration and her frightened anger into her shapeshifting. Within two seconds, she was too large to hold, and dropped to the floor, expanding rapidly until she stood as high as his thigh. And kicked him hard in the shin.

"*OW! Bloody buggering bollocks!*" the giant shouted, hopping back and grasping his shin.

"*George! Watch yer language!*" the giantess yelled from the kitchen.

Myal smacked the edge of her fist into his elbow, numbing the nerve there with another hard blow, then punched him in the gut when his arms and knee shifted out of her way. The moment he doubled over, she grabbed his ear and hauled him down nose-to-cage, pinching it as hard as she could to control him.

"*That,*" she asserted, her voice booming at half the volume of his and over four times its normal tone, "*Is Master Kerric of the Tower, and you* will *pay attention to what he has to say!*"

"*. . . Did you say Master Kerric of the Tower?*" A woman about as tall to George as Kerric was to Myal hurried out of the kitchen doorway, hastily wiping her hands. Like George, she had medium brown hair, though hers was a bit curly; unlike him, her nose was thin and pointed. Both had complexions someone back in Penambrion had once called "strawberries and cream" and clothing which, while outlandish in its cut, was quite conservative, save that her skirt ended just below the knee, yet wasn't shaped anything like a gauntlet-runner's armored skirt.

At the same time, squinting at the furious mage in the cage, George tried to rear up in surprise. Myal kept a tight grip on his earlobe, though. She might be the size of a young child to him, but she had enough mass and he was enough off-balance that she knew she could keep him like this with less fuss than in any other position.

"*Blind me wi' ferrets! It IS Master Kerric. Mandy! We almost ate th' master! Red light, my royal arse!*" he added, trying to twist his head to look at his companion. "*You must be goin' color-blind in yer old age, woman. We don't eat th' Master!*"

"*I* know *we don't eat th' Master!*" Mandy argued back. "*An' I'm* not *going color-blind—and watch yer language*—oh, and mind yer volume," she added in an exaggerated murmur, tucking the dirty hand towel into a pocket on her apron. Dropping to her knees with two floor-thudding jolts, she braced her mostly clean hands on her skirt-covered thighs and smiled at the now impatient man in the cage. "Coo-ee, Master Kerric! How've ye been, eh?"

"*Thank* you, Mandy," Kerric sighed, relieved he wasn't about to see Myal ripped open and popped into a stew or something. "I've been fairly well, thank you. I hope you have, too. Now, I do hate to be a bother, interrupting your supper preparations and rushing my visit like this, but my companion and I are in a hurry. We need to get to the top shelf exit."

Mandy's hazel green eyes widened. "Th' *Seraglio?* Good Lord!" Her hand went to the base of her throat, where a string of

creamy white pearls the size of . . . well, on Mandy, the size of a
pinky-nail, and to Kerric, the size of pumpkins, rested on a silken,
knotted string. It reminded Myal very much of the plain pearl
necklaces she had abandoned in one of the earliest traps they had
slogged through, taking instead the one with rainbow pearls and
diamonds.

Leaning down, the giantess scolded Kerric at a not quite ear-
aching volume. "An' what's a nice bloke like th' Master doin' with
a lady, heading for a naughty lil' segment of the Tower like that,
eh? I thought you were a gentleman, I did!"

Kerric sighed and rolled his eyes. "Someone tried to wrest
control of the Tower away from me on the one day I went out
shopping in another town, Mandy. The Tower's in lockdown
mode. I have to get back to the heart to restart everything, and
the fastest way is through the Seraglio—which means I'll need
you to *not* eat the woman I love, thank you very much."

Myal blushed at his choice of words. She didn't know if he
actually meant it, or if he was just tossing off a useful phrase to
get the giant couple's cooperation. She wasn't going to protest it,
though; these giants could still decide to change their minds, fight
the pair of them, and pop them into a baking dish or something.

Still caught in her grip, George craned his neck as best he could,
peering up at Myal. "'Zat true?" he asked. "D'you love 'im, too?"

Blushing again, she nodded.

"Oh, well, f'r Heaven's Sake—you can let go a' me now, girlie,"
he added, fluttering a hand near the fingers gripping his ear.
"We'll pop you right up t' the top shelf, right quick. Word of a
Terry," George stated.

Myal released him with a shake of her other finger in his face.
Mindful of her much-larger lung-power, she spoke in a murmur,
too, for the sake of Kerric's ears. "Don't go back on it, or I'll bake
you for our supper."

"Ooh, she's a feisty one, isn't she?" Mandy giggled, briefly covering her mouth. "Bit of a warrioress? 'Ere, Master Kerric, I'll give you a lift up to th' shelf myself," she stated, reaching for the cage latch.

"Yer too short, woman," George protested as he straightened and rubbed at the small of his back. "I'll lift 'im!"

"You gotta get th' little lady," Mandy pointed out, sticking her hand inside with her palm up and her fingers flat. Kerric climbed onto the proffered platform, avoiding a spot of dough that hadn't been completely wiped off. He sat down and braced himself on her skin as she pulled her hand back out, latching the cage against any future arrivals.

"Little, my foot! She's done grown herself up to a tyke!" Looking down at Myal, he lifted his brows. "Can you get back t' little-bitty size?"

Myal folded her arms across her armored chest, trying her best to look stern and intimidating. "I'll wait until Master Kerric's safely on the top shelf. *Then* I'll shift shape and join him."

"Definitely a fierce one," George muttered. He turned to watch his wife stretching up on her toes, palm angled awkwardly to get Kerric up to the right height. "I told y' you were too short, woman."

"Oh, sod off!" Mandy muttered under her breath. She waited until Kerric scrambled free, turned, and waved at them, and fluttered her fingers in return, grinning. "There you go, Master Kerric. You're next, young lady—if you'll both excuse me, *somebody* likes his soda bread, 'e does, an' I don't dare let it wait too long between kneadin's."

George gave Myal a sheepish look. "It's really *good* soda bread. Now, shrink yerself down, poppet."

Wary, but willing to give him a chance, Myal released her ink-magic. Shrinking all the way down, she found him following her in a stoop. Like Kerric, when he offered her a flat palm, she climbed up into it and sat down for better balance. A thought crossed her mind even as he crossed the floor.

"*Why* do your people eat our kind?" she asked. "We're very small, maybe three bites' worth. Surely you have farm animals that are bigger?"

"'F course we do," George told her, lifting his wrist to the level of the knickknack shelf. "But mini-man meat is sweet an' tender. S'a shame to be givin' up the two o' you, really."

"I don't believe you," Myal muttered, still not quite ready to trust him. She meant, she didn't believe he was going to leave the two of them alone. However, it seemed the two males misinterpreted her disbelief.

He gave Kerric a furtive look while Myal crawled off his hand and onto the shelf board . . . which at their comparative sizes was not very furtive at all. Kerric rolled his fingers in an encouraging gesture. "Go on, tell her. She won't tell anyone else—and nobody's scrying this. All the lines got shut off, which is why I'm in a hurry to get things back under control."

"Right. That 'splains why I had to listen to th' cricket match. . . . See, th' thing is, we usually just transfer 'em to a new cage, spell-proof an' such," George whispered, turning to face Myal. His breath gusted across the shelf when he did that, smelling of toffee and nuts, oddly enough. "Then we use th' evil-o-meter on 'em.

"If they're really bad, we cast a memory-erasin' charm on 'em first. But if they're just bad at adventurin', Mandy works wi' the Master, 'ere, to open a portal back to their home town, an' off they go, bad or good. We tell th' good 'uns they're too stringy for the stew pot." He grinned, showing teeth as long as her forearm. "Most of th' time, we let the little blighters escape, an' just enjoy watching Tower episodes on th' telly in between runs, in exchange for some really faboo anti-scrying wards.

"Anyone else in this realm would eat you with a bit o' trifle for pudding," George explained. "But then they hate anythin' extra-dimensional. See, magic's not allowed in this universe legally, even though it exists, but me an' Mandy are from long lines o' mage-sorcerer type families, and . . ."

"George! Haven't you got that girl up to th' top shelf yet?" Mandy hollered from deep in the kitchen. *"While you're up an' about, dearie, could you get me a couple lamb patties from the icebox in the garage, since we're not having mini-man tonight?"*

"Yes, dearie, she's up! An' I'm comin', hold yer bloody horses!" he hollered back, thankfully turning away from Myal and Kerric, who both quickly clapped their hands over their ears, since his voice was still overly loud at that range. "Love of my life," he muttered, "but I swear t' God she can't find 'er own arse without me. Anyway, off you two get, an' send a note 'round when you got everything settled again, eh?"

ELEVEN

"I'll do that," Kerric promised, lowering his hands from his ears. "Thanks, George."

Moving over to a wooden toy cottage set against the back wall, he pulled out his lock picks and started working on the cottage door. Myal watched George retreat, grousing under his breath about lamb versus man-meat as he went. She didn't completely lower her guard when he was out of sight, but she did relax somewhat.

She relaxed even more when Kerric opened the door, revealing the familiar pale granite floors, walls, and suncrystal-streaked ceiling of the Tower on the other side. Again, she felt a tingling prickle as she passed the threshold. Shutting the door, Kerric slumped against the panel. It took him a few moments to speak. When he did, he glared at her.

"Don't *ever* scare me like that again! George wasn't being completely honest," he warned his bemused partner. "A 'red light' means they're supposed to *kill*, not capture, particularly the moment you tried to fight him . . . except you surprised him by growing that large, and those two honestly *don't* like eating mini-man meat . . . but there *was* a chance they'd do it." Rubbing his hands over his face, Kerric scrubbed for a moment, then peered at her. "You surprised *me* when you grew that large. I've never seen you do that in all your gauntlet runs."

Myal shook her head. "Most chambers in the Tower are a bit small for it. It's also very exhausting, and difficult to control exactly how large I grow. Plus, a *good* adventurer always keeps a hidden trick up her sleeve. Or down my pants," she amended, flashing him a grin. "The tattoos are below my waistline in back."

"I'll have to have a closer look at some point," Kerric quipped dryly. He stayed resting against the door for a few moments more, then gathered himself with a deep breath. "Right. We have one spike trap to navigate, then the second door on the left is our third refreshing room. We tidy up, eat a little bit, and then strip off our armor for the three challenges of the Seraglio run."

"Our armor?" Myal repeated, frowning. "Why?"

"The gauntlet section imposes feelings of lust and arousal upon an adventurer. It's kind of hard to, ah, take care of such urges quickly if there are lots of obstacles in the way," Kerric explained, blushing. He moved a few paces up the hall, then stopped and nodded. "Here's the trap. Trip it by sliding your sword just past that line in the stone blocks there. We'll get a five-second window while it resets for us to slip past, one at a time."

"Ah. Don't dawdle," she murmured.

"Exactly. I'll go first, if you'll set it off," Kerric said.

Drawing the blade at her hip, she crouched next to the wall and slid it past the subtle, hair-thin crack. Spikes shot up, knocking the blade aside with a loud *tang*, though not hard enough to knock it out of her grip. Kerric hopped across the trap zone quickly even as the five spears reset back into their illusion-hidden holes. Tensing her muscles, Myal counted slowly to five, then slid her blade across. The spears snapped up, sank down, and she leaped. Landing, she steadied herself and resheathed her weapon.

Or started to; Kerric caught her wrist, and pointed at the blade. That was when she noticed something yellowish and oily smeared on the steel. "What's that?"

"Poison," he said. "You'll want to wash it off in the refreshing room before sheathing it."

"Lovely." Following him into the refreshing room, Myal ducked into the ladies' portion. She didn't touch the stuff directly, just angled her blade in the sink so that the water from the tap slowly rinsed off all of it, then used the facilities.

By the time she had all of her armor off and stowed in her now bulging backpack, the sword looked clean. Gingerly washing it with soap, she dried the blade and returned it to its scabbard, then debated whether or not to keep wearing her sword belt. *On*, she decided. *It won't be that much in the way, I think. And it's like my boots; I'm not going anywhere barefoot in this place if I can help it.*

She felt a little odd wearing just her padded vest and skirt, but with the sword at her hip, she didn't feel completely defenseless. Shouldering the pack, she returned to the lounge. It took her partner a few more minutes to emerge from the gentlemen's room, but then she suspected he wasn't as accustomed to donning and removing armor as she was. Adjusting her scabbard, she sat down to wait for him, and tried not to think too much about the previous stuffed leather couch they had used.

When he did open the door, his appearance riveted her. Kerric had stripped down to a pair of shorts, the belt with his pouches, and his boots. With the straps of his backpack looped over his shoulders, he looked very . . . odd. Myal quickly bit her lip. At least he didn't have that stupid-looking helmet on his head, but the plain, padded muslin shorts were little more than undergarments, covering him from waist to mid-thigh and hanging baggily off his hips. He had nice thighs, yes, with a fair bit of muscle on them, but the loose garment made them look skinny whenever the muscles weren't being flexed.

Kerric, catching sight of her flushed face, nibbled lip, and bright eyes riveted on his legs, sighed. "I look ridiculous, don't I?"

She chewed her bottom lip for a moment, then admitted very, very quietly, "You have since I first saw you in armor. I'm sorry."

He didn't take umbrage, but instead nodded and sighed again. "I know. Not everyone can look like Nafiel."

"No," she agreed in a tiny voice. Her shoulders shook and her face reddened. "Sorry."

Not at all offended, Kerric quickly flexed his limbs, twisting one knee out and lifting his hands up on either side of his head, letting what muscles he did have bulge. Her helpless laughter, bursting from her before she quickly slapped both hands over her mouth, made him grin. Strolling over to her, Kerric gently pulled her hands away from her mouth. She blushed and tried to cover her face, but he wouldn't let her.

"It's alright, Myal. I know very well who and what I am." Bending over, he brushed his lips over her forehead. "And I am quite certain Nafiel doesn't make you laugh nearly as often as I do."

She blushed again and mumbled, "No, he doesn't. Sorry."

"Well, if you're really that sorry, you can kiss it and make it feel better," he offered. At her bemused look, he flexed his left arm and pointed at his bicep. "Kiss it, and make it feel better?"

"Oh." Leaning forward, Myal pecked it. "Is that better?"

"Somewhat." He flexed his other arm and pointed. She promptly kissed that, a smile teasing at the corners of her mouth. Then he flexed his knee, and pointed at his thigh. Her jaw dropped and her eyes widened in mock-outrage, but she couldn't hide her smile.

Kerric pointed again, firmly. Insisting she follow through. He received a roll of her dark brown eyes for his troubles and a press of her lips just below the hem of his shorts. The tingle that raced up his leg to his groin had nothing to do with mirror-Gates to other worlds. Clearing his throat, he pulled back, mindful of their surroundings. The Hairy Naked Thing wasn't the only possible random wanderer in the Tower. Not that they'd wander into a refreshing room, but . . .

"Right, then. Have you had something to eat?" he asked, breathing deep to clear his head.

Myal unfocused her gaze as she turned her thoughts inward for a moment, gauging how hungry she was.

"I could go for a bit of sausage," she finally said. A moment later, she heard him cough, looked up from the level of his thighs, spotted how red his face was, and blushed hard herself. The innuendo implied by her line of sight was honestly inadvertent. Licking her lips, she added, "That, too. But I meant the summer sausage."

"Right." Fetching out the remnants of their food supply, Kerric shared it with her, a bit of bread, a hefty chunk of cheese, and a couple inches of the spicy meat. Sitting beside her on the couch, he chewed and swallowed the first few mouthfuls before bringing up the subject of the Seraglio. "Now, uh, normally the Seraglio is most easily run by people who've been courting a while. Obviously, I haven't had anyone in my life like that."

"Never?" Myal asked, curious. She nibbled on her hunk of cheese, enjoying the tangy-smooth taste, with a hint of being smoked somewhere in the curing process. "Not ever? Not a single girl?"

"Well, of course I did," Kerric told her, side-tracked. "I did my share of lighthearted courting back when I was young and still being tutored in magic, same as any other young man. But there were no feelings strong enough to bind me permanently to any particular woman, and I've never been attracted to other men. So when I started journeying, I didn't leave behind any regrets, relationship-wise. Other than family ones.

"I do miss my parents from time to time," he continued, "but Father's a teacher, and Mother's a lace-maker, and they never knew quite what to do with a powerful mage for a son, other than give him—me—lessons. Father teaches for a high noble family up north, so they could afford to get me lessons in my youth, but other than that . . . They have my brother, Barric—no relation to that wall of meat in Torven's group—and my sister, Althea, to take after them, and some grandchildren to cosset by now. We chat by mirror every few weeks, but it's a bit far for them to travel, and I never could justify leaving the Tower for more than a day at most . . . and you've seen the mess made of that this year."

She nodded. "Which one of your siblings teaches, and which one makes lace?"

"Barric teaches, though he has a fair hand with the threads. Althea helps Mother, when she's not chasing down little ones. Yet another reason why I don't want them visiting," Kerric added dryly. "Which brings us back to the needs of the Tower. Now, the first chamber we'll enter is actually a couple of rooms rolled into one. And the first obstacle involves the inner of those two rooms. It's called Seven Minutes In Heaven."

Myal gave him a blank look. "Is it a doorway to another universe? Like the Giant's House?"

"You mingle—*we* mingle," he corrected himself, "at a party with several people—highly complex illusions of succubi and incubi, actually—with drinks, snacks, music, and lust potions perfuming the air. And we get numbers assigned to each of us when we enter. At some point, those numbers will be randomly drawn and two people will go into a closet for seven minutes. The first trick is, the more you lust after someone, but haven't done anything about it, the more likely you'll be paired up with their number when the slips are drawn from the hat."

"I see. The second trick?" Myal asked. "You implied more than one."

He grimaced. "The trick is *not* to give in to our lusts in the closet. If we can last for seven minutes without consummating anything, then the door opens to the *next* gauntlet chamber. Which is the trap Anything But The . . ."

"Anything But The . . . What?" Myal prompted him.

He grinned. "Anything but the bed. We can make love in the next room so long as we don't touch the bed." His grin faded into a grimace. "If we touch it, we get chained to it, and won't get released until the Master of the Tower releases us."

She gave him a disconcerted look. "I hope this bedchamber is larger than the one at my tenement. If it is the same size, we will be in deep trouble."

"Oh, there'll be options. The bed will just be the most appealing surface, that's all," he dismissed. "Plus there will be distractions. If we're sufficiently aroused and into each other, we'll be able to ignore them. The trap after *that*, that one will be a little bit difficult. You will see an illusion of twelve Kerrics lined up in a room," he stated. "And I will see an illusion of twelve Myals. Each of us has to pick out the real Kerric or Myal from all the fakes, and kiss the real one to break the spell so we can move on to the last half-dozen non-Seraglio traps."

Myal quirked her brows. "I think I've heard this story. Something about a king with twelve identical daughters, and the youngest one helps the hero, but he has only three passes to pick her out from the rest or he'll be beheaded?"

The grin he gave her was lopsided, not quite a grimace.

"That's the right story, and that's the right trap. But I do have a shortcut." Digging into his pouch, he pulled out the last two pieces of food, saved all the way from the storerooms of the Adventuring Hall. Handing one of the papery-wrapped objects to Myal, he held up the other. "We have to eat this after we enter the third trap—the room will scry us the moment we step inside and create the illusions; the moment right *after* they're created is the moment you eat this. It's the only thing that will differentiate reality from illusion so that we can break the spell with a kiss."

Taking the highly recognizable object, Myal wrinkled her nose. "*This* thing? I thought the original story called for a bit of honey to be eaten, so there would be a bee on the princess' lip."

"There won't be any bugs in that room available," Kerric said, shaking his head. "So honey wouldn't work. The best part about this solution is, there's no reason whatsoever for an illusion-princess—or prince—to consume one of these when looking for his or her lover."

"You are right about that," she mused wryly. Tucking it into her cleavage, she nodded. "I'll do it. But you owe me."

Placing his hand over his heart, Kerric grinned. "My word of honor, you can collect after I resume my place as Master of the Tower and things get settled back down . . . which will probably be two or three days later. Or as many as four or five," he added dryly. "But you can collect, eventually. Anyway, once we identify each other, then we'll be free to take on the last leg of the journey."

He finished the food in his hand and rose, dusting off his palms. Myal, thinking on what lay ahead of them and what they had just done, frowned softly. "Kerric?"

"Yes?" He turned, giving her his attention.

"When we were in the Giant's House, you said 'the woman I love' . . ."

That was as far as he let her get. Shrugging, he spread his hands.

"Mostly a figure of speech. But . . . partially a truth. A growing one. You're very lovable, Myal," Kerric admitted, gazing at her. "You make me laugh and smile, you're smart, capable, articulate, sexy as hell—all of that in that order of importance—and I've been kicking myself for not getting to know you better before this gauntlet run. I would *like* to get to know you better after everything is done, here, but I won't pressure you into it."

A smile blossomed on her lips, at first shy, then growing in warmth. Rising to her feet, she beamed it down at him for a moment, then impulsively leaned down and kissed his forehead. "I feel the same way. I'd like to get to know you better after this, too."

Picking up her unoccupied fingers, he kissed them gallantly, then nodded at the bread still clasped in her other hand. "Finish your meal, and we'll be on our way. We haven't seen Torven or his lot in a couple hours, but that doesn't mean others aren't working their way inward. This first room in the Seraglio section could take us anywhere from half an hour to three or more."

"Three hours?" Myal groaned. "It took us almost two hours to get through the Chess Match trap."

"Only because we had to actually fight each of the piece-to-piece battles, turn by turn," Kerric reminded her. "Now eat your bread. You'll need your strength."

He gave her another kiss on her fingers in sympathy. Myal dutifully started chewing on the bread. When her mouthful was gone, she washed it down with a drink from her half-empty waterskin, refilled that in the ladies' room and returned it to her backpack, and shouldered the pack as she joined him at the door.

The entrance to the Seraglio section had one obstacle Kerric had forgotten about: an ornately carved, glowing archway with a misty-pink barrier glowing between the marble columns. Myal eyed it, then the man at her side. "Is this supposed to be here?"

"Yes. It'll ask you two questions. Just answer honestly. I'll see you on the other side," Kerric reassured her. Stepping through, or rather, into the mist, he paused for a moment, stated something which she could not hear, paused again, stated something else, and continued through the archway to the far side. It was hard to see him, but he turned and beckoned her forward.

Trusting him, Myal took a deep breath and stepped into the mist.

"Are you physically, mentally, and emotionally mature?"

The voice startled her a bit. It didn't sound at all like Kerric for all it was male—the voice was deeper, almost a full bass instead of a light baritone—but it did have the same confidence and sense of competence about it.

"Yes, of course," she said, eyeing the archway. It was about as deep as her arm was long, enough to encapsulate her in the mist, which smelled faintly of both vinegar and flowers, an odd combination.

"Do you enter into the sexual activities of this sector of your own free will, aware of and accepting any and all possible consequences?"

"Yes, I do. There is no way I can get pregnant," she added bluntly, if under her breath.

"You may pass." The section of mist in front of her parted, allowing her to rejoin her partner. Kerric grinned and clasped her hand, pulling her down the hall.

The pink haze seemed to extend to the very walls, until she realized they were nothing more than smooth-polished slabs of rose granite instead of pale or dark gray like elsewhere. Faint, subtle friezes had been carved into the polished surface, ones depicting increasingly amorous scenes of opposing genders, same genders, couples, trios, and even whole orgies of delights. Indolence, gluttony, luxury, and lust guided each image she saw as they moved further into the Seraglio.

"Everything on this level is dedicated to the Seraglio scenarios, save for physically unconnected passages leading from one floor to the next, and a few maintenance tunnels, which we won't touch," Kerric told her. "There aren't even any windows or balconies to the outside on this level. But since there's still a chance for an immature person to get this far into the Tower, the law-sayers ages and ages ago insisted the Guardian of that era put up a Truth Gate to keep those who cannot handle themselves in mature, physical relationships out of this floor.

"If you'd lied, or simply hadn't been capable of handling yourself, you'd have probably been dumped into the Chuting Gallery or something," he added. "We want to go down this left here, and take the second set of doors in an alcove on the right."

Myal eyed the increasingly lurid images flanking them as they followed his memorized directions. She slowed, peering longer at one particular scene. She had a tattoo that just *might* be able to make herself that limber, but as for Kerric . . . A tug on their interlaced fingers got her moving again.

"Saw something you want to try?" Kerric asked, curious. She blushed, and he smirked. "I must say, working Maintenance has certain perks. You can actually spend time looking at all these lusty carvings. I know I certainly furthered my own erotic education in my second year of working here. Ah, here we are."

Pulling on the handle, he opened one of the two doors into a lushly appointed gathering hall, one with various cushion-strewn platforms around the edges. A plethora of lit candles provided illumination, scattered at platform level, in wall sconces, and hanging in chandeliers; the flames danced with sultry warmth and perfumed the air with whiffs of exotic, stimulating perfumes. The predominant colors were a velvety red for the carpeting and golden trim on everything, but there were also silken violets, plush blues, and luxurious greens.

Gilded columns twisted up into the vaulted ceiling, and life-like statues dotted the hall, candelabras held aloft in the muscular arms of mostly-naked, marbled men and curvaceous, alabaster women. Three locations held trays of fruit, bread, meats, and sweets all arranged in finger-food sizes, while pitchers of chilled drinks, their rounded sides beaded with sweat, waited next to stacks of goblets. Five more doorways led into other parts of the Tower, or seemed to, but it was the shrine-line structure at the far end of the hall that held the place of honor. Deeply carved with very erotic figurines in blatantly sexual poses, it held a single door instead of the pairs of double doors spaced down either side of the cushion-strewn chamber.

A chamber which was not unoccupied. Men and women in scraps of cloth just big enough to qualify as swimwear, never mind Aian-style outfits, looked up at their entry. Goblets were raised in greeting, someone waved a hand bearing a bunch of grapes, their intended recipient snapping his teeth on thin air instead of thick, juicy fruit, and a cry went up from dozens of throats, a babble from which a few phrases could be heard.

"They're here!" "The last members of the party are finally here!" "Send for Senya!" "Huzzah!" "Finally, the party can start!" "Party, like Netherhell—finally the *fun* can start!" "Someone get Senya!"

A youth with a lean, toned body and skin dark enough to have been an Amazai pelted for one of the far doors on the left. He disappeared through it even as Kerric nudged Myal to the right. "Put your things over by the near right-hand set of doors. Any time you take off anything, even if it's to put on something else in its place, make sure it ends up with your belongings, or it'll get left behind," he murmured in her ear. "Remember, all of this is an illusion. You walk out of here without your real clothes, and you'll wind up embarrassed."

"No, worse," Myal corrected him. "I walk out of here without my underclothes, and my armor will chafe."

He chuckled, nodded at a few of the women smirking and fluttering their fingers at him, and helped Myal stack their things next to the indicated doors. A moment later, more people poured into the room, easily doubling the fifty or so people already counted inside. Some of them were carrying a litter, upon which reclined a dark-haired woman in a deep green dress edged with embroidered silver. All of the newcomers were chanting, a chant swiftly picked up by the rest.

"Senya! Senya! Senya!"

Hand drums were carried in, along with reed pipes, flutes, and even a stringed instrument or two. The musicians quickly scattered to either side of the presumed closet-shrine, and began thumping and wailing and strumming a soft, sensual, infectious rhythm. Myal found herself swaying with the music, and even Kerric—familiar with this scenario—moved with the beat as well.

The chanting reached a crescendo as the woman was carried to the center of the chamber, and the litter lowered. Two strong, tall, muscular men assisted her to her feet, which she attained with a graceful swirl of her shapely legs. When she stood, she was no taller than Kerric, but commanded the attention of all with as much of his self-confidence, if not more. Not that Myal could blame her; the dark-haired woman had lush curves like the forest-covered mountains ringing the many inlets back home, and a smile to match.

"Welcome," she purred, her lips a rich, dark red normally seen on ripe, sweet cherries. "Let the numbers be picked, let the fruits be sweet, the wines fragrant, the players lucky . . . and let the games begin!"

A flutter of her gloved hands dispersed a quartet of maidens in layered, pink, diaphanous gowns which flowed from one shoulder to the opposite thigh, barely covering pertinent bits, their hair twined with chaplets of flowers. They moved around the room in pairs, one of each pair dispensing little lottery tickets from cloth-lined baskets, half of which were retained by the selectors, half of which were tossed into the gilded urn carried by the other woman.

More servants followed. Men in layered blue loincloths came around with platters of food and wine-filled goblets. Women scattering blossoms out of woven baskets, grinning and teasing people by trying to trickle them onto heads, cascade them over shoulders and breasts, arms and bellies and thighs.

By Aian standards, they were all very underdressed with arms and legs covered only by bracelets, anklets, sandal straps and armbands. Many sported bared bellies. By Mendhite standards, Myal had seen similar garments during beachside festivals; there were only so many ways to cut and drape less than a yard of cloth, after all. Myal glanced at Kerric, wondering what he thought of all of this. It took her a few moments to spot him, for he had wandered off while she wasn't looking.

Kerric, familiar with similar displays from past scrycastings, had moved over to one of the flower-petal girls. A few murmured compliments, a courtly bow, and he fished a fistful of petals out of her basket while she giggled and simpered. Carrying it back over to the wide-eyed Myal, he deliberately scattered them over her skin, even rising up onto his toes to dust her hair. She shivered under their touch, and gave him a questioning look.

"This is all about sensuality, the pleasure to be found in sensations," Kerric murmured, smirking at her. Leaning in, he pursed his lips and blew at one of the petals clinging to a bit of her skin above the neckline of her undervest. It fluttered and lodged for a brief moment in her cleavage, before flipping free under a little too much blowing and dropping toward the floor. Glancing up, he shrugged. "You can do whatever you like to tease me, but I'd recommend not touching me very much. Remember, the more we sate our desire for each other, the less likely we'll both be picked in the end."

Breasts tingling from the stream of air and the caress of petals, Myal blushed. His words did remind her of the ticket she had been given. She looked at it in her hand. "Oh—I'm a 53. What is your number?"

Checking the slip of paper, Kerric nodded. "47. Tuck it into your top, so no one else can claim it."

She complied, cheeks warming a little as she slid the scrap of paper into her quilted armor undervest. Triple thumps of the drums interrupted them. The drummers struck their triple-beat again, and a third time, before beginning a new song, one that encouraged many of the others to get up and begin swaying, undulating, and hip-shaking. Myal found herself swaying and undulating; the music was a bit odd compared to back home, but just as infectious as she remembered from the old beach and village festivals of her youth.

She swayed a bit more, smiling, then realized her sword was bouncing awkwardly on her hip. Leaning over, she murmured a question in Kerric's ear. "Do I need a weapon in this room?"

He shook his head quickly. Then grinned and rose on his toes, until she leaned over so he could speak in her ear, too. Kerric poked a thumb at his chest as he did so. "Nah, I'm the one with the only sword you'll need."

A blush stained her cheeks. It was followed by a chuckle. "Yes, but you said you couldn't swing it in this one."

"True. Not if we want the right door opened," he muttered back. Shifting away from her, he pulled off his belt, draping it over the backpack he had set by the door. Holding out his hand, he nodded at her waist. Myal hesitated, her adventurer's instincts warring with her trust in his claims for a moment. Unbuckling the sword belt, she passed over. Kerric set it on top of her pack, then caught her hand and drew her onto the main floor area, urging her into joining the dancers.

This wasn't the normal sort of dancing. No lines, no rings, no patterns or any sort of formality to it. This was just a modest sea of bodies moving as the thrumming, wailing, syncopated thumping of the instruments impelled them to move. Most brushed against their nearest partner. Someone tried to step up behind her to undulate his torso against her back. At the first hint of a startled, irritated frown, Kerric scooped his arm around her waist and spun her away. Catching her hand, he pulled her back into him, thumping their bodies together a little.

That placed his face at the perfect height for a grin and a brief, sensual nuzzle along the neckline of her top. Myal shivered. Let other women keep taller partners than themselves; the Master of the Tower was just the right height for her. She curled her hips in a slow figure eight, brushing up against him, teasing him with her belly and the tops of her thighs. He retaliated by ghosting his hands up and down her sides in skimming little brushes that made her wish he would touch a little firmer, a little longer with each ticklish pass.

"Okay, everybody!" Senya called out, her voice a laughing, joy-filled accompaniment to the music. "It's time to play Basilisk's Delight!"

The musicians brought the current song to a close and gave her their attention. So did the dancers, about half of them cheering and half of them groaning. Several headed for the tiered platforms to either side, finding cushions or a server with a platter of food and drink. Myal frowned and whispered to her companion as they did so. "I thought we were supposed to play Seven Minutes?"

"It's a party. We'll play a number of games," he reassured her, falling silent just as their "hostess" began to speak again.

"This one's a simple one, darlings," the curvacous woman in green drawled. She swivelled her hips and undulated her arms. "We dance until the music stops—" Freezing in place, she smirked. "And whatever position you are in is the one you hold. If you wobble and drop," she mimed staggering, then straightened, "you're out of the game, and must go off the floor to await . . . a punishment.

"That means, as there are . . . it looks like sixty dancers left, so we'll play until thirty of you lose." Smirking she turned and gestured to the musicians. "Play something vigorous!"

Kerric caught her hand and tugged her into murmuring range. "You don't want to be a loser; you'll get tagged for a punishment— quick, dance!" he added as she stood there. "You don't want to be tagged out for *not* dancing, too."

Quickly undulating, Myal danced. Mindful of the balance rule, she made sure she had herself well-positioned, resting her weight on one leg while she lifted the other onto its toes and swirled her hips forward, arms up and moving like slow flames. In front of her, Kerric rocked and twisted side-to-side, hands on his waist, hips thrusting to either side in syncopation with the music . . . which stopped. They both froze.

Movement heralded failure on the carpet-covered floor. Senya *tsked*. "You know the rules! Off you go to await your *punishment*."

A few embarrassed giggles, a couple of groans, and about five players moved off to the side. She clapped her hands and the musicians began playing again, the tune still lively, still fascinating enough to dance. When it stopped again . . . nobody staggered or wobbled. Senya restarted the music with a flip of her hand, stalking through the scattered dancers, her dark eyes flicking here and there. She tapped two on the shoulder and poked her thumb, indicating they had lost for not dancing enthusiastically enough, given the way the man and the woman slumped and scurried off to the sidelines, but did not yet sit.

When the music stopped again, this time four were caught off guard and had to move out. The music picked up its tempo, forcing Kerric to snap his hips and Myal to wiggled hers. A sheen of sweat built up on Myal's skin as she concentrated. More fumbled and were removed. Kerric glowed as well in the candlelight, a few beads trickling as he worked his body in time to the melody and the rhythm, taking care to move fast but with every shift keep himself balanced.

A couple more were tapped out for not being enthusiastic enough, but most of the rest staggered. When it looked like thirty had dropped out, Senya held up her hands. The hostess made a show of counting on her fingers as she strolled through the remaining dancers . . . and strolled right up to Myal. She poked the tall woman in her tattoo-inked belly. "You're out, too."

"Why?" Myal asked, puzzled. She hadn't moved from her stance, back arched, arms out to either side, hips caught mid-thrust. Her muscles trembled from the strain of holding the position, but she didn't wobble. "I'm perfectly balanced."

"You're too tall. And we have only twenty-nine out. You!" she ordered, looking at Kerric. "Punish her. The rest of you, grab a loser and drag them to the cushions!"

TWELVE

odies scattered at the flip of her hand, free to move. Kerric wrapped his fingers around Myal's wrist and tugged her toward a particularly broad, fat scarlet cushion. Myal's face burned, and she muttered under her breath. "Too tall? I ought to *too tall* her right in the face!"

"Shhh, love," Kerric soothed her. He stroked his thumb along the inside of her wrist, tickling her skin to distract her ire. "Remember the end-goal . . ."

Subsiding, Myal waited next to him and the cushion he had selected, as did the others. When the last giggling "loser" had been "dragged" by her grinning partner to an unoccupied spot, Senya turned in a slow circle and smirked.

"The winners will now spank the losers thirty times on the body-part of their choice with their open, flat palm. Points will be given for both location originality and impact . . . but you are *not* allowed to seriously injure the loser. Head, throat, and scrotum are forbidden. All else is fair game. Take a few moments to decide what you're going to do, and to get into position," Senya instructed the participants. "Failure to comply will only bring down a worse punishment."

Myal blushed brightly, eyes wide. A spanking? She hadn't been spanked in ages, and to be spanked now just because of a silly party game . . . ! A yelp escaped her as she found herself tugged sharply downward. Catching her balance, Myal followed Kerric down onto the cushion. Unfortunately, he got to sit on his rump, while she got tugged over his thighs.

"I'm afraid I'm a bit of a traditionalist," Kerric murmured, glad his partner wasn't taking a swing at him for this. Rubbing his hand over her rump and thighs, he added, "This will be the area I strike."

He honestly didn't know how Myal felt about being spanked, but they had to play along. This was the Seraglio. There were consequences for not playing along. That was the trap; if they didn't play all the way through to winning Seven Minutes In Heaven, the right door wouldn't open, the wrong ones would unlock, and these lighthearted games would turn increasingly dark and dangerous.

Face burning at the thought of being spanked in front of all these people—even if her mind knew they were simply magical illusions wrought by the Tower—Myal struggled against the instinct to rise up and protest. She was a grown woman, she was in charge of her own life, she hadn't done anything wrong . . . but the feel of his fingers gliding over her cloth-covered backside and down to her thighs wasn't frightening. More like exciting, particularly when, on the return trip up toward her waist, he pushed up her padded skirt, baring the legless undershorts covering her mound and most of her rump.

Breathing a little fast, she reminded herself there was a purpose to this game, licked her lips, and nodded. "I trust you."

Kerric slid his fingers up the inside of her thigh, high enough
that the edge of his index finger brushed against her cloth-
covered mound. "I will do my best not to betray that trust," he
promised as steadily as he could. It wasn't easy; the moist heat
radiating from her flesh made his groin ache and harden with the
need to explore it. Fingers, lips, other flesh . . . He didn't dare go
that far. They had to play the game. "I will still have to spank you."

". . . Understood," she murmured. Mindful of Senya's conditions about uniqueness of location and the strength of each hit,
she swallowed and added bravely, "I can take some pretty strong
blows, you know."

Fingers squeezing and jiggling one buttock, Kerric grinned.
"With this much cushion? I should think so."

"Oh!" She started to rise up to confront him for daring to suggest that her rump was fa—

"Everyone ready? Too bad!" the hostess called out, amusement lacing her tone. "Thirty spankings, and you have two minutes to deliver them. Begin!"

The musicians began playing a lively little tune Myal recognized as being exactly two minutes long; she had heard it several
times before in certain other gauntlet runs, usually the comedic
ones, but hadn't expected to hear it here. *Thirty spanks in two minutes . . .*

*The local Aians divide their minutes into sixty seconds—important
for timing events in the gauntlet runs—which means he'll have to make
an average of one strike every four seconds. Which he will . . . he's not
striking? Why isn't he—AIIEE!* The yelp escaped her as his hand
smacked into her rump, sheltered at this point only by a single
layer of cloth, and not by the quilted skirt that went under her

armor. That was a harder blow than she had anticipated, given the gentle way his palm had stroked her nether-curves a moment ago. Craning her neck, Myal struggled to peer up at him—and flinched as he smacked her again.

To her surprise, he looked like *he* was the one suffering. Biting his lower lip, he cupped the buttock he had whacked, then smacked it a third time, meeting her gaze. "Ah . . . you might want to help me keep count. That was three. We don't want to go over *or* under thirty."

"Right . . ." Facing the broad cushion again, Myal expected another strike, which would have made four. She got six stingingly fast swats instead, divided evenly between her two nether-cheeks. "Sssev—er, nine!" she counted.

"Focus, Myal," Kerric chastised her. He slid his hand over her rump a few times, soothing away the sting, then tugged and pushed at her knees, parting her legs. Once they were wide enough to work, he spanked her left inner thigh four times, then slapped the right side another four.

"Thirteen—seventeen," she managed. The left patch stung more than the right, but that was the angle working against him. Her muscles quivered and her legs squirmed when he tickled his fingertips over all that sensitive, sensitized skin. "Kerric, this . . . this is . . ."

"Are you enjoying it?" he asked quietly, brushing his thumb-nail up against her cloth-covered folds. She licked her lips, not responding fast enough. He slapped her rump hard enough to make her yelp, then teased her through her undergarment once more. "I asked you a question."

"Eighteen," she panted. "And . . . yes?" Her head spun. Myal hadn't ever really associated pain and pleasure in the same way, but there was something about how her flesh throbbed after each blow that . . . that transferred it straight to her loins.

Mindful of their dwindling time, Kerric fondled her just a little bit more before stating, "Because you took so long to respond, I am going to apply the next few blows to your sweet little nether-lips. Now part your legs wide."

Blushing, aroused beyond sense given the circumstance, Myal shuffled her knees as wide as she could, given her position. The first few slaps made her hiss and tense in anticipation, but he started with gentle blows. Started being the key word. Each one increased in its intensity, until by the eighth one, the *smack* of his fingers into her crotch was louder than the other swattings happening around the room.

"How many was that?" Kerric asked, pausing not just to ask, but to give himself a moment to calm down. His fingers throbbed, yes, but his manhood strained against the fabric of his loincloth and the quilted armor-shorts sheltering her belly from his thighs. He wanted to strip off the fabric separating his fingers from the liquid heat dampening the material, to inhale her musky perfume not just from the air, but directly from the source.

Her reply dragged his mind back to their task. "Eight. Ah . . . a total of twenty-six," Myal managed.

"Good girl," he praised, and spanked each inner thigh once, stingingly loud . . . and then twice more at their crux, as hard as he dared.

"Thirty!" she gasped, hips rolling to ease the throbbing tingle. Her breath caught in her throat at the feel of his fingers sliding between her nether-cheeks. Biting her lip, she tried to muffle her moan, but the way he cupped her mound only made things worse. Pain was there, yes, but the tender way he touched her transformed the pain, making her flesh incredibly sensitive. Without conscious thought, she arched her back, lifting her pelvis up into his touch.

The music came to an end, signaling that their two minutes were done. Reluctantly, Kerric removed his fingers.

Senya inhaled deeply, as if she could smell the rising lust in the air. Kerric wasn't the only one who had combined pleasure with punishment for his or her partner. Sighing—purring, rather—she smirked. "Good job, everyone."

A swirling flick of the hostess' hand and a spin of her body flung rippling lights out through the air. They landed on all thirty "losers" and separated. Myal craned her neck, following the lights. Transparent green circles appeared on Myal's rump. They tingled a little, too, almost as if someone had applied mint to her skin. Her partner shuddered; a glance at his face showed him sitting there with his eyes closed, his cheeks red.

"What is it?" she whispered.

Senya answered for him, announcing it to the entire hall. "Of course," she drawled, "it wouldn't be at all fair to the losers to take all the punishment and receive no reward . . . so now the winners must apologize for each and every spanking they gave . . . by kissing the spots they spanked. You have two minutes to 'apologize' properly."

A snap of her fingers ordered the musicians back into play. Myal froze for a moment, absorbing the implications, then quickly scrambled off Kerric's lap so that he could move into position. Except he didn't move. Shifting onto all fours beside him, mindful of the marks glowing on her skin, Myal nudged her partner and hissed, "Move—you're wasting time!"

"I am in a Netherhell . . ." Kerric muttered. Eyes rolling upward, he struggled for self-control, wasting a few more precious seconds.

When he felt he could control himself, he twisted onto his knees behind her, grateful she had moved far enough forward that he, too, knelt on the nearly bed-sized cushion. *Bed . . . don't think about beds. Don't lose it*, he silently ordered. It was hard—*he* was hard—but he gripped her hips and lowered his head to her rump. One kiss . . . two. Three, four five . . . Her cloth-covered rump was one thing, but when he got to the target-circles on her thighs, that was another. Musk and heat, delicate-soft skin.

Groaning, he kissed her fervently, chasing down each of the bright green glows not to count them down and remove them, but because they were exactly where he wanted to press his lips. They didn't fade immediately, either; apparently the force of the blow used required a certain length of time to dismiss the targeting marks. They could be removed in any order, but they had to be thoroughly removed, and that took time.

He almost didn't make it. Not just from the ache in his groin, the muscle-shaking urge to just strip down her last defense and plunge into her—the others were merely illusions, it wasn't technically in public—but because that last sharp-stinging smack took a long time to dissolve. He was forced to use his tongue, just managing to banish the mark a bare second before the drummers thumped out the last two beats.

Still kneeling before him, Myal had dropped her face into the cushion. At some point, she had bit at the velvet in order to stifle not only her moans, but the urge to push back into his face, to reach down between her thighs, tug the damp crotch aside, and let him kiss the real thing. She had no clue if he had managed to kiss away all the marks by the time the music ended, and the Mendhite did not care. His lips marked her flesh as surely as any tattoo.

When the melody stopped, she was left with a burning need for more. Struggling against the urge to push back into his now absent lips, she kept her teeth locked on the scarlet velvet, until the party hostess spoke up once more.

"Oh my," the green-gowned woman drawled. "It seems things have gone quite a bit far. Some of you were *very* inventive in where you spanked, and very thorough in apologizing. Numbers

64, 78, 13, and 2 are to be penalized for not clearing their marks immediately. All four of you will go through the blue doors," Senya stated, pointing at the back left doors, the ones which she had been carried through.

Myal realized now that their frame had been painted blue, and the panels tinted that color. The others were red at the near left, gold at the entrance Myal and Kerric had used, purple by where they had dropped their packs, and green at the back right set of doors. The shrinelike closet with the single door, that wood had been tinted silvery gray.

"You will submit to anything done to you in that room, for your punishment," Senya continued. "The rest of you . . . I do believe it's time to play Seven Minutes In Heaven. Let's start drawing the numbers!"

Kerric didn't know whether to pray that they get paired together right away, or that they not be the very first couple. The way his body ached, seven minutes in the closet with Myal, unable to sate his hunger, would be seven minutes in a Netherhell.

"Numbers . . . 53 . . . and 47! Oh, my, the two of you must *really* be on edge," Senya teased, drawling the words. She held up the two tickets in her hand. "The selection picks the people who are the closest to, ah, 'losing,' as it were. Now remember," she added as Myal slowly pushed to her feet, and Kerric gained his, "if only one of you sates their desire, you go to the green room, where the sated one will be punished and the unsated rewarded. If both of you do, you go to the red room, where you'll both be punished. And if you hold out the full seven minutes without touching or trying to arouse each other even further . . . you follow the losers into the blue room, where you will be punished *most* thoroughly.

"But if you do touch, yet do not sate . . . then you get the purple room." A flutter of her fingers shooed the two toward the shrine room. The hostess turned her attention toward the rest. "While we wait to see if they're in Heaven or a Netherhell, the rest of us get to play Move The Egg!" A clap of her hands summoned maidservants with baskets of eggs. "The object is to press them between you and your partner's bellies, and 'roll' them up the body to the mouth of one or the other without crushing or dropping the egg or using your hands . . ."

One of the loincloth-draped manservants opened the door to the richly carved room. Inside, there was nothing but a candelabra overhead dimly lighting the chamber with four flickering flames, a single padded stool, and even more lewd carvings than the outer walls held. Unlike the outside of the shrine, these weren't just carved in stone; someone had taken care to paint every limb and curve in a full palette of colors.

Worse, unlike a room lit by suncrystals, the candle flames danced in the breeze stirred by their entrance. That made the luridly erotic figures seem to dance and sway as the shadows cast by their relief-carved surfaces moved and shifted in correspondence. Kerric looked around at the images of men and women conjoined in exotic and athletic ways, of thrusting bodies and suckling lips, caressing hands and curled toes, and groaned again. "Oh, yes . . . I *am* in a Netherhell."

Licking her lips, Myal nodded slowly in agreement. Behind them, the servant closed the door, murmuring a polite, if wicked, "See you in seven minutes . . ."

The moment the door closed, Myal grasped Kerric's wrist. She pressed his palm to her breast, her eyes wide with both passion and determination. "We have to win. That means doing— enduring—whatever it takes."

"Right. Right," he nodded, licking his own lips. "Just . . . ah . . . be careful on rubbing our loins together." Catching her free hand, he pulled it to his chest, letting her palm cover his nipple. The way she blushed and shifted her hand, caressing him, made him give her a lopsided smile and gently plump her breast. Moving up against her, he looked up into her eyes. "This may be a Netherhell of unrequitable lust, but I'm glad I'm suffering it with you."

Myal *snerk*ed, caught off guard by his quip. She couldn't help it; Kerric just made her laugh. Big guffaws, little snickers, it didn't matter. She smiled down at him, letting herself enjoy that acknowledged fact. "Kerric, I cannot imagine anyone else I'd be willing to endure this kind of torment with, either."

Dipping her head, she brushed her lips against his brow in a kiss more tender than sensual. Somehow, that seemed the right thing to do. Abandoning his chest, she slid her hands up to his cheeks, tilting his head back so she could dust his face with little kisses. He lifted his chin, nuzzling her in return, peppering her throat and collarbone with little pecks, while his own arms wrapped around her waist, pulling her close.

Eventually their lips met and nibbled, mingled, kissed . . . but the position put a strain on her neck. Pulling back, Myal looked around, gauged the height of the stool, and nudged Kerric over to it. The padded leather seat was tall enough that, once he hitched himself up onto it, their heads were level. Kerric pecked her lips and grinned. "Remind me to fetch out this stool for use elsewhere in the Tower, when we're through."

She squinted at it a moment, gauging the faint glimmer to it that didn't come from candlelight, then shook her head. "It's an illusion. Copy the spell, and you can have it with you day or night, without having to carry it anywhere."

"Good point." Pulling her close, he nibbled on her bottom lip, then rested his forehead against hers. "Does this mean I get to enjoy more of your kisses once we're done with this run?"

"I'd run a gauntlet to get to you for another kiss," Myal confessed, stroking her fingers through his soft, delightful curls. Mendhite hair was long, and sometimes wavy, but never this curly.

"I'll see about keying you to access my quarters, once I'm back in control," Kerric promised. Tilting her jaw with a caress of his hand, he nibbled on her throat. "I would run a gauntlet, too," he murmured between suckling, slow bites. "But why should we bother, if we don't have to?"

A wicked thought made her chuckle and offer, "I think I'd like to run the Seraglio again with you."

He laughed into her neck, and swatted her rump. "Tease!"

Her breath caught at the sting-and-throb. "Don't do that," she groaned, nipping at the curve of his ear with her teeth, evoking a groan of his own. "It's making me ache for more."

He spanked her again, this time for daring to arouse him via his surprisingly sensitive ear. The angle wasn't good for a truly throbbing hit, but it did tease the woman in his arms, making her catch her breath and moan. Spreading his knees, he pulled her firmly between his legs, loins and bellies and chests pressed together. Fingers buried in her hair, he tilted her head, angling her mouth for a deep, plundering, commanding kiss.

Myal permitted it for a little while. His confidence and his competence pleased her as much as his sense of humor. But she wasn't a doormat woman, content to always follow, never lead. Tangling her fingers in his hair, she tugged his head back and attacked his throat, licking it in long, lascivious strokes of her tongue . . . and attacked his ear again, this time suckling it.

"*Damn* you!"

Kerric hissed the curse, his hips jolting forward with the instinctive imperative to thrust. He could feel the tip of his shaft growing wet with need and knew he was getting too close to losing the game. Swiping his fingers up the inside of her leg, he cupped her mound and rubbed.

"Don't you *dare* make me climax just yet," he growled, pressing her soaked underclothes up against the little nub sheltered in her folds. Her gasp soothed some of his anger, but he didn't stop until her knee threatened to buckle, then he stopped his fingers. Just stopped them, until she whimpered and squirmed, instinctively seeking more stimulation. "That's right, don't you *dare* come. You will just whimper and beg me to finish. You will *beg* me and I will *deny* you."

That was a little too self-confident. Arrogant, even. Panting for breath, Myal struggled with her aching need. After a moment, she slid her fingers over his chest, and pinched a nipple. The curse that escaped him was a lot more graphic, and it made her chuckle. "We can't *do* that just yet," she purred into his ear, letting her lips brush against all those sensitive little nerve endings she had discovered. "We still have to endure our Seven Minutes in a Netherhell . . ."

Knowing she was right, hating it, Kerric recaptured her mouth with his, kissing her deeply. The door opened behind Myal, spilling warm candlelight and fresh air into the room, along with the chatter and laughter of the illusionary party-guests.

"Congratulations!" Senya crowed. She wasn't the only one peering inside, but she was the hostess, so it was her place to speak. "Your seven minutes are up, and you're *almost* in a compromising situation. There's the purple door," she added, nodding at the panels near their discarded things. "Now go use it. You've earned it. Come back here when you're through, and we'll have more fun and games to do." Moving away from the shrine-closet, she held up her hands. "Alright, let's draw another two numbers for Seven Minutes In Heaven!"

Aching, Kerric eased himself off the stool. He followed Myal across the room as the numbers 17 and 5 were drawn, this time for a pair of men who blushed but headed eagerly for the closet.

Even knowing they were nothing more than complex illusions, Kerric found himself envying the pair. He wanted nothing more than to make love to Myal in that closet, to stay in there and shut out the rest of the world until he could exorcise his need for her out of his blood.

The only problem is, I think she's seeping into the marrow of my bones, with the intent to stay there. It wasn't an unhappy thought, realizing he was falling for her hard. Shaking his head to clear it, he stooped and gathered up his discarded belt and backpack. She picked up hers, they both checked the ground to make sure nothing was being left behind, and another servant opened the nearby doors for them.

The room beyond . . . was a lot smaller than Kerric remembered. He blinked, swallowed, and cleared his throat. "Right . . . this must be the lethal version," he muttered under his breath. "Whatever you do, don't touch that bed."

"Got it," Myal agreed equally quietly.

The man at the door fluttered his hand, shooing both of them inside the modest-sized bedchamber. There were two doors, placed on opposite walls. The wall to the left held the head of the huge four-poster bed, and a night table to either side. The wall to their immediate right was just five feet away from the foot of the bed, the same distance given for the nightstands.

Those little tables were delicate, flimsy, and placed right up against the bed. They were fine for holding a glass of water, but would break under their combined weight for lovemaking. At the foot of the bed sat a chest with a padded lid, but if they used *that*, they'd brush up against the footboard. The floor was an option, but it was cold hard stone with only a narrow strip of carpet.

Myal narrowed her eyes. The double doors they had entered through were placed down by the foot of the bed and that chest, giving her a good view of their exact positions "Kerric . . . that chest isn't touching the bed."

"Yes, but if we use it, we'll brush up against the blankets or the footboard, and that counts," he reminded her.

Smiling, she shook her head. "No, it won't . . . because all we have to do is pull the chest over to the far wall, and use *that* to lean against."

He opened his mouth, closed it, and tipped his head, acknowledging her point. "Brilliant. Simply brilliant. Be *very* careful in moving it."

Nodding, she dropped her pack in the nearest corner and moved to the far side of the chest, knelt down, and grasped it solely by the nearest leg, the one away from the bed. Kerric did the same on the other side, since the chest didn't have handles to tug upon, and they hauled the heavy thing over to the other side. The effort cooled their mutual desire a little, but that was alright.

Sitting down on the chest, Kerric tugged her over to him and guided her into straddling his lap. That meant her head was much higher than his, but that, too, was alright. It left her breasts at the perfect height for lovemaking; all he had to do was remove her remaining clothes. He would have to aim her padded vest into the corner with their packs of gear, not wanting even a single scrap of their clothing to touch that luxurious-looking, heavily trapped, potentially deadly-by-starvation bed.

Realizing what he was trying to do in plucking at her vest, Myal dismounted from his lap and stripped, tossing everything at their packs. She, too, wanted to avoid the bed; she didn't know how it would react, other than that it would bind whoever touched it, but she was too experienced an adventurer to risk carelessness even in the face of her still-high desire. He rose, too, and under her eager gaze stripped off the last of his clothing as well.

As soon as he was naked enough, Myal pushed him back down

onto the padded lid and climbed back onto his lap. "You do realize this room is a lot smaller than you promised."

"Well, I hadn't seen the lethal version played before," he murmured wryly, wrapping his arms around her waist. He started to bury his face between those luscious, tattooed curves, but she tugged on his hair.

It wasn't easy for her to think, given how his shaft was now resting between her folds; her body kept urging her to rock against it. But not for nothing was she one of the top female adventurers. Focusing through her desire, Myal asked, "What, exactly, are the conditions for successfully moving on from this room?"

Her voice was breathless at certain points and her hips couldn't stop moving. The sway of her breasts just a breath away from his lips was equally distracting, but Kerric was a fully trained mage, with a fully trained will. That, and the answer was exactly what he wanted to do. "We must take care to fully sate our desire for each other, without touching the bed. Once we are sufficiently sated, the far door will unlock and open."

He rolled his own hips, pushing up against her, prodding to find the entrance to her sheath. Myal moaned, head dropping back. "Thank the Gods. Something I can do without thought!"

Kerric chuckled and wrapped a hand under her buttock. Lifting her a little, he positioned himself with his other hand, and then pulled her slowly down onto his shaft. "Tight . . . hot . . . can't think, either."

She laughed, and the pulsing clench of her inner muscles was both subtle and perfect. Wanting more, Kerric tickled his fingers down her ribs, making her squirm and squeeze him again from her tensing. With a groan, he buried his face in the valley between her breasts, nuzzling her. Myal stroked her fingers through his hair, playing with his curls, and began rolling her hips to slowly, seductively capture the last few inches of him.

Slowly didn't last long. Not with his mouth tormenting her nipples, not with the feel of his shaft filling her down to the last little bit. She had only made love with him once, with an interruption before their second chance, and a long hour of erotic seduction before this moment. Just thinking about being here with him made her shiver with need.

Bracing one hand on the wall for support, the other arm around his shoulders, she flexed her thigh muscles, rising and falling in hip-rolling strokes that made both of them groan. Kerric wrapped both his hands under her backside, encouraging her into deeper, faster movements. Sweat started to slick their skin as they moved. Feeling dizzy with mounting desire, Myal almost missed the uncomfortable tingling, until her kidney tattoo on her back flared hot in warning.

"*Poison!*" she gasped, eyes snapping wide.

He stopped moving, his concentration on his own pleasure broken by that one word. "What?"

"Poison! Contact poison," Myal explained, struggling to think through the mix of panic and pleasure addling her wits. The left tattoo had activated, which meant it was a poison or toxin of some sort, but the right one had yet to burn in the effort to cleanse her body of whatever it was, suggesting it wasn't immediately lethal. "My knees—bench seat!"

Kerric heaved both of them up off the chest. He was too aroused to pull out now, and that meant carrying her. Shuffling sideways until he could lean against the wall for support, he cast out his left hand, the right tightly gripping her rump.

"*Faddershou spesifica!*" Golden light zapped the padded leather top, sank in, then burst upward in glowing runes. He sagged against the wall in relief. His body clamored to pound into her, making it hard to think. "Thank the Gods. Just a lust potion.

Activated by sweat . . . which explains why I'm, *nngh*, so hard right now. Nothing . . . nothing deadly."

"Good. Good," she panted. She had wrapped her legs around him when he lifted them off the chest, but could feel his body straining to hold her up. Extending the left one, she touched the floor with her toes, curling them into the pile of the rug laid over the stone floor. "Don't think the . . . the rugs are trapped."

Shaking his head, he rolled them along the wall, putting her back against it. That gave her support and allowed her to bend her knee a little, lowering her pelvis into better range for him. It meant he had to either ignore her breasts since they were now a little too low to nibble or free a hand to plump one up . . . except she did that for him, cupping one in the hand not busy holding onto his shoulder.

Grateful, he returned to pleasuring it with tongue and lips even as he flexed his lower body. In this position, she didn't have much leverage to move; it was all up to him. Kerric didn't disappoint. There was something erotic about taking this gorgeous woman up against the wall. An erotic image crossed his mind, a future possibility. Leaning back a little, though he continued to thrust into her down at the hips, Kerric shared it with her.

"I'm going to invite you to my office, here in the Tower," he growled softly, "and show you everything . . . and then have my way with you just like this, up against a wall, where no mirror-scryings can reach . . . Dammit!" Frustrated, he pushed deeper, faster. "This potion . . . I was *ready* to explode when we came in here, but now I can't!"

Myal groaned, head thumping lightly against the wall behind her. She was glad he had put in the no-scryings caveat. The last thing she wanted was for all those patrons to watch her making love to the Master of the Tower. Still, it was a hot image. *She'd* have paid to be able to watch the two of them together, if only in a very private, exclusive viewing.

Which led to the irreverent thought of, *I wonder if he would allow it, if it was just for the two of us to watch? It's not like I've spent a lot of gold on other things* . . . It was illicit, it was unusual, she wasn't sure he'd go for it, and there would have to be safeguards against anyone else getting their hands on the scrycasting crystals which would record it, but it was a titillating thought. *I thought I was too shy to even think of such things. I guess not!*

Though she loved the way he was making her feel with his hands and his mouth and his . . . the position itself wasn't entirely comfortable for her. She had to slump and angle her legs, and the one thigh supporting most of her weight was starting to ache. His inability to be sated at this angle and speed might have a solution. Tugging lightly on his brown curls, Myal tipped her head to the side once she had his attention. "How about the floor? Better traction, faster speed?"

He slowed his thrusts and released her breast, giving it a last lick. Considering the risks, he nodded. "Right. All fours?"

She blushed but grinned. Disengaging, the pair repositioned themselves. Unsure if the rugs scattered on the stone floor were safe or not—as the cushioned lid of the chest had not been—she positioned herself with one palm and knee on stone, the other pair on the colorfully patterned, soft, thick, red-and-cream pile. Her poison-detecting tattoos would let her know which was dosed with something, if there was anything.

Settling behind her, Kerric widened her stance a little with touches on her inner thighs. He, too, knelt half on a rug and half off. *Such annoyances . . . I can't wait to get back in charge, so I can make love to her without having to* think *about potential dangers.* Gently, he gripped her hips and pressed back into her depths. She had a magnificent rump, one with a few tattoos on it. A corner of his mind wondered what the sun-in-glory one was about, but only a small corner. The rest was dizzy with the feel of her snug, slick heat clasping his flesh.

Slowly, he rolled his hips, snapping that last little bit into her so that their bodies ground together. Pulling out partway, he swept his fingers over her rump, massaging and kneading it, then thrust in fast and deep, making her gasp. One thrust slow and prodding. Two thrusts fast and strong. He repeated the first pattern, then the second, and on the third slow invasion, he added three fast.

The sound of her moans, the hoarse panting of her breath, the flush of sweat beading on her skin were all signs of her rebuilding arousal. She shuffled her hand and knee onto the carpet, so he did the same, and tormented her with one slow, four fast, one slow— and slammed into her hard and fast, not stopping for a dozen strokes. He started to resume a leisurely roll, but her inner muscles trembled and clenched, gripping his shaft.

Instinct seized both of them. The angle was perfect, the range of motion unhindered, the balance and stability excellent, the bed far enough away that nothing short of the wildest movement would brush against it. Worries melted away. It was all hot, sweet, swift, deep. With her hips tilted down just so, she could feel his flesh slapping against hers in just the right way, as well as rubbing deep inside. Fingers clenching in fists, she moaned loudly, letting her pleasure sweep over her.

The lusty sound that emerged from Myal's throat tipped him over. Groaning deep, Kerric stiffened, pressed deep, and let his bliss drain out through his loins. Dizzy, breathless, he came back to himself, ears first picking out the sound of her heavy breathing, then his eyes the sight of her sweat-slick back. This room was lit by suncrystals overhead, not candles; it wasn't bright, but it was enough to see her flushed, inked skin.

Moving a little bit inside her, Kerric reached under and teased the little peak of flesh at the front of her folds. Myal jumped and sucked in a sharp breath, then let it out in a sound that might have been a curse in Mendhite, if she'd had a little bit more presence of mind behind it. Instead, she shuddered in a second orgasm. Smiling, he coaxed a little more out of her, then just cupped her flesh, feeling the little twitches that signaled a properly sated woman. He knew he was.

However, if the far door—well, nearest by now—had unlocked at some point, Kerric hadn't heard it happening. Sagging back onto his heels, he gently pulled on her hips as he moved, keeping them conjoined. She moved with him, settling her cheek onto her crossed forearms with a sigh.

"You are really good at that," she half-purred, half-sighed. "Thank you."

Kerric, hands gently rubbing her from the small of her back down to her hips and her rump, chuckled. "My pleasure, believe me. So, the floor has a lust potion smeared on it, too?"

"What?" Myal asked, blinking a little at the question. The way he stroked back up toward her spine made her want to melt into a little puddle and ask him to keep rubbing up the length of her back. She focused her thoughts on his question. "Uh, no. The rug just gave me more padding to rest upon."

He snickered. She rose up on her elbows, twisting to look back at him. Kerric patted her backside. "There's a saying out at Senod-Gra, the City of Delights." He deliberately squeezed her nether-cheek and smirked. "It rhymes in their language, which makes it funny, but in Aian, it just basically means 'more padding for the thrusting.' Personally, I can see why a lady's bottom should be so pleasantly rounded . . ."

Since his fingers were still caressing *her* bottom, tracing out its roundness, Myal decided she would be more flattered than offended. She did, however, express her earlier desire. "Could you . . . rub further up my back? Up along my spine?"

It was not the first such request he had received, though it had been a long while. Nodding, he rubbed his palms along her muscles, kneading and stroking them. That pressed their groins together, though he had softened considerably, and she was no longer quite as slick. The angle didn't allow him much length, though. Carefully parting their flesh, Kerric knelt up and leaned over her for a more thorough, if brief, massage.

Mindful of the passing of time, he only gave her a minute or so, then patted her rump. "Up you get, and mind the chest and bed. The next section is an empty hall, so you can check the door if you like. Of course, I do feel rather sated, and you look it yourself."

"I feel it," she agreed in a murmur. Stretching a bit like a cat, she shifted and regained her feet. Padding to the door, she tested the knob. It turned freely, the panel opening a little. "It's unlocked . . . toss me a boot or something?"

Searching briefly, Kerric tossed her one of her boots. She wedged it in the now open doorway before returning to join him. He didn't question why; many of these traps reset if a door was opened and shut just once. In fact, he thought it rather clever of her to remember that, despite the way she kept smiling to herself in a silly, happy way.

That smile plagued him. He struggled to put on his armor, trying not to be affected by it. Not just because of the threat of his lust being re-aroused, but because he wasn't supposed to . . . Wasn't . . .

Kerric almost sat down on the chest lid again as the realization struck him. *I don't have to avoid a relationship with her.* She's *not interested in children,* I'm *not interested in children, we both agree little floor-rats aren't what we want in life, though neither of us would deny they're necessary for the survival of our kind . . . I could court her, date her, be with her, and not have to worry about contraceptives this, parental longings that.*

The thought was strangely liberating. Exhilarating. He finished dressing in a much lighter mood, almost jolly, and even leaned up and kissed her on the cheek as he passed through to the corridor beyond. Then helped steady her while she pulled her boot on, completing her outfit. When she straightened, and sighed, he asked, "Ready to go?"

Myal nodded. She wanted another bath—she wanted a real bed for her and him—and she wanted this too-long gauntlet to be over. She had plans, vague but slowly forming, on what she wanted to do with her life once this particular run was over. If Kerric was still willing to explore the possibilities she could see. "Right. What room is next?"

Wordlessly, he dug through his gear and held up the crinkly-wrapped object from earlier. Myal wrinkled her nose and dug out her own. It took her a full minute to find it. When she did, she tucked it into her cleavage.

". . . Ready."

Nodding, Kerric opened the door. The two of them stepped through . . . and each from the other's perspective vanished. Myal found herself in a plain but oddly triangular room with a creamy, plush carpet woven with intricately detailed plants. Three giant trees sprawled out of each corner, eventually forming a lacework bower in the center of the design. Lifting her gaze, she saw that the walls had been paneled in subtle patterns of wood, making the place feel sort of like a chapel or a cathedral. Movement off to her left showed a line of Kerrics striding in through the other door. They lined up along the diagonal wall and gave her grim looks.

She had the sneaking feeling she would have to face off against at least eleven of the twelve in a fight if she couldn't pick out the right one. As soon as they stopped, she counted slowly to twenty, just to be sure, then pulled out the object tucked into her cleavage. Unwrapping the papery skin, Myal bit into the fat clove and chewed. Chewed, and rolled it around the inside of her mouth until her eyes watered. Only then did she swallow it down, and rinsed her mouth with several swallows from her waterskin. It wouldn't get rid of the smell, but at least it cleared out the little bits of chewed-up garlic.

Carefully approaching the first, she covered her mouth, leaned in close, and sniffed at the illusion-Kerric's face with her unblocked nostrils. She didn't pick him, just moved to the next, and the next. Number Seven smelled extra garlicky, but she didn't pick him right away. Continuing on to the remaining five, she checked them, then went back down the line again. Taking a third pass to be absolutely sure, Myal kissed Kerric Number Seven . . . and sighed in relief as the others vanished.

Relief, and a wave of dizziness. Instead of standing along the diagonal edge of the triangular room, both she and Kerric now stood in the center, over the lacy vines patterning the center of the odd carpet. Both of them reeked of garlic, and he had the temerity to reach up and plant a kiss on her chin.

"Good job! I'll make it up to you later. Now, can you do that sound-masking thing?" he asked. "You don't have to pick me up; I just don't want the details scryable, later."

Nodding, she reached up and touched the tattoo at the base of her skull, then clasped his hand.

"The Twin Triplets of Confusing Doom," Kerric said, listing the first one as soon as she nodded. "We have to enter three rooms; the moment the first of us starts to go from the second room to the third room—let's say it's me—then I will appear to be entering from the first room to the second room behind us . . . and there will be a duplicate of you ahead of me and a duplicate of you behind the copied me, back in the first room. Both my evil twins and your evil triplet pair must be dealt with before we can continue."

"Evil twins and triplets?" she asked. "How evil?"

"They will be able to do everything that *we* can do," Kerric warned her. "All abilities, all spells, all tattoos . . . and the spells animating them will have learned from the techniques, weapons, and magics you and I have used throughout this whole gauntlet run. But they will not be created until the moment the second door is opened into the third room. Before that point, we'll be able to lay the traps of the Comb, the Mirror, and the Ring on them, since we didn't have to use them on George and Mandy—another reason for talking to that couple, instead of sneaking and fighting.

"Beyond that is the Wine Press, which is a simple matter of you manipulating the lever back and forth quickly while I work on teasing open a very complex, spell-resistant lock. You'll have to work quickly and watchfully to avoid us getting crushed to death by the rise and fall of the ceiling," he murmured grimly. "That trap will be followed by Confrontation."

"So what is Confrontation?" Myal asked, peering up the hall when he paused for a drink from his waterskin. "A massive battle with something?"

"A single foe, but an enemy that grows stronger, the more we fight it. So . . . we don't. We refuse," he instructed. "The next one after that is called the Printer's Trap. We will have to cross it one at a time, and I will tell you the riddle now, so you have a chance to guess it before we get separated—since like some of these others, it will be as if I vanished and you were left alone, from your perspective. You'll be confronted with a hallway of a certain length, covered in medium-large floor tiles, each one carved with an Aian rune-letter. Step on the right ones, and you're safe. Touch the wrong ones, and they will crush you against the ceiling literally faster than you can blink."

Myal blinked at his claim, then blushed, realizing how fast a blink truly was. "Oh. What is the riddle?"

"What belongs to you, yet others use it far more often than you yourself do?" Kerric recited from memory.

"Oh! I know this one. Your name," she stated, smiling. "Or rather, *my* name. So I spell out my name in Aian lettering?"

He nodded. "And I will have to spell out my own. The walls are trapped to crush sideways if you try to climb them, and if you tried to fly or climb to the ceiling, the tiles will strike anyway. After that, it's This Is The Ladder That Never Ends, but we already disabled the trap on it with, ah, Rick's Favorite Fireball Trap. We just go up three floors, then back down one, and the door will open," he paused, grimaced, and finished, ". . . onto another one of those Magic Will Not Help You corridors. On the bright side, that is literally the last stretch of the gauntlet to be run. On the far side of that corridor, the door opens up onto the Fountain Hall.

"As soon as I've recovered from the corridor, I'll be able to regain control of the Tower, and *that* will be that," he finished, spreading his arms with a shrug. "You can relax in my quarters, have a meal and a bath, maybe a nice nap . . . and, luck willing, I'll be able to join you relatively soon. That is, if you would like to stick around? You don't *have* to, but I have been enjoying your company a lot. I'd like to enjoy more."

Myal blushed and ducked her head. She nodded. "Same here."

Kerric grinned. "Good! Then we just have to survive, and pray there's no one waiting in the Hall to attack us the moment you drag me through. The Twin Triplets room is the first door on the right, here."

"Is there anything dangerous about the Fountain Hall itself I should know about?" Myal asked, following him to the door, which he started unlocking with his tools. While he worked, she dug around for the three objects collected much earlier in the run, the little silver hand mirror, the wooden hair comb, and the golden ring.

"Don't try to push past the shield wall. It'll look like a curved bubble, but there'll be more room between it and the outer walls than in that whole bedroom behind us," he said. A glance over his shoulder allowed him to spot what she now held in her hands. "Good! You found them. Put the mirror on the threshold of the first-to-second door, leaving it open. It'll form a lake which will suck the magical energies out of the air. That'll take care of my evil twins' attacks, and blunt the attacks of your triplets. The comb has to be dropped the moment the twins appear, when I jump back from the second-to-third doorway. That'll put up a tough bramble thicket between us and the lead member of your triplets."

Myal peered into the first of the three rooms, though like her partner, she didn't yet enter. They were largish, about twenty feet by thirty. Plenty of room for a fight, or a magic-made pond. "And the ring?"

"Set it on the floor behind you before you lay down the comb. Then pick it up and throw it at each twin or triplet in turn—mine first, then whichever of yours makes it through the first barrier. Probably the lake one behind us," he said. "It will bind them and render them instantly helpless the moment it hits, at which point we can kill our alternate selves. But we'll have to move quickly and be ready to re-cast the ring. I've seen you in action, and I'd rather not have to fight you directly, even if it's only an evil version of you."

"Same here," Myal murmured, letting her respect show in her eyes. "You've proven you're a top adventurer. As good as I am, and the others."

Kerric grimaced. "I cheated. I have all the shortcuts and right answers memorized."

Lifting her hand, she tapped him lightly on the nose. Just the once, to get his attention. Smiling slightly, she explained herself. "I speak of *execution*, not just knowledge. You can say 'roll under the first volley of spears, and leap over the second wave, then kick down the door, all within five seconds' but to actually *do* so takes skill and steady nerves. You are a true adventurer, Kerric Vo Mos. I, Myal the Mendhite, say so."

Tapping him on the nose again, she leaned down and kissed him on the lips. He returned it, then sighed. "Alright, so I'm an adventurer. One with a very short and very private, non-scrycasted career, since I've learned enough on this one trip that I do *not* want to have to do this again—Seraglio segment with safety features reinstalled not withstanding, of course. Ready with the enchanted items?"

She nodded, then winced. Her head was beginning to throb. Reaching up behind her head, she pressed on her tattoo again, shutting it off. "Hopefully that's the last time I'll have to do that."

"Hopefully, yes," Kerric agreed. One last, quick kiss on her cheek for good luck, and he led the way into the last of the traps.

THIRTEEN

The first thing she did was peer warily through the door. The Fountain Hall shimmered with swirling, pearlescent green energies, making it difficult to tell what sorts of stone lined the chamber, other than several of them. Sizzling noises reached her ears, sparking the worry that someone was trying to invade the heart of the Tower besides them. But she saw no one.

The second thing she did was shove the door wide and prop it firmly open with both Kerric's and her backpacks. Once it was secured against shutting, she pulled Kerric partway over the threshold, then checked for outsiders again. Only when she was fairly certain nothing would attack either of them immediately did Myal finish sliding the recumbent form of her lover and friend from the anti-magic corridor into the Fountain Hall. Hand on her sword, pulling the packs away to let the door shut, and tired from the long gauntlet run, she waited for him to recover. There was certainly enough time to take in her surroundings in more than just a few fast, wary glances.

The most spectacular feature was the Fountain itself, though it was hard to see through all the other things in the way. The singularity-point, a tiny rip in reality that allowed magic to stream into their world, was a single bright spot of light not much bigger than a large spark cast from the snapping flames in a campfire. It sat just above floor height, in a specially made basin beneath an odd, arching projection, and below a vast glob of dimly lit sun-crystal shafts acting as a chandelier.

The Fountain was the brightest thing in the room, though there were plenty of other sources. Multihued light spewed forth in all directions from that spark-point, streaming in pastel veils reminiscent of oil on water, or perhaps the flickering hues found in polished opal stones and sunlit rainbow pearls. All of that poured into a bubblelike sphere twice the length of a man in diameter.

Normally the glow of all that energy would have blended into a shimmering white light, but it was all confined behind curved walls of greenish energies. Jade green, mint green, algae pond with a hint of aqua, she didn't know quite what to call it, other than that the various intensities cycled through in a soothing ripple of color. Those energy-walls also bulged slightly, like soap bubble films blown upon by an unseen wind. They clung to the columns, to white lines in the floor and to equally arched ribs in the vaulted ceiling, as if sails caught in an unseen, unfelt breeze.

Or rather, they clung to the outermost and middle layers of three concentric rings of columns. The innermost ring had curved but vertically straight walls filled with a gauzelike mesh of silvery, cobweb-thin filaments. On that mesh, images from hundreds upon hundreds of scrying mirrors were flickering, many of them familiar from her years of running Tower gauntlets.

The basin holding the Fountain bubble had been built up out of black marble, forming a sort of stair-step platform about shin-high to her. From one edge, a strange armlike structure jutted up and out, following the curve of the singularity-field. It formed a black stone projection more akin to a faucet pipe than a pedestal, a faucet tipped with a long-stemmed, narrow-cupped goblet. It took her a few moments to realize the "cup" had an uneven rim. It took her a few more to realize that it actually formed a sort of high-mounted chair.

Myal stared at it, frowned, then tilted her head, gauging the size of the thing and its distance from the bubble-sphere. If she wasn't mistaken, that chair seat was positioned at just the right distance to dangle a mage's feet into the top of the bubble, when those feet weren't resting on the stirruplike supports. From the look of it, with the short edge of the rim twisted to face the curved arm, it probably swiveled in a full circle.

This truly was the control-center for the Tower. The Master—or Mistress—would simply climb the somewhat stepped support arm, sit in the chair, and swivel it to face whatever projected scrying image he or she wanted to cast out to the many patrons awaiting their doses of entertainment. Not that she'd ever climb those steps; she wasn't a mage, and held no pretentions of being able to tap into that much power, never mind actually control it.

The floor was marble, as were the columns, and the ceiling as well, but no type of marble she had seen before. Where the walls and columns were pure white, and the ceiling pure black, the floor was different. Somehow, the normal striations, veins, and veils found in marble had been controlled, corraled, and recrafted into new shapes. The base color for the columns was white, but the polished floor underfoot was not.

It *looked* like it was intricately inlaid in swirls, curves, and lines, some black, some blue, some green, or cream, or white. There were golden bits and brown bits and pink as well. Every possible hue of marble was represented at some point, in triangles, rectangles, ovals, circles, squares. Spirals and undulations, arrows and loops. But the longer Myal stared at the floor, the more puzzled she grew. Finally, she crouched and fingered the dividing line between two colors, a bit of black and a bit of gold.

Nothing. No seam. It was one continuous piece of solid stone. Myal knew very little about stonework; she knew how to bash through it with her tattoos if needed, but not how to sculpt it, and definitely not how to tint it.

"Mmm . . . I take it we're safe?" Kerric murmured, capturing her attention. Myal twisted to look over her shoulder, still crouched on the ground. He smiled sleepily up at her, lying on his back and looking too cute—silly helmet notwithstanding—for words.

"Yes. As far as I can tell," she added, speaking quietly. The energies from the Fountain continued to sizzle, as did the shields.

"Mm. Good. Do me a favor?" Kerric asked, peering up at her. "Back up about three paces . . . and shift about one and a half to your left? That's the only thing I could think of which would improve my view."

Back up three paces and shift over . . . Oh. Blushing, Myal pushed to her feet. She did her best to frown down at him, though once again his sense of humor was threatening to make her laugh. "I'm not here to position myself just right for you to look up my armored skirt. *This* time," she added tartly, though she was amused by his audacity. "If you want there to be a *different* sort of time, you'll have to get up and reclaim your throne."

Gesturing off at the arch-suspended seat-thing with one hand, she planted the other on her hip in a no-nonsense way. Sighing, Kerric heaved himself over and up onto his knees. The move made him groan a little. He rested there for a few moments, letting all that shifting blood resettle into the new position, breathing deeply to control the impending associated headache. Once he was sure his skull wouldn't split open from a head-rush effect, he pushed to his feet.

"Well. The Gods are on our side. We're the first ones in here," he murmured, glancing around the pleasantly empty Fountain Hall. "Good."

"So how do you reclaim it?" Myal asked, curious. She kept her eyes roving around the edges of the broad, round chamber, not sure how long they'd stay alone in here. Too many hours spent looking for and dodging dangers, enemies, and lethal threats had her feeling a bit paranoid, and not without undue cause.

"Each Fountain has a unique . . . tone to its magics, for lack of a better explanation," Kerric told her, still working on recovering from the anti-magic corridor. "To master the Fountain is not to make it change itself to suit you, but rather to shape yourself to match it. Once a mage is accepted into the Fountain's energies, *then* he or she can influence its behaviors, subtly altering its tone. But left alone, the Fountain reverts to its true nature. So. I attune myself to each layer of defense, then step in through the screen gate over there," he stated, nodding at a column that was actually a slender archway with a mesh door in it, giving access to the innermost section. "Climb up, attune myself to the Fountain itself, and there you have it. The Tower has a Master again."

"Well, get to it," Myal directed him. "I don't trust that Torven fellow to stay away at this point. They say that in all the adventure stories in the Great Library, the hero only narrowly saves the day. I don't want him to show up and attack while you're only halfway through because you were somehow delayed. So go save it."

Squinting a little, Kerric eyed the reversed, curved images on one part of the projection mesh. He smirked. "If those scrying spells are right, Torven and company are busy dealing with Pookie the Giant Polka-Dotted Elephant. If they are, then it looks like they wandered off course when we smashed the maintenance tablet and concealed our presence from being tracked. But you're right. I've been away from my work for long enough."

Removing his helmet, he dropped it on the floor, gave his scalp one last, semi-satisfying scrub with his fingernails, then shed a few more layers of armor. When he was ready, Kerric walked up to the shields. They crackled with a lethal amount of energy, but that didn't matter. He wasn't going to force his way through.

"Guard me, just in case," he told Myal over his shoulder. "I'll need all my concentration for this."

Nodding, she drew her sword and started studying the room in earnest. She moved a little as she did so, both to provide herself with full fields of view around columns and to keep her tired body awake and moving, but didn't move far from his position. Satisfied he would be well-protected, Kerric returned his gaze to the barrier. The trick to getting through wasn't brute force; it was cooperation. Harmony.

All he had to do was find the frequency thrumming beneath everything, and match his own inner vibrations to that peculiar not-quite-a-note that was the Fountain's resonance. A mage could be tone-deaf and still be good at shaping and casting magic, but a Guardian had to be more. Thankfully, the purity of those shields' green hue told him that any influences imbued into the energies by the interloper had long since faded. He wouldn't have to try to match any other mage's powers. His task would have been nigh impossible if another powerful mage had gotten in here and attuned him- or herself first.

For almost ten years, Kerric had worked with these magics. Studied them. Molded his inner energies to vibrate along similar lines. Altering his normally golden-hued aura to something green was easier than a lesser mage might think . . . but then Myal didn't think about how she drew, swung, or sheathed that sword she wore. Not anymore. Not because she was just that good, but because being that good came with a lot of practice. With the ease of a lot of practice himself, Kerric altered his inner tone and pressed into the barrier, meshing and merging with it

When fully attuned to the Fountain, his aura affected it in turn, changing it from a bright aqua jade to a deeper forest hue. This was something similar, save that he altered himself first, suppressing and squeezing his own energies into the right shape. Like trying to describe a chord played on crystal bells, words couldn't define what he did; he just did it, played himself like a handful of familiar chimes. It only took him a minute to stretch far enough for the right effect. A single step brought him physically up to the barrier; a second stepped him through unharmed.

Tired, but unharmed. It took effort to match such complex frequencies, particularly without the use of a chime forged in the heart of the Fountain to help attune his mind via his ear. But he got through.

Myal's soft sigh of relief at his safe passage almost distracted him. Setting aside thoughts of her, ignoring the sight and sound of her, Kerric continued to the next layer. Keeping the purity of his purpose as Master of the Tower uppermost in his thoughts, to guard the singularity, to not abuse its power, to not harm the world itself with the power he was about to command, he passed through that layer as well. Pushed through it, rather; this layer had a physical component as well, one which clung to his unarmored body. More of his inner energy drained away. He staggered on the far side, then recovered, squaring his shoulders.

The third layer of protection was a simple locking mechanism on the mesh door. He might have discarded his armor, leaving him in his scuffed leather boots and sweaty, grimy padded tunic and calf-length trousers, but he hadn't discarded his lock-picking tools. Pulling them out of the pocket of his pants, he worked on the latch, swung the panel open, and stepped inside. Turning to shut it was merely a habit of tidiness; by this point, between the outer protections and Myal's fierce abilities, no one would be able to get in here to challenge him fast enough.

He didn't climb the slanted pedestal, however. Instead, he stepped up to the knee-high wall, sat on the edge, and swung his legs over. Energy washed up over his skin, blinding his inner senses in that first shock wave of power, like how the chill of a swimming pond shocked the outer senses. Part of it revived him, but more of it taxed him, like trying to fight a strong river current with his mind. Pushing off from the black marble edge, he jumped into the sphere.

Energy instantly reached up to grab him, floating him in pure magic. Locks fluttering in the not-wind stirred by the spewing energies, Kerric emptied himself of all thoughts, all notions, all sensations. He embraced the peculiar chiming energies of the singularity, let it all wash through him, absorbed into every pore, every muscle, every bone. The moment he was one with the outer energies, he opened his eyes and drifted toward that spark.

Shifting his hand forward, he touched it. The power at the source-point was a thousand times worse than the outer shield walls and a hundred times stronger than the bubble-sphere. But like those shields, it was a familiar power. He remembered it very well, and in its own limited, unthinking way, it remembered him. So what took him a minute to attune to outside the outermost ring now took him only a few seconds to do here in the heart of pure power. The moment he did attune, the coruscating energies refreshed and revived him as nothing else could, outside of maybe a fine meal and a great night's sleep.

On the far side of that outermost shield, Myal strove to keep one eye on the rest of the Fountain Hall, doing her duty in the face of her rampant curiosity. Seeing Kerric jump into that bubble-thing worried her; the sheer amount of magic it took to run all the traps, tricks, monsters and illusions of the Tower would surely turn any lesser man to ash, or an unprepared man. But within moments of him swimming into its waterless depths, the mint-green spark at the very center flared against his fingertip, the bubble pulsed into a darker shade of forest, and the aqua green shields vanished as if made of roiling steam from a kettle taken away from a fire.

To her surprise, he didn't climb back out. Instead, he floated up out of the sphere. The chair-seat swiveled without being touched, and Kerric turned and floated back and down, settling into place. For a moment, his feet continued to dangle inside the bubble, then he lifted them up onto the footrests. Even from several yards away and through a misty screen of shifting images, she could see his chest rise and fall with a deep breath, see the slumping of his shoulders and arms against the side-rests of his odd chair.

"Kerric?" she called out carefully. "Is it safe to approach?"

". . . Hm? Oh, yes."

Flicking his hand, he opened the mesh door with a spell. The final two traps were that the gate had to be opened without magic, and the seat claimed without touching the pedestal supporting it. Either would kill the unwary. Not because they were part of the original protection system, but because they were two traps he himself had laid before heading out of the area to go shopping in Sendale. Dismissing those spells with a second flick of his hand, he nodded politely to her.

"I think I'll just get everyone out of the Tower, then shut it down while I go through the Topside Control staff and truth-spell them for loyalty, then have them truth-spell everyone *else* in the various layers of Maintenance for loyalty. The Tower will have to remain off the scrycasting channels until I know we haven't any more adders hidden in our midst like that Torven rat . . . who is managing to survive rather well despite the ferocity of the Pookie scenario spells." He gestured at the mesh screens, enlarging one of the images with a practiced, wordless bit of power.

Myal glanced that way as she ducked through the arch-pierced column. Not that she would hit her head on its lintel, but it did feel a bit low compared to the high ceiling around them. Sure enough, Torven and company were battered, bloody, and besting the giant, enraged, long-nosed creature. She shook her head. "I don't know what could kill him, given the luck he's displayed."

"True. And until the Fountainways can be reopened for business, I cannot exile him anywhere far, far away." Rubbing at his chin, he thought a moment on what to do with them, tapped his lips as he sorted and discarded possibilities, then dipped his boots back into the sphere and flicked out his finger.

Torven, Barric, and the rest swirled up into the ceiling with startled yells. Not that Kerric or Myal could hear them yelling, since the sound spells weren't activated, but they watched the quintet hollering with wide mouths and wider eyes, flung this way and that through the suction chutes, until they landed in a completely white, completely blank, brightly lit chamber. Nodding in satisfaction, Kerric swept his hand to the side, shifting the view of the brightly lit, utterly empty room and its captives away from the center of his attention, and called up three new images, enlarging them in a vertical row.

The bottom image was of a middle-aged male with blond hair and shadows under his blue gray eyes. The middle image was a fresher-faced, deeply tanned man with a black moustache and close-cropped black hair, and the top image the very tired-looking Jessina, his lead controller.

"Wake up!" Kerric stated heartily, flashing the startled trio a smile. "Good morning, Tower Maintenance. Kerric Vo Mos is back in the house, and the Tower is once more firmly under my control.

"Oh, thank the Gods!" Jessina breathed, her smile so big, it was almost enough to overlook the tears of weariness in her eyes. Brennan looked like he was so relieved, he was going to faint, while the fresh-faced fellow, a mage named Caros, simply grinned and nodded several times. It should have been Heral at this hour, but undoubtedly he had stayed up extra-late, which meant Caros was now covering for him. Base Maintenance was one of the few locations the employees of the Tower could get to relatively safely. The same could not be said for the other two locations.

Kerric didn't let them speak. Holding up his hand, he silenced what Jessina was going to say. "First priority, I want to see the senior-most in all three Maintenance sections up here for a mandatory Truth Stoning. Now, I've worked with all of you for years, and I trust all of you with the running of the Tower . . . but one of our recent Maintenance mage recruits decided to use a map tablet to try to find his way to the heart of the Tower and take it over by guile, stealth, and force.

"That means you have to undergo trial by truth-spell so that when you apply it to everyone *else* who works for the Tower, you can honestly say I'm requiring it of everyone, period. I don't want to wake up tomorrow morning having to do this manure pile of an obstacle course all over again just because that mage has accomplices I didn't know about," Kerric stated dryly. "Once you've undergone the test, then we will open up all the mirror-Gates in all the rooms and halls with people in them so that they exit directly out of the base of the Tower. Third priority, getting those people the food and healing attention they may need, and compensating them for the discomfort of being stuck in the Tower for however many hours it's been."

"Eighteen," Jessina told him quickly. "We've all been stuck in here for just over eighteen hours and two minutes."

"Good. Caros, contact the Adventuring Hall exchequers and have them compensate everyone, worker and adventurer alike, for . . . ten gold per hour?" Kerric glanced at Myal. "You think that's a fair amount?"

She nodded. "That sounds fair."

"Good. Once everyone has been 'sent home,' so to speak, you and the other senior leads will start interrogating maintenance personnel. Hopefully there won't be any conflicting loyalties about who they work for, how they use the tablets, and what information they'll give to outsiders. If there are, however, knock them unconscious, lock them in a White Room, and search their homes, lockers, and belongings for maintenance tablets, maps of the Tower, and any other information which could be used to disrupt the smooth running of this business."

He gave his mirror-linked leaders a stern, sober look, ready to silence protests. Thankfully, they did not arise. This was not a city or a region subject to an outside king. The Master of the Tower was also the Master of the Adventuring Hall, the Master of Penambrion, and the Master of the outlying farms as well. He wasn't a king in a traditional sense and he wouldn't have taken on the title, the responsibility, or the trappings of a traditional king, but Kerric's commands were as good as law when he chose to exercise his powers locally.

The deadly dangers of an un-Mastered Tower had just reminded them why he had that kind of power and authority. Not to wield all those dangers against others, but to keep it from being wielded.

Most of the time, he was content to let the region be governed by a council of the Maintenance leads, the mayor and his burgher, selected members of the various farming and crafting guilds, so on and so forth. This was not one of those moments. A flick of his hand activated the Gateways embedded in every threshold. "Jessina, bring a Truth Stone from Topside. The sooner we get this over with, the sooner we can get back to scrycasting and earning all that income we've been losing. Brennan, contact the creativity teams at the Adventuring Halls and have them start thinking of ways to make up all the lost scrying time for our patrons."

"They're already on it," Brennan reassured him. "As soon as we realized that a hostile takeover was in effect and that a shutdown was possible, I directed my daughter Menissa to start thinking of ways to make up for the lost time."

"Good. I'll see you up here within a few minutes. The sooner we can get everyone truth-tested, the sooner we can clean up the Tower and reopen it for business. Jessina, you want to handle the evacuation announcement?" Kerric asked her. "You have such a lovely, reassuring voice for it."

"Of course. I'll be up there in forty seconds," she promised, shifting as she fetched something below her scrying mirror's field of view. "I'll go first, and bring Bradell up with me. I could use some sleep, but between the two of us, we'll get everyone currently in Topside tested before they'll be let go. Jessina out."

The others murmured their own excuses. Kerric nodded and put his feet back up on the resting bars. A wave of his hand collapsed the mirror-views being projected around him. Glancing at Myal, he found her eyeing the Fountain pool and its bubble warily. ". . . What's on your mind?"

"Does it hurt?" she asked him, lifting her gaze to his. "All that magic pulsing through your body?"

"Like plunging into a cold bath. Once you get past the shock of it, you get used to it," he reassured her. "I truly expect this truth-scrying to be a formality. These are men and women I've worked with and trusted for years," Kerric added in an aside. "They've had ample opportunity to betray me, to mess things up, even to seize control. A good half dozen of the strongest ones could've stayed in here and taken over once everything shut down, but they didn't.

"Unfortunately, the Tower employs a couple hundred people. Not everyone can be personally vouched for through years of loyal service in the face of opportunity," he finished.

Myal nodded. "This shouldn't take long, though. Would you like me to take a Truth Stone oath as well?"

He smiled, one corner of his mouth twitching up higher than the other. "You're like Jessina. I know you wouldn't betray me. Unfortunately, that's not the point . . . and you do bring up a good point. I *should* have all the adventurers tested as well. But if I did that, it might be bad for business. After all, part of the point *is* to brave the hazards of the Tower to get to the treasures hidden deep within. Of which, this is the biggest prize."

"The biggest prize, yes." Jessina's voice rang out, echoing across the hall. She had emerged from an alcove-shaped depression not far from the hidden door Myal and Kerric had used. "But not exactly a portable one. Most adventurers come here to make their fortune and *leave* with said fortune. The Fountain, praise the Gods, is not at all portable. Hello, Myal," the darker-skinned woman added in greeting, smiling at the tall Mendhite. "I don't know what tricks and traps you had to put up with to get Master Kerric here, but I thank you deeply for your efforts.

"Nothing personal, Myal," she added, before turning to Kerric, "but will you test her to make sure she won't sell the secrets she knows of how to get in here?"

"I'll do so freely," Myal stated, holding out her hand for the white marble disk in Jessina's grip. Sensing Kerric was about to speak, she shook her head as she looked his way. "Don't protest, Kerric. It's a completely valid concern. One which I am happy to allay." Accepting the Stone from the other woman, Myal gripped it. "My name is Jessina."

Black fingerprints outlined the lie. She waited for the marks from her fingers to fade, then gripped the rounded white disc once more.

"I will *not* tell anyone else the full details of the correct path to the heart of the Tower and its Fountain Hall, nor write about it in full, nor reveal the full sequence of events in any shape or way," she stated. A touch of humor quirked up the corner of her mouth. "Though I reserve the right to joke about some of the more amusing details, such as the Hairy Naked Thing."

A flash of the Stone showed it pristine white. Jessina nodded in approval; behind the other woman, the other two men appeared from similar alcoves. More would arrive soon. Myal didn't relinquish the Stone immediately, as she did have one more thing to add.

"I have one request. I would like to write a heavily *edited* account of our passage to the heart, with the understanding it will be heavily censored for content by Master Kerric and his topmost trusted staff, and only cover a few of the traps we met. But Herding Cats and the Battle for the Banqueting Hall are too amusing not to share . . . and I think too harmless to be denied. But that is my opinion. I will let the decision rest in your collective hands," she finished, finally handing the all-white Stone back to Jessina.

Brows lifting, the older woman considered Myal's request, then shrugged. "I've read some of the Mendhite's little booklets. They're entertaining, popular, *and* heavily edited. She hasn't covered more than a quarter at most of the traps she's run through. I think it's safe enough."

"What, Myal the Mendhite?" Caros asked, reaching their

side. He stuck out his hand, offering it to Myal. "If she wants to write an edited account of what happened while we were all offline, that would be fantastic! Master Kerric, I'd strongly suggest getting this little . . . er, this *big* lady under contract. The exchequer is already demanding to know if we got any footage of your run through the Tower. They said they've had a tonne of requests for it, and that if we can provide them with a scrying of the Master of the Tower running the gauntlets, they'll pay five and ten and *more* times the going price.

"I know the Adventuring Hall tried their best to block out news of what you were doing, but obviously the rumors ran wild, and *everyone* wants to buy a scrycasting of you in action," Caros added. He shrugged and scratched at his mustache. "But since we *don't* have any active scryings from the blackout period, and we wouldn't *want* a scrying to get loose, one of Myal's booklets will probably sell *huge* if she covers a tiny fraction of it in text. Not just here around the Tower and in the closest kingdoms, but I think with our patrons all the way around the world as well."

"That does make sense," Jessina agreed. She half laughed to herself a moment later as Brennan finished his own approach, trailed by two more, who emerged through the alcove-Gates. "We might even start a new fashion in Senod-Gra, the 'sinful' vice of *reading* for pleasure."

Myal choked on a hastily smothered laugh. Despite the fact that Senod-Gra stood more or less on the far side of the vast sphere that was the world, everyone associated with the Tower had heard of the City of Delights and its many, many vices. Reading was not considered to be one of them.

"I'll consider it. I'd write it myself, but I'll concede my literary skills are more technical than narrative in nature," Kerric admitted. He lifted his chin at the stone disc in Jessina's hand. More people were arriving, making the transition through the hidden

Gateway links. Most of them looked as tired as the trio of Maintenance leads did, though one of the Middle Maintenance seniors, Heral, looked literally as if he had been awakened mid-sleep, for he wore only a pair of loose trousers for clothing, and was still yawning mightily behind his hand. "Alright. Start stating where your loyalties lie."

Mindful of her lowly place as a mere adventurer, Myal moved back as the dozen or so people came forward. She didn't leave—it wasn't as if she *could*—but she did give the others some respectful distance. Recommended or not, she wasn't yet a part of the Tower staff, and this was clearly a top management staff meeting. As she sat on a blue-colored bit of the floor, Myal noticed an occasional searching look from Kerric, seeking her exact location as if seeking reassurance she was still there. Seeing him do so every once in a while kept her from feeling forgotten.

Those little looks gave her a warm spark of her own to hug deep inside her chest while she waited. It was no Fountain-style singularity, empowered with enough magic to have been shared out across a thousand lives, but it did warm her spirits and empower her sense of hope for her personal future. No spoken promises, just a few implied and several unspoken ones, but they were enough to keep her patient.

"And your City's patience has been deeply appreciated during our little maintenance and scrycasting difficulties," Kerric repeated as smoothly as he could without sounding either unctuous or impatient. From this seat, it looked like he was connecting the scrying from within a book-lined room, as a point of discretion to protect the true nature of the Fountain Hall, as all such calls were screened. A similar spell had been set up for Guardian Keleseth to use in far-off Senod-Gra. "As I said, we're quite happy to credit hour per hour of lost viewing time toward your next bill, Guardian, but I cannot issue a refund at this time."

"It's been almost nineteen hours, Guardian Kerric," Guardian Keleseth groused, her wrinkled brow furrowing deeper as she scowled. "Just refund us nineteen hours' worth and start shipping out the next 'casts!"

It was a good thing his toes weren't dangling in the singularity-bubble underneath his seat. Rubbing his forehead, Kerric exercised some mental patience to keep from scowling back at her, and to keep his tone from being snappish. "As much as I would love to do that, Guardian, I am unable to at this point in time. We've restored power, but we still have to do a full sweep of the Tower to fix various issues that were affected by the outage. Then we have to finish reworking the scheduled gauntlets, *and* the Tower scrycasts have to be restarted by the Guardian.

"That would be me, and that would require me to be at my full strength. Since I *personally* had to attend to the problem, my reserves are a little low. Senod-Gra will just have to wait until I've had a chance to eat and sleep—you can distract your people by laying bets on exactly how long it'll take for the first scrycasts to resume, and which gauntlets will remain the same and which will have been replaced."

Seeing her draw in a breath to argue the point, Kerric held up his hand in a curt gesture, cutting her off. His patience was almost at an end.

"*Please*, Hostess," he added, addressing her by her formal title. "Your account has been our biggest and best customer for hundreds of years, yes, but you are *not* our only customer. You can make requests on which gauntlets your people would like to see, and we have been good suppliers by doing our best to fulfill those requests, but you do *not* control the Tower. You are *not* in charge, and you can turn yourself blue from lack of breath in protest, but that will *not* speed up the delivery of the next scrycasting. Have a good whatever-time-of-day it is out there, and I'll contact you when I *officially* can tell you the moment the 'casts will resume."

A slash of his hand, a pulse of will-backed power, and her image vanished. He traced a trio of runes in the air and pushed it toward the mesh, ensuring that any further attempts at communication would go into a series of recording crystals for later viewing. Slumping back in his seat, Kerric rubbed his forehead again, then his temples. Off to his left, the image of Jessina's face—back at her desk in Topside Control—gave him a wry look.

"Not exactly the most diplomatic of endings, there," she murmured, "but at least *you* can get away with doing that. If I tried, you would not only get the original arguments, but a diatribe on uppity underlings as well."

"I know. I also know that I am done for the day. I am done with contacting these people. I am done dealing with problems, and I am *done* working. Set up a standard 'Please wait while we perform maintenance on the Tower; your patience is appreciated' message as an automagic response to all incoming calls, and then . . ." He sought for something tactful to say, and gave up with a shrug. "Well, unless the Tower is melting, or on fire, or crumbling to pieces, *don't* call me. I'm going to go eat, and sleep, and excrete, and who knows what else that rhymes with those three 'eet' things, and I'll be doing them for the next several hours. Try to get some rest, yourself."

"All we've been doing is resting. Well, resting and worrying. Now that power has been restored and our biggest clients reassured, we can manage the smaller details for you," his senior-most lead reassured him in that unflappable way of hers. "I took the liberty of ordering food prepared for everyone, including several dishes sent to your quarters. Will Myal be joining you for a meal? There should be enough for her as well."

He glanced at his gauntlet partner, who had settled on the floor at the base of one of the innermost columns to rest. At the sound of her name, she glanced over at Jessina's image, then looked up at him. Kerric, catching her interested gaze, nodded. "Yes, I do believe she will be."

"Then I shall wish you a good rest," Jessina stated. "Enough was sent under stasis domes just a few minutes ago to feed around five or six people, from what the Tower kitchen staff said. They grew bored during the lockdown and started experimenting with new recipes, and have sent a couple variations of each final dish for your approval."

Kerric bowed slightly, pleased that not everyone had spent the time during lockdown worrying or fretting or bored out of their minds. "Thank you. Remind me to raise your overtime bonus for going the extra mile . . . and the kitchen staff's bonus, for being productive in spite of the lockdown. Goodnight, Jessina."

She smiled. "Good day, Master Kerric."

A spiraling slash of his finger ended the link. A second one dimmed all the images on the screen, leaving behind rectangular and oval frameless views of various rooms, corridors, and one still brightly lit room filled with five disgruntled would-be thieves. Kerric started to spin the chair around, then turned it back, dipped in his toes, and opened a connection to a small closetlike room with a sink, a vending cabinet stocked with dried meats, crackers, and the like, and a toilet.

He watched the smallest woman, the one with the thick accent, look up, jump to her feet, and gingerly test the door. When it proved to be a simplified refreshing room, her shoulders slumped and she returned to the others. They were still prisoners of the Tower, and would remain so until Kerric, Master of the Tower, decided what to do with them.

Right now, he had far more pleasant thoughts on his mind.

Spinning his chair around, he walked down the now-trap-free ramp and headed over to Myal. He reached her just as she pushed to her feet. "Ready for a meal almost as good as the Banqueting Hall? And I say 'almost' because there won't be quite as much variety, but it'll be equal in quality. Far better than what you've been eating at the Honey Spear."

Myal nodded. She was tired, her backside hurt from sitting on the hard marble floor, and she wanted a bath, but the mere mention of food made her stomach rumble, protesting the delay of its implicit delivery. "Where are we going now?"

"My personal quarters. You are invited to dine with me, relax with me . . . bathe with me, so we can help each other get those hard-to-reach spots," he added lightly, "and sleep with me. And possibly at some point make love again with me . . . if that is your desire."

She blushed and ducked her head at the blatant invitation in his tone as well as his words, but nodded. "Yes." Catching his hand, Myal twined her fingers with his. "Please."

FOURTEEN

The grin he gave her was brighter than the White Room. Myal found herself tugged through the mesh door and toward one of the many alcoves lining the edges of the room.

"There aren't many physical doors into this place, but there are plenty of doorway-Gates, and they're all functioning. If you'd like to keep visiting me—and I hope you will, as I cannot remember enjoying a woman's company as much as I have yours," Kerric added over his shoulder, "then I'll see that you're attuned to the exterior ground-level door that leads to Topside Control, and from there, the doorway that leads to my quarters. There's a physical path, too, but mostly we just use the Gates."

"Is the physical path trapped?" Myal asked him, curious. They detoured to pick up their discarded bags and armor. She had removed hers while waiting for him to finish the most urgent pieces of business, and now hoped that wherever they were going, it would include a hot bath as well as a hot meal.

"Yes, and for good reason," Kerric told her. "It wouldn't do for anyone to have an easy path to assassinate the Tower Guardians in their sleep, after all." He pointed at specific triangles from among the colored marbles underfoot, one each per alcove, then reclaimed her hand in his. "Black leads to Base Control, that medium gray leads to Middle Control, the white leads to Topside Control . . . and this pale blue triangle here leads to my quarters. Since you're with me, holding my hand, you'll be passed through the Gate. If you choose to leave without me, you'll be automagically deposited in one of the external alcoves at the base of the Tower—all exits from the control centers do that for unauthorized personnel under normal operating conditions."

"I don't see a hallway or a door in the alcove," Myal said, peering at the curved recess in the white marble surface. "Aren't I supposed to?"

"Nope." Tugging her into the shallow alcove, he vanished beyond the wall. There was no resistance, no hitting a wall, and no tingling or burning or chilling sensations, since all the Gate-frames were spaced so close together. She also didn't actually hit the wall. An arm's length from reaching the back of the alcove, the view changed.

The hallway on the other side of the hidden transfer point was dimly lit, though that didn't last long, In response to their presence, the suncrystals slowly brightened, so that by the time they emerged in the large sitting room at the end of the passage, their eyes had time to adjust to the bright sunlight streaming in through the huge, crystal-glazed windows covering one wall of the large room. Overstuffed seats, elegantly carved tables, and artwork from a hundred cultures decorated the walls.

Kerric released her hand and gestured at the paintings, scrolls, carvings, masks, weapons, and so forth hung on his walls. "A lot of this is a legacy from past Guardians—go ahead and set your things down anywhere," he added in invitation. He dumped his overstuffed pack of armor and adventuring gear next to one of the couches. She dropped hers next to it as he continued to speak, introducing her to his home. "Almost all the furniture is provided by the previous owner, though the retiring Guardians do sometimes take a few items when they retire. And I can swap out something if I prefer. Like a really big bed. I like to sprawl when I sleep, just to warn you."

"As do I," Myal admitted. "Though I had to get my bed custom-made, just to be long enough for me."

"I don't think you'll be disappointed by the size of my bed if you choose to stay overnight. Well, technically into the afternoon. It's about noon now," he added, squinting at the sunlight. "Four hours from when the scrycasts cut off to when sunset happened—most of it spent researching for a qualified partner— eight or so hours of fighting our way through traps in the night, another six hours tramping around in the daytime until we finally got to the heart . . . yeah, about eighteen." Sighing, Kerric spread out his arms, stretching his back as well as his limbs. "Gods, it's *good* to be home again."

"I wouldn't know yet," Myal quipped dryly. And then flushed as he dropped his arms and turned to look at her. The mood between them soured a little, making her regret she had said it. "I didn't mean . . ."

Rubbing at the back of his neck, Kerric waved off her awkward apology. "I know what you meant. You've been away from your own refuge from the world a bit too long as well. Would you rather head back to your place? I could open a mirror-Gate to your front door if you'd like, so you don't have to walk all the way home."

She bit her bottom lip, wondering how to word her reply. Slowly, Myal stated, "What I would like . . . is to eat a fine meal with you, and see the rest of your home, and . . . and see it through *your* eyes. To then have a chance at some point soon to show you my home, for more than a single conversation, to show you it through *my* eyes. And . . . to see what each home has in common. To also see what we can learn from each other."

The mood wasn't broken anymore. Kerric felt relief that it had been merely slowed. Nodding, he walked back to her side and clasped her hand. "That much, I can do right now. The food, I mean; the rest will take time. This way. I don't cook, so I don't actually *use* the kitchen—one of the privileges of power is being able to order someone *else* to cook my meals—but I do tend to eat at the breakfasting table in there."

Myal gave him a bemused look. She had thought she'd learned more than enough about Aian ways in her five years here, but this was a new thing. "An entire table just for breaking one's fast? Is it illegal to use it for lunch, or supper?"

Kerric laughed. "No, I think it's just that breakfast is considered casual, merely for family, and supper is when you formally invite guests over for a meal. So the table for breakfast is smaller and often in worse condition, because no one needs to impress their own immediate family. But as it's usually just me, why dirty a big fancy table?"

"Why haven't I heard of this Aian custom before?" Myal asked him.

He answered as he led her down a corridor, bypassing a room with a large, fancy table indeed. Myal had an impression of dark wood with an intricately carved edge, matching high-backed chairs with cream cushions, and an ornate suncrystal chandelier before he led her into the bright, homey, clean kitchen. "It's not an Aian custom, so much as it's a semi-wealthy family custom. The very wealthy always dine formally with great care for their manners and their surroundings, and the modestly wealthy down through the poor often only have the one table for eating.

"Penambrion hasn't many of the truly poor; most people are modestly wealthy, since most work for the Tower. Of the adventurers, those that make enough money to be wealthy usually leave to go live rich lives elsewhere, and most of those who stay usually follow the lives they lived before coming to the Tower to make their fortune," he stated, guiding her to the breakfast table, which sat in a sunlit, window-filled nook. It was old and scratched, and cluttered with dome-covered dishes, but the sanded oak planks were otherwise clean beneath their waiting meal. "The farmers have the least security, since they're at the mercy of the weather, but most years they do reasonably well."

"Yes, I've helped with their flooding fund," Myal admitted. The bright smile he gave her at that bit of news warmed her down to her toes. She resolved to keep supporting his farmers. Their farmers, since Penambrion was now her home, and had been for the last few years.

Courteously assisting her into one of the chairs on either side, Kerric seated himself across from her, passed out two plates from a stack and some cutlery, and began removing lids. "Roast beef, peppered squash . . . steamed *kaoli* greens, buttered onions and green beans, all valley-grown . . . and I'm not sure what this is. Something in a pastry wrapper."

Myal leaned over the bared plate, sniffed at the little cylinder-shaped wraps, finally broke one open between her fingers to examine the steaming contents, and grinned. "Egg rolls. They're a bit small, which is why I wasn't sure. We make them back home with cabbage and other vegetables, sometimes with meat, and the wrapper is brushed inside with scrambled egg before they're folded and fried—this smells like chicken, and cabbage, and slivers of mushrooms. Most visitors in Mendhi love it . . . unlike *hagas*."

"*Hagas?*" Kerric asked. Most things translated well with the Ultra Tongue potion he had consumed years ago, but certain things did not. All he had was a vague impression of something lumpy in a bed of what looked like multi-hued brown rice. "What's that?"

"Well, first you take a calf's stomach—the fourth one, which is the one you squeeze the rennet out of for making cheese," Myal stated. At the scrunching of his nose in disgust, she grinned. "I know you like cheese, Kerric. But as I was saying, you take the fourth stomach, rinse it and leech it and set aside the liqueur made for cheese making, then you take mushrooms and rice, barley and spices, black beans, peppers, spinach, toasted nuts, and *fatah* cheese—it has a strong flavor and a crumbly texture—and a little sour cream, and you mix it up and stuff it into the stomach, put it in a baking pan, and pack in more of the stuffing mixture around it with some more peppers. Oh, and you also add . . ."

The look of revulsion twisting his face made her trail off into a chuckle. Kerric couldn't blame her for laughing at him, but he couldn't accept that the dish she described was food. "I think I'll have to agree with your visitors to Mendhi. I'll take everything *but* the calf-stomach, if you please."

"But that's what gives it its unique flavor," Myal teased him.

"I like *your* unique flavor, and that's the only unique Mendhite flavor for me," he stated firmly. He did take one of the egg rolls, though. The smells wafting up along with the steam from the one she had broken smelled delicious. Not at all like the *hagas* thing she described—not that Kerric had smelled one, yet, but he could imagine the weirdness of it.

"Are you comparing me to a calf's stomach?" Myal asked him dryly, scooping some squash onto her plate and adding a few slices of the beef.

"Certainly not. The entire calf—no, the entire *herd*," Kerric corrected himself, "couldn't compare to you." He served some vegetables and the steamed greens onto his own plate, then several slices of beef.

She quirked her brows, then chuckled. "I do believe that is the oddest compliment I have ever received. Thank you—for the compliment, not just the uniqueness."

He grinned and cut into his meat. "Then stick around; I get even odder."

As he had guessed she would, she laughed at the absurdity of that. Kerric was beginning to get a feel for what pleased Myal, and that pleased him.

Gently teasing and joking with her—for the more time she spent with him, the more she gave back as good as she got, which pleased him even further—the two finished their meal. Replacing the domed lids to stasis-preserve what they hadn't eaten, he showed her his command of cleaning spells in soaping, scrubbing, rinsing and drying the dishes in just a few minutes, then took Myal on a tour of his home.

Myal enjoyed seeing more than just the kitchen and formal sitting room. The personal library of the Guardians of the Tower, past and present, impressed her beyond words; it was larger than her entire tenement building, and required stairs and ladders to reach all the books and scrolls. Kerric teased her by playfully dragging her out of the room and mock-dabbing at imaginary drool on her chin. She stooped a little and pinched his backside for that, then kissed him. That made them a little late for the tour of the small conservatory, with its broad glazed windows and plethora of flowers. Plucking an orchid no bigger than his thumbnail, he tucked it behind her ear. She gave him a kiss for that, too.

His workshops also impressed her. With the vast energies of the Tower at his disposal, he had clean-burning, spell-fueled forges for metalsmithing, glassmaking, woodworking, even some pottery. The latter puzzled her. Eyeing the clay-stained equipment, Myal glanced at him. "Why pottery? I thought you worked primarily with mirrors."

"The frame a mirror is set in can be just as important as the mirror itself," Kerric told her, warming up to one of his favorite subjects. "Same as the mirror's shape, thickness, clarity, even the components of sand and ash and so forth that go into making it. Pottery frames are heavy and cumbersome, but they provide more stability than wood or metal frames do for Gateway construction. Wood frames dampen some of the shock-waves of the Shattered aether that makes long-distance transportation so difficult these days, but metal is a better stabilizing agent for the actual spell, allowing it to stay open longer with less loss of energy under similar aether conditions. You can't reach as far, but you can hold the Gate open longer.

"You see, I'm getting closer to re-creating the old Portals in a new way that can reach past the ruptures in the world's energies," Kerric added, waxing enthusiastic about his non-Tower work. "The old ones were made out of stone, which is very stable and enduring, but the resonances they work at are along the same span of frequencies as the energies released when the last Convocation of God and Man turned the old capital city of the Aian Empire into a giant crater."

Myal, leaning back against a stained but otherwise empty workbench, lifted her chin. "You know, I don't even think the librarians of the Great Mendham Library know why the old capital exploded, and they gather information from all over the world. Do you know?"

He shrugged and spread his arms. "Even after two centuries, we still don't know what went wrong that day. We *do* know that whatever energy was released, it was a big enough blast to rupture all the great Portals that were standing open, allowing pilgrims from all over the world to travel to the Convocation. Now, this next room on the tour contains what I like to call my thinkshop, as opposed to my workshop.

"I know you Mendhites love the written word," he teased as he clasped her hand and led her toward a pair of double doors on the far side of the room, "but this contains numbers and mathemagical symbols as well as letters, so feel free to be bored."

The angle was very awkward since she had to use her opposite hand, but Myal still managed to swat at that gorgeous rump. Even if it was still clad in stained and sweaty under-armor padding. "Behave. I am capable of understanding a mathemagical formula. I just cannot *use* the magics . . . involved . . ."

Her voice trailed out. The room he led her into was filled with chalkboards scribbled on in dozens of hues of chalk, huge pads of paper bound along the upper edges and perched on easels, walls of that same fine metal mesh from the Fountain Hall, and mirrors. Over half the formulae scribbled on the boards and projected onto the mesh screens were moving. None of the writing on the paper pads moved. Most of the mirrors were blankly passive, reflecting back the scenery around them, but one very large mirror in the distance had the Mendhite adventurer grabbing for her sword. Which she had left in the front room, along with her pack and her armor.

Kerric, noticing her reflexive twitch-and-grab, tensed instinctively in her wake. He searched his think-room for signs of the many dangers they had faced during their long gauntlet run to the heart, and frowned when he spotted the cause. "It's okay," he murmured, reassuring her even as he relaxed a little. Only a little, though. "That's just a special scrying mirror. It's not a doorway onto the traps of the Tower or anything. Though why it's showing scenes of battle . . . I don't . . ."

Leaving Myal to either stay back or follow, Kerric hurried through the half-maze of boards and screens. The closer he got, the more details he could see in the great cheval mirror standing against the back wall. One segment of his research had led him into exploring ways of scrying into the past. Pools of water, specially crafted glass, even trays of personally spilled blood, though blood-magic was always inherently dangerous. If it wasn't the mage's own blood, that weakened the Veil, the barrier between this world and the Netherhells, where demonic creatures roamed, beings of evil made manifest. Only a self-sacrifice countered the negative energies of such a use.

This mirror, however, wasn't designed to scry into the past. It was his greatest triumph, a mirror that scryed into the future. Perhaps it wasn't wise to have bargained with the priests of various Aian deities for some bones from deceased Seers to grind up and use as a stabilizing agent in the crafting of the glass. But his calculations, however morbid, had suggested that the use of such intrinsically, divinely blessed ingredients would allow for success. That was what Seers did; they peered into the future and related what they saw. Sometimes in verse, sometimes in spontaneous outbursts, sometimes in dreams or waking visions.

Sometimes, in mirror-based scryings. This mirror had been carefully crafted, every step of its construction carefully gauged, to give him a glimpse into the future of the Tower approximately one year ahead. The only problem was, with an actual Seer, one received words which could be interpreted. Sometimes those words could be misinterpreted, or assigned several possibilities, and the details were usually very sketchy . . . but they usually contained explanations of how various things led to the conclusion being discussed.

This mirror simply showed what would happen to whatever land he focused it upon approximately one year from the moment in which he looked, based purely on current events. Anything could change the image, though most of the time it simply showed the most likely events, which rarely changed drastically. It was still being tested for accuracy, and Kerric had left it focused on one of the most stable images he knew, the High Temple of Fate in the Empire of Fortuna. Undoubtedly the image had been paused during the Tower's lockdown, but with the reopening of the communication channels embedded in the Fountainways connecting various singularity points to each other . . .

Myal stopped next to him, staring at the massive scene of bloodshed and chaos. Great war machines stomped across the landscape, crushing smaller buildings as they fell. They faced off against giant beasts and vaguely humanlike beings covered in dark scales, claws, and battle armor. Tiny by comparison, humans fought against what both realized at the same time were demons, given how they both gasped at the same moment. Denizens of the Netherhells, preached against in both many religious lessons and many mage lessons around the world, the monsters attacked without mercy. Overhead, an ugly stain of clouds, purples and browns and muddy greens, spread across the sky instead of the usual shades of white through gray. The very air itself seemed tainted.

"Where is this?" Myal asked in a whisper, heart racing in alarm. "Where in Aiar is this? I don't recognize any of the building styles."

"It's not here. It's in Fortuna . . . and it hasn't happened yet." Kerric flinched as a six-armed demon disemboweled some armor-clad, brave, but outclassed warrior. Turning, he faced another mirror, one set to record everything the larger mirror had seen. Stroking the edge of the frame, he backed up the recorded scryings, watching for the exact moment in time when the placid view of Fortuna had changed.

Myal, holding her tongue while he spellcast, watched the new, smaller mirror as the images of the demonic invasion flowed backward, eased, and retreated. She'd seen reversed recordings of scrycastings before. Usually, such things fascinated her, watching time flowing backward. This time, the images were too gruesome and disturbing to enjoy. They also started to blur, they moved so swiftly. Grim-faced humans—Fortunai—retreated from clashing with the demons. They stood in formation as their leaders rode their horses backward back and forth, no doubt giving stirring speeches. They gathered in the great plaza before their Temple, first in mighty ranks, then in grim-faced formations, then in straggling groups, until there was nothing but a plaza of unhappy people hurrying back and forth under a sickly-looking sky—

The grim, overcast image vanished. Bright blue sky overhead, peaceful daylight, and a placid plaza filled with priests, petitioners, and average citizens took its place. Kerric jabbed at the forescrying mirror, freezing its image, and slashed out his hand. A mesh screen rolled his way on metal casters. As Myal watched, he muttered strange sounds and scratched glowing lights on first the surface of the mirror, then on the blank, unlit mesh, until a modest rectangle blossomed on its surface, showing the frozen image had been captured by the board for manipulation.

"I don't know what changed in the world to create such a horrible future possibility," he murmured, aware that Myal was silently watching and wondering what was going on. He was wondering, too. "But I do know I can quickly rule out whether or not it was something *we* did."

A scooping slash of power connected the board to a couple others, which lit up with images of their own. Myal peered past the first to get a better look at the rest, then looked back at Kerric. "What are you doing?"

"If my regaining control of the Tower did this, then . . . no, I can rule *that* out very quickly," he dismissed. "This change happened too far back in time. So now," Kerric stated, streaking his fingers across the board, calling up images from the internal scryings of the Tower, "we see if my thwarting or keeping Torven alive is what caused . . . no, still too recent. The life or death of the idiot thief isn't the cause . . . Here is a time stamp calibrated to the approximate time of day it is in the capital of Fortuna," he explained, pointing at a set of tiny symbols down in the corner of the first image on the mesh screen. "And here is a time stamp of when events happened here in the Tower.

"Whatever happened, it happened . . . an hour or two after lockdown occurred. *Before* I picked you," he added firmly. "So it is an unrelated event. Not related to the Tower locking down, not relating to my selecting you to run the gauntlet with me, and not related to anything that happened while we were restoring my control."

"That's . . . good, I suppose," Myal murmured, eyeing the images. "But if this mirror can predict the future—"

"Based strictly on current events," he interjected. "Whatever is happening around the world when an exact image is shown in the forescrying mirror has an influence on that image. I don't know *what* event in our current time frame caused this, but if it was scryed upon by any mirror or Fountainway that touches the Tower, I'll be able to find out what the triggering event was, and . . . and maybe figure out a way to undo it." He turned to look up at the original looking glass. "Because a demonic, Netherhell-based invasion *must* be stopped."

"Yes, it must," Myal agreed. She grimaced in the next moment. "I don't know what I can do to help you, though. If this were a *physical* foe, I could take it down, or at least try. But this?" She gestured at the mirror, then let her hand flop against her thigh. "I am unable to help."

"Yes and no," Kerric countered. He moved around her, heading for one of the blank easel pads. "If there is one thing I have learned about you during our gauntlet run to the heart, it is that you are *smart*. You see things from not just one viewpoint, but from many." Hefting the entire easel, he brought it over to her side as he spoke. "You consider lines and angles of attack, you size up opponents for their weak points . . . In short, you *think*.

"Which is a huge point of arousal for me," he added. Pulling her head down into range, he kissed her cheek, then her lips. "So, together, you and I will think. I'll do all the hard work, scrying and sorting, and you write down all of our observations and try to figure out connections of cause-and-effect." He paused and wrinkled his nose at the task ahead of them, eyeing the recording mirror and the mesh board. "Of course, if *anything* in the world set this disaster in motion, then I'm not quite sure where to begin in conquering the problem it caused."

His words triggered a thought. Myal pounced on it mentally. "Divide and conquer. We start with, as you said, every connection this mirror has in the Fountainways. Everyone knows the Tower scrycasts to every known continent, and even to some kingdoms that are underwater. Perhaps there are spells you can use to . . . to trace *vibrations* in the aether connected to this evil? Netherhell energies are different from our own, after all, and anyone who dabbles in dealing with them . . ."

"Would leave a trace in the aether, yes—wait, underwater—Menomon!" Acting on his idea, Kerric summoned another cheval mirror on rolling wheels. Angling the mirror so that it faced away from the rest of the room, he plucked a piece of chalk from a nearby board and scraped several runes on the edge of the frame. "Jessina said the attack came from the Fountainway connection with Menomon. That attack *ended* at some point, because I didn't see any danger-runes from that channel while I was seated over the heart, checking up on everything. Right . . . this should be warded enough for a quick contact . . ."

Focusing the mirror with a murmur, he activated it . . . and found it blocked. He tried again, and received no connection. Brow creasing with a frown, he turned and headed for one of a trio of alcoves tucked into one of the sidewalls . . . then swung around and stalked back. Catching Myal's hand, he hauled her in his wake.

"Come. We're going back to the Fountain," he told her. Then released her. "Wait, grab the drawing pad and a pencil from that table there, so we have some way to write down our observations."

The moment she came back with pad and writing implement tucked under her arm, he caught her wrist and led her through the hidden doorway-Gate. Emerging in the Fountain Hall, he led her through the mesh door and stamped his foot three times on one of the rounded brown sections of marble near the black-lipped edge of the singularity pool. The moment he moved back, the surface of the stone shifted, stretching up into a swivel-style chair like his own.

"Have a seat," he directed her. "All of this started because *something* happened in Menomon, an underwater city located far to the south of us. I cannot say exactly where, other than that it's located somewhere in the Sun's Belt Reefs, but I can say that the people of Menomon are odd, isolationist, and paranoid. The Mistress of their Fountain, however, is open-minded, common-sensical, and a delight to deal with.

"Guardian Sheren would never attempt to attack the Tower Fountain, however. Menomon is an underwater city, built under a protective bubble of air," Kerric told Myal, mounting the steps to his own seat as she took the offered one, pad balanced in her lap. "Sheren's Fountain is used specifically to keep the city it shelters from being crushed and its occupants drowned by the weight of the water over their heads. She would *never* risk a retaliatory attack from a fellow Guardian upset at her trying to wrest away control of a second singularity. It would literally kill her and everyone living with her."

"So it had to have been someone else. Someone who challenged her and took over the Fountain, perhaps? You said the attack was stopped," Myal reminded him. "Perhaps the city's rulers or its citizens protested, and got whoever it was to stop? Or . . . did the Tower counterattack automatically?" She bit her lower lip at the possibility of all those people crushed and drowned deep underwater.

Kerric shook his head quickly, curls bouncing around his head as he negated that awful thought. "The Tower doesn't attack through the Fountainway. All of its defenses are *here*, so all it did was cut off all contact, until I regained control and re-awakened the connections. The *connection* is fine. With centuries of scrycasting research behind everything, the Tower's diagnostic spells proved that much when I checked the status of everything, including that. I'm just getting *blocked* by something which seems to be deliberately cutting it off, and I need to check on that."

Dropping his feet into the bubble, he flicked his hands through the air, summoning up curving veils of light that didn't need any mesh for projected stability. It took him a few minutes to double-check all the connections. When he was through, Kerric rubbed at his jaw, feeling a hint of stubble beginning to grow. As much as part of him wanted to shave it off so he could rub his face all over Myal's tattooed belly, preferably while the two of them were rolling around on his oversized bed, Kerric knew this had to come first.

Great power demanded an equal level of care and responsibility. Not just in how it was wielded, but also in how it *could* be wielded. Stopping a Netherhell invasion counted high on the To

Be Done list, even if Penambrion was on the Aian continent, an entire ocean and a couple kingdoms away from the ancient Empire of Fortuna. Demons didn't give a damn about kingdom or continental boundaries.

"Have you found something?" Myal asked. Some of the runes were hard to read because she was viewing them backward from her position. Others were hard to read because they were purely magical signs, esoteric with meaning known only to mages. Mathemagics was the only branch of writing that translated across language barriers because it used mathematical symbols, which always bore the exact same meaning from culture to culture.

". . . It's been closed off from the inside. Someone inside Menomon closed the Fountainway channels. These runes here say it was done several hours *after* the attack ended," Kerric added, pointing at a vertical line of glowing, bluish lights, then pointing at a set of gold lines that squiggled a bit, with a darker blob in their center. Map symbols, not runes. "These show that the attack ended because of something farther down the line. Farther to the south, if I'm gauging the channels correctly."

"Who or what lies to the south?" Myal asked.

"Guardian Rydan . . . or possibly Guardian Saleria, though she's more to the southwest. They're Guardians of singularities found somewhere in the Katanai Empire, south of Sun's Belt. I have a second-hand connection at best with Guardian Rydan's Fountain, but Guardian Sheren has spoken of his great power. If anyone broke into her Fountain Hall and attempted to take over our Fountain, it's possible he detected it and attacked from outside."

"Which could have caused the collapse of the city," Myal muttered grimly.

"What? No, *that* wouldn't cause the channels to be cut off," he dismissed. "I'd *see* the city having been crushed, because the unique nature of the Tower's scrycasts allows me to project scrying spells along the channels. Normally the vibrations of the energies involved make the connections sound-based only. And for good reason, since if you can see a place, you can attack it with enough power to push a mirror-Gate through the aether. Our biggest client, Senod-Gra, permits three times the normal visual connections because, well, they *are* our biggest client. Our service flows to them, and they send money to us.

"No, the connections were closed from the inside. I suspect it's a result of the paranoia of Menomon's ruling Council, which Guardian Sheren has complained about time and again. 'Sodden old sticks-in-the-mud,' as she calls them," he added in an aside. "Which is ironic, her calling them 'old.' She's older even than Guardian Keleseth, who *is* an old stick-in-the-mud. Doubly ironic, for her to be in charge of a city renowned for its ability to relax inhibitions. If you ask me, the Guardian of Senod-Gra needs to get out of her Fountain Hall and go play in her own city for a day. Or maybe a whole week."

Myal didn't quite successfully smother her laugh; it emerged as a *snerk* sound. Kerric grinned at her for a moment, then sighed and rubbed at his chin again, thinking. So did she. Within a few moments, Myal had another question. "You said some of the energies involved came from either Guardians Rydan or Saleria? Perhaps they know why the city of Menomon has sealed itself off from contact."

"Good point. I do have a direct connection to Saleria. I don't for Rydan. He's fairly new as a Guardian, only a few years' worth, and rather isolationist. Not paranoid, exactly, but not interested in interacting much with others." Twisting his chair a little, Kerric activated that line, literally a line that appeared on one of the mesh screens across from him. No image formed, since this was a voice-only line. Whatever else she did with her days, Guardian Saleria wasn't interested in watching scrycasts from the Tower.

Much like her counterpart, Guardian Rydan. *". . . Guardian Kerric to Guardian Saleria, are you available?"*

That was all he said, but that was all he needed to say. Most Guardians had catch-spells for recording and preserving such messages. It could take anywhere from a matter of seconds if the Guardian was on hand and not busy, to several hours before one might reply. But it was now daytime across the breadth of Aiar, and that meant day for the continent of Katan as well. Just as he started to wonder if he should try establishing a communications channel directly with Guardian Rydan's Fountain, he got a response.

"Yes—yes, I'm here," a familiar, if distorted, feminine voice replied, making the coppery-hued line wiggle rapidly in time with her words. She sounded a bit breathless, and a bit tinny, but he recognized the Guardian. *"This is Guardian Saleria. Guardian Kerric, you said? I was just getting into the Bower when I heard you call. What can I do for eastern Aiar?"*

"We were attacked by unknown forces using the powers of the Fountain of Menomon, which has since been closed down from the inside. Were you assailed as well?" Kerric asked.

Saleria's voice, tinny and echoing, bounced back to him with an answer. *"Attacked? No. This is the first I've heard about it. Is everyone alright at the Tower?"*

"Yes. It took a while to settle down the defenses, but we're fine. Do you have a connection to Guardian Rydan?"

"Guardian who? Rydan, you said? No, I don't know anyone by that name," Saleria replied.

"You don't?" Kerric repeated, bemused by that revelation. *"He's located down somewhere along the west coast of Katan. Surely you know your own fellow Katanai Guardian?"*

"No, I am the only Guardian of Katan that I know of . . . and it's Kah-TAH-nee, not Kah-tahn-EYE," she added dryly. *"It's possible there is another one—I'm told Fountain Guardians are an especially*

secretive lot. But then I only connect to four other Guardian-centers. You're the one with a hundred links."

"*It's only twenty-three,*" Kerric dismissed. "*Right . . . I've spoken with him through Guardian Sheren's Fountainways. I'll see if I can establish a connection myself, since I know the vague direction to head.*"

"*I'm sorry I couldn't help. Anything else? That is, if it's brief,*" she added. "*I need to begin my mid-morning prayers soon.*"

"*Just one thing. I have reason to believe someone in the world is plotting to open a Gate or even a Portal to the Netherhells,*" Kerric warned her. "*I cannot guarantee the accuracy of this information, other than that if current events remain as they are now, it will happen within the year.*"

The connection echoed badly, distorting her voice by a bit, but he could still hear the teasing chuckle lurking in her tone. "*Now now, Guardian Kerric, you know as well as I that no mage can be a Seer. Even one powerful enough to handle the energies of a singularity-rip.*"

"*It's information from a Seer. Sort of,*" he muttered under his breath. "*Just keep your eyes and ears open. I'll let you know if the visions change, but if you can spare some prayers for averting a Netherhell invasion, or perhaps for searching out energies influenced by such efforts, and are willing to share your findings, I'd appreciate it.*"

"*I'll pray to avert it. That, at least, is a part of my job description. Gods bless you, Guardian Kerric. Guardian Saleria out.*"

"*And you,*" Kerric murmured as the copper-hued communication spell vanished from his projection screens. "Well, that's that. What are your thoughts?" he asked, lifting his feet out of the bubble and turning his chair to face Myal. "Anything?"

"She sounds sincere," Myal said, "though I don't know why this other Guardian wouldn't want to have a connection with her Fountain. Particularly if they're on the same continent. Don't Guardians usually cooperate? I know you connect to the other two on Aiar, along the north and south coasts. Everyone in Penambrion knows that, even if we don't know who or where exactly they reside, but we do know they're the ones who help relay on all the scrycastings to some of your far-flung clients."

Kerric shrugged. "Knowing what little I do of Guardian Rydan, I suspect the choice was entirely his. A couple years ago, Guardian Sheren was contacted on a very, very old Fountainway channel, one which hadn't been used since the Shattering of Aiar . . . though it came from south of the Sun's Belt, and not from up here in Aiar. I've spoken with him via her connection only a handful of times, and he's left me with the impression he's more or less an antisocial hermit. But he is a Guardian, and he will occasionally chat with the rest of us."

"So how do we do that?" Myal asked, looking up at him.

FIFTEEN

Kerric smiled at the "we" she used, because she had automatically included herself in their task. Tucking the toe of his boot back into the sphere beneath his seat, he opened up a set of controls, and a spotlight more or less centered over her chair. "Prop the drawing pad on your lap so the light lands on it, and you can help."

Bemused but trusting him, Myal nodded and squirmed in her seat. She finally settled on crossing one ankle over the other knee for a more or less flat support surface. As soon as she settled, Kerric centered the light projected from the suncrystal chandelier overhead with a few thoughts and a flick of his fingers. The spotlight vanished, and control runes appeared on the now shadowed page, lit by the projection spells overhead.

"Can you read that?" he asked. At her nod, he relaxed. "Good. It's touch-activated. Tap the page or slide your fingers over the surface to maneuver the viewing angles for the images. You won't be able to alter anything you see, but if I'm to patch a connection channel around Menomon, I'll have to close my eyes to 'feel' my way through the world. Establishing a new Fountainway is a very visceral process. I'll need you to talk me through it, if I don't want to take a full hour getting it right."

"Understood," she said. Tapping the square with the runes for Fountainway Map on it, she expanded the image with a slide of her hand. It was easy enough; it made her smile. "This is fun. I always thought that if I ever did retire and get a non-adventuring job, it'd be on my feet as a combat instructor at the Adventuring Hall . . . but if this is how Tower Control interacts with every-thing, I could get used to a sitting job."

"The interface is simple. The Tower's Fountainways are marked in green, Menomon is marked in blue, and Guardian Rydan's channel is marked in gold," he told her.

"What about this faint white line?" she asked. "It parallels the gold. Is that a flaw in the display spell?"

"No, it's not; you can see when you magnify the view that it doesn't follow the gold line exactly," Kerric told her. "That's why I need your help. The controls along the right edge of the pad adjust the tilt of the viewing angle and the focus elevation, plus north, south, east, west, zooming in or swinging out, the usual for scrycastings. The white line is brand-new. It wasn't there before we went into lockdown, though it was there when I re-opened everything.

"It's some new channel that follows the old one to Menomon. I don't know where it originates from, and at this point, it's irrel-evant because I *know* the gold one is the one I need. That's the one I need you to direct me to. Tell me north, south, up down, whatever it takes, and remember to think in three dimensions. I'll let you know if I run into anything that I cannot put a channel through, and we'll just back up and reroute around it. The new patch will grow a brighter green than the old."

"Patch?" she asked, looking up at him.

"The easiest way to connect to Guardian Rydan's channel is to drive a patch-channel around Menomon, being careful of its local aether and protective spells—all that stuff in blue—and connect to his channel on the other side," he told her. "We'll see if we can get some news of what happened to Menomon out of Guardian Rydan first, then attempt a connection to the new Fountainway if he doesn't know what happened, either. Zoom in and hit the multihued button. That will pull up what my Fountainway can sense of the local aether around Menomon. Red is bad, green is good. Try to stick to the chartreuse side of yellow at the very least."

"Understood." Sliding and tapping her fingers across the light-infused pad, she marveled for a moment that her hand wasn't casting a shadow. But then that was the essence of magic, bending the laws of the universe by the power of a mage's trained will, confined and shaped by runes and words and who knew what else—tattoos, in her case—to perform things not normally physically possible. Or things that were physically possible, but without physical labor being involved.

As she magnified her view of Menomon and its surroundings, however, she frowned and zoomed in further. "Kerric . . . the white line? It goes to the heart of what I presume is the Fountain Hall, since that's where the green and gold lines connect, but . . . it doesn't actually connect."

Pausing his preparations for channel-making, Kerric pulled up his own copy of the map, floating it in the air in front of him. Zooming in, he peered at the bubble-filled section where his line and Guardian Rydan's line met Guardian Sheren's Fountain. Sure enough, the white channel went *almost* all the way, but stopped short. "Huh. That's a Fountainway channel, alright, capable of communicating, scrycasting, and even sending objects through . . . I'm honestly surprised it's not connected, and even more surprised Sheren hasn't cast it out. It's just sitting . . . There, see the power levels? It's almost completely shut down. Whoever built it isn't using it."

"Was it used to take over her Fountain?" Myal asked.

Kerric frowned in thought. "No . . . I don't think so. Not directly. It might have delivered someone into the Fountain Hall, but not a direct takeover, no. And it had to have been pushed into that room *after* the Menomon Fountain's defenses had been weakened or altered. The more I look at this situation, the more curious I grow. Ready to guide me?"

"Ah . . . yes. The terrain around the eastern side of Menomon is less hazardous than the west," she stated, double-checking the hues being displayed. "You'll have to dip over or under the white line, but you should be able to reach the gold with fewer problems from the east," she told him.

Fixing the images in his mind, Kerric nodded and closed his eyes. A touch of his hand on the edge of his chair lowered it further into the Fountain, soaking him in magic up to his knees. The further into the singularity-well he delved, the stronger the magics he had to play with, but the more it affected his physical senses from the sheer power coruscating through his mind.

Eyes closed, he surged his thoughts out to the edge of the underwater city's limits, and bulged out a portion of the channel. Splitting channels for disparate scryings meant for distinct points of delivery was an easy task; the spells built into the Tower after so many centuries of scrycasting made it easy. And with Myal murmuring directions, watching what he could only feel, it only took a few minutes to craft a channel that detoured around the city, under the low-powered white line, and tapped up into the golden one.

Tapped was the right word for it. Kerric "knocked" on the side of the channel, as if it were a door and he a guest coming to request a visit. This one took a little bit longer to get a reply than contacting Guardian Saleria had. He spent the time reinforcing his channel, warding the sides of the tunnel, installing protective spells that would filter out excessive energy or potentially danger-ous packages. Such spells were equally familiar to him, since they were part and parcel of the Tower's contract-signed promises to its many patrons that nothing harmful would be sent to them.

It was also a reassurance that a patron could not send any-thing harmful to the Tower, though there were provisions for patrons to ship gold through the live scrycasts to shower upon their favorite adventurers. Sometimes the gold, which appeared literally flying through the air down at the adventurers, caused bruises and cuts when it struck, but they were always minor inju-ries when that happened, and the adventurers were usually grate-ful for the monetary praise.

In this case, he just wanted a communications channel to start with, though he did build in future points of access. The rest could be opened up later; maybe Guardian Rydan felt lonely and bored, and would like to chat with someone. Or maybe he wanted to enjoy the sight of adventurers tackling difficult traps and dan-gerous monsters. The only reason why Guardian Saleria wasn't herself a customer of the Tower was that whatever her tasks were, she spent a lot of her days in spell-backed prayer. She relayed along some of the scrycastings to a few wealthy Katanai... *Katani* patrons, Kerric knew, but that was it.

Someone knocked back, forming a starting-point bulge of their own. Kerric finished attaching the channel and opened it. As soon as he did, he got a male voice. A stranger's voice.

"Who is this?"

Opening his eyes, Kerric stared at the new copper line on his mesh-screens. *"I was about to ask you the same. Where is Guardian Rydan?"*

"Ah. Guardian Rydan has retired. I am Guardian Dominor. Who is this, and how can I help you?"

Eyes narrowed in suspicion, Kerric asked, *"What happened to Guardian Rydan? Where is he?"*

"I told you, he retired. Currently, he is asleep. Or making love to his wife, I'm not sure which."

Wife? Kerric thought. Of all the possible replies the stranger could have made, that wasn't on the list of things he would have guessed. Kerric had thought this Guardian Dominor person had forced Rydan out of the position, but if he was talking about Guardian Rydan sleeping with a *wife* . . . *"When did Guardian Rydan retire?"*

"I'll tell you that, if you tell me who you are. This channel connects to Menomon, but the last thing we heard was that the Council of Menomon ordered it shut down. So who are you, and how did you get into this conduit?"

"Ah—This is Guardian Kerric, from the other side of Menomon. I've patched a channel around Guardian Sheren's Fountain, because it seems to be shut down and I cannot get ahold of anyone in the city. I would like to speak with Guardian Rydan, please, to confirm that you are who you say you are, and have the right to be in control of his Fountain."

There was a long pause, then the man's voice came back. *"You know, I would argue that point with you, except I suspect you're feeling belligerent because of the same problems we had about a day ago. Your own Fountain must have been attacked by the one in Menomon, am I right?"*

"Yes. Where is Guardian Rydan?" Kerric asked. *"Him, I know. You, I do not."*

"*I've called for him. He's not going to be happy about it, but he's on his way. He did mention the whole paranoia-protocol thing to me when I took over, but didn't mention your name. Of course, we were in a hurry at the time,*" the stranger, Dominor, added in a tinny-sounding aside, "*but given the circumstances, it's understandable.*"

"*We've only spoken a few times, but I'm sure he will remember me,*" Kerric admitted. "*Can you tell me why the switch in Guardianship, while we wait?*"

"*He got married. An event which shocked the Netherhell out of his brothers, since we never thought he'd lower his prickly, isolationist defenses long enough to even look at a woman,*" Dominor stated dryly, voice echoing through the line.

Off to the side, Myal listened with a touch of amusement. She whispered to Kerric, "He sounds like a true curmudgeon, if that's his own brother saying bad things about him. I wonder what woman took pity?"

"Shhh," Kerric hissed back, though he grinned. He addressed the other man. "*So you are his brother?*"

"*One of them. Here he is. Rydan, a man named Guardian Kerric is calling . . . Stop glaring and stick your damned finger in the communication stream.*"

"*I know very well how to operate my Fountain, Brother,*" a much more familiar voice echoed through the line. "*This is Guardian . . . ex-Guardian Rydan. Identify yourself.*"

"*This is Guardian Kerric. Last time we spoke, it was in a joint channel with Guardian Sheren about importing food via the Fountainways. You said the best you could send her were some seeds for growing trees of her own, as you were running low on stasis-spelled fruit. I said I would send her a cartload of . . . ?*"

"*A cartload of pears, yes, I remember you. Now why the hell are you interrupting my sleep?*" the ex-Guardian growled.

"*I am interrupting because the Tower Fountain was attacked* through the Fountainways from either Menomon's Fountain or a spot beyond it," Kerric stated, "which caused the Tower's defenses to shut down for over eighteen hours. When I got everything back to being operational, I found Menomon shut down tight, a stranger claiming to be in control of your Fountain, and a strange new channel paralleling yours in its approach to the city from the south. These are all things that any Guardian would find alarming, particularly when they all happened more or less at once. So. What has been going on?"

"Ask Domin—Guardian Dominor," Rydan corrected himself. "He knows everything. I'm going back to bed. Guar . . . Gah. Rydan out."

"I'll answer any questions you have," Guardian Dominor reassured them, speaking up as his apparent brother fell silent.

"Old habits do die hard, don't they?" Myal murmured, feeling sympathy for the married curmudgeon. "I hope he's kind to his wife, at least."

"I heard that." The voice belonged to Guardian Dominor. He wielded it with a tone laced with humor. "It was more like his wife being kind to him. She's very good for him, and he loves her very much. I suspect his current crankiness is from lack of sleep. Or unrequited lust. They are newly wed, as of yesterday. So . . . you wanted to know what happened with Menomon and the attacks?"

"Yes, please," Kerric said, wishing he could see the other man's face. "What happened?"

"A mage named Xenos was rescued by the Menomonites when his ship crashed on the Sun's Belt Reefs. They helped rescue a lot of the passengers on board the wreck, while others ended up floating south down to Nightfall, here. At any rate, this Xenos fellow was ambitious and cunning. He managed to lull the city officials into thinking he would be a good citizen, and somehow managed to work his way into the system far enough to poison Guardian Sheren, all to gain access to her Fountain Hall."

"Poison?" Kerric asked, alarmed. He wasn't the only one; Myal gasped in shock. He quickly asked, *"Is she alright? Did he kill her? Is that why the Fountain was shut down? How did you learn all of this?"*

"She was poisoned, but she managed to get help, and will be spending the next few months recovering. One of her apprentices, some woman named Danau, was ordered to shut down all magical access to the city in the Guardian's absence. Once the Guardian has recovered and the Council has stopped being a pile of petrified fish dung, we should be able to communicate with her again," Dominor stated. *"As for the attack itself . . . Xenos was using controlling scrolls on all the Fountainway terminus points. We knew at the time that we were under attack via some very subtle yet strong subversion spells, and suspected that the other Fountains were being subverted as well.*

"Rydan and I switched the Guardianship to buy us more time, since Xenos was using aura-matching spells in his takeover attempt. We created the second channel to form a second angle of attack, and disrupted his efforts—speaking of which, do not attempt to make contact with that second channel. Rydan is still a vastly powerful mage, and that channel connects directly to his, ah, his own personal energies, shall we say. He'd be extremely upset if you attempted to contact or tamper with it in any way."

"Understood. I'll leave it alone—I'll even set up some warning sigils around it, in case anyone else tries," Kerric offered. *"Though it might be easier just to remove that channel entirely, if his powers are bound to it. I'm quite sure your Katani mage instructors have told you never to leave a conduit into your personal energies out where anyone can access it."*

"I'll warn him about that. Anyway, Xenos was then sufficiently distracted that the apprentice Danau and a group of Menomonite guards were able to get inside the Hall and kill him directly. So he's dead and gone, but Menomon doesn't have anyone who can step up to take Sheren's place, so they've shut it all down."

"Well, the Tower owes you a debt of gratitude for taking out the interloper," Kerric stated, seizing on the opening made by a new Guardianship. *"I don't know how much Guardian Rydan may have*

told you about what we do, but we provide scrycastings, live and previously spell-recorded entertainments of adventurers running gauntlets through rooms and halls filled with puzzles, tricks, traps, monsters, plus damsels and gents in distress, ranging the gamut from light comedy with little danger to literally lethal situations.

"If you're interested, I can connect a scrycasting channel to your Fountainway so you can view a sample of what we do on a mirror. We have patrons from all around the world who pay our modest viewing fees for our unique form of entertainment."

"I . . . don't think that's something the citizens of the kingdom of Nightfall would be interested in at this point in time," Rydan's brother hedged, his voice echoing not only with the odd resonances of Fountainway communications, but with bemused doubt as well. *"But I'll keep it in mind for later."*

"Kingdom of Nightfall?" Kerric asked. *"Aren't you in the Empire of Katan?"*

"Not anymore. We're an incipient kingdom, with all the headaches that entails. Now, is there anything else I can do for you?" Guardian Dominor asked.

"Yes, actually. Did you have a recording of the exact time when Xenos was killed, and the exact moment the Fountainways for Menomon were sealed off? We're not just trying to establish what happened in Menomon that caused our own defenses to activate, but to track down a sort of Seer prophecy about . . . well, we've been given a vision of a Netherhell invasion, and the nature of the Seeing is such that if we can track down what event triggered it, we can alter those events so that it doesn't actually happen."

"Ahhh, yes, the meddlings of a Seer. My twin's wife's first husband was a Seer—I don't know if you know Guardian Serina, but she worked with him for a while. Actually, he was a Guardian, forgive me for forgetting that part. My extended family has been through a lot in the last few days."

"*Guardian Serina . . . that would be Guardian Milon?*" Kerric asked. "*Yes, I knew him. We used to talk about what being a Seer is like, and how magic can sometimes duplicate similar efforts in the short term through temporal scryings. And I can imagine you've been through a lot, between an attack and a Guardianship change. But back to my question. Do you have the exact timing of those events?*"

"*Ah . . . I don't actually know. I'm very new to this Guardianship thing. Tell you what; give me a few hours to let Brother Grumpy sleep a bit longer, and when he wakes up this evening, I'll see if he can help me track down any such abilities. I think Serina accounted for exact timing of everything in her monitoring spells, but I'm not completely sure. I'll ask her, too.*"

"*Did the Fountain of Koral-tai get attacked as well?*" Kerric asked, concerned.

"*No, but she did resume the Guardianship of it yesterday, and she's still packing to head back to Natallia for a longer stay—it's a long story,*" Dominor dismissed. "*I'll tell you about my courtship of Guardian Serina another time. Suffice to say she's the Guardian of Koral-tai, I'm the Guardian of Nightfall, and we're married as well. We have been for a few months, though, so we're not quite as grumpy about interruptions as Rydan and his wife might be.*"

"*That sounds like one heck of a story,*" Kerric offered, bemused by what had been happening on the other side of the Sun's Belt while he had been busy risking his and Myal's lives. "*How about we arrange for a shipment of fine Corredai tea, and schedule a time where you and I can sit down, maybe open up a scrying mirror channel—away from your Fountain Hall, since safety is the Tower's number one priority in its scrycastings—and we can have a nice long discussion about it over a hot cup or three?*"

"*You have a deal. Let me go track down my wife, have a bit of a chat, and then wait for Rydan to wake up, feed himself, and maybe*" *resemble something close to civilized. I'll get back to you tonight—ah, it's not quite an hour before full noon locally. So in about five or six hours?"*

"It's just after the noon hour here," Kerric stated. *"Make it eight. I've had an extremely long day of my own, and need to sleep, even though it's the middle of the day. We can synchronize timing systems at that point, since hopefully you'll have the information I need by then. Until then, I'm going to go rest."*

Guardian Dominor chuckled. *"Well, don't take after Rydan's other bad habits. Sleeping during the daylight hours is merely the least obnoxious of them."*

Kerric laughed. *"Now* I know *you're brothers. Guardian Kerric out."*

Extracting his feet from the Fountain, he lifted the chair back up with a touch of the spell runes subtly carved into the chair arm, then turned it so that he could dismount. A glance at the pad in Myal's lap made him quickly shut it off with a flick of his hand and a pulse of his will, honed through long attunement to the Tower's many spells. Others had to use runes and such to interface with those spells. He was the Master. The hardest part for him was disciplining his mind enough to *not* trigger the wrong effect.

"Thank you for that expert guidance, Myal," he praised her, descending to the floor. "Since it looks like we'll have to wait to get any results . . . would you like to retire with me to my quarters? Or should I send you to yours, so you may bathe and sleep?"

Myal tucked the pad and unused pencil under her arm and rose. Cheeks flushed with her thoughts, she asked as boldly as she could, "Will we have time to make love again when we awaken, if I stay?"

Catching her hand, Kerric lifted it to his lips. "My dear lady, it would be my distinct *pleasure* to fulfill your request, if you stay."

Lacing her fingers with his, he tugged her toward the alcove with the pale blue marble triangle embedded in front of it. Myal didn't protest in the least. She remembered a conversation from back when she was a girl bordering on becoming a woman. A clutch of older cousins had been giggling and gossiping about young men, and all of them had agreed: the taller, the better. *What fools they were*, she scorned mentally, silently as he led her through to his quarters. *As if height has anything to do with a man's abilities in bed!*

The bed in question was as large as promised. Larger than Myal had imagined, actually. She had expected something that was a little longer than she was tall, wide enough for two people to sleep comfortably, maybe three. Instead, Kerric's bed was a big, square, feather-stuffed thing twice as long as he was tall, and equally as wide. She stared at it blankly as soon as they entered his bedchamber, trying to figure out how many could sleep on it.

"Six people," Kerric stated, making her blink. "That's if you put one down at the bottom crosswise to the rest."

"How did you . . . ?" Myal asked.

He shrugged and gestured at the massive piece of furniture. "Because that was *my* first thought, too. Who wouldn't be wondering?"

He had a point. Myal tipped her head, considering the massive mattress, then turned to him and asked, "How many *have* you had on it? Six?"

"Two. But mostly just the one, me."

"All that space, for just you?" Myal asked.

He shrugged. "I get hot, I roll over and find a cool spot."

"I get cold, and wrap myself in blankets," she countered. A thought crossed her mind, making her smile and elbow him. "Maybe I'll wrap myself in you?"

Blushing, he grinned. "Maybe. On with the tour. This door

leads to my dressing room—yes, an entire room for clothing, how absurd," Kerric said dryly, mocking his lifestyle, "when my bed-chambers alone are almost as big as whole tenements in Penambrion. I didn't build this place, though. *That* door leads to the refreshing room, and this one in the middle is for the bathing room. It connects to the other two."

Opening the door, he gestured for her to enter. Myal's tenement was luxurious in one respect: she had a bathing tub of her own. Sometimes she used one of the town's two bathhouses, but mostly for swimming in the big pools. This tub wasn't quite large enough to swim in, but it was five times as large as the one she used, making it not quite half the size of Kerric's bed. It was also already full.

A glimpse through the open door to the right showed shelves of clothes and other belongings in a well-lit room. "Whoever built this place loved to bathe and admire his clothes. Or her. What is the little tub in the corner for? The one with the scrolls on the edge?"

She nodded at a tub not quite large enough to bathe in, but bigger than a kettle. Kerric, following her gaze, chuckled. "That's a clothes-washing tub. It's an Artifact, enchanted with several complex spells. Put your things into the tub, twist the knob on the faucet to add water, pour in a dollop of softsoap, tap the starting rune, and put a basket on the floor behind those 'scrolls' to catch the clothes. Which aren't scrolls, by the way. They're drying presses; they press and suck the moisture out of the clothing when the washing and rinsing spells are done.

"Speaking of which . . ." Without any show of modesty, Kerric started stripping off his remaining clothes and tossed them into the tub. "If you want to add yours, now is the time. My plan is to wash these, take a bath, and then curl up on that big bed of mine with you. Since we have time to kill before we find out what the new and old Guardians of Nightfall know, and we might as well spend it doing pleasant things, right?"

About to agree verbally, Myal found herself distracted into merely nodding. The sight of his naked body distracted her from higher thoughts. Tight buttocks, great thighs and calves, trim waist and hips, flat stomach . . . Nothing rippled with over-bulging muscles, but then she wasn't one of the female adventurers—or the many, many lady patrons—who swooned over someone like Nafiel. Kerric's muscles showed when he used them, and relaxed when they weren't needed, giving an overall impression of strength with the ability to yield.

He nudged her elbow. "Myal? Strip. You must be more tired than even I am."

Blushing, she started removing her garments. "I was thinking about your body. Physique. That's the word."

"I'll take that as a compliment, then. Do you like really hot baths, hot baths, or merely warm baths?"

"Medium-hot. I don't want my muscles to tighten after such a long day," she admitted. "I wouldn't be able to move in the morning."

"Done," he promised, twisting a lever on the edge of the tub. Runes started glowing in golden-orange hues along the inside. "One minute to the perfect temperature . . . You know, I heard a rumor that some lands don't even have a sense of time beyond a vague grasp of 'morning,' 'mid-morning,' 'noon' and the like. I couldn't work that way—the *Tower* doesn't work that way."

"Mendhi is that way. We have hours, and quarter-hours, but no minutes or seconds," Myal stated. "We're very close to the Sun's Belt, so our days and nights are similar in length all around the year. When I came here, I had to practice counting how long a second was, and memorize how many in a minute." The air in the bathing room grew warm and humid as she spoke. Myal relaxed a little. She sighed in a soft hum, closing her eyes. "This feels like home. Heat and moisture."

"If I could afford the time away—which obviously I cannot," Kerric lamented dryly, "I'd love to visit Mendhi. I'd love to visit the Great Library in specific—what mage wouldn't? But I'd love to see it through your eyes as well. I mean, I'd show you Penambrion, but you've already lived here, so you know all about it already." Testing the water, he cut off the glow with a twist of the lever. "There, that should be good."

At a gesture from him, Myal tested it, then quickly climbed in. It was good; hot enough to relax, but not hot enough to overheat or even turn their flesh pink. The tub was also deeper than she was used to; it had a bench seat with a comfortably sloped back. She shook her head, then quickly worked on unbraiding her now-damp hair. "I feel like this is for soaking, not for cleaning—is there a current?"

She could feel the water moving past her skin. Kerric nodded. "You can see the small holes here and there for the water to flow in, and to flow out again. The whole thing gets cycled in about half an hour, I think."

Thinking about that, Myal finished unplaiting her hair. When Kerric picked up a comb—silver, not wooden, and not likely to turn into a dense bramble thicket—she turned her back to him so that he could brush out the tangles.

"I think, before this last day, I would have wondered at so much luxury for such a seemingly easy job. You, the Master of the Tower, do not run the gauntlets day after day. Yet when you *do* have to adventure into the Tower, it is in the most deadly of runs. So perhaps this luxury is earned," Myal asserted. She peered back over her shoulder, smiling at him. "Thank you for sharing it with me."

Leaning forward, Kerric hugged her with one arm . . . conveniently cupping her bared, floating breast. "You're welcome. Thank you for getting me back in charge. Now with that said," he murmured in her ear before kissing the curve of it, "remind me to have you put on that fancy pearl and diamond necklace you picked up. *Just* the necklace. Since I haven't found you the perfect outfit to wear with it, yet."

She grinned at that, leaning back into his arms. "Mmm, I think I'll do that. I do suggest you apply soap to your hand, though."

"Oh?" he asked, setting the comb aside in favor of cuddling her against his upper body.

"If you do not focus on bathing, we will never get clean," Myal warned him.

"You have a point," he conceded . . . then pulled their lower bodies into closer alignment. It was obvious he wasn't thinking about soap anymore. "But I suggest getting very, very dirty first, so we don't waste all that good soap."

Chuckling, Myal twisted in his arms, turning so that she could give him a kiss . . . and another . . . and both of them forgot all about the soap for a good while.

SIXTEEN

Kerric didn't get much sleep. Not naturally, at least. He honestly wasn't used to *sleeping* with anyone, lovemaking aside, and the way Myal cuddled him in her sleep, seeking the warmth of his body, was a bit distracting. Very distracting. But he could not bring himself to move her away, and his thoughts turned and tumbled the idea of keeping her with him, at his side, for more than just a gauntlet run. For more than just a day.

After a handful of hours, he gave up and speed-slept, then dozed lightly in her arms. Eventually, he knew he would get used to her cuddling; all it would take was constant exposure. Practice, as it were. That thought left him smiling as he napped. He woke when she stirred, aware that she held herself still for a moment in that way that said she was assessing her surroundings warily. The feel of her muscles relaxing against him a few moments later made his heart skip a quick beat in pleasure.

She didn't stay cuddled up against his side for long, however.

After several long seconds, she sighed and squirmed free. Lying there, feeling and listening to her squirm to get out of the bed, Kerric kept his eyes closed. He didn't want her to see him, just in case his expression looked as abandoned as he felt. The sound of the door to the left of his bed told him why she had crawled free: that was the refreshing room door.

Relaxing, he snuggled into the bedding as best he could on his back, given his sprawled position. He had visited that room earlier, himself; he couldn't blame her for taking advantage of the peace and quiet. A faint frown creased his brow. Peace and quiet was something he wouldn't have, once he rose and faced whatever remained of the day. *Restarting the scrycasting channels will be interesting, if not an outright headache. Normally they're staggered in the gauntlet runs, so that we aren't trying to get everyone in and out all at the same time. Maybe if we staggered these ones as well?*

She came back, crawled under the covers, and scooted her way back over to him. Kerric started to open his eyes, but felt the sheet and blankets shift oddly on his chest as she drew close. She was up to something. Unsure what it was, but willing to trust her, Kerric opened his eyes to the barest slits. Myal wasn't visible as anything more than a lump under the covers.

For a moment, he thought it was because she had grown cold during her trip. A moment later, he felt the real reason why she had ducked so low that not even her head showed. Her head, he discovered by the warmth of her breath and the tickling of her hair, was too busy centering itself over his hips.

Clever gi—uhhhrrl oh Gods. Even with his eyelids closed, his eyes rolled up in his head at the soft, warm caress of her lips along his shaft. Heart thumping, he felt blood rushing to his nethers, filling and thickening the formerly quiescent flesh. They had made love in the oversized bathtub, they had snuggled in the bedding, they had slept together in the literal sense as well as the lascivious, and now she was making his favorite daydream come true. That a truly smart, sexy woman would worship his manhood first thing in the morning.

Even if it was technically late afternoon.

She also hummed as she did so, happy little noises as she nibbled with lip-covered teeth, before wrapping her tongue around the underside in a way that made his eyes roll up again. Kerric couldn't hold still. Back arching, he pushed the covers down out of his way. Catching handfuls of her hair, he rubbed it over his stomach and stroked it back from her face in movements far more sincere than smooth-practiced.

The head-bobbing did him in, it felt so good. Groaning, he dug in his heels and arched his body, her name a strangled grunt. "Myal!" If she kept going, it would be over too fast. "Myal, please!"

Myal blushed at his plea. Not from embarrassment, but rather from an unexpected and rather heady sense of power that rose at his words. *He's begging* me *for something? The most powerful mage in . . . in hundreds of miles, and dozens of lands?* The thrill that rushed through her veins at that realization was purely feminine, and it pooled warmth low in her belly faster than the taste and the feel and the thought of what she had been doing to him.

Rearing up onto her knees, she pushed the covers completely off. The air in the bedchamber was a little cool against her flushed body, but all that did was intensify the ache in her flesh, drawing her nipples into tight little buds and making her hips want to rock. The quickest way to sate her own need as well as his was to climb over his lap, which she did. And to grasp his shaft, which she did . . . and to position it just so, so she could sink down onto it. Which she did.

Her lover lifted his palms, elbows braced on the bed and fingers spread, a pleased smirk curling his mouth. Despite her very physical position, the thought of clasping hands with him seemed very intimate. Smiling shyly in return, Myal slid her fingers through his until their hands interlocked, giving her some support and stability. Which she used, guiding herself while flexing her leg muscles to slide up and sink down. It felt good, so good that her brief shyness evaporated with each greater, quicker roll and flex of her body.

Kerric couldn't think of a sexier sight. Myal still had an uneven red line on her cheek from sleeping on a crease in the bedding, her long black hair desperately needed a brush, and her delightful breasts, each just barely a nice handful, were too far away for him to lick. But she was beautiful in her desire . . . and certain other parts were close. Freeing one hand, he reached between her splayed thighs and started murmuring.

Bemused by the change, Myal slowed down her rocking on his shaft. She didn't understand magical phrases, but she did recognize when a spell was being cast. Wary, she stilled, only to find him touching a finger to his tongue, then that same finger to her clit, and returned it to his tongue for a lick. He rubbed and stroked all around the erect little peak on the return touch, making her moan and shift, pausing every so often to touch his tongue, until it felt like he was still rubbing her when his finger wasn't toying with her flesh.

No . . . Not rubbing, she thought, eyes widening in amazement. *Licking!* She could see his tongue stroking around his lips, and *feel* it stroking between her nether-lips. *He's—oh Goddess—licking me!* Pleasure bucked through her body, first tensing her muscles, then weakening them. Slumping over their rejoined hands, she moaned, but he didn't stop.

In fact, he freed his hand again, forcing her to brace herself partly on his chest, and touched his finger to his tongue and to her breasts. Not just the nipples, either, but the sensitive line of her sternum, and the creases underneath each curve. Feeling his tongue flicking and teasing and licking was too much. Groaning, she dropped both hands to the bed, overwhelmed by the pleasure shuddering through her flesh.

It was enough for her, but it wasn't enough for him. Bracing his heels once more on the bed, Kerric grabbed her hips and thrust up into her, all while licking and flicking his lips. That drove her over the edge. Crying out, she rode him like a wild thing, rearing up and dropping down, clawing at the bedding.

That's more like it, Kerric thought, in the corner of his mind still capable of rational thought. His smirk changed into a gasp as she raked her fingernails down his chest, onto his stomach. That was . . . erotic. When she did it again, then dropped down once more into range, he grabbed her by the back of her head and pulled their mouths together. With his tongue playing against hers, every move from it echoing against the other, spell-touched parts of her body, she cried out against his lips, inner muscles pulsing around his shaft in ragged, delicious squeezes.

That was enough to trigger his own orgasm. Head pressed back into the bedding, he let himself go. Holding her close while his flesh filled hers, he gradually shifted his grip to soothing strokes while both of them recovered. Both of their bodies were sheened in sweat, and the air had the heady, musky perfume of their lovemaking. A beautiful feeling, and a beautiful smell.

As limp as his limbs felt, Kerric couldn't stop smiling. Making love to this extraordinary woman energized him even as it relaxed him; he felt ready to take on a second Tower gauntlet, if need be. Thankfully, another run wasn't necessary. Even if it had been, there was a physical way to access the Fountain Hall from this bedchamber, one without any tricks or traps in it, though it did involve several flights of narrow, barely lit stairs, and was only to be used in the most dire of emergencies. But getting *to* the Guardian's quarters involved circumnavigating far more lethal traps than the much easier route he had picked, and more people than just a single, fantastic partner.

He licked his lips, preparing to thank her once again for helping him. Her faint shiver and soft moan stopped him. Curious, he did it again. She moaned a little louder, breath hitching and body squirming. *Oh. Right*, he realized. *The tongue-touch spell*. A slow grin spread his lips, prompted by a very wicked thought.

"What's the matter, Myal?" Kerric asked his beautiful bed partner, enunciating each word carefully. "Is something bothering you? Like, say . . . the ssssssensation of air blowing acrossssss your nipplessss and nether-ssssssentinel?" he inquired slyly. "Or perhaps the rapid flicking and licking and lapping of the tip of my tongue against your favorite bitsssss?"

"Damn you," Myal groaned, feeling exactly that. She was sated from riding him, but still incredibly sensitive in the post-bliss lethargy of lovemaking. "I need . . . *ungh* . . ."

"Yessss," he purred, "you *need*. You need me to make love to you. You need me to show you how beautiful and strong and glll-lorious you are," Kerric added, taking the time to press his tongue on the *L* in *glorious*, as if pressing his tongue to that special little nubbin between her legs. "And *I* need to tell you, word for word, how wonderful I think you are. How brave, and strong, and compassionate, funny, delightful, intelligent, brilliant, quick-witted, sexy, magnificent . . ."

He didn't stop describing how he felt about her. Each word from his damnable mouth teased and touched her in ways only possible via magic. Dizzy with pleasure, Myal moaned and writhed on top of him. Words like *succulent* weren't quite as effective as *titillating*, but some of the more base phrases he used stimulated her ears and her mind even more than her body. And all of it blended into a glorious, teasing ache that drove her back up into delirious delight.

He didn't move beneath her. His flesh re-thickened, holding her in place, but the Master of the Tower did not move. He did not have to; instead, he proved himself the master of her desires via his words. Dazed, aching for repletion, for relief from the pleasure hazing her mind, Myal felt his hands stroking her hair back from her sweat-dampened face. Felt him lifting her face from where it rested next to his ear on the pillow. Blinking, she gazed down at him and forced herself to focus on what he was saying. It helped that he paused for several long seconds before speaking.

When he was sure he had her attention, Kerric stated slowly and clearly, "I would love to spend the rest of our lives together in getting to know you better, Myal of Mendhi . . . because I am falling in love with you."

Overwhelmed, she dipped her head and kissed him, putting into the efforts of her own lips and tongue what she couldn't think coherently enough to say.

He hadn't expected such a fervid reaction. She didn't have to speak; her response was eloquent, arousing his hunger and feeding it simultaneously. Buried in her body, his shaft pulsed, hardened, twitched, and spilled. This second climax didn't rock his body; it simply rocked his soul. Their kiss slowed, until she finally broke free and nuzzled her head down next to his ear once more, breathing deeply, softly, in her repletion.

Smiling, Kerric hugged his woman. "So," he finally murmured a minute or so later. "What do you think of my sp—"

Striking as fast as she ever did in a Tower run, Myal clamped her hand over his mouth.

"End. The spell," she ordered hoarsely, flesh too sensitive to continue. Not unless he wanted to leave her a puddle of sated goo in his bed, unable to move. At his nod, she cautiously released his mouth.

"I do indeed love you," he murmured. She groaned and moved to silence him again. Capturing her wrist, Kerric gently pulled her fingers free, muttered the termination words with a push of his will behind them, then kissed and licked her fingers. Only her fingers. Feeling her slump against him in relief, he grinned and kissed the side of her head. "So," he murmured, "do you love me? Or perhaps think you could?"

"Very, very easily," Myal groaned. She did not want to move. Unfortunately, she was too experienced an adventurer to think that either of them could stay in this moment of bliss. Still, it didn't hurt to ask, ". . . Do I *have* to let you go back to work?"

He chuckled, amused by her complaint. "Yes, unfortunately. Hopefully, Guardian Dominor has more news for us. And hopefully between Tower Control, Maintenance, and the Adventuring Hall, everyone has sorted out the various employees' loyalties and fixed the new scrycasting schedules. And *hopefully*, you'll be able to recover your strength, head home, and plan on inviting me over for . . . hm . . . what do you call supper when it'll actually be served around breakfasting time?"

"*Food.*" She stated it flatly, like an epithet. She also snuggled closer over him, pinning him down. "I am *not* moving."

"Yet," he warned her, putting a time limit on her cuddling, though he did tighten his own grip a little.

". . . Yet," Myal conceded, enjoying the feel of him beneath her, around her, holding and supporting her. She could be as strong and powerful as anyone could wish when running a gauntlet, but there were times when she just wanted to hold and be held. After a few more moments, she sighed and loosened her grip. "Dinner, you said? At my place?"

"Can you cook?" Kerric asked her. "If not, we can go out to eat, or eat here. I'd offer to cater, but the food would have to arrive outside your doorstep, since those tenements are thoroughly warded."

"I can cook a few things," she admitted. "Not as well as your chefs, though. Usually, I eat out."

"Ah, yes, the Honey Spear. We can go there tomorrow morning, if you like," Kerric offered. "I'd offer the evening version right now, but I have to grab something to eat on the way to the Fountain Hall to check in and see how ready we are to resume scrycastings."

She thought about it, mind working away while her body rested over his, still recovering from their lovemaking. Out of consideration for Kerric, she had braced some of her weight on elbows and knees, but he didn't seem to mind the rest of it. Finally, she dipped her head, kissing the tip of his nose. "Only if you do not think it will cause problems, for the Master of the Tower to be seen courting an adventurer."

Kerric knew what she meant. "Only if *you* don't mind that everyone will be taking bets on everything from whether or not there'll be a second date, all the way through to bets on how long this will last."

This, she knew, meant their current relationship. Whatever it was. The only thing she objected to was the word *last*. That implied this whatever-it-was would end, and she did not want it to end. Adventuring was a male-dominated profession, mostly because of the physical needs. She was respected for her skills, and admired for her skills, and relied upon for her skills, but very few men gave her all three as freely as Kerric did, and *he* was familiar with scores of women adventurers just as capable as she was. That implied she rated high in his esteem.

Shifting her position, she crossed her arms on his chest. He winced briefly from the pressure as she moved, but didn't protest once she settled back down. Not that Myal was trying to hurt him, just pin him down. Physically, that was. Magically, he had her beat by a Tower to her tenement building, and could have levitated her off of his torso with a thought. But no, he merely arched a brow in silent inquisition.

"I give it forty-three years," she stated, doing her best to sound confident. "With three major fights. Are you going to argue, or will you hold off until the first ten-year mark?"

The laugh that burst from his throat moved his whole body, jostling her a little. Shaking his head, Kerric caught his breath and countered, "Only forty-three? I'd have picked at least *sixty* years."

"You're just being greedy," she mock-admonished, tapping the tip of his nose again. He kissed her finger, then nipped it playfully. She allowed it for a moment, then removed her finger from his reach and gave him a sober look. "*Will* we be giving this a chance? A long-term chance?"

"Considering how much I enjoyed your company when in the midst of great peril, and am *still* enjoying your company in a moment of rest? When I'm supposed to be concerned for the resumption of the Tower's normal operations and eager to get back to work?" Kerric asked her rhetorically. He shook his head slightly, banishing negative thoughts. "Well, I am eager to get to work, but I, for one, am also going to court you in earnest. If you don't mind?"

"I'd like that," she agreed, giving him a contented cat sort of smile, shy and smug and deeply pleased all at once.

Kerric thought it was adorable. In the privacy of these moments alone together, she was showing him a softer side than the competent, straightforward Myal the Magnificent she normally displayed for the scrycasts. It was, he decided, a rare privilege. He combed her tangled locks back from her face, enjoying the moment, then sighed. ". . . As much as I could spend a year in here with you, I do have work to do. And you should go to your home, to relax, to rest, to see if you'll be called up for a gauntlet run any time soon. Though that does bring up one big problem."

"Oh?" Myal asked. She moved as she did so, reluctantly dismounting off to the side, but he did have a point about getting back to work.

Holding up thumb and forefinger close together, her lover grimaced and said, "I'm going to have a slight problem with nerves, every time you adventure through the Tower from now on." Sitting up, Kerric scrubbed his hand through his locks, then rose and turned, facing her. "I respect you and your skills, and the years you spent honing them. I will not stop you. I just . . . I'll have a hard time not lowering the challenge rating when you go in, even knowing you'd probably win. It's the *probably* that still carries a slight chance for failure, and the . . . the thought of losing you is not one I'm willing to contemplate."

His concern warmed her from the inside out. Myal snuggled into the heat left by his body in the bedding and propped her head up with one hand. "Thank you for respecting my choices. For being honest, too, about how you feel." She paused, then smirked and said, "Goddess . . . the *nerve* of some people—you sleep with a person only once, maybe twice, and next thing you know, you find that you actually *care* about them!"

Snickering, she watched him gape at her, until his shocked look made her laugh out loud. Giggling madly, Myal buried her face in the bedding. It didn't help that with each inhale, she could smell pure male mage. Her mage. Her man.

The next thing she knew, her right buttock stung painfully as a soundly struck *thwack* echoed through the room. Myal popped her head back up to gape at him. "You spanked me!"

"It was *three* times," Kerric mock-growled, swatting her

delightfully rounded, inked rump a second time, and a third. "Once in the Tower, once in the tub, and once in my *bed*, woman."

"*Twice* in your bed," Myal argued, wiggling her rump in an attempt to avoid being smacked again. He still managed to spank her twice more. Then made her moan from the way he rubbed his palm over the warm spot left by his hand. As she stilled, his fingers slid down between her thighs, boldly claiming the right to touch her nether-folds. ". . . Three times?"

Groaning softly, Kerric removed his fingers. "Temptress . . . I really do have work to do. I'll contact you later about supper, yes?"

Myal nodded. Then looked around. "How do I get out of here?"

"When you're ready, just leave through the same door we entered. I'll set it to the Adventuring Hall foyer from the Fountain, to shorten your walk home. Just give me ten minutes before you leave—though you're free to stay here as long as you like," he added quickly, reassuring her. For a moment, his gaze lingered on her strong, beautiful body. Tongue flicking over his lips, he dragged in a deep breath and dragged his gaze away. In fact, he put his hand up at the edge of his eyes to shield himself from the sight of her. "Right. Clothing. Work. Scrycastings. Angry patrons getting angrier at every second of the delay . . ."

She snickered again. Guardian of the Fountain, Master of the Tower, the most powerful man in the region, and she could distract him just by being naked in his bed. "You are good for my self-esteem."

For that, he leaned over and swatted her one last time, just a glancing blow on her buttocks, enough to tease as well as sting. "Behave, woman, or I'll trap this bed like Anything But The . . . ! Feel free to help yourself to the food under the stasis domes, and like I said, give me ten minutes to dress, get down to the heart, and reset the front exit of my chambers."

Nodding, she watched him duck into the refreshing room, no doubt to clean up before heading over to the dressing room to don clothes for the day. Once she was alone in his bedroom, Myal rolled onto her back, savoring the faint, lingering sting. Pain wasn't new to her; it was never new to a seasoned adventurer. But the pleasure that accompanied the way he spanked her, that was a strange and wonderful treat.

Not something for every day, of course, but she wouldn't mind it on occasion . . . particularly when coupled with that tongue-touch spell of his. A shiver rippled through her, an aftershock from the memory of him working his linguistic will upon her. Lounging in the too-luxurious bed, Myal contemplated staying right where she was for a while longer. *She* didn't have to be anywhere or do anything.

Except she was curious about what it took to restart the scrycastings. Climbing out of the oversized bed, she padded for the refreshing room and knocked on the door. "Kerric?"

"Yes?"

"Can I come watch you work?" she asked. She could hear running water and raised her voice. "I've always been on the scryed side of the mirror, not the scryer's side."

"Can you be not-sexy?" he called back through the door. A moment later, the panel opened, allowing him to poke his head out. "Because I'll need to concentrate on my work, and not your legs."

She blushed at the compliment, but gave him a quelling look. "I do have Aian-style clothes. Fabric from neck to ankle, even. I'll need to visit my home, though. I didn't pack it in my adventuring bag."

"I'll send you there from the Fountain Hall. When you're ready, come back to the Adventuring Hall and go through the staff door," he instructed her, exiting the refreshing room so that she could use it. "I'll have someone escort you through the doorway-Gate in the back office to Topside Control, and another will guide you from there to the Fountain Hall."

Nodding, she closed the door.

"*My wife is rather peculiar when it comes to mathemagical puzzles, I'm afraid,*" the unseen Guardian Dominor drawled. Unlike his brother, ex-Guardian Rydan, he had an actual sense of humor. Dry, but extant. "*She'd like to see a recording of this 'Netherhell invasion' if that's possible, and copies of your notes. As if she needs* another *global problem to address . . . but I'll admit there are few who can think as well as she can.*"

"I am aware of Guardian Serina's reputation," Kerric allowed. "*Give me a moment to copy my notes. Have you chalkboards or enchanted scrolls standing by to receive the information? And a flawless crystal about the size of a goose egg?*"

"*Yes, and yes. I'm actually going to relay this on to the Koral-tai Fountain,*" Dominor stated. "*And we always have spare crystals lying around, locally. We're not a diamond mine, but Rydan is particularly good at manipulating stones of all sorts.*"

"*Excellent,*" Kerric praised. He glanced over at Myal, who was busy at work in the black chair again, this time with a proper crystalline tablet hovering in front of her. Her task was to pick a location for the lying, cheating, secret-stealing mage Torven and his companions to be shipped to, since they couldn't be held in a White Room cell forever. Once that task was complete, Kerric had another for her, if she was willing to accept it.

The Adventuring Hall staff had arranged for five fresh gauntlets to be run, three of them particularly dangerous, on top of the original schedule of twelve lesser scrycastings. Thankfully, Myal was not on the list for any of them. It was Hall policy to allow at least two days of rest between runs, and three following the multi-

day ones, though if a patron made a particularly strong request—
accompanied usually by a substantial bonus for the adventurer in
question—some might forego their rest period. Myal was not
under consideration at the moment, though that was probably
because the patrons out there did not yet know she had personally
helped him get back into the Tower heart.

Aware of his scrutiny, she glanced over at him and smiled for
a moment, before returning her attention to her work. "Almost
finished. I am negotiating for one of two possible places. Either
Darkhana, across the Eastern Ocean from here, or Arbra, which
is east of Fortuna, which is east of Darkhana. The latter would be
the better option, as it would place them very far from Aian
shores."

"The farther away, the better," Kerric muttered, accessing his
thinkshop and the Arithmancy spells tying many of his chalk-
and mesh-boards together. Summoning images of each board, he
sorted through the ones he wanted, setting them aside as glowing
runes, then opened a scrycasting window to the mirror in question, ready to extract what was needed. From the heart of the
Fountain, he could breach any anti-scrying ward in the whole of
the Tower at need, though he did not do so casually. No one else
could do so, however.

The Netherhell invasion was gone. A placid, untouched, people-
strewn plaza met his gaze. "Alright . . . that's a *little* odd."

"What's odd?" Myal asked him, looking up from her platter-
sized tablet.

"The Netherhell invasion. It's gone. *Guardian Dominor, it seems
we have another anomaly. The Netherhells image is gone,*" Kerric stated,
activating the channel again even as he started reversing the scrycast recordings. "*I don't know what happened, but in the time we
rested . . . huh. It just changed a few moments ago. I don't know what
happened, but it's no longer a possibility.*"

"Hm. You're going to disappoint my wife if you keep that up. May she look at your research notes anyway? She's expecting, and anything I can do to distract her from the nausea would be appreciated."

Kerric nodded, though the movement couldn't be seen on the other end of this connection. He didn't yet have as strong a bond of trust with this Guardian Dominor as he'd need to suggest linking scrying mirrors, but at least with this one, there was hope for it. Guardian Rydan . . . no. *"Of course. Sending it through now."*

Bundling the lot of runes into a cube-shaped mass of light and energy, he sent it swirling down into the sphere beneath his feet.

". . . Got it—nice encapsulation spell! Any chance I can trade a crate of fruit or something for instructions on how to re-create it?" the other mage-Guardian asked. *"We're a little strapped for cash at the moment, locally, but food, we have."*

Myal read the written message sent to her through one of the minor channels, nodded, and tapped her stylus on the crystal. "Kerric? I have an agreement for the five to be shipped out to Darkhana and dumped on their northern coastline. As it's still very cold up there despite being summer, they'll be more concerned about finding shelter than in seeking revenge."

"Price?" he asked.

"Five free hours of scrycasting."

He wrinkled his nose. "What's the Arbran offer?"

"They're asking for a full day's worth."

"Go with the Darkhanan," he directed.

A moment later, he got an exclamation through the Fountainways. *"Hey! Guardian Kerric, I thought you said the scrying wasn't showing a Netherdemon invasion anymore."*

"It isn't," Kerric started to assert, checking the mirror. He blinked and stared at the forescryed image: gone was the placid day, shaded toward evening, and in its place was a mass of demon-wrought destruction and carnage. *"What the . . . ?"*

Quickly backing it up, he counted seconds from the moment of change, then frowned. Peering over to the left, he found Myal scribing notes with the stylus on the tablet in glowing lines.

"Myal . . . I've changed my mind. Go with the Arbran exile."

"Alright," she agreed. Distracted as she was by her task, she had heard the exchange, and the changes. "Give me a moment to offer apologies . . ."

A minute later, she tapped the rune for sending the message across the Fountainways. A quick glance at the mesh panel showing the scrycast of the Seer's Mirror . . . showed it switching from the horrible aftermath of a lost battleground to . . . a beautiful, tranquil sunset in the High Temple Plaza in far-distant Fortuna. Myal looked up at Kerric. "That's interesting. Such a swift change would suggest this Torven group is responsible."

"Guardian Dominor, I do believe we have found our keystone for the event in question, though you're welcome to pass on our information to Guardian Serina for review anyway," Kerric stated, tapping into the Nightfall communication channel once more. He included a timescale of Myal's actions, though not a visual recording; what happened in the Fountain Hall stayed in the Fountain Hall, after all. *"Here's hoping it distracts her from her nausea. And congratulations to both of you; may your children be born healthy, smart, and wise."*

"Thank you. Guardian Dominor out," the new Guardian stated.

"Guardian Kerric out." Sighing, Kerric rested a moment, then looked over at Myal. "When can we send the quintet of idiots through?"

"Finalizing . . . now. All the contract needs is your signature," she stated, tapping the stylus as gracefully as if she'd been working with one of these Topside Control tablets for months, not a matter of hours.

The glowing packet-run leapt off the crystalline surface and swirled up in front of him. Reaching up into it, Kerric "signed" it with a twist of his personal magics, and a touch of the Tower, stamping it with both sets of power. Contract complete, he watched it fly down into the sphere. A few moments later, an acknowledgment came back from the Guardian of the Vortex in the form of a similar spell-aura signature. With the transaction complete and the Tower bound to give a day's worth of free scry-castings, he shifted to the controls for the White Rooms.

Sometimes things went wrong in the Tower; rooms broke down, doorway-Gates didn't function correctly, or just some magical hiccup in the system happened. When that happened, adventurers and maintenance personnel were usually shipped automagically by preset spells into a blank, brightly lit, white-washed chamber not connected to any other place.

It was completely safe, if completely boring and completely inescapable. No one would die in a White Room; it had a modified stasis spell on it, should they start to grow too thirsty or too hungry. It just wasn't meant for more than temporary storage for safety reasons, until the adventurer or worker could be recon-nected to a safer spot somewhere in the rest of the Tower.

Thankfully, he didn't have to connect the White Room to one of the alcoves ringing the Fountain Hall. He could connect it directly to the Fountainways, the channels connecting the various singularities. They didn't always follow logical, land or surface routes, but they did connect, and that was all that mattered.

One moment, the quintet were sitting in the White Room, clearly bored out of their minds. The next, they yelled and fell through the holes that opened beneath their resting bodies, van-ishing down into the swirling maw that would lead to the Vortex Fountain, wherever that might be. An expensive exiling . . . but a necessary one.

Kerric smirked a little as they tumbled out of range. Torven and Barric, the archer Kellida, the would-be thief Unsial, even the Healer-mage Crastus, would be flung thousands of miles away, dropped somewhere on a foreign continent where none of them spoke the local tongue, without weapons, without gear, and with only the clothes on their backs. Everything left behind would be confiscated by Tower personnel and used to pay for the replacement of the lost maintenance tablet, as well as any other damages incurred.

It was a fitting punishment, without having to be a lethal one. If the five of them wished to be adventurers for real, they were going to get a real adventure. Satisfied, he closed the Fountainway funnel and restored the White Room to its normal blank state, then connected the attached refreshing room to a corridor set for Base Maintenance personnel to check and clean. He turned to address Myal next, but no sooner did he twist his seat around than Kerric found himself interrupted by an incoming mirror-call from the mayor's office.

Swiveling back to face it, he sighed and opened the connection. Burgher Sylva. Kerric barely managed to catch his wince as it started. He shifted it into a smile. "Sylva, how are you doing?"

"Just fine!" the middle-aged woman replied brightly. She let her smile slide into a smirk, her tone attempting to turn sultry. "I was wondering when we'll be going on that date you owe me. Obviously not tonight, as you're still putting things to rights up there, but . . . perhaps tomorrow night? Or the night after?"

Or how about never? an uncomplimentary corner of his mind thought. An incoming message from Jessina provided a grateful distraction. "One moment, Sylva; something's come up." Sending the link with the mayoral assistant into a soothing holding spell, all shades of blue and green with slow-pulsing patterns, he opened Jessina's mirror-connection. "Yes?"

"We're ready with the simulacrums for the new trap rooms,

Master Kerric," Jessina stated smoothly. She looked a lot better for having gotten a decent amount of sleep in the intervening hours. "Is Milady Myal ready to test them?"

Glancing over at Myal, Kerric found her sitting with squared shoulders and a firm nod. He answered for her "She is. Send the illusion-tests to Myal's crystal pad. Once they've been tested and basic flaws worked out, we'll run a mock-up. Hopefully the rooms will be fully enchanted and ready for testing within a week. New hazards are always popular."

Nodding, Jessina ended the connection. Kerric almost forgot the pending call from burgher Sylva, but Myal apparently hadn't.

"What is this date the assistant mayor mentioned?" she asked, her tone calm, if curious. She tapped the stylus on the broad tablet, activating the incoming information. Back home in Mendhi, there were similar such spells for chalkboards and smaller slates; these strange crystal tablets with their clear bodies and glowing images embedded within the mineral were exotic by comparison.

"Ah . . . it's just a bit of nonsense," he said, trying to dismiss it. "A bet about her trying to use a pair of rumors to quell suspicions on why the Tower went into lockdown and why I went inside, in the hopes of preventing anyone from trying to wrest control of the heart for themselves. Apparently it was only somewhat successful.

"The wager itself was that I'd regain control, and if I did, she'd take me on a date . . . and if I didn't, but survived, I'd take her on a date. For dinner. Or something like that," he said, not really remembering the details. "To be honest, I didn't pay it much attention. I just . . . need to figure out how to let her down. Gently. She's not really my type."

Myal considered that, since his tone implied that *she* was his type. She preferred thinking things through when there was time. Finally, she asked, "Did you *promise* to go on a date with her?"

"I . . . Yes, I suppose I did," Kerric admitted, not wanting to lie to Myal. "But I don't really want to . . ."

He trailed off as she gave him a quelling look. "It's just the two of you sharing a meal together," Myal stated. "I know you get along with the burgher, because everyone gets along with her. She's very nice. If you promised a meal with her, you should follow through. This isn't something which will harm you."

Kerric knew she was right. Still, the way he felt about Myal, he had to ask, "You wouldn't mind?"

"Of course, I'd mind," she scoffed, frowning at him. "A part of me is deeply thrilled we've been meshing so well, and that part of me wants to keep you entirely to myself. Most of the rest of me knows I cannot cage or confine you and expect you to still be yourself. Just as you cannot keep me from being myself whenever I go adventuring."

"I'd hardly compare a date with Sylva to a gauntlet run," he pointed out. "She's much too sweet. I may be interested in you, and not her, but that doesn't mean she deserves any scorn."

Myal rolled her eyes. "I didn't mean it like *that*. I meant your sense of honor and responsibility. Your sense of duty—not that *she's* a duty that has to be endured—I can't explain it well!" she finally said, catching the way he rolled his eyes. "My words are better when written down. Just . . . go arrange to have dinner with her. As you both promised."

She couldn't explain that it was an odd sort of fear that compelled her to push him on the date, even as she hated the idea deep inside. The fear that, despite how well they had gotten along on the gauntlet run, how they were still getting along well, he would somehow prefer someone else. He'd worked with the burgher for years, after all, and it was quite possible Kerric might prefer Sylva's company now that he wasn't being forced by circumstances to get along with one gangly, shy, awkward-feeling foreigner.

This wasn't a gauntlet run, or a sailing ship, or anywhere she felt comfortable, competent, and secure. This was a relationship, an area where she had always failed, thanks to her long-standing desire to become a Painted Warrior. None of the men she had tried courting back home had wanted much to do with her as a woman after finding out she was a woman who had deliberately chosen not to be a mother. As if it somehow made her *not* a woman anymore.

This relationship thing also felt like a far bigger risk than merely running the Master of the Tower through a lengthy maze of lethal traps. He was brilliant, strong, and skillful with his magic, and could easily have the pick of any woman in the region—or any man, if he were so inclined, though he didn't seem to be. Outside of her own specialization, Myal still didn't quite see what he saw in her of all people. So, to be fair, she would give him a chance to look at another woman. Sylva *was* nice. A real woman.

She bent her head over the tablet, focusing on the information she had been sent regarding new traps and danger scenarios.

Kerric knew something was bothering her, but if Myal couldn't put it into words, he couldn't address the problem directly. Re-activating the mirror-link with the mayor's office, he summoned up a smile for Sylva. "Sorry about that. Tomorrow night will be fine. I'll take you to the Honey Spear for dinner."

"Actually, I was thinking of cooking you a meal in my own home," Sylva countered, giving him a coy smile meant to coax him into changing his mind.

He wasn't coaxed. A meal in Sylva's home would be far too intimate, far too suggestive of things he simply wasn't interested in, with her. "No, that's alright. You deserve a chance to relax, not dash around cooking everything. I'm told the food is worthwhile at the Honey Spear. It's not the Tower kitchens, but it will make a nice change, I think. You did help quell rumors in the town while I was occupied, so you've earned a meal. How about eighth hour, tomorrow?"

Her face fell a little at his counteroffer, and he could guess why. The invitation sounded businesslike, not romantic, which was how Kerric was determined to keep it. If the mayor of Penambrion ever stepped down, the burgher was the one who would step into the position, and mayor and Master had to get along as business partners for the good of everyone in the region. Jilted lovers did not always get along.

Sylva sighed and nodded. "Alright. Tomorrow night, eighth hour. Would you like to come over to my home early for a drink?"

"I'll probably still be working. Jessina wants to upgrade several rooms with new dangers, which means a lot of spells have to be integrated in new ways into the system," he demurred. "Particularly if there are opponents designed to chase adventurers further than their origination-point chambers. But I'll come to your door at eighth hour sharp. See you then?"

"Yes, I'll see you then. I'm looking forward to it," Sylva added flirtatiously.

Kerric nodded politely, ended the spell connecting him to her mirror, and slumped in his chair, wondering what sort of business-related topics he could dredge up to fill a whole meal. The impact of the loss of a full day's worth of scrycastings, of course, but possibly also the spring plantings and the possibilities of late-season flooding in the valley.

A glance over at Myal showed her frowning down at her tablet. Thankfully, he knew that frown; he had seen it several times during their gauntlet run. She was merely concentrating on a new problem, not worrying over his dinner arrangements. The opening of another mirror scrying distracted him from the thought of telling her he'd take Sylva to dinner as prearranged, but that he'd save dessert for her. The call came from Jessina, who smiled wryly at him when he acknowledged the link.

"Sorry to interrupt yet again. I'm about to hand Topside Control over to Grador and the night shift, but I've just received a pair of participation requests for Myal the Magnificent. I thought I'd run them past the two of you, since I knew she was still in the Hall with you."

"Go on," Kerric said, as Myal glanced up in curiosity.

"The first," Jessina stated blandly, "is by a consortium of wealthy patrons in Senod-Gra. They have included Myal's name in a list of participants for a requested Seraglio gauntlet."

"Absolutely *not*," Kerric asserted crisply, without even having to think about it. When he did think, a heartbeat or two later, he glanced guiltily in Myal's direction. If she *wanted* to, that was her business, not his . . . *No, she does not*, he realized, spotting the relief in her eyes at his flat denial, along with the quick shake of her head that confirmed it. Relieved as well, he returned his gaze to the projected scrycasting. "What's the other request?"

"A scrycasting club down on the southern coast in Amaz wishes to see a series of Scavenger Hunt gauntlet scenarios. They're willing to pay extra for solo runs of competing adventurers, and want to pay for at least one big name. Myal makes the top of the list because she's a Painted Warrior, which is like a mage as well as a warrior. The rest are sword-and-spell types of lesser fame, since most of our big names are already booked for making it up to the patrons for the lost scrycasting time. It's a contract for eight short runs, no more than two hours apiece, once a day; live scrycasting time would start at ninth hour of the morning, local."

Again, he glanced at Myal. She had her thinking look on, and nodded within a few moments. He did as well. "She is willing, and the scheduling of it would give her plenty of time to rest between runs and still finish her evaluation of the newly proposed rooms. Veto her place in the first list, and draw up the standard adventuring and scrycasting contracts for the second.

"Remind the requesters in Senod-Gra that all adult-oriented gauntlet runs require at least three days' notice to track down and receive responses from all requested participants, and that participation of any one particular adventurer is *not* guaranteed. Tell Grador that if they have a problem with that, he can transfer their scrycall to me, and I'll handle it," Kerric finished.

That made his Topside Control lead chuckle. Jessina shook her head, her teeth white against her dark lips as she grinned. "I suspect they won't have any problems with it. Not when you put their City Hostess in her place. I'll handle this before I go—and take heart, Master Kerric," she added. "I can finally see the top of the task pile from here, which means we've been making excellent progress in catching up."

"Most thanks to you and the rest of the team. And I'm very grateful everyone, except the idiot Torven and his friends, passed their interrogation tests," Kerric added. "I was hoping everyone would, and am deeply grateful they did. I'll have to figure out what to do to thank all the staff for such strong loyalty."

"Invite them all to the Banqueting Hall for a feast," Myal offered, speaking up. "A feast, and a food fight. Offer to scrycast it as a bonus free present to all the patrons who lost service while the Tower was shut down."

Overhearing Myal's comment, Jessina widened her grin. "I like it. And I think it'll work. If you don't hire her for Tower Staff soon, *Master*, I'll have to smack you on the head. I'll chat with you tomorrow. Jessina out."

Kerric chuckled. It wasn't often the unflappable woman issued a threat toward him, but then it wasn't often he was idiotic. And he wasn't going to be an idiot. "Well, you heard the lady. She's the smartest person on my payroll. Care to work for the Tower, instead of just in it? At least, for part of the time?"

"I'll consider it," Myal murmured, though she smiled as she said it, warmed by the welcome and the admiration from both him and his colleague.

SEVENTEEN

yal hated everything in her clothes chests. It was not a happy thought; she was not normally a woman to fret over how she looked, but here she was, fretting. At least, outside of a scrycast she normally didn't care. During a gauntlet run, she wanted to look strong, competent, and a little bit sexy, since that contributed to her popularity, but this wasn't a run through the Tower meant to be viewed by hundreds, if not thousands, of wealthy patrons—she wasn't really sure how many people watched each individual mirror scrying, but she knew at least that many mirrors were involved.

Instead, this was a . . . well, she wasn't going out to dinner with Kerric, so it wasn't a dinner date. But she was determined to show up at the Honey Spear. To reassure herself that Kerric wasn't . . . That he wouldn't . . .

Just admit you're jealous! She finally demanded of herself, scowling at her dimly reflected image in the windowpanes of her bedchamber. *Admit you are jealous, Myal, that he's taking Sylva to dinner, and not you. And . . . and then admit you told him to do it, so it's your own fault.*

That was the worst of it. She had poured the salt of this evening onto her own wounds herself. Kerric had said he wasn't interested in Sylva, and that he *was* interested in her, Myal. He had all but whined about having to honor his bargain with the burgher of Penambrion, and showed enthusiasm for the adventurer with whom he had just run the worst of Tower gauntlets. Her brain, calm and logical in the face of danger, understood that Kerric wanted to be with her, not Sylva or someone else. That he'd had plenty of opportunities to pick someone else, yet had not, until her.

Her heart wasn't nearly as big and tough and brave and strong as her physical self. Nor as wise as her head. Proof of it lay in her acceptance of the serial scavenger hunt gauntlets. She should have taken an extra day of rest, but the bonuses for her patron-requested appearance this morning had been too good to turn down. There had been a few tense moments earlier in the day when she had worried as much for what Kerric must be thinking of the risks she was running—and almost distracting herself dangerously by it—as she'd been worried herself for her actual safety. She still had a mottled patch of bruises along her left side from catching an ogre's club, though the bruises would be gone by tomorrow.

The relief in those gray eyes when the Master of the Tower had congratulated her team via mirror upon their return to the Adventuring Hall told her he had fretted quite a lot during her trip. If she kept doing it, she'd keep worrying him. Yet Myal wasn't quite ready to retire yet. She wasn't entirely willing to continue running the riskiest excursions anymore, but she knew she'd miss the excitement of it. *Some of that* could *be soothed by Jessina's suggestion this afternoon, by test-running the new gauntlet sections the Tower's research mages have been creating. She thinks I'd be a perfect test-adventurer for such things, since I'm still young and fast enough for it, and Kerric did admit there'd be many safety features lined up to protect me from any malfunctioning traps or spells . . .*

In the light of the expensive but worth-every-thronai light-globe illuminating her tenement bedchamber, Myal stared at her reflection in the glazed window. *He was trying hard to be encouraging and supportive in spite of his concerns . . . and I threw him into a dinner-date with a woman he's not interested in. I should go be there to support him . . . except I still don't know what I should wear.*

Mindful of the passing of time, Myal finally gave up and drew out one of her older outfits, a Mendhite style vest and kilt set. Both were woven from silk, a little creased with age, though at least the laundry shop two streets over knew how to keep them bleached white. They were rather daring for Aian society; the vest had no sleeves, showed off a good portion of her cleavage, and didn't quite meet the waistband of her kilt, which in turn just barely covered her from waist to knees. But the outfit was flattering, and made her colorful tattoos stand out in contrast to the plain white fabric.

A pair of white—well, almost white, slightly scuffed from use—knee-high boots completed the outfit, covering just enough of her legs to satisfy most Aian sensibilities. Not that Penambrion was very conservative; the entire region depended upon the scry-castings of the Tower, a very visual medium, for its best source of income, but Myal didn't want to offend. Or attract the wrong attention; some male adventurers assumed that if a woman showed up in a less-than-conservative amount of clothing, they were looking for an adventure of an adult nature.

She didn't want to attract the wrong attention. That would be disruptive for Kerric's meal, which wasn't the point of going to the Honey Spear at the same time as his dinner with Sylva.

She almost left her apartment with just her clothes and a belt with a coin pouch attached. But when she went to fill it with enough silver scepterai for her supper, Myal found the necklace she had salvaged from the Tower. Glittering rows of diamonds had been chained together between three large pearls, all of it strung together with links of white gold. The necklace would not clash with her outfit, and actually didn't look bad when she checked her reflextion.

A bit flashy, perhaps, and very wealthy-looking. Myal added a dagger in a gray-dyed sheath to her belt as a visible warning she wasn't to be trifled with, then checked that her braid was still neatly plaited down to her waist. Ready, she left her tenement. As she walked down the steps, the folds of the kilt brushed against her thighs and knees, giving her an extra touch of confidence. The knife in its sheath was a familiar weight, counterbalancing the coin purse strung opposite it. And the necklace drew startled, appraising looks from the adventurers exiting the Honey Spear when she reached its entrance.

Confident in herself—she was a popular, wealthy adventurer, filled with stories both written and verbal waiting to be told—she pushed open the door and stepped inside. The noise of the place washed over her, not as a babble of voices, but rather as a rushing tide of whispers. No one spoke above more than a murmur, but it seemed as if everyone had an opinion to share, however hushed that sharing might be. Seated off to one side at a table just big enough for two, the Master of the Tower and the burgher of Penambrion were the focal points for all those whispers, and their accompanying stares.

Until she walked in. After no fewer than five people did a double take, glancing her way in idle curiosity, then whipping their heads back and forth between Kerric and her, Myal decided *someone* had spread a rumor that her trip into the Tower with the

Master had ended up being a romantic one. It was the only reason why she could imagine people being so keenly interested in, yet wary of, her reaction at seeing the Master with the burgher. Unfortunately for them, she already knew, so she really didn't have a reaction for them to gossip over. Unfortunately for her, she didn't know who had started the rumor, so she didn't know who to thump for their impertinence.

Finding an unoccupied seat was a bit difficult, even though a handful of men and women had left when she entered. Even just wading through the tables, trying to look, was hard; Myal had to back up and detour a few times. A large hand lifted and waved as she came close to one table, beckoning her over to it. The hand belonged to Nafiel, who removed his leg from the seat next to his and gestured for her to take it instead. Also at the table were two others she knew. Shalia Truehand, her downstairs neighbor, was one. She was seated on the lap of the other, Rick the Archer of all people, the most laid-back, yet second-most successful, adventurer in the Tower's history.

That was the face she hadn't been able to place, the evening Kerric had come to visit both of them in his quest for a gauntlet partner. Normally, the man smiled a slow, goofy, relaxed grin at best; he didn't leer. Except he was leering openly at Shalia now, and she was smirking right back. But as much as she was curious about the pair—Shalia was infamous for being rather intense and Rick famous for being very mellow—Nafiel's choice of a greeting snagged her attention.

"Ahhh, Myal the Magnificent! Marvelous to meet you this evening," the large, muscular, bare-chested male stated. He grinned at her, no doubt amused by his alliteration. The same hand that had beckoned her close slapped one meaty thigh below his fur-covered loincloth, a garment shaped something like a kilt, only scandalously short by anything but swimming standards. "If you sit on *my* lap, we can get in another one, maybe two people at this table, yes? Everyone wants to be here tonight."

"No, thank you," Myal replied dryly. Her gaze wasn't on the handsome, overly muscular, brown-haired man next to her, tall and gorgeous and barely dressed just so he could show off all those carefully maintained muscles. It lingered instead on the handsome, modestly muscled, brown-haired man about five tables away, who was fully clothed from the neck down.

Kerric had decided to dress in a deep blue tunic accented in swirling patterns of silvery gray and black silk, with black cloth buttons-and-loops for the closures, local-style. She couldn't see his trousers from here, but she knew the outfit from seeing it in formal scrycast announcements in the past; the trousers would be a solid blue, the boots and belt black accented with silver trim. His shoulder-length hair had been pulled back on the sides and top with a silver clasp, leaving every expression on his face fully visible as he chatted animatedly with the burgher.

It was not the outfit she had last seen him in, post-gauntlet. That had been shades of dark to medium gray, and made out of high-quality but common linen, not expensive imported silk. A twinge of jealousy stung at her thoughts the moment she realized he had actually dressed up for his dinner with Sylva. *Of course he dresses up when I tell him to dine with another woman . . . I shouldn't have told him to do this.*

Naturally, she *dressed up, too,* Myal acknowledged silently, cattily. *Man-thief, baiting her trap with no doubt her best outfit.* Part of her wanted to find something wrong with the woman's choice. Unfortunately the shades of deep rose, light pink, and subtle accents in pale blue on her *chosam,* the local formal tunic-dress for women, actually flattered her light complexion and her feminine curves. With her blonde hair piled up on her head and her expression delighted in whatever they were talking about, she looked very beautiful. Alluring, even.

Except Sylva's delight was too genuine to really feel catty over it. The woman was sweet, and competent, and nice, and . . . Myal couldn't hate her for capturing Kerric's attention. *In their conversation. Just in their conversation*, she struggled to reassure herself. *He's just being nice because she's a business colleague, a fellow leader of the region—no, he's being nice because* he *is nice, and* she *is nice, and I really need to stop thinking catty thoughts.*

Nafiel leaned in close enough that she could feel his body heat. "You really shouldn't look so jealous in public," he murmured in her ear. "People will start taking bets on whether you'll try to pick a fight with Sylva over the Master. As much as we're in the business of entertaining, that sort of public spectacle wouldn't be scrycast, so you wouldn't be getting paid for it."

"Sorry I'm late getting to you," the tavern maid stated, reaching Myal's other side. "By the Gods, it sure is crowded in here tonight! Word spread fast that the Master was dating a woman, and *everyone* wants to come see," she added in a quiet but chatty tone. "Tonight's big meal is roasted beef with glazed onions, mashed tubers, and all the buttered squash-bread you could want, but we also have a goose that's just come out of the baking oven with a nice stuffing, if you're willing to wait a few more minutes, or a hearty fish soup if you're not. That, I can get back to you within . . . um," the woman hedged, peering through the crowd. She chuckled ruefully. "Well, another five minutes just to wade through all the tables, maybe. I think half the town is trying to get inside, tonight."

"Beef," Myal ordered. "Please."

"I'll be back as soon as I can with your plate. Anything to drink?"

"She'll have cider," Nafiel stated, upturning one of the clean mugs on the table as he reached for a pitcher. "That way you don't have to carry extra."

"That'll be a blessing—I'll be back shortly," the server promised, already wiggling and edging her way back out from between the tables toward the kitchen.

Myal frowned at Nafiel. "I don't wish to get drunk."

He leaned in close again. "It's fresh, not fermented." He fixed her with a pointed look, his hazel eyes looking more green than blue or gray at this distance. "People like you and me, with all our strengths, should not get intoxicated in public. Particularly when our emotions are running strong."

"I am fine. I am under complete control," Myal asserted—and squeaked in shock when the Pashai barbarian reached over and scooped her onto his lap without warning.

"Then you'll not smack me for this," he murmured in her ear as she perched there in shock. She didn't have to worry about him being after her expensive necklace; Nafiel was easily the wealthiest adventurer in the valley, though a stranger would never know it from the way he dressed and acted. Raising his voice, he greeted two people who had moved up to take the barmaid's place. "Zevra, and Salonnei—Adventuring Hall staff, yes? I thought I recognized your beautiful smile. Come, sit; Myal has generously given up that nice comfortable chair to sit on my lap, just for the two of you!"

"One chair, for two of us?" the stripe-clad Zevra asked, while his companion giggled and blushed at Nafiel's compliment. The adventurer grinned, seated himself, and pulled her onto his lap as well, though he didn't nibble on her ear as Rick the Archer was doing to Shalia, both of their dinners all but forgotten.

There wasn't much Myal could say otherwise; Zevra was a friend and fellow adventurer—as was Nafiel, even though she did want to smack him—and there really weren't any spare chairs to be had in the tavern. She was lucky she could even see Kerric and Sylva from this angle, though she suspected Nafiel had perched her on that leg, facing in that direction, so that she wouldn't have to strain to see the Master and the burgher enjoying their meal.

Even as she thought about Kerric, he looked around the room in an idle fashion while his dining companion drank from the red wine in her goblet. Their eyes met. A warm, happy smile lit up his face—the previous ones had been honest smiles, but this was a genuine one. Just then, Nafiel leaned forward, cutting off Myal's view of her lover. When he sat back, offering her the mug he had poured, Kerric's brow had pinched in a frown. Not an outright scowl, but not a happy expression, either.

The gossiping whispers and speculative murmurings picked up in their intensity as people followed the line of that frown from Kerric to the Nafiel-seated Myal and back. That did it. Myal was no dunce when it came to public entertainment. She was now the focus of far too many eyes, far too many thoughts, and far too much potential for harmful gossip to dare push off the showman barbarian's lap, or slap him, or stalk out of the tavern . . . or confront Sylva in anything but the most polite of fashions.

"Good girl," Nafiel murmured in her ear, praising her. He almost sounded like Kerric when he said it, but his voice merely irritated her. "Nothing stirs a man's resolve like thinking another man is courting his woman."

He's deliberately *provoking Kerric with jealousy?* Myal realized with a shock. Turning, she eyed the strong, powerful, highly skilled fighter. Hissing into his ear to keep their conversation as private as possible, she demanded, "Are you insane? You do *not* provoke a fight with the Tower Master!"

"Actually, I'm looking forward to seeing how he'll handle this," Nafiel returned calmly, picking up his own mug. He did so in the same dry tone he often used during a gauntlet run to describe encountering yet another very lethal trap. Myal recalled him having used it once to describe the Scales of Justice, in fact.

"Adventurers!" she huffed, unable to believe that he could be such a danger-addict as to taunt the most powerful mage in the land.

Nafiel, in the middle of a sip of his cider, choked on it with a laugh, and started coughing. Apparently, he hadn't expected *her*, a fellow adventurer, to be so scornful of her own profession. The Hall worker, Salonnei, reached over and whacked the large man on the back a couple of times, hard enough to rock his torso. "—Enough! Gods above, woman! They should put *you* in the Tower as one of the dangers. Zevra, I hope you have some good healing talismans in your home, with *her* strength to deal with."

The commotion drew Sylva's attention as well as Kerric's. She glanced their way, studied Myal, Nafiel, and the others, then looked back at Kerric, only to swiftly follow his frowning gaze back to Myal seated on Nafiel's lap among the others. Her brow furrowed as well, clearly not happy that her companion's attention was more focused on another woman than on her.

The gossip level intensified around them when the other patrons in the tavern noticed *that* as well. A modest distraction for Myal came in the form of the tavern maid heroically making it back to her table in record time with a tray of plates and baskets of the sweet, moist squash-bread that everyone locally liked. She gave Myal her plate, accepted the handful of coins thrust her way without being counted, and waded off to deliver other food to other customers. Leaving Myal to sit there on another man's lap and pick at her meal while *her* man didn't have to share a chair while he conversed and dined with another woman.

A nice woman, whom she honestly could not hate or even think of harming, though Myal heartily wished she were gone.

Halfway across the room, Kerric dragged his attention back

to the woman seated at his own table. He did not like seeing Myal seated so . . . so acceptingly in the big adventurer's lap. *Why isn't she elbowing him, or walking off, or . . . Well, it is very crowded in here,* he acknowledged, watching her accept her plate of food, barely able to make room for it next to Nafiel's. *And there are two others sharing seats, though it looks like they're actual couples . . . and I really wish she had a seat of her own, dammit. They look far too good together like that.*

I also wish he were wearing some actual clothes, dammit—even in the winter, he barely puts a fur throw on his shoulders. But now it's summer, and with all those enchanted amulets and such to keep him safe and warm or cool, whatever the weather, which means she's sitting there on his naked thigh, and . . .

"Kerric?" Sylva asked, her tone edged enough to recapture his attention. Turning back to the burgher, he offered her a polite smile.

"Sorry—I knew it'd be crowded when I brought you here, but I didn't think it'd be quite this crowded," he apologized. "Any time I take a woman out for a meal, everyone always speculates on whether or not I'm developing a love life."

She smiled again, mollified. Bracing her elbow on the table, Sylva rested her chin on her fingers in a flirtatious pose and purred, "Should we give them something to *really* gossip about?"

Stifling the urge to wince, Kerric shook his head. "I'd rather not give them that kind of speculation. You and I are colleagues, and one day you will be the mayor of Penambrion. I wouldn't do anything to jeopardize such a good working relationship between the Tower and the town."

Her smile fell. Straightening, she picked up her fork and stabbed at her mashed roots, before asking, "Yes, well . . . surely you *do* want a personal life, yes? With the right woman? Someone intelligent, and cultured, and . . ."

"And I have found that woman," Kerric told her quietly, aware that the men and women seated at the two nearest tables to theirs had fallen quiet, straining to hear their words. "She is the right woman for me, and I am the right man for her." *Even if she's sitting in the wrong man's lap*, a corner of his mind snarked. Kerric kept his expression and his tone gentle. "But as much as many people out there could try to wish it otherwise, I am not the right man for *you*, and you are correspondingly not the right woman for me—you want children, Sylva," he reminded her. "You've alluded to offspring at least three times so far this evening.

"I do not. And I would never limit a woman's right to choose for or against such things in a matter as important as that, or force her to change who and what she wants herself to be, just as I wouldn't care to have a woman try to change me so radically." Picking up fork and knife, he cut into the last few bits of beef on his plate. "Each of us deserves a partner in our lives with similar viewpoints and goals. There will be a man out there who is perfect for you—many men who would be perfect.

"I, however, am not listed among their number, and never will be. Our most basic preferences are too different," he asserted as Sylva drew in a breath to protest. "I respect you too much, Sylva, to demand anything less than your happiness with the *right* man."

She subsided, scowling a bit, though her distress didn't last long. "Well, I can honestly say I tried. I've had feelings for you for quite some time, Kerric. A pity they're not returned."

"If they're feelings of admiration and respect, they are," he pointed out, popping a forkful of beef into his mouth. An expressive shrug dismissed any chance for more romantic-type feelings while he chewed.

Sylva sighed and toyed with the remains of her meal. "I suppose I'll die an old maid, then."

Kerric snorted, coughed, and cleared his mouth with a sip of his cider. Like many mages, particularly powerful ones, he avoided drinking much in the way of alcohol for the sake of self-control. A small beer here, a light ale there, a single glass of wine sometimes, but tonight, nothing but fresh-pressed cider from the apples grown here in Penambrion. "The only thing you have to worry about, Sylva, is making sure that you can get along for the rest of your life with *yourself*. Once you take care of that part, you'll be happy no matter who comes or goes in your life."

"Hmphf," she scoffed, though she didn't otherwise protest. Eyeing the rest of the crowded tavern, her gaze fell on Myal, seated on Nafiel's lap. This time her frown was a puzzled one. "Wait . . . you said you thought you'd found the right woman for you . . . and you've been rather close with Myal the Magnificent ever since your Tower run . . . but she's cuddled up with Nafiel. If *she's* the one you're interested in, how could you hope to compete with *him*? No offense," Sylva added quickly, looking back at Kerric, "but he *is* the dreamiest man in the whole region."

Kerric knew Sylva had a point. He also knew Myal's feelings on the other man; she had sworn she and Nafiel were merely colleagues and friends, nothing more. Pricklings of jealousy bothered him every time he glanced their way . . . but the mage knew that he had to trust her word. She believed in giving one's word and following through on it, which was why he was here dining with Sylva instead of with her.

Shrugging, he switched the topic back to the needs of the region, avoiding that particular subject. "Speaking of Myal, she did put up a good suggestion yesterday. With so many people in the Tower and the Hall and the town itself working hard to set everything back to rights and on schedule again, it was suggested we hold a big feast-and-food-fight in the Banqueting Hall in the

Tower to celebrate their efforts, and to turn it into a free bonus scrycasting—hence the food-fight scenario—to make up for all the lost entertainment time.

"Obviously we cannot get everyone into the actual room itself in the Tower, but there is the Penambrion Market Hall. If we pick a few days before the Spring Planting Festival next month, would it be permissible for us to hold the feast-and-fight in there? With the appropriate spells for safety, pre- and post-cleanup, and a brief suspension of the anti-scrying wards, I think it could be managed," Kerric offered, "but I wanted to know what you think of the idea. Using the Market Hall for public events is your area of expertise, not mine."

Perking up a little, the burgher considered his request with a thoughtful look while she sipped her wine. A sidelong glance showed Nafiel once again leaning his brutish barbarian head far too close to Myal for Kerric's comfort, murmuring something in her ear. Something which made her laugh. He knew he didn't have exclusive rights on making her laugh, but Kerric didn't like watching another man managing it.

Myal, halfway across the room and snickering so hard she snorted, quickly covered her nose and mouth. Panting to recover her breath, she twisted just enough to elbow Nafiel subtly in the chest. He grunted and winced slightly, but otherwise didn't register the hit openly. "That is a *terrible* pun," she admonished, trying to sound stern instead of silly. "Stop trying to cheer me up just to make Kerric jealous!"

"It does seem to be working, though," Nafiel pointed out. "He keeps glaring at me between ogling you and trying not to frown at her."

"You exaggerate," Myal stated, forced by honesty to admit that much. She picked up her mug for another drink between bites of tender beef. "He's just frowning slightly. That's hardly a glare. And there's no need to make him jealous. I'm pretty sure he'll still like me more than her when his dinner arrangements are done."

"Ah, but it's not just for your sake," Nafiel sighed, resting his chin on her shoulder for a moment, staring in the same direction as Myal, though not at the same target. "I'd very much like to date our Town burgher, if I could. I do love older women . . . so sexy, so confident, so ready to be loved thoroughly by the right man . . ."

"Why don't you marry her?" Myal quipped dryly. Hearing his sigh, a sincerely regret-filled sound, she realized why he couldn't in the next moment. ". . . You're serious about her?"

"I'd like to be," he murmured, picking up his own mug. "But if I did that, my career would be over because I couldn't be an effective husband and father if I kept risking my life and limb every day . . . and *she'd* be fielding death threats from outraged patrons. For that matter, you might have taken yourself off the Seraglio list, but I'm firmly on it. That's too much money to pass up, and I have a whole village with serious problems I'm trying to support, back home."

That was the first time she'd heard him mention such a thing. Myal gave him a curious look. Everyone knew Nafiel loved his home village and spoke proudly of the people he had grown up with, but this was the first time he'd mentioned any difficulties among them. "Is everything alright, back home?"

"You didn't hear?" he returned. At the shake of her head, Nafiel shrugged. "The old king of Pasha is dying, and his sons and nephews are all fighting to be named his next heir. Literally fighting. My home village has been raided three times this winter by the so-called armies the various factions have been raising. They've been forced to eat the grain set aside for seed just to survive, they have so little left, so I've been buying extra food and seed and shipping it to them under armed guard . . . but there's only so much I can do from several hundred miles away. I may have to leave the Tower to go home and fight, if it comes to an actual succession war. So it looks like I might lose my favorite job anyway."

"I can't imagine the Tower without you, Nafiel," Myal murmured. "But I do understand why you'd have to go. If Mendhi were as close, and *my* family were threatened, I'd be heading home, too."

He smiled wistfully at her understanding, then pulled her into a hug. Not a romantic one, just a thankful one for her sympathy. Myal couldn't quite hug him back in her current position, but she did curl an arm up around his, squeezing the muscular limb in return.

A moment later, the Master of the Tower stood . . . and the tavern fell deathly quiet within the span of three heartbeats. Dozens of eyes flicked between the short but powerful mage, and the tall, muscular warrior. Myal stiffened, worried, but Nafiel didn't let her go. "It's okay," he breathed in her ear, mindful of the sudden silence. "It's just that they've finished their dinner. He hasn't seen this little hug. *Yet.*"

The amusement in the barbarian's voice told her he was looking forward to the explosion when Kerric did. Rolling her eyes at Nafiel's addiction to adrenaline, Myal waited to see what Kerric would do. As she—and the whole of the crowded tavern— watched, he bowed to the burgher and spoke. "Thank you for a lovely dinner, Sylva. Your company, as always, is most enjoyable. I'll look forward to the arrangements for renting the Market Hall for that party."

With another slight, polite dip of his head, he turned as if to leave, though his gaze swept through the silent, watchful crowd and spotted Myal snuggled in Nafiel's burly arms. One brow lifting silently, he headed their way.

Chairs scraped and bodies shifted, clearing a better path between the Master of the Tower and his target. Some of the mage-adventurers whispered under their breath, auras lighting up with protective shieldings, clearly getting ready to defend themselves from the impending fight. No fool, Kerric knew they had seen his many glances at Myal, both happy and unhappy, during the meal. He knew what conclusions they were drawing, and how most of them expected a fight, or at the very least a challenge to a duel of some sort. *Or maybe they're secretly taking mental bets on how quickly I'll get him fired from the Adventuring Hall roster . . . or how fast I'll strike with a ball of fire or something.*

He did none of those things, however. Stopping next to the couple, he bowed slightly to Nafiel and stated clearly, calmly, and almost cheerfully, "Thank you, Nafiel, for keeping my beloved company while I was occupied with town and Tower business. I trust I can call on you again, should another such need arise?"

Nafiel first grinned, then chuckled, then laughed heartily. He released Myal, holding out his large, callused hand for the shorter man to grip. "If she doesn't find me too boring! I can hardly compare to you, milord. Myal, I'll see you tomorrow at the Adventurer's Hall. Master Kerric, I'll see you for the debriefing on that Seraglio run."

That little comment reignited the gossip mill, and Kerric almost could have kissed the other man for it. Now all the whispers were about the salaciousness of a Seraglio gauntlet, and the fact that the highly eligible Nafiel had agreed to compete . . . though there were still several murmurings discussing the diffusion of tension between the two men. Those who had expected a fight relaxed their bodies and their powers with relieved looks. Others—mostly women, but a few men—gave both Kerric and Myal dirty looks when she placed her hand in his, allowing him to assist her to her feet.

"If you're done with your dinner, my dear lady," Kerric stated, not bothering to hide his words, "I've prepared a special dessert for you in my quarters. Would you care to partake?"

"Always," she replied, deeply relieved there wouldn't be a fight. She liked but didn't love Nafiel—not like she loved Kerric—but she didn't wish him to be hurt, either. There was no doubt in her mind who the winner would be in a fight between the two men, even accounting for all of Nafiel's enchanted charms and baubles, each of which was meant to either level the playing field or give him an advantage in a fight, much like her more visible tattoos.

Gossip followed them as Kerric entwined his fingers with hers and led her out of the tavern. Once they were outside in the cool night air, the noise of everyone whispering and murmuring swelled into outright, open talking. The Master of the Tower sighed and said, "They're taking bets on our relationship, you know. It's like a regular Senod-Gra in there."

"They can take bets all they want. I'm the one who's going to win," Myal stated. She had seen how Sylva looked at the end of their meal, a little disappointed perhaps, but not at all devastated or resentful that she'd been turned down. Somehow, Kerric had dealt with the burgher as gracefully as he had dealt with the barbarian. That satisfied her, though she did have one comment to make. "I do wish to change my bet, however."

"Oh? You mean the forty-three years bet, on how long we'll be together?" he asked, wanting confirmation they were on the same topic.

"Yes. I want to make it *sixty*-three years. Three years longer than your bet," she stated.

Kerric laughed and shook his head ruefully. "You're making it very difficult for me to out-bet you. Not even the most powerful mage in the world can make himself and his beloved live forever, you know."

"True, but I do like the odds of living a very long and very happy rest-of-my-life with you," Myal stated.

"Mm, yes," he agreed, loosening his grip on her hand in favor of slipping his arm around her waist. She draped hers around his shoulders. "In that case, I'll make my bet for Happily Ever After."

Myal started to sigh happily, enjoying the night with her beloved at her side. Then frowned. "Wait, I thought you wrote technical books, not romantic stories."

"True, but I'm willing to give it a try—and, dammit, I knew there was something I forgot to do," he groused under his breath. Giving her waist a squeeze, Kerric said, "Remind me after we make love to start reading your story booklets."

"What, you're not going to read any of them for at least a week?" Myal mock-worried.

Kerric chuckled and hugged her close as they walked side-by-side. "Silly woman, you're under contract, remember? I'd have to stop making love to you for at least a few hours every day for your scrycastings. Though I won't stop loving you, just to warn you—and let me tell you, my heart was pounding when you faced off against the Choking Shadows trap. Could you please move a little faster when facing off against such things?"

"I was worried about whether *you* would be worried, and *that* distracted me," Myal admitted. She shrugged and added, "Now that I know you'll be worried about me, I can relax."

He snorted. "Oh, is *that* how that works? I sit there in the Tower fretting over you being harmed, like that horrid whallop you took this morning, and you're *happy* about it?"

"I am if it means you love me," she pointed out.

Stopping her with a squeeze of her waist, Kerric turned to

look up at his beautiful, tall, tattoo-painted warrior. "Myal, I love you, I want to share the rest of my crazy life with you, and I want to share the rest of yours, too. '*If*' that means that I love you," he scorned, repeating her doubt. "Have I finally made myself clear enough for you?"

She thought about it a few moments, then nodded. "Yes. You have."

Kerric started to head toward the edge of town again, then stopped mid-step. He faced her fully again. ". . . Well?"

"Well, what?" Myal asked.

"Well, do you love me that much in return?" he prodded her, rolling his eyes.

There weren't enough street lanterns close enough to see the movement of those gray eyes of his, but she could hear it in his tone. Myal looped her arms around his shoulders, pulling him close. "What do you think?"

"I think, if you don't answer me promptly, I'm going to turn you over my knee and spank you again," he stated impatiently. Then paused and added honestly, "Actually, that was rather fun for both of us, so I might do it anyway."

She blushed, remembering how much both of them had indeed enjoyed it. Kissing her lover on the forehead, she stated firmly, "Yes, Kerric, I love you that much, too. I look forward to the next sixty-three . . . wait, we haven't settled what the wager is for, have we? Who gets what, if we win?"

"We will *not* discuss that on the city streets," Kerric stated, nudging her into moving again. He did lift his head for a quick, soothing kiss on her cheek as she complied. "We've just fed all of Penambrion, the valley, and the Tower enough gossip fodder for the next dozen weeks. They only need to know there's a bet on us making it all the way to Happily Ever After. They *don't* need to know what the prize is if we do."

Nodding, she released him from the loop of her arms and laced her fingers with his once more. A minute later, a thought crossed her mind. "Kerric?"

"Yes, my love?"

She liked the sound of that, and decided to use it herself as well, but carefully did not let it distract her from her question. "Kerric, my love, *is* there a trap, or room, or gauntlet or whatever, called 'Happily Ever After'?"

"Yes, there is. And you've just triggered it," he told her. "It's a timed trap, too. You'll have sixty-three years to figure a way out of it."

Her laughter rang through the night-cloaked streets, mixing well with his chuckle.

THE SONG OF THE GUARDIANS

When serpent crept into their hall:
Danger waits for all who board,
Trying to steal that hidden tone.
Painted Lady saves the lord;
Tower's master's not alone.

Calm the magics caught in thrall:
Put your faith in strangers' pleas,
Keeper, Witch, and treasure trove;
Ride the wave to calm the trees,
Servant saves the sacred Grove.

Cult's awareness, it shall rise:
Hidden people, gather now;
Fight the demons, fight your doubt.
Gearman's strength shall then endow,
When Guild's defender casts them out.

Synod gathers, tell them lies:
Efforts gathered in your pride
Lost beneath the granite face.
Painted Lord, stand by her side;
Repentance is the Temple's grace.

Brave the dangers once again:
Quarrels lost to time's own pace
Set aside in danger's face.
Save your state; go make your choice
When Dragon bows unto the Voice.

Sybaritic good shall reign:
Island city, all alone
Set your leader on his throne.
Virtue's knowledge gives the most,
Aiding sanctions by the Host.

Faith shall now be mended whole:
Soothing songs kept beasts at bay
But sorrow's song led King astray.
Demon's songs shall bring out worse
Until the Harper ends your curse.

Save the world is Guardians' goal:
Groom's mistake and bride's setback
Aids the foe in its attack.
Save the day is Jinx's task,
Hidden in the royal Masque.

—AS PROPHESIED BY THE SEER HAUPANEA

TURN THE PAGE FOR A
PREVIEW OF JEAN JOHNSON'S NEXT
GUARDIANS OF DESTINY NOVEL

THE GROVE

COMING IN DECEMBER 2013
FROM BERKLEY SENSATION

ONE

Calm the magics caught in thrall:
Put your faith in strangers' pleas,
Keeper, Witch, and treasure trove;
Ride the wave to calm the trees,
Servant saves the sacred Grove.

WESTERN KATAN

Aradin Teral eyed the priest tottering with uneven steps from altar to altar in the Westraven Chapel. The man was ninety if he was a day, with hair not only white but wispy and thinned with age, a face with more seams than a student tailor's practice piece, and two canes to hold himself upright. Still, the man was revered by the locals, some of whom stood in the center of the eight altars. The rest, including Aradin, stood or sat on the benches placed outside the eight altars and watched while the new father toted his infant daughter from altar to altar in the priest's wobbling wake.

In accordance with local customs, the newborn was to be blessed by both the God Jinga and His Wife Kata at each of

Their four altars, representing the four seasons, four aspects, four this and four that. It was an interesting religion, one of the older ones around, and apparently a conglomeration of two individual sets of worship combined many centuries ago into a single faith in a single, unified nation. Enough time had passed that the two different styles of worship for the local God and Goddess had been successfully and smoothly blended. Normally, Aradin would enjoy it, as he enjoyed learning about any manner of new cultures and faiths in his travels.

This time, however, he wasn't traveling abroad for the usual reasons. If he had been, Aradin would not have been in a large chapel like this, watching a newborn receive an elaborate set of blessings. The Darknanan sighed under his breath, wondering how long this service would take. At the moment, the most elaborately decorated, flower-wreathed altars were the ones for summer, given the actual time of year down here below the Sun's Belt. Unfortunately, the age-stooped priest was only just now moving on to the blessings for autumn. Those would be followed by the rites for winter, and then spring, before closing the "year" with one last rite at the summer altar.

(. . . *This won't do at all,*) Aradin thought. Not to himself alone, but to the Guide he bore inside the Doorway of his soul. (*He's kind and thoughtful and everyone respects him . . . but I seriously doubt Prelate Tomaso could survive a trip through the Dark. He'd be liable to die physically in there from the shock of it. That's never a good idea.*)

Teral shrugged mentally. It was all the older male could do, since Aradin was the one in command of their shared body. (*So we look at the next on our list. Or better yet, ask him who he thinks would be a good representative before their local Gods. Just don't mention politics.*)

(*I have to. We almost picked Priestess Tenathe. If we hadn't been there the day word of the Corvis brothers' claim for independence reached her ears, we would've picked a woman enraged enough to sabotage everything,)* Aradin reminded his Guide.

(Yes, yes, I know,) Teral dismissed, clasping a mental hand on his Host's mental shoulder. *(The Seers have predicted this Nightfall place will be the focus for the new Convocation of the Gods, if all goes well, and it is vitally important that Orana Niel speaks before the reconvened Convocation. But it's hardly our fault the Katani government cannot stand these Nightfallers.)*

(Only the politically active ones,) Aradin thought back, snorting softly under his breath. *(I don't envy Cassua, having to deal with the Mendhites. They've been seeking a Living Host since before the Aian Convocation fell.)*

(Heh, feel sorry for our Brothers and Sisters who have to pick out a Mekhanan priest,) Teral joked back, though it wasn't much of a joke. Official Katani policy might have been anti-Nightfall, but at least this was a civilized and polite land. The kingdom of Mekhana was not. Or rather, its government was not.

The priest's voice, wavering but rich with belief, rose and fell in cadences that were familiar, even if the rituals themselves were not. Both males could understand the words being said; Aradin wore a translation pendant, which allowed him to read, write, hear, and speak in a specific language—in this case, Katani. But while the actual words of the blessings and aspects being invoked were unfamiliar, there was something soothing about being in a fellow priest's presence.

Then again, after having spent almost four months roaming this land, Aradin and his Guide Teral were becoming increasingly familiar with the Katani way of life.

Like Darkhana, both lands had a God and a Goddess. The priesthoods of both lands accepted both males and females, mages and non-mages. Then again, both lands had a fairly even ratio of one mage born for every fifty without any added powers, their numbers more or less evenly divided among males and females. Of course, the Katani religion was a bit more lighthearted about some things, following in the wake of their so-called Boisterous God Jinga, who served as counterpart and foil for the more Serene Goddess Kata.

Back home, their God was Darkhan, the slain deity who had formerly been the Elder Brother Moon. Millennia ago, His Highest Priestess, Dark Anna, had bound her very life to His out of love and worship. When the third and farthest moon had been destroyed by demonic efforts, shattering His original power-base, she had managed to salvage the God of their ancient people. Now, He served as the God of the Dead, He who guides lost souls to the Afterlife.

The High Priestess's sacrifice had directly aided the world's effort to thwart an invasion attempt by the denizens of the Netherhells, and the upswelling of faith and gratitude had elevated her to Goddess level, forever bound to the Dead God. A new faith had been born, rising out of the ashes of the old, and the people of Darkhana had moved on. That background and its resulting mythos didn't exactly lend itself to an overly cheerful or buoyant religion, though the Darkhanan faith wasn't completely somber.

Since all lives, all souls around the world went through the cycle of being born, eventually dying, and of traveling through the Dark on their way to the Afterlife, home of the Gods, Darkhanan Witches didn't think of themselves as being the one true religion, or the only faith worth following. Their entire philosophy when traveling abroad was based around being an adjunct to whatever beliefs a person might hold while they were alive, and an advocate for that person when they were sent to the Gods for judgment on how they had lived their lives, whether that judgment would end in a punishment or a reward.

(We celebrate life, and we do not fear death,) Teral murmured,

following his Host's sub-thoughts. The newborn squirmed a little in her father's arms, emitting a *mehhh meh* sound that said she
would need nursing soon, but otherwise cooperated. *(So while
this ceremony is going on a bit long compared to some we've seen . . . it's
an auspicious day whenever we can celebrate life, even if it's in a foreign way.)*

(Dark Anna, you're feeling preachy today,) Aradin groaned. He
stifled another sigh, since he didn't want to seem impatient or
bored with the proceedings.

(I'm feeling my mortality, such as it is,) Teral admitted. *(Which
is odd, because I died in my fifties, and not my nineties—as you well
know—but I suppose it's just a touch of envy, seeing this aged gentleman
still getting around, doing what he was ordained to do.)*

(I should be so lucky, living to be so old,) Aradin replied, irritation
fading as quickly as it had risen. It had to fade; if it didn't, their
shared life would have quickly become unbearable. Both men had
lived together, two spirits in the younger man's body, for well
over a decade now. Learning tolerance was one of the key require-
ments for being a Darkhanan Witch, if an unspoken one.

(Well, you shouldn't be much older in a few moments,) Teral
pointed out, looking through Aradin's hazel eyes, *(because it looks
like the ceremony is coming to an end.)*

Sure enough, as the priest's voice wavered and rose in a
final benediction, the gathered worshippers chanted a mass—
" . . . *Witnessed!*"—that rang off the vaulted ceiling. Naturally, it
startled the infant, who immediately began squalling. The father
brought her over to the mother, who had been placed in a cushioned seat of honor at the center of the eight altars. While the
new parents fussed gently over the infant, an assistant-type
priestess urged everyone to head for the tables laden with food
around the outer edge of the church, food which everyone else
had brought as an offering to the Gods and to the new child.

Not hungry, Aradin watched the locals mingle and gossip. He smiled and dipped his head in a friendly way when people came near, but otherwise dismissed his presence as being ". . . just here to chat with Prelate Tomaso," and, "I'm in no hurry; I'll get to my business once you're all done celebrating this new life."

One of the older women sat down next to him after a while, and proceeded to talk Aradin's ear off about this, that, the other, all of it local gossip about the family with the newborn, their family members, the history of the village . . . all things which Aradin had no clue about. Patience was another trait favored by Darkhanan Witches, as was politeness. Though he hadn't originally intended to become a Witch-priest, he had learned how to be patient, polite, and kind. Which meant listening to the elderly woman prattle on until her middle-aged daughter came to collect her when the post-blessing party began to wind down.

(I'll be happy when we can get back to trading and talking herbs again,) Aradin thought, smiling politely in farewell as the village gossip moved off with her family. *(Searching for holy representatives is rather tedious. Though I did like her story about her nephew and the pig down the well.)*

(Only because we didn't have to help rescue it,) Teral agreed, chuckling. *(Ah, I see through the corner of your eye that the priest approaches.)*

Sure enough, when Aradin glanced to his right, he saw Prelate Tomaso hobbling their way, using his two canes for balance and a touch of support. A quick glance around the chapel hall showed it was now nearly empty, and that the assistant priestess had grabbed a mop and rag to start cleaning off the now emptied tables. Without fanfare or fuss, the locals had gathered up their food and their belongings and taken themselves out, leaving only a bit of scrubbing and sweeping to be handled by the local church staff.

The elderly man smiled a semi-toothy smile—several were missing from old age—and wobbled over to a spot on the bench next to the foreigner. With a few audible creaks from his joints, he sat down, sighed in relief, then turned toward Aradin.

"Well, well, young man! To what do I owe this honor? It isn't every day a priest of distant Darkhana comes to visit our far-flung land," Tomaso stated without preamble. His voice was light and strong with energy, despite his age.

Aradin let his brows raise in surprise. He spoke quietly, not wanting his deep voice to echo off the walls now that there weren't any other noises to muffle and mask it. "I wasn't aware anyone in this region was familiar with my Order. Katan is very far from my home."

"*I* and not *We*?" the local chief priest asked, in turn surprised. He poked an arthritic, age-spotted hand at the broad-sleeved robe Aradin wore. On the outside, the robe looked to be a plain, sturdy, travel-worn shade of tan linen. The inside was lined with a very tightly woven, stark shade of black. "Is this not the robe of a Darkhanan Witch-priest? The lining, I mean? It may have been sixty or so years, but I do distinctly remember meeting with one of your order."

Aradin smiled wryly. "Forgive me. Yes, it would be 'we' and 'our' home. I speak in the singular out of habit so as not to confuse the people in the lands we travel. I am Witch Aradin Teral, a procurer of priestly paraphernalia and magical mundanities for the Church of Darkhana, and thus something of an emissary in foreign lands." He offered his hand, palm up and mindful of the older male's swollen joints. "You are Prelate Tomaso of the Holy House of Kata and Jinga, correct?"

"That is correct," the elderly priest agreed. He rested his fingers on Aradin's palm for a moment, then squeezed with a bit of strength. "And a pleasure it is to meet with you. The last—and only other—one of your kind I met was a Witch named . . . Ora Niel?"

"High Witch-Priestess Orana Niel, yes . . . and now that you mention her name, I am not surprised you would remember her and her Guide after all these years," Aradin chuckled wryly. "I am actually in Katan on her behalf."

"Oh, indeed? How fares the young lady?" Tomaso asked.

Considering the "young" lady in question was technically older than both of them combined, Aradin grinned ruefully at the label. "Still more than a match for any man or woman alive, and still as young-looking and lovely as ever. That is, the last I saw her, which was . . . two full turns of Brother Moon ago, if I remember right. I was—sorry, *we*—were wondering if you could help us with a little quest we're on?"

"Well, that would depend upon the nature of the request, of course," the Prelate cautioned. He patted Aradin on the knee. "But I'm sure it will be something manageable, or at least not too unreasonable. What is your quest, young man?"

Aradin cleared his throat, consulting swiftly, silently with Teral on a good way to word their request. Finally, he sighed. "Well, we need to find a priest or priestess who would be the best possible emissary between your Gods and your people . . . without politics getting involved. Someone who has the holiness to speak with blessed Kata and Jinga," he stated, nodding at the eight altars, "but also some level of authority with which to bring back the words of the Gods to your people, and have them be heeded. But, again, without politics muddying the issues. The perspective of a . . . to put it politely, a bureaucrat, would only make the situation difficult to manage properly, and possibly make it prone to failure."

Tomaso wrinkled his brow in thought. He had plenty to spare, and the pouty look of his half-scowl was almost cute in a way. Brows working, he mulled it over, then asked, "Perhaps what you need is a Seer, not a priest?"

"That would be more of a one-way form of communication, from the minds of the Gods to the mouths of Their chosen vessel, to the ears of us mere mortals," Aradin corrected gently. "That is also a matter for warnings of the future. What we seek is a two-way communicator who can work with those things we mortals already know about. An arbiter and an advocate. Someone who is used to speaking with your God and Goddess, bringing the concerns of your people to Them, and bringing back whatever rulings or prayer-effects They may choose for Their replies."

"Well, I don't know about rulings, exactly," Tomaso mused, scratching at his wrinkled, stubbled chin, "but if there's any priest or priestess in the Empire who speaks with the Gods on a daily basis about the concerns of their parishoners, and manages the sheer power of prayers on a daily basis, all without dabbling in politics . . . then it would be the Grove Keeper. That's about as far as you'll get from politics for a holy intermediary who also possesses a distinct level of authority."

"The Grove Keeper?" Aradin asked. He could feel Teral's confusion and curiosity as well as his own. "I don't think either of us have heard of that position before. At least, not outside of the land of Arbra, where their deity is the Goddess of Forests . . . and I'm not sure if that is one of their titles or not. What do they do?"

"He . . . actually, I think it's a *she* right now," the elderly priest corrected himself. "She is the Guardian of the Grove, a place which used to be the Holy Gardens where Blessed Kata and Jinga were wed, uniting the two main kingdoms of this continent into a single empire ages ago. Unfortunately, when the Convocation of the Gods destroyed the Aian Empire two hundred years ago, give or take, the Grove became a place of untamed, uncontrolled magics. Energies too powerful to allow pilgrims to visit or betrotheds to wed."

"That sounds like yet another location in need of healing,"

Aradin muttered dryly. *(Which means it is all the more imperative Orana Niel speaks at the Convocation of the Gods,)* he added silently to his Guide.

Tomaso continued, patting Aradin's knee. "If there is anyone who is an expert on judging the merits and turning the petitions of the people into the quite literal power of prayer, it would be the current Grove Keeper. If you will indulge an old priest in the lengthy process of rising and retiring to my study, I will see if I can find a map showing you how to get to the Grove. That is, if you are prepared to travel that far, and to face the dangers which make it an ill-advised place to visit for the unprepared, never mind the unwary."

"I am a well-trained mage, and a cautious man by nature." Aradin comforted him, clasping the older priest on the shoulder. Rising, he turned and offered his hand to assist the elderly clergyman to his feet. "And my Guide is even more careful than I. If it is not forbidden for a foreigner to visit such a holy place, then we will go."

"Forbidden? No, not at all," Prelate Tomaso dismissed. "But difficult? Yes," he grunted, struggling to his feet. "It is no longer the garden of delights it was—one more tug, young man! Ahhh, there we go. This way . . ." Canes in his hands, the priest headed for one of the doors leading into the wings of the church. "My body may be getting old, but the Gods have given me a still-sharp mind. I remember your fellow Witch's visit. She brought the most lovely, delicate tea from some place in Aiar. A mountainous land . . . Cor-something . . ."

Aradin perked up at that. "Oh, yes, I've had a variety of Aian teas in our travels. And other things. Studying plants is one of my specialties. I'm always eager to find out what plants are being harvested and used in various ways locally for magical, medicinal, and culinary uses wherever I go."

"Heh! You'll find the Grove a terrifying place, then," Tomaso chuckled. "But before you go, I think I can find a tin of spell-preserved tea somewhere. Will you stay and have a cup, while I dig for those maps? And perhaps, could I have a chance to meet your, erm, Host? No, sorry, your Guide, was it? You would be the Host, yes?"

"Yes, and we'd be delighted," Aradin agreed, following him through the door. Privately, he wondered what the elderly priest meant by that quip about the Grove, but knew he'd either learn it in conversation or learn it when he got there. The polite thing was to let his host dictate their conversation. "Teral would be happy to meet you in person as well, so to speak. At least with you, we won't have to explain what to expect first."

Chuckling, the Prelate continued to lead the way, his pace slow but otherwise steady. "I suspect you'll have to explain it to the Grove Keeper, if she has the time to meet with you to discuss your request. They're usually wonderful people, the Grove Keepers, very trustworthy, but they're often far too busy with their duties to bother with learning about foreign lands and exotic oddities."

Aradin smiled wryly. "That actually fits in with what we're looking for. I can only hope she'll suit our needs."